THROUGH THE GLEN
SPECIAL EDITION

THE HIGHLANDS SERIES
BOOK THREE

SAMANTHA YOUNG

Through the Glen

A Highlands Series Novel

By Samantha Young
Copyright © 2024 Samantha Young

Cover Design By Hang Le
Edited by Jennifer Sommersby Young
Proofread by Julie Deaton

ALSO BY SAMANTHA YOUNG

Other Adult Contemporary Novels by Samantha Young

Play On

As Dust Dances

Black Tangled Heart

Hold On: A Play On Novella

Into the Deep

Out of the Shallows

Hero

Villain: A Hero Novella

One Day: A Valentine Novella

Fight or Flight

Much Ado About You

A Cosmic Kind of love

The Love Plot

On Dublin Street Series:

On Dublin Street

Down London Road

Before Jamaica Lane

Fall From India Place

Echoes of Scotland Street

Moonlight on Nightingale Way

Until Fountain Bridge (a novella)

Castle Hill (a novella)
Valentine (a novella)
One King's Way (a novella)
On Hart's Boardwalk (a novella)

Hart's Boardwalk Series:

The One Real Thing
Every Little Thing
Things We Never Said
The Truest Thing

The Adair Family Series:

Here With Me
There With You
Always You
Be With Me
Only You

The Highlands Series:

Beyond the Thistles
Among the Heather

Young Adult contemporary titles by Samantha Young
The Impossible Vastness of Us
The Fragile Ordinary

Titles Co-written with Kristen Callihan
Outmatched

Titles Written Under S. Young

About the Author

Samantha is a *New York Times, USA Today*, and *Wall Street Journal* bestselling author and a Goodreads Choice Awards Nominee. Samantha has written over 55 books and is published in 31 countries. She writes emotional and angsty romance, often set where she resides—in her beloved home country Scotland. Samantha splits her time between her family, writing and chasing after two very mischievous cavapoos.

ACKNOWLEDGMENTS

For the most part, writing is a solitary endeavor, but publishing most certainly is not. I have to thank my amazing editor Jennifer Sommersby Young for always, *always* being there to help make me a better writer and storyteller. Your encouragement and support mean the world!

Thank you to Julie Deaton for proofreading *Through the Glen* and catching all the things. I'm so glad Theo surprised you in the best way!

And thank you to my bestie and PA extraordinaire Ashleen Walker for helping to lighten the load and supporting me more than ever these past few years. I really couldn't do this without you.

The life of a writer doesn't stop with the book. Our job expands beyond the written word to marketing, advertising, graphic design, social media management, and more. Help from those in the know goes a long way. A huge thank-you to Nina Grinstead, Kim Cermak, Kelley Beckham and all the team at Valentine PR for your encouragement, support, insight and advice. You all are amazing!

Thank you to every single blogger, Instagrammer, and book lover who has helped spread the word about my books. You all are appreciated so much! On that note, a massive thank-you to the fantastic readers in my private Facebook group, Samantha Young's Clan McBookish. You're truly special. You're a safe space of love and support on the internet and I couldn't be more grateful for you.

A massive thank-you to Hang Le for creating another

stunning cover in this series. You are a tremendous talent! And thank you to Regina Wamba for the beautiful couple photography that brings Sarah and Theo to life.

As always, thank you to my agent Lauren Abramo for making it possible for readers all over the world to find my words. You're phenomenal, and I'm so lucky to have you.

A huge thank-you to my family and friends for always supporting and encouraging me.

Finally, to you, thank you for reading. It means more than I can ever say.

When the moonlight's on the mountain
And the gloom is on the glen,
At the cross beside the fountain
There is one will meet thee then.
–"When the Gloom is on the Glen," William Makepeace
Thackeray

PROLOGUE
SARAH

Ardnoch Castle, Scotland
October

The castle seemed hushed. Not just because it was evening at Ardnoch, but because many of its members had returned to their film and television projects a few weeks ago. Summer was their season off, and we saw many members descend upon the estate only to depart in droves come September.

They'd been gone for a month and the castle had grown gradually quiet, just as I liked it. *Not that it matters*, I thought as I hurried down the carpeted corridor toward Theodore Cavendish's room. I technically no longer worked here. It was the end of an era. But it was time.

Before I left, however, I was going to use my proximity to the rich and famous to get what I wanted.

Drawing to a stop outside of Mr. Cavendish's door, I

sucked in a breath and pushed down the sudden swarm of fluttering nerves in my stomach. Seriously, I felt a wee bit sick.

Fueled by a newfound confidence in myself and a promise I'd made to my now-deceased grandfather, I didn't turn away. I would not run from this opportunity. Even if it meant putting trust in someone I wasn't even sure I liked. Mr. Cavendish wasn't just a droll, flirtatious son of an English viscount. The cynical bitterness within him might be my ruin. How did I know these things about someone I'd never actually spoken to?

I was very observant.

Because I was shy and introverted, some people assumed I lived in my own world and didn't pay attention to what was going on around me. It was the exact opposite, actually. I paid close attention. I watched people. I read them. Attempted to understand them. And realized that because of the last three decades of doing just that, I had a pretty good gut instinct.

Years ago, when someone was threatening my boss Lachlan Adair and terrorizing the estate, I'd come under fire as a suspect because of the bad blood between my grandfather and the Adairs. The fact that I blushed in his presence because I found my boss attractive didn't help matters. Yet, I'd forever be angry with myself for never voicing my suspicions. I'd always suspected the real culprit. The actor Lucy Wainwright.

Everyone thought she was a sweetheart, but she'd often been erratic toward me when I cleaned her room. One moment she was kind and generous and the next yelling at me for some misdemeanor for which I wasn't to blame. I'd also observed her from a distance and noted her intense preoccupation with Lachlan. Moreover, I saw her talking with her partner in crime, Fergus Ray, more than once and thought their interactions odd and cagey.

I didn't speak up because I thought no one would listen to the opinion of a shy housekeeper. How I regretted that after they kidnapped Lachlan. Thankfully, Lachlan's now wife Robyn and my grandfather were there to save his life.

So, aye, I had good instincts about people. And my instincts told me to be wary of Mr. Cavendish, even if he was my first choice.

I raised my fist to knock on his door but before I could, it flew open and the man himself jolted to a stop.

"Fuck!" Mr. Cavendish clasped a hand to his chest in fright. His alarmed expression immediately darkened to a glare. "I almost defecated in my trousers, thank you very much." His Eton upper-crust British accent made even the most disgusting sentences sound charming.

Uncomfortable under his glower, my cheeks grew frustratingly hot. As did the sight of him up close. Theo Cavendish was annoyingly attractive. Tall, at least a few inches over six feet with a swimmer's build, he wore clothes well. Like a model. Even just in his current sweater and jeans, he looked like he'd stepped off a photo shoot. The sweater molded to his taut physique and accentuated his broad shoulders. His pale gray-blue eyes complemented a face that was almost too pretty due to his full, pouty mouth. The sharp angle of his jaw and cheekbones, along with his designer stubble, attempted to make him a little more rugged.

I knew I was probably gawking, but thirty-one years down the line and I still hadn't quite figured out how to act around handsome men. I think taking the job at Ardnoch was an attempt to make myself immune to them. After all, it was a members-only club for film and industry professionals, and a lot of the members were good-looking. Including the behind-the-scenes people like Theo, who was a screenwriter and director.

However, it didn't make me immune and instead, I'd shrunk further into my shell, allowing my old insecurities and traumas to dictate my introverted behavior. Or so all the podcasts I'd listened to on therapy and mental health told me.

"May I help you?" Theo snapped impatiently.

There. I saw and heard it in his voice. His contempt.

My cheeks flushed even hotter, and I wanted to run away.

Don't you dare, treasure. I heard my grandfather's growled words in my head as if he were there beside me. *It's time to go after what you want. You've already proven to yourself what you're worth.*

Okay, Grandpa, I thought. *For you and for me.* My keen perception might tell me that Mr. Cavendish was a wounded, cynical aristocrat who would lash out at anyone who dared get too close to him ... but it also told me he was the right man for the job. I might not be a fan of him as a person, but as a creator, there was no one quite like him. And finally, I was beginning to believe in myself. Moreover, I'd promised Grandpa that I'd start *living*.

I threw back my shoulders. "I—I'd like to speak with you, Mr. Cavendish."

He searched my eyes, and I noted the spark of curiosity glinting in his. Suddenly, he looked taken aback, like he'd never seen me before. His perusal grew so intense, I could feel my nerves getting the better of me again. I nibbled nervously on my lip, trying to draw from that well of courage the memory of my grandfather had opened inside me.

"Well?" Mr. Cavendish grimaced. "Sarah, is it?"

Despite his obvious impatience to be rid of me, I was shocked he knew my name. "Aye. Sarah McCulloch."

He gestured for me to hurry up.

"Oh." *You can do this, Sarah!* "Um ... May I come in?"

Raising an eyebrow, Mr. Cavendish leaned against his door, arms crossed over his chest. The pose caused his slim but muscular biceps to flex. "Wishing to follow in the boss's foot-steps, my love, and bag yourself a member?" He referred to

Aria Howard, the estate manager, who'd recently gotten engaged to the Scottish actor North Hunter.

The sneer in Cavendish's words sparked my ire. That's what people seemed to think of me. Some pitiful creature that scuttled around Ardnoch, crushing on the male celebrities. A good percentage of those members were entitled arseholes who weren't worth a damn. Theodore Cavendish was the last person I'd ever crush on. I had a crush on his brain. That was it. "That's not why I'm here."

He pushed off the doorjamb. "Then why are you?"

Do it! I licked my lips again, looked him straight in the eye, and stated, "We have business to discuss, Mr. Cavendish."

I'd shocked him. And intrigued him. That gave me courage. "Well?" I gestured to his room.

A reluctant smile tugged at the corner of his mouth and he waved me inside. "This I have to hear."

Forcing my feet one step in front of the other, I smoothed a hand down my housekeeping tunic. Tonight was the last night I'd ever wear this uniform. Clutching my handbag strap, I forced my grip to loosen. My nails had probably left crescents in my skin.

Licking my lips nervously again, I stared out the large window of the bedroom suite, watching the rain lash the pane, wondering if I could have this entire conversation with my back to Cavendish.

He cleared his throat, indicating that wasn't going to happen.

Turning, I squared my shoulders and decided to go for it without overthinking. "I'm about to tell you something that very few people are aware of, and I must ask for your discretion, no matter the outcome of our conversation."

He shot me another amused look as he crossed the room to sit on the end of the bed. Leaning back on his hands, I ignored the visual feast he'd created with the unconsciously inviting pose. "Good God, little mouse, have you killed someone and need a partner to bury the body?"

I frowned at the horrendous pet name that brought back terrible memories. "Please don't call me little mouse."

Cavendish huffed. "Yet no denial of murder. Should I be worried? Is there really a corpse somewhere decaying as we speak?"

"Well, considering I only committed the murder an hour ago, I very much doubt it's decaying just yet."

For a moment, Cavendish blinked at me warily. Then he let out another huff of air. "You almost had me there, little mouse."

Scowling at his continued use of the pet name that spiked the ire in my blood, I decided to push through the indignation and get to the point. "I want to write a screenplay with you."

Something like disappointment tightened his features. "Of course you do." He moved to get off the bed, his body language turning dismissive in an instant. The man was more temperamental than the Highland weather, unpredictable and quickly changeable.

"No." I stepped forward to explain. "I mean, I want to write a screenplay with you for the adaptation of my book series." Tilting my chin back in defiance of any coming ridicule, I continued, "I write under a pen name. No one knows but my cousin. My grandfather knew too ..." I drifted off, still unable to talk about losing him. "I write a thriller series about a detective inspector called Juno McLeod." Opening my handbag, I pulled out the paperback copy of book one, *Hollow Grave*, and held it out to him.

Cavendish attempted to mask his shock when he realized I was serious, but I saw a flicker of astonishment in his eyes as he took the book from me.

The first time I held a copy in my hand, I'd burst into tears. I couldn't believe I'd finished a novel. My e-books were self-published. I'd done a lot of research on how to do it, on how to run ads, and as I wrote more books in the series, my income started to increase in very healthy increments. Enough so, if the industry wasn't so unpredictable, I'd have considered quitting my job. Then, something miraculous happened, and word of mouth on social media platforms led to the series going viral in the US and UK a year ago. I hit number one and even now the first five books were still in the top 100 charts in several countries.

I'd made more money than I knew what to do with. Moreover, I'd gained a literary agent, sold foreign rights in twenty countries, the print rights to a publisher in the US and UK, and I'd been approached by two different and well-respected producers interested in film and television rights.

Which brought me here. With Cavendish. The mind behind one of my favorite TV shows of all time, *King's Valley*.

I knew in my gut that Cavendish was the right person to bring Juno to life. She was a complicated human, driven by her trauma and darkness. Her relationship with the main antagonist in the story was twisty and dark, with an underlying sexual tension that would require a nuanced and delicate hand to pull off on-screen. Cavendish knew how to make those kinds of relationships work on film. I'd seen everything he'd ever done, and while he'd directed movies and guest-directed episodes of TV shows here and there, he'd only been the creator of TV shows brought to life from his own screenplays and ideas.

Until now.

I hoped.

In a blushing ramble, I spewed all this to him as he read the blurb on the back of the book.

Heavy, mortifying silence fell between us as Cavendish turned the book over to its front cover. "S. M. Brodie. Interesting pen name."

"It's my initials and my grandmother's maiden name."

He didn't react. Instead, he ran his fingers over the embossed tagline along the top of the cover and read, "'The Multimillion-Copy Bestseller.'"

When I didn't respond, he looked up from it. "I'm to believe that an author who has sold several million copies of her series continues to work as a housekeeper?"

The idea that I might lie about my secret career made me clench my hands into fists at my sides. I didn't inform him that today was my last day on the job. What was the point if he wasn't going to believe me, anyway?

However, his eyes narrowed at whatever he saw in my expression. "No, you're not lying, are you?" He stood, gazing down at my book again. "You really are S. M. Brodie. How surprising."

I swallowed nervously. "Like I said, I've had two producers contact my agent about buying the film rights. I can show you the emails."

Cavendish shook his head and held out the book for me to take.

I waved him off. "Keep it."

To my irritation and hurt, he sighed and threw it on the bed as if it was an inconvenience. "Sorry, little mouse. I don't do adaptations. I write my own stories."

Even though I'd known there was a good chance he'd tell me that, I fought through the crushing disappointment. "You won't say anything to anyone?"

He raised an eyebrow. "Who would believe me? I barely believe it."

I huffed, disheartened but not surprised by his carelessly hurtful attitude. "Right. I am used to people underestimating me, Mr. Cavendish. Sorry for taking up your time."

"No apologies necessary," he said to my back. "And congratulations on your secret success."

The mocking tone made me stop at the door. I glanced over my shoulder at him, holding his gaze. "Congratulations on your wonderful work," I told him sincerely. "I suppose as surprising it is that a 'little mouse' such as me is a *Sunday Times* best-selling writer, it's astonishing that such a cliché of entitled aristocracy with your pathetic ennui and cynicism ... is capable of writing television characters with such complexity and depth." I strode out of Cavendish's room, legs trembling from my daring insult, heart racing, skin flushed.

However, as I reached the staff elevator, a smile tugged at my lips as I remembered the way Cavendish's expression slackened with furious shock at my volleying his mockery back at him.

ONE
THEO

I loved women. The silk of their skin beneath my hands. Their breathy gasps. The bite of their nails on my back, my arse. The way they can be pliant and submissive beneath me or ride me like there's no tomorrow, mindless to everything but their passion and need. I loved their laughter, their easy affection. Give me soft, hard, voluptuous, slender, short, tall, redhead, blond, brunette, black, brown, white ... I had no type. *Woman* was my type.

The only kind of woman I avoided like the plague was the innocent kind. The ones who didn't know how to play the game. Because as much as I loved women, I would never fall in love again. I'd made that decision long ago, and once I made up my mind about something, I was the most stubborn bastard a person did meet.

I'd encountered enchanting, intelligent, funny, beautiful women from all over the world. I'd even fucked a fair few of them. And in the last fifteen years, I hadn't fallen in love with a single one. If they couldn't do it for me, no one could.

I was immune to the emotion.

Which was why I sought out women like actor Angeline

Potter when I needed a distraction. Angeline would most likely talk my ear off about the minutiae of her day at the spa, all the while bitching about everyone in her life, but she would offer me a small reprieve from my concerns.

My writer's block was still very much in force. It was driving me up the wall. It was scaring the shit out of me.

And I remembered seeing Angeline arrive at the estate for the weekend. I might have gone down on her at the last Ardnoch Christmas party. She seemed open to another recurrence of my head between her toned thighs, so I'd thought, why not?

I'd gone to her room and part of me admired her honesty when she agreed to fuck under the condition that she was a selfish lover and I wasn't to expect reciprocation.

Thinking she meant she expected to receive head but not give it, I agreed. I went down on her, she came, and then when I was inside her, she came again. I did not expect her to then hurry me up to orgasm like an impatient harpy.

"Oh, for fuck's sake, just fucking come already," she'd snapped multiple times, lying there with a bored expression beneath me.

I'm afraid it rather killed my urgency to climax.

On the contrary, I pulled out of her and fell onto my back, staring at the ceiling, balls blue, wishing like hell I'd just stayed in my room and masturbated my boredom away. Limpid jade eyes that darkened with an unexpected fire filled my vision, and I scrubbed my hand over my face in frustration.

Sarah McCulloch had entered my thoughts far too often these past few days since her clandestine visit to my room.

Long, elegant fingers smoothed over my chest. I turned to stare stonily into Angeline Potter's now soft countenance.

"Stay. Cuddle."

What the fuck? I hadn't even come and she didn't give a rat's arse. Again, part of me admired her selfishness and sense of worth. The other half disliked her greatly for it. What can I say? I'm complicated.

"I don't cuddle." I pushed up off the bed.

"Fair enough." She shrugged and snuggled back down under the bedcovers, eyes drowsy.

I smirked in disbelief, shaking my head. I wondered how many men had treated Angeline the same way and if she'd finally just decided to hell with all of them. If they were going to treat her as disposable, she'd do the same. If that was true, good for her.

After I returned from the bathroom where I disposed of the somewhat used condom, I pulled on my underwear and trousers. Angeline's eyes popped open. "Oh. My friend, Kitty —Kitty Lawson."

I nodded. I knew of Kitty. She was a respected British actor, and I'd put Kitty on a list of actors I wanted to work with. You know, whenever my writer's block ended and I had a bloody script ready for development.

"She fancies you and has been going on and on about finding a way to meet you ... but I'd rather you didn't dip your wick in my friend pool now that we've fucked. And Kitty's one of my best friends, you know."

Pulling on my shirt, I tried to mask my irritation. I was an imperfect man. I knew my faults. But I liked to think disloyalty wasn't one of them. Friendship was the one state of human pairing that meant something to me. "You fucked me even though your best friend has a crush on me. How very catty schoolgirl of you, darling."

Angeline shrugged lazily, brushing her sex-mussed hair off her face. "I like taking what others covet."

Feeling the sudden need to shower, I shoved on my shoes, my expression a mask of cold boredom. "You didn't take a fucking thing, darling. But I'll be sure to tell Kitty how much her friendship means to you when we cross paths." Turning, I strode to her door, hearing her outraged gasp.

"You wouldn't dare!"

I glanced over my shoulder. "Oh, if the mood strikes me, I can be a bit of a shit-stirrer. I absolutely would dare." Flashing her a dark grin, I marched out of her room, ignoring the curse words she threw at me. They were muffled as the door closed behind me, and I made my way toward the stairwell.

I should have gone to the gym instead. I liked using the rowing machine in light of the fact that I was so far away from the Thames River, where I rowed regularly. I'd been part of a rowing team at Oxford, and we'd tried to keep it up after graduation. Sometimes we still got together, but mostly I rowed in a single scull these days. With no scull or river, I worked off that energy in the gym. It should have been my first choice instead of Angeline.

While the great hall and reception rooms of Ardnoch Castle reminded you that you were somewhere stately, the upper hallways felt like they could belong in any luxury hotel. Except for the turret. The turret on the guest wing had been converted into a reading nook, and it had all the atmosphere of a medieval castle, even though the castle itself was built in the nineteenth century.

I'd grown up in a home only somewhat smaller than Ardnoch. Haleshall Manor in Suffolk. My father's viscountcy was one of the oldest in England, dating back to the sixteenth century. Haleshall sat on the Suffolk Coast, and for all its grandeur, it had been fucking freezing to live in during the winter. Not that I'd spent more than a few weeks at Christmas every year at our ancestral home. I was sent to Eton College at thirteen years old and lived there for most of the year.

During summers, I'd join my family at our townhouse in Belgravia, London. A place filled with my best and worst memories. As a child, I'd lived there during the school year to attend a preparatory school in Notting Hill before my father demanded I leave everything behind for Eton. Not a single Cavendish male had failed to attend Eton, and I wouldn't be the one to break tradition.

My footsteps made no sound on the plush tartan carpeting as I walked to my room. Lachlan Adair had renovated this castle to within an inch of its life. I couldn't even imagine the fortune he'd spent. As wealthy as my father was, he'd balk at the cost of renovating Haleshall Manor to this level. It would remain as grand and aristocratically cold as the old bastard himself.

I followed the tartan up wide, elegant stairs to the lavish Gothic windows along the landing. It was a clear night as the rain had given way a few days ago to sunshine.

Following the familiar hallway to my suite, it bemused me how much Ardnoch had come to feel like home this past year. Never would I have believed I'd join a members-only club. As the second son of an English viscount, I'd grown up in a world of members-only clubs. My father and brother were members of White's, an exclusive, centuries-old gentlemen's club in St. James, London. King Charles and Prince William were members. I'd refused my invitation to join.

I'd taken my inheritance from my mother and left that world, as much as it was possible to leave it behind. I didn't want it if it meant being close to my father or giving him anything that might make him happy.

Ardnoch was different. It was salt in the wound to my father. A reminder of what I'd become. Not a respected barrister and member of Parliament like my brother Sebastian or a viscount turned wealthy investment banker like my father.

I was a creative. A writer. I made movies and TV shows.

It didn't matter if my work was important to me, that it made me happy. Or that it was a respected career in the twenty-first century.

It wasn't worthy of the son of a viscount. And that son buying membership to a club for film and television professionals while snubbing a membership to White's ... oh, that pissed the old man off.

I felt a petty resurgence of pleasure that I'd angered the old fucker by buying into Ardnoch. Maybe my reason for doing so was childish, but I'd grown to love the Highlands. The people here weren't too bad either.

Immediately, my mind returned to Sarah. I hadn't seen the little mouse around the estate these last few days. My gaze zeroed in on my bedstand where her book lay unopened.

She'd taken me by surprise with her bold request to write with me. Even more so that she was a successful crime fiction writer. In fact, I'd been so shocked that someone still could knock me off-balance that I might have lashed out a little. It was just ... how could someone so guileless and innocent astonish me?

And in return, I'd treated her with sly superiority, thinking her too ignorant to sense it.

How wrong I'd been.

Moreover, she didn't let it lie. She called me out. She got me wrong, but she also got me right, and I hadn't known whether to rage at her well-targeted skewering or clap.

In the end, I mentally applauded the little mouse.

Good for her.

She'd need that ability to fight back. Someone whose books were that successful couldn't stay anonymous forever.

A piercing ring sliced through the quiet of the bedroom suite, startling me out of my thoughts. Hurrying across the room to where my ringing phone sat on the desk beside my discarded laptop and career, I grabbed the mobile. There was no caller ID. Not in the mood for a sales call, I picked up and answered with lazy boredom, "You've called Hot Boys

Twenty-Four Seven, Fabio speaking. How can I help you with your kink?"

There was silence. And then a huff of annoyance. "Still haven't grown up, I see."

The familiar voice tightened my fingers around the phone. "Seb?"

"Hmm, yes," my brother responded with impatience. "I'm surprised you recognize my voice it's been so long. I tried calling you from *my* phone, but I have a sneaking suspicion you blocked my number."

I had blocked my elder brother's number. "What do you want?"

"We haven't spoken in four years and that's all I get?"

"Seb, what do you want?" I repeated, trying to remain unaffected and relaxed.

Sebastian hesitated, and then his heavy sigh crackled the line. "Father is ill. Cancer. You need to come home."

Rage filled me at the *C* word. The memories it evoked. "You mean, the way he didn't come home while our mother was dying?"

"You need to forgive him, Theo."

Like hell. "Is he dying?"

"You need to come home."

I took an inner breath, refusing to reveal my anger. My repeated question came out calm and uninterested. "Is he dying?"

"We're not sure."

Liar. My brother had always been a terrible liar. "What kind of cancer? What stage?"

Seb cleared his throat. "It's not something one talks about in polite conversation."

I grinned darkly. "It's his fucking balls, isn't it?"

Sebastian snarled, "Do you have to always be so crude?"

Laughing, I shook my head. "That's bloody brilliant. He

spent his whole life dipping his wick in places he shouldn't, and now he's got ball cancer. Perhaps Karma exists, after all."

"I cannot believe you are mocking our father's cancer."

"Oh, I'm not mocking cancer, Sebastian," I drawled. "I'm applauding a universe that respects justice."

"There's a very big difference between justice and revenge, Theodore. To wish this on anyone, most especially your father, is outrageous."

His indignation did nothing to me. "I didn't wish this on him. I'm just not going to come running to his side to shower him with sympathy. And frankly, I doubt very much he needs me to hold his hand while he loses his balls."

Silence greeted me for a few seconds and then Seb said quietly, "Your bitterness will eat you alive if you're not careful, brother."

His words found their target, and I wanted to hurt him back. "I'm not your brother, Sebastian. You stopped being that for me a very long time ago." I hung up, throwing my phone on the bed as memories rose from the corners of the room, pressing in on me.

A bright, agonizing flame of pain scored across my chest, and I dragged a hand down my face, trying to push the memories back.

Distraction. I needed a distraction.

Usually writing was my distraction.

Opening my eyes, the first thing I saw was her book.

Hollow Grave by S. M. Brodie.

It suddenly looked more like a life raft than pages bound together, so I kicked off my shoes and clambered onto the bed. Picking up the hefty tome, I pried it open and hoped like hell Sarah McCulloch was about to surprise me some more.

Two

SARAH

"Are you sure about this?"

Closing the boot of my car where Jared had just placed my suitcase, I turned to look up at him. When my cousin arrived on the farm almost five years ago, I wasn't sure what to expect. Never in my wildest imaginings would I expect us to become best friends, for Jared to be like the younger brother I'd never had. Even if he acted like my big brother most of the time. The thought brought a tender smile to my face, and I reached out to squeeze his arm in reassurance. "I'll be fine."

He gazed down at me with green eyes the exact shade as mine. We'd inherited the unusual color from our fathers, who'd inherited them from our grandmother. "I don't like you being so far away by yourself."

"I'll be two hours away."

Jared's handsome face tightened. "Aye, in a cottage, by yourself."

"I hate to break this to you, Jar, but I'm thirty-one years old and I can take care of myself."

"I know. But I worry."

With the staggering new fortune I'd amassed in the last year, I'd purchased a small cottage in a coastal village in the North-West Highlands, in a pretty, wee village called Gairloch. It had a beach like Ardnoch but was much smaller, and the waters turned turquoise like the Mediterranean. Our grandpa used to take me to that beach every summer when I was a wee girl. Now I'd packed my bags, intent on spending a few months there writing the next book in the Juno McLeod series.

What Jared didn't say, yet I knew was behind part of his agitation, was that he'd miss me.

I was twelve years old when I officially moved in with my grandpa and Nana. Their eldest son, my father, died in a farming accident when I was a baby. Afterward, Mum left Ardnoch and took me home with her to Dundee. But she was devastated after losing my father, and she struggled with depression and substance abuse. I spent summers with my grandparents, but when I was twelve, things got so bad at home, I plucked up the courage to call my grandpa. He didn't just come to collect me this time. Grandpa brought the police and social services.

After that, Mum didn't put up a fight. Custody was granted to my grandparents. A few years later, Nana died, and it was just me and Grandpa. He was my whole world.

Over the years, my cousin Jared would stay with us during the summer holidays, but he was a very angry young man, six years younger than me. We didn't have much in common. Or so we thought. My uncle, my dad's younger brother, hadn't wanted anything to do with the farm and left Ardnoch at eighteen. He'd spent most of his life abandoning anything that required responsibility and commitment. Including Jared. And we discovered Jared's life with his mum in Glasgow wasn't easy in a very similar way to mine.

Jared called Grandpa when he was twenty-one and asked if

he could come work on the farm. He was heading down a dangerous path and was smart enough to know he needed to make a change. Grandpa didn't even have to think about it. Jared moved into the farmhouse a few days later. And he threw himself at the work.

I think even he was surprised by how much he grew to love the farm. Grandpa left the farm to both of us. Fifty-fifty. However, I gave my half to Jared. The farm to me *was* Grandpa. And he was gone now. But the farm was in Jared's blood, and I wanted him to have it.

"I'll miss you too," I promised him. "I'll call and then I'll be back at Christmas." Our first Christmas without Grandpa. Tears stung my eyes at the thought, and Jared's face softened with understanding.

"Come here." He pulled me into his strong embrace, resting his chin on top of my head as we held on to each other. "If you get lonely out there, you come back. No persevering through it because you think you should or because you think I need space."

I smiled against his chest. "Okay, big brother."

He snorted at that, kissed the top of my head, and released me. "And don't worry about me. I've got plenty here to keep me busy."

My brow furrowed. I doubted many people realized that farming was one of the most stressful jobs ever. When your income depended on the climate and you lived in the Scottish Highlands, it could be utterly soul-destroying. We'd seen crops fail because of inclement weather, crops my grandpa and Jared had poured their sweat and blood into.

"I've got Georgie and Enzo," he reminded me, referring to the farmhands who'd worked on the farm for the last three years. I'd seen a few farmhands come and go, but Georgie and Enzo were closer to Jared's age, and the three of them worked well together and enjoyed each other's company.

"And whatever girl you take a fancy to this week," I teased. Jared had a bit of a reputation in Ardnoch for being a player. It didn't matter if he was no longer quite so much the playboy he'd once been, especially as he had such little time to do so now. He'd garnered the reputation during those first few years when he'd slept with every eligible woman in the village and beyond, from here to Inverness.

Jared rolled his eyes. "Aye, like I've got time for that."

"Make time." I patted his arm. "You know what they say. All work and no play …"

He grinned. "Aye? You planning on taking your own advice, Sister Sarah?"

I punched his arm this time. "I'm not a nun!"

"If you say so."

Grimacing, I turned to round the car. "That's my cue to leave."

"Have you got everything?" he called after me.

"Yup." I pulled open the driver's door and glanced back at him. "I'll phone you when I get there." Melancholy threatened, a deep, yawning loneliness that I knew was mostly born of grief. "If you need me to come back, tell me, aye?"

Sadness tightened Jared's features. "Aye, wee cuz."

"Big cuz," I countered, my smile wobbly.

His return smile was forlorn. "I'm proud of you, Sarah. Grandad would be proud too."

"I'm proud of both of us. *We're* doing Grandpa proud."

Jared nodded and hit the roof of the car before stepping back. He wore his usual work gear of flannel shirt, jeans, and green farm boots. The farmhouse I'd grown up in stood behind him. The two-story home was built a hundred years ago in sandstone brick with slate tile for its roof of multiple pitches. Grandpa had gone into the attic space so he'd added dormer windows and a third floor. Jared had taken that space for himself when he came to live with us, but I'd finally talked him into taking the primary bedroom now that Grandpa was gone. That third floor got too hot during the summer.

Knowing it would be strange for him, I used my earnings to have my grandparents' bedroom furniture removed and put in the attic. I bought a whole new bedroom suite for Jared and redecorated the room. He cried quietly when he saw it. Jared had rarely cried in all the years we'd known each other, but we'd both been extremely emotional these last few months since Grandpa's death. And poor Jared had been with him. Had held him in his arms as he died. Heart attack. No time to save him.

The two of us were like a raw wound; the slightest thing reopened the pain and tears.

For not the first time, I questioned leaving Jared so soon after. It had only been six months since we lost the only real father we'd ever known.

"I can stay," I whispered.

Jared swallowed hard but shook his head. "He'd want us both to start living again."

Pushing down the tears in my throat, I nodded and gave him a wee wave. "Off I go, then."

He smiled. "Go write another bestseller, superstar."

"Talk soon?"

"Call me as soon as you get there."

"Love you, Jar."

His mouth trembled and he looked away, composing himself, before he turned back to me. His words sounded like stone under sandpaper. "I love you, too, Sarah."

Afraid I might burst into painful sobs, I hurried into the car and slammed the door shut.

About a year after Jared arrived, he got a phone call from his mum that had set him off. He was acting like a shit to everyone, and he did something stupid and dangerous with the tractor. Yet Grandpa didn't yell at him, didn't rage. He knew something was eating away at Jared, and at dinner that night, he'd told him that he could destroy the whole farm if he liked, but it wouldn't stop Grandpa from loving him.

Jared turned as white as a sheet, and it was the first and only time I saw my cousin cry—until our grandfather died. Grandpa had got up from the table and pulled Jared into his arms, holding him tightly as he promised him nothing could make him stop loving him. Jared cried like a small child and returned the sentiment, though the words sounded wrenched from him.

He'd never been able to say those three words easily, but Grandpa had made it safe for him. For both of us.

Knowing that man who'd protected and loved us as fiercely as any good father would was now gone from the world still tore through me like a serrated knife.

I hit the gas and drove faster down the drive than I should because if I didn't, I wasn't sure I would leave the farm or Jared behind.

THREE
THEO

For the first time in months, my fingers itched to type. To transport the ideas and scenes in my head onto the page. Except, also for the first time, they were inspired by someone else's story. Many of the scenes were already written by someone else, but I could visualize how they'd work on-screen and which part of the dialogue was perfect for adaptation and the parts we could take out without affecting the story.

I dropped my phone and stared unseeing at the bedroom wall. Well, I had wanted the little mouse to surprise me. She'd shocked the fuck out of me. After devouring her first book in one night, I'd downloaded the next book onto the e-reader app on my phone. Then the next and the next and the next. I'd read the first nine in her series this past week. According to the online retailer, the Juno McLeod series had eleven books so far.

When I wasn't reading in the library, I read during meals at the dining table as I binged the atmospheric world Sarah created in her Juno McLeod books. The only time I took a break was to use the rower in the gym and to get a sexual health check at the clinic in Thurso, thanks to the timely reminder I'd set on my phone.

Otherwise, I was all about Juno.

Juno, a detective inspector, was based in Dundee, the crime capital of Scotland, but her cases took her around the country. A main plot wove throughout the entire series while a secondary subplot opened and then was resolved by the end of each new book. Juno's primary antagonist was the serial killer she was hunting, and the dark connection between them was intriguing and nuanced and, to be frank, bloody brilliant. That alone would enthrall audiences. But so would the intelligent, complex, funny Juno. The stories were gritty. And Sarah often explored real-world social issues many would find relatable.

Moreover, she took the reader all over Scotland, and her prose brought the country to life. So much so, I envisioned epic cinematography via drone camerawork.

"Bloody hell," I muttered to myself. Sarah's depth of writing was astonishing. It would be fantastic on-screen if the right person wrote and directed it. Also, casting would be essential. The right actor for Juno was pivotal. She was in her late thirties and had the confidence and realism that came with age. I could already think of a few actors who might fit the bill.

All week I'd been waiting to see the little mouse in her housekeeper uniform moving around the castle. I wanted to see her reaction when she realized what I was reading. But we'd never crossed paths, which seemed strange because I felt like I'd caught glimpses of her often in the past.

I wondered who else had approached her for the film rights. She'd mentioned they were two well-known producers. A flash of urgency and something unpleasant crawled through my chest.

Was that ... jealousy?

Did the thought of someone else adapting these books fill

me with actual jealousy? That both amused and pissed me off. I was never possessive. Over work or humans.

But if I was honest with myself ... I wanted this bloody series for adaptation.

Fuck.

There was my own rule to consider, however—that I always write my own screenplays. But if I went off and wrote something similar to Sarah's series, I'd feel like a failure from the start. Juno was not my idea ... and, truthfully, as much as we (shockingly) shared a similar sense of character development and portrayal, Juno was Sarah's. Only Sarah knew Juno to her core.

If I adapted the series, I'd need Sarah on board.

But did I really want to work with the little mouse? With her blushing and lack of assurance?

Her writing, however, did not lack confidence.

It still astonished me that she was S. M. Brodie.

Picking up my phone, I opened my text messages to the latest text from my writer and producer friend Colleen. She knew I was struggling with writer's block and said she had a short break in her schedule if I wanted to come to London tomorrow to brainstorm with her.

My thumb hovered over the keys to reply.

With a sigh of frustration, I exited her text, and my eyes snagged on another two rows down. The contact wasn't saved because it was my brother. Although I'd blocked him several times this week, he just found new numbers to message and call me from. I had several voicemail messages from him that I'd deleted without fully listening to.

A knock sounded on my suite door.

"Theo, you there?" The familiar Scottish accent made me shove off the bed.

Opening the door, I gave my friend North Hunter a droll

look. "Finally dragged yourself out of Ms. Howard's bed, have you?"

We both knew the reason I hadn't seen him lately was because he'd started filming a new Scottish crime series in Glasgow. He was only here at Ardnoch now to visit his fiancée, Aria Howard, Ardnoch Estate's manager. North had been the star of my most acclaimed and award-winning TV miniseries, *King's Valley*. We'd become good friends after working together. The lovesick bastard now spent what free time he had with his fiancée. So I was surprised to see him at my door.

He smirked at me. "Aria has work to catch up on, and your last few texts sounded almost manic. I thought I better check on you."

I grabbed my room key and turned to pick up my phone, too, and instead eyed the paperback from Sarah. Taking hold of it, I turned it toward North. "Have you read this series?"

Stepping into the room, North took the book from me. "No, but I've heard of it. Jack Irving, the guy producing the new series I'm on, told me about it. I think he might be in negotiation with the author's agent over the rights. Is it any good?"

The level of my agitation at that news was alarming. I had to clear the irritation from my throat as I answered blandly, "It's not bad. Better than most of the penny dreadfuls that saturate the genre fiction market these days."

North snorted. "You do know this is the twenty-first century, Theo? Penny dreadfuls are no longer a thing."

Ignoring his sarcasm, I shrugged and gestured him out of the room. "Let's get a drink." I wondered how far into negotiations Jack was with Sarah's agent. Had she just decided to sell it to whomever when I said I wasn't interested? I huffed.

"What?" North asked as we strode down the castle corridor.

"What, what?"

"You just made a sound of exasperation."

I did? I flicked him a look. "No, I didn't."

"I'm fairly certain you did." North narrowed his eyes. "In fact, you seem off in general."

"Don't be ridiculous," I drawled. "I am never off. I am the sun."

"What? Bad for the skin?"

"Fuck off, old boy." I usually was in the mood to banter with North, but I was distracted. Little mouse was nowhere in sight and Jack Irving might be producing my adaptation.

"Well, that sounded sharper and more sincere than usual." North stopped on the stairwell. "Theo ... I am here to talk if you ever need me."

The truth was I knew I could probably trust North with ... well, with anything. But I didn't want to give voice to the fact that my brother was plaguing me and I couldn't tell him Sarah was S. M. Brodie because it wasn't my secret to tell.

But ... "I'll explain over a drink."

Five minutes later, we were seated in a quiet lounge in the castle, each with a whisky in hand. "How is Ms. Howard?" I asked first.

An infatuated curl tugged the corner of North's mouth. "She's perfect. I am blissed out on her utter perfection."

I rolled my eyes because he was being deliberately saccharine to annoy me. "I'm going to need more than one drink to listen to your lovesick piffle."

"Fuck you," North said without rancor. "Now tell me what's going on."

Eyeing my friend, I shrugged. "I ... well, you know I've always had a rule about writing my own screenplays, but you also know I've been struggling with writer's block."

"Aye." North leaned forward. "Any progress there?"

"No. But ... the S. M. Brodie books ... I've read nine of them in a week."

He raised an eyebrow in question.

"They're damn good, North. Damn good. The author ... they reached out asking me if I would be interested in adapting them, and I turned them down."

"But now you're rethinking it?"

"Yes. Yet I'm not sure if it's because I want to or because I can't write a thing of my own."

"What if it's both?"

"I pride myself on writing my own shows. It's the one thing I take seriously, don't you know."

North didn't return my smirk. "It's the one thing you're not afraid to admit that you take seriously, you mean."

A flare of temper caught me by surprise, but I shoved it back down. My amused tone held an edge. "Don't psychoanalyze me tonight. I'm not really in the mood."

My friend studied me carefully. "Adapt the books, Theo. The entire time we've known each other, I've never seen you this distracted or on edge. Others might not see it, but I do. And you need a purpose or you'll become an even bigger prick than usual. Adapt the books. No one else cares if it's an adaptation or not. Especially if you write the screenplay."

"And if the author wants to help me write the screenplay?"

North snorted. "I say hell mend them."

I chuckled. "I'm not that bad."

"Anyone who spends even a wee bit of time around you requires a thick skin, Cavendish."

"It seems your friend knows you well."

I froze at the voice. Glancing to our left, I was startled to find Sebastian with Aria. For a moment, I was so shocked to see him after four years, I didn't speak. He looked the same, if a little older. He'd inherited my father's looks while I took after our mother. He was dark while I was fairer. Black eyes, so like our father's, glared back at me. There was no sign of the boy I'd once hero-worshipped.

That snapped me out of my stupor. "What are you doing here?" My accusing glare went to Aria because she'd obviously let him in.

Aria's brows drew together. "Your brother claims there's a family emergency."

Glowering at Sebastian, I wanted to rail at him. I wanted to physically throw him out of the castle. However, I didn't want anyone to know anything about me or him or our family. Smoothing my expression, I stood slowly. "Let's talk in my room."

I gave North a nod and my friend stared at me in concern. With another nod to Aria, I marched out of the lounge, sensing my brother behind me.

"Theo—"

"Don't speak until we get to my room."

Tense, chilly silence fell between us. I wanted to sneak glances at him, but I forced myself to keep my gaze straight ahead and used the time to compose myself. There was no way I could let him see how angered I was by his arrival.

As soon as we walked into my room, I strode across it to sit casually in an armchair. Crossing my legs, I gestured lazily to him. "Well, you've obviously come with a purpose."

Sebastian grimaced as he straightened his tie. Since he graduated university, I'd never seen my brother in anything but a three-piece suit. A gold wedding band glinted on his ring finger before his left arm fell back to his side. Of course. I'd almost forgotten he'd married two years ago. According to the papers, she was the daughter of a colleague. Ten years Sebastian's junior. Very pretty too. He'd probably married her because she came from a suitable background and was young enough to give him children. I doubted it was love.

And North and Aria might think love is real, but in a few years, they'd realize they were wrong.

"I need you to come back to London to see Father."

It felt like a hand fisting around my throat.

Sebastian took my silence for indifference. Fury flushed his cheeks and he took a step forward. "It is time to put the past behind us, Theo. Father needs us. My wife is pregnant, work is demanding, and as much as I hate being here to ask this of you ... I can't do everything alone."

For a moment, I saw the boy and not the man, and a niggle of guilt worked its way past my guard. I forced another memory to the forefront of my mind. Of him shoving my feelings aside. Of him protecting Father over me. It took me a minute, but I worked off the invisible fist around my throat. I was grateful how unaffected I sounded as I remarked, "Congratulations on planting your seed. Let's hope it's a boy." The Cavendish viscountcy was still one of the peerages that could only be inherited by a male heir.

Sebastian's face tightened with distaste. "Sometimes I cannot believe the man before me is the same person as my little brother."

"Funny, I was just thinking the same about you."

He had the audacity to wince. "Theo ... I know I've made mistakes with you—"

"Let's not go over old news. I don't care about it anymore."

"If that were true, you'd forgive Father. You'd forgive me."

"Why forgive when I can just forget?"

"You are a swine," Sebastian spat. "And I hate that I've had to leave my pregnant wife back in London to chase after you like you're an errant child."

"Then go home to your poor wife."

"Unfortunately, I promised Father I would bring you back."

"You'll have to break that promise, Sebastian. Because I'd rather have every inch of my body pierced with acupuncture needles dipped in the juice of Carolina Reaper peppers while lying in a bare white room with *Grease*'s "Summer Lovin'" pumping continuously through the stereo than go back to London with you."

My brother gave a long-suffering sigh. "I can see you're in a mood this evening, so I will return in the morning. I'm staying at the Gloaming in the village, and I'm not leaving until you come home with me."

A few minutes later, Sebastian was gone and my heart rate still hadn't slowed.

My fingers drummed the armrest as I took another few minutes to gather my thoughts. Then I practically jumped out of the chair and marched from the room.

There was a possibility she'd finished work for the day, but it was worth checking. I searched upstairs first but no sign. It was only on the first floor that I had any luck when I saw a housekeeper's cart disappearing into the staff elevator.

"Wait!" I called out.

A hand stopped the door from closing, but to my disappointment, it wasn't Sarah who stepped out of the lift.

This young woman with rich dark hair gave me a flirtatious smile. Was she new? "Can I help you, sir?"

"Uh, yes. I'm looking for your colleague. Sarah McCulloch."

"Oh." She seemed bemused by my interest in Sarah. "She no longer works here."

Stupefied by this, I rasped, "What?"

The housekeeper shrugged. "Sarah quit."

"When?"

The girl blanched at my angry tone and even I was surprised by how irritated I sounded. Even more so how strangely furious I was that Sarah had left without a word.

"Last week was her final week."

"Where is she?"

"Oh. I'm not ... I don't think I can tell you that, sir."

Digging into my pocket, I pulled out my wallet and then a hundred quid and offered it to her. "Now can you tell me?"

She stared greedily at the money and then glanced past me.

I looked over my shoulder to see another housekeeper strolling down the hall. Turning back to her, I ushered, "Make up your mind."

The housekeeper quickly snatched the money from my hand and stuffed it into her pocket. "I overheard her telling Mrs. Hutchinson she was staying at a cottage in Gairloch. She called it Haven's View Cottage."

Satisfaction eased my indignation, and I gave her a nod before turning on my heel. It seemed I had some Google Mapping and packing to do.

Four

SARAH

Gairloch, Scottish Highlands

The first time I walked down Gairloch Beach, I fell in love. It was a warm spring day back then, the sand perfectly soft and golden, the waters near shore a vivid turquoise because of the warm Gulf Stream that hit this part of the coast. There was only Grandpa and me on the beach, and I thought this was what peace, true peace, felt like.

I suppose that's what I was looking for when I bought my wee cottage up on the cliff overlooking Loch Gairloch.

When I arrived at the cottage, I was still raw from my goodbye with Jared and I cried myself to sleep that night. The next morning, however, I woke up determined to embrace my new home and the words I hoped to find there. After cleaning up a bit, I went grocery shopping and even drove farther north to shop in a village that held a weekly market. It was surprisingly busy. Upon my return, I got stuck into my new book.

The cottage was a two-bedroom midcentury bungalow, and it had spectacular views from its large windows. I set up my desk in the living room, facing the view. Unsurprisingly, I got swept up in Juno's world in the coastal city of Dundee. It felt good. I felt like I'd made the right decision coming here.

Today, however, when I decided to take a break from writing and walk the beach to clear my mind, I noted my legs trembled a little as I got out of the car. Now, twenty minutes later after sitting by the shore on this rare, splendidly sunny October day, I had to admit I wasn't feeling great. Physically. I stared out at the water, watching it ombre from turquoise to sky blue, my eyes drifting over the coastline to my right, peppered here and there with white homes up the cliff, and to my left a rugged collection of hills. Lifting a trembling hand, I pressed a palm to my clammy forehead and grumbled under my breath.

Perhaps I caught a bug at the market. I'd best return to the cottage.

I pushed up onto my now very weak legs and trudged back along the beach. By the time I reached my car, I felt like I'd run a marathon. My head was pounding and my stomach was sick.

Muttering expletives, I got into the car and tried not to panic at how light-headed I was as I drove along the coast. My bungalow was along from the center of Gairloch, just off the coastal road and up a wee winding lane into the hills where a few homes had been built to enjoy the loch view. The older woman who owned the home next to me was out in her garden, and she waved as I practically slid out of the car. Giving her a half-hearted wave back, I got inside the cottage just in time to make it to the bathroom where I promptly threw up my breakfast.

After I'd purged as much as I was going to from my stomach, I got up on even shakier legs than before. Shivers wracked my body as the room spun and my hair felt damp against my neck. The thumping in my head, along with the dizziness, made it hard to concentrate. How had this come on so quickly?

Stumbling into my bedroom, I clumsily kicked off my shoes and yanked free of my coat and sweater before face-planting in the bed.

———

FIRE EVERYWHERE. I couldn't get out. And looming like the gatekeeper to hell was a mammoth black demon, at least two hundred feet tall. It lunged for me and I screamed.

My eyes flew open, my pulse throbbing in my ears.

Slowly, my vision adjusted to the dark, and I remembered where I was. The room wasn't quite familiar to me yet, but I recognized it as the primary bedroom in my new bungalow. It was then that I slowly became aware of everything else. Sweat drenched my body. My skin was on fire, and my head still pounded like the devil from my fever nightmare was banging drums inside my skull.

My nose and head felt stuffy, and as I moved to check the time, my limbs seemed to be made of rocks instead of flesh, muscle, and bone. Forcing myself out of bed, I had to lean a palm against the wall to steady myself. It took me twice as long as normal to get to the living room and to my handbag to retrieve my phone. I couldn't remember the last time I'd felt this poorly. A look at the screen told me I'd been asleep for hours. It was nine o'clock in the evening.

I needed water, so I pushed myself to get up to fetch a glass from the kitchen. I also forced down some paracetamol and changed into a nightdress. It wasn't the weather for night-dresses, but a touch to the skin on my chest told me what I already knew. I had a fever.

That was never more obvious than a few hours later when

I woke up again with chills. I chittered miserably in my bed, pulling the duvet covers tight around me, too weak to do anything about it, and hoping it meant my fever might break soon.

———

I FELT DRUGGED.

The room wouldn't stop spinning, and I could do nothing but lie in misery in my bed the next morning. My fever hadn't broken, my headache hadn't abated, and I kept drifting in and out of consciousness. I knew I should probably call Jared. I'd had the flu as a child and this felt the same. It wasn't just a bad cold. I was really unwell. But I could barely make myself move.

Do it, Sarah, I heard Jared's voice say. *Get on that phone and call me now.*

Groaning, I rolled over and was just reaching out a heavy arm for the phone when a banging sound reverberated through the cottage.

Is that my head? I thought on a moan.

The pounding continued.

Then ... "Sarah? Sarah McCulloch?"

Why was that voice familiar?

"I know you're in here because your neighbor said she saw you go in and you haven't come out since yesterday."

What the ... Somehow I got out of bed, listening to that familiar posh accent I couldn't quite place rattle on about his long drive and how I better be in here. Sickness rose as the world spun, and it felt like I was on the deck of a ship in the worst storm ever as I made my stumbling way through the bungalow to the front door.

With trembling fingers, I opened a door I realized I'd forgotten to lock.

And standing on my doorstep was Theo Cavendish.

"Oh, great," I muttered as black spots crawled around the edges of my vision. "I've progressed to full-on hallucination."

"Dear God," I heard him say just before all the lights switched off.

FIVE

THEO

The last thing I expected to happen when I arrived at Haven's View Cottage was for its owner to open the door and faint in my arms. I lunged for Sarah as her eyes fluttered closed and her knees buckled. Holding her off the ground, I deducted, using my sharp observational skills, that Sarah was ill. She was drenched in sweat, her skin feverish, and she was currently unconscious. Bending down, I slid an arm under her knees and lifted her. Carrying her into the bungalow, I noted how light she was as I searched the house for the bedroom. Although average height, she looked and felt tiny and fragile.

There were two bedrooms, but the one with the rumpled curtains and half-empty glass of water on the nightstand told me this was Sarah's. I laid her down on the bed, my heart racing a little that she hadn't woken up yet. Noting her thin nightdress had pulled down at her chest, almost revealing her nipple, I tugged on the strap, restoring her modesty. The last thing she bloody needed was a strange man ogling her. She shivered in her unconsciousness, so I pulled her duvet over her.

"Sarah?" I murmured, brushing her sweat-soaked hair off her face. "Sarah, are you conscious, little mouse?"

She whimpered in her sleep, and I bit out a curse. It had been years since I played nursemaid but needs must. Tugging my phone out of my back pocket, I did a quick search for doctors in the area. Surprised to discover the small village had a health center, I called them.

"Gairloch Health Center, Jan speaking," a woman answered.

"Ah, yes, good morning. I've just arrived at my ... my friend's home here in Gairloch to find her stricken with something flulike. She just passed out and I can't rouse her."

"Is she a patient with us?"

"I have no idea. She's not long moved here, I think."

"What's her name and date of birth and I'll check for you?"

Impatience rose as the little mouse's eyes suddenly opened. They were glazed with fever. They fluttered closed again on a moan. She was in a bad way. "Sarah McCulloch. I ... I'm afraid I don't know her date of birth."

"Address?"

"Haven's View Cottage."

"Ah, yes, Ms. McCulloch just registered with us."

Thank God. "Do you do house calls?"

"Let me put you on hold while I speak to a doctor."

Reaching out, I pressed the back of my fingers to Sarah's forehead and she pushed into my touch as if seeking the cool. Staying on the phone, I marched across the hall to the bathroom we'd passed and found a facecloth. After running ice-cold water over it, I squeezed it out and took it back to Sarah, where I carefully laid it over her forehead.

She seemed to sigh in her sleep. Tracing my fingers over her flushed cheeks, I murmured, "Poor little mouse."

"Sir?"

"Ah, yes?"

"Has Sarah woken up yet?"

"She opened her eyes, but she wasn't cognizant of her surroundings and she's passed out again."

"Okay. Dr. Garroway will pay a house call. He'll be there within the next half hour."

Relief filled me. "Excellent, thank you."

Hanging up, I stood over the patient, uncertain what to do next.

"No," Sarah moaned and then mumbled something I couldn't make out. Her tone was distressed.

I leaned over the bed, pressing my palms into the pillow on either side of her head. "Little mouse, you're okay," I murmured in her ear.

"No, don't. Please don't."

"Sarah, wherever you are, it's not real. I'm here. You're fine."

Her eyes flew open, still glazed with illness, but recognition lit them. "Mr. Cavendish?" she croaked.

I smirked wryly. "I think you can safely call me Theo, little mouse."

"D-don't ... don't call ... me ... that." Her eyes fluttered closed again, and I would have been amused if I wasn't low-level alarmed by how bloody ill she was.

Thankfully, I only had to wait nervously by her bedside for another lengthy ten minutes before there was a knock at the door.

A tall, elderly gentleman with very long limbs stood on the other side. "I'm Dr. Garroway," he told me in a clipped accent almost as posh as mine.

"Dr. Garroway, I'm Theo. Come in. Sarah is this way." I closed the door behind him and gestured for him to follow.

"And you say you just discovered the patient?" he asked behind me.

"I arrived less than half an hour ago. She opened the door to me and fainted in my arms."

I stepped aside as soon as we entered Sarah's bedroom, and Dr. Garroway marched past to the bed.

"You have no idea how long she's been like this?" he asked as he bent over and gently lifted her lids to check her eyes with his penlight. She groaned and tried to bat his hand away.

"I assume she was well enough three days ago. According to her very talkative neighbor, that's when she arrived." I'd need to have a word with Sarah about the old woman next door. She didn't know me from Adam, but she'd practically told me Sarah's entire itinerary since her arrival three days ago.

The doctor flicked me a look, a frown between his brows, but he didn't say anything before turning back to Sarah. He checked her heart rate and then her temperature.

"Hmm." He straightened and looked at me. "Her temperature is at 39° C. A little higher and I would suggest hospitalization, but for now, just keep an eye on her. Do you have a thermometer to monitor her fever?"

I shook my head.

"I'll leave this one with you, then." He placed it on the bedside. "If her fever spikes past 39.4°, call either the practice again or call NHS 24."

"Is it the flu?"

"Yes, I believe so." The doctor sighed. "I'm afraid there's been a rather bad outbreak in the area. A few of the elderly have been hospitalized. Sarah has been hit pretty badly by it, but she's young, and according to her records, she has no history of respiratory problems, so I'm optimistic she'll be able to fight it off. You'll need to make sure she's drinking plenty of fluids, even if that means rousing her. Try to get her to eat, even if it's just a bit of toast."

He pulled a pad out of the folder he carried, along with a pen, and began scribbling. "There's a pharmacy just up the road." He pointed in the general direction of the village. "Here's a prescription for paracetamol." The doctor handed it to me, and it finally hit that I was going to have to play nursemaid to this stranger. "Sports drinks with electrolytes in them will help too. I can't reiterate how important fluids will be in the speed of her recovery."

"Fluids." I nodded, looking down at the prescription. "Will she be okay while I nip out for these?"

"It's just up the road," Dr. Garroway repeated. "And remember, call if her fever spikes."

Bloody hell. I looked at her small form and flushed face. How on earth had I become responsible for this human being?

ANY SLIGHT INDIGNATION at the predicament I'd landed myself in I shoved away and got down to the business of making sure Sarah McCulloch didn't end up in hospital. I pondered whether I should call her family, but then I remembered her grandfather recently died. There was a cousin, but I couldn't remember his name. Her phone needed charged, so after I collected the paracetamol and some groceries, I returned to charge it. Unfortunately, she had a passcode, so I couldn't get in to look at her contacts to call someone who would be a more appropriate care provider.

Instead, I made myself familiar with the small kitchen and filled one glass with water and another with a sports drink filled with electrolytes. I then climbed onto the bed beside Sarah and eased her light weight up against me.

"Wake up, little mouse."

She groaned. "No."

A smile tugged at my lips. "Come on. I need you to take paracetamol and some fluids."

Another groan as she nuzzled her hot cheek against my throat. Something like tenderness made my chest ache a bit. I ignored it. "I will shake you awake, little mouse, for your own good."

"Go away," she mumbled even as she burrowed closer.

"You asked for it." I shook her and her eyes flew open.

For a moment, I felt caught in her surprising jade-green gaze. Her brow furrowed. "Mr. Cavendish?"

"Yes, as we've already established, I am, in fact, Mr. Cavendish. Now"—I reached for the two paracetamol on my lap—"open up and take these."

"Why ... w-why are you here?"

"That's a discussion for another day. Take the pills."

"W-what are they?"

"Paracetamol. The doctor said you need to take two every four hours to help bring your temperature down."

"Doctor. Is ... is that who stuck that thing in my mouth?"

I stifled my laughter. "That thing was a thermometer. Don't worry. I wouldn't let strange men stick things in your mouth for no reason. Now, take the tablets."

"You're filthy," she muttered weakly, making me grin. Then she parted her lips and took the paracetamol.

"Water. Head back." I pressed the glass to her lips and helped her swallow some down. She winced and tried to pull away after a second. "No, darling, you're going to drink the whole lot."

It seemed to take a huge effort, but thankfully, she drank it. Then just as quickly, she fell asleep against me. I lay there in the bed, watching her flushed chest rise and fall in calm breaths, my arm going numb. My belly grumbled. I needed to eat and so did she.

Somehow, I couldn't quite force myself to move, however, as this was the most restful I'd seen her since my arrival.

I'd sit a little longer with her, let her rest a bit more before I shook her awake to force-feed her. I chuckled at the thought. If she hadn't liked me before this, the little mouse was going to hate me by the time she recovered.

Six

SARAH

All I wanted to do was sleep. So it was extremely irritating when that dreadful man kept waking me up to force pills and water down my throat, and then he made me chew on bland slices of buttery toast. I was cognizant enough to know it was Mr. Cavendish, but I didn't have the energy to ask him why he was here or mistrust his intentions.

However, I woke up during the night, shivering and shaking so badly, I must have made a noise because suddenly, Cavendish was in the doorway. He hurried to the bed as my eyes adjusted to the dark, and I vaguely noted his rumpled, sleep-creased appearance.

"Bloody hell, little mouse," he muttered. "You're shivering enough to start an earthquake."

"S-so c-c-cold," I chittered, my teeth clattering together as I shook.

"Maybe your fever is breaking," he murmured.

Suddenly, Cavendish threw off my duvet and sat down on the bed. Alarm cut through my daze. "W-w-what are y-you d-d-oing?"

"Body heat," he explained with surprising patience. "Turn on your side and pretend I'm someone you like."

"I-I don't th-think s-so." I had enough presence of mind to remember I didn't know this man.

"I'd have to be the worst sort of reprobate to take advantage of a sick woman. And while I am actually a reprobate, I'm not the worst sort. I promise you, I just want to warm you up. It's all very innocent. But I'll get out of the bed if you want me to."

I wanted heat badly enough to trust him just a wee bit, so I turned onto my side. I jolted as his arm wrapped around me, tugging me close to him. He pulled the duvet back over us.

To my astonishment, the heat of his body soaked into mine and while my shivering didn't entirely abate, I did feel warmer.

"Go to sleep, darling," Cavendish murmured against my hair as he tightened his arm around me.

THE NEXT MORNING, my eyes opened to find sunlight spilling in through the cracks in the window covering. My mind felt clearer and as I checked myself, I realized while I was still sticky with sweat, I didn't feel feverish. I pressed a hand to my chest and the skin was much cooler to the touch than before.

I tried to breathe out in relief and realized how stuffed my nose was. My head still ached too. And when I swallowed, it hurt like hell.

A memory of last night hit me.

Theo Cavendish was here ... and he'd slept in this bed beside me.

No.

That couldn't be right.

Could it?

I pushed up with a groan, and the room swayed but not as badly as before. The movement, however, set off a tickle in my nose and I sneezed. It wasn't pretty. Ugh, I needed a hanky. Turning my gaze to the bedside table, I was surprised to see a fresh glass of orange juice, two paracetamol, and a box of tissues.

I'd just wiped my runny nose when a familiar, deep, extremely posh voice said, "Ah, good, you're awake." Looking up, I watched Cavendish stride into the room, fully dressed and hair slightly damp, as if he might have showered. He looked well-slept and not at all disheveled. "How are you feeling?"

This man had spent all day yesterday and last night looking after me. Why? Confused, I replied in a thick, bunged-up voice, "I think my fever has broken. What are you doing here?"

"Let's test that, shall we?" he replied instead and reached for something on the bedside table. I realized it was a thermometer. "Open up."

I took it from him with shaky hands and stuck the instrument into my mouth. We stared at each other, his gaze searching, mine questioning, as I let the thing sit until it beeped. Taking it out, I read the digital screen. "Says 37.3°."

"Congratulations, little mouse, your fever *has* broken."

"Yay," I replied sarcastically. "I sound like hell."

"Yes, you do. But the worst is over." He gestured to the paracetamol. "Take those, drink up, and I'll bring you something to eat."

"Did you ... did you sleep in here with me last night?"

"You were shivering quite badly, so I provided body heat. You warmed up almost immediately." He smirked. "I have that effect on women."

I attempted to roll my eyes, but it hurt so I stopped. "Aren't you worried about catching what I have?"

"You have the flu. The doctor said there's been an outbreak in the area."

Groaning, I slumped back against my pillow. I bet I caught it at the market the other day. The place was packed with people. "And you're not worried about catching it?"

Cavendish shrugged. "I have a remarkable immune system. I can't remember the last time I was ill. I've been on several film sets where almost the entire crew has come down with something, and yet"—he gestured to himself—"nothing. Healthy as a horse."

"Fine. But can you explain what you're doing here? It's a wee bit surreal that, of all people, you're the one taking care of me."

Cavendish crossed his arms over his chest. "I read your books. They're rather good. I came to write the screenplay."

Shock froze me to the pillow. I was not well enough to deal with this. "M-my agent is reading through the contract a producer has sent. It's almost a done deal."

"*Almost* being the operative word. These things take forever. But we can have this conversation later. Right now, you have the flu, and you need to get better. And you need to eat something."

"Why?" This was a man who treated everyone with careless charm and if you were unlucky, like me, a bit of arrogant mockery. Why on earth was he looking after me?

Understanding my question, Cavendish gestured to the room. "Is there anyone else here to look after you?"

I could call Jared, but it would take him away from the farm and he needed to be there. "What do you want in return? The adaptation rights?"

His gaze narrowed and he opened his mouth before his lips pressed together, as if he'd thought better of it. A tense silence passed between us before he drawled lazily, "You need to eat and then if you're able to stand, I'd suggest a shower, little mouse."

NOT LONG LATER, I took small bites of the fried egg on toast Cavendish had cooked up for me, all the while eyeing him while he eyed me. He'd pulled a chair into the room to sit by my bed and was now on guard, making sure I ate every bite of the breakfast. The whole thing continued to be surreal. I'd also never met anyone who didn't squirm when you stared constantly at them without speaking, and weirdly, I found myself almost enjoying the challenge of staring him down. Cavendish was unmoved.

He'd been a little surlier when he'd returned with my breakfast, and I had a feeling I might have hurt his feelings when I'd suggested he was caring for me with an ulterior motive in mind. But that couldn't be right. He never crossed me as the type who anyone could truly hurt. Or someone who would take care of another human being unless there was something in it for him.

He liked my books.

I tried not to show how much that meant to me. Even though he was a prick, he was still a talented prick whose work I admired.

And he liked my books.

I'd eaten almost the entire slice of toast and egg when I started to feel nauseated and exhausted again. "I'm done."

Cavendish shook his head. He sat with one leg crossed over the other, his hands clasped together on his washboard stomach, totally casual, as if looking after a flu-addled stranger was a normal occurrence.

Oddly, he didn't feel like a stranger. I didn't feel threatened by him in my space or awkward that he'd held me last night. Usually, the very thought of a strange man in my personal space would have sent me into shy convulsions.

"Aye, I am," I insisted, pushing the plate away from me on the bed.

"You have two bites left. You can do it. Be a good girl."

I scowled at him. Patronizing arsehole.

His lips twitched. "Food and fluids will help you recover faster."

The thought of my manuscript, lying barely started on my computer and the deadline that loomed, made me reluctantly drag the plate back and quickly stuff down the rest of it. I'd barely finished when Cavendish reached over to take the plate, and I felt a violent tickle in my nose. I hurriedly reached for a hanky and managed to hold back the sneeze just long enough for Cavendish to get out of range.

And then I sneezed like it was a frickin' Olympic sport. There was so much mucus, I wanted to die as I scrambled to wipe my nose and face. My cheeks flushed at the sudden knowledge that the Honorable Theodore Cavendish, a specimen of physical male perfection, was here to witness me at my worst. Right now, I probably looked like someone had rescued me from a hot, phlegmy swamp.

"I didn't know that much noise could come out of such a little thing," Cavendish teased as he strode from the room. "Get some sleep. I'll be back in a few hours and then we'll see about cleaning you up."

Confused and mortified, I slid back down my bed and buried my face in the pillows. I didn't have long to feel embarrassed or bemused by his continued presence because exhaustion pulled me deep into sleep.

"I don't want to," I grumbled a few hours later, feeling crabbit and out of sorts upon Cavendish waking me.

"You'll feel better if you have a wash, little mouse."

I glowered at the pet name, but I'd given up on telling him to stop calling me that. I think I'd realized quite quickly that if you told Cavendish not to do something, he took perverse pleasure in doing it even more. Such a child. "I don't think my legs will take it."

"If that's true, you can get right back in bed. C'mon. You must be needing the loo."

As soon as he said it, I felt the pressure on my bladder. Bloody Nora.

"Fine." I weakly shoved aside the duvet and hurried to push down the hem of my nightgown.

"Let me help." Theo offered his arm.

Stubbornly, I stood without aid. My legs shook and the room swayed. I felt so weak, it was almost shocking. I panted for breath and leaned, without meaning to, into Theo.

He quickly slid an arm around my back and took my clammy hand in his. "Come now, I've got you."

Quietly, I marveled at his patience and cavalier kindness as he accompanied me from the bedroom and across the hall into the bathroom. My hair stuck to the back of my neck, and I wanted to scoop it up and out of my way. Sweat clung to my armpits, and while I couldn't smell a thing through my stuffed nose, I gathered that I stunk after sleeping two days away and sweating out a fever through most of it.

If the smell was bad, Cavendish thankfully didn't mention it. He took me into the bathroom. "Are you okay from here?"

Cheeks so hot, I knew I was cherry tomato red, I nodded, unable to meet his gaze. The bastard dared to chuckle at my mortification. "Fine. I'll be outside if you need me."

As soon as he closed the door, I used trembling fingers to situate myself on the toilet. Knowing he was out there, listening, however, I couldn't go. Finally, I croaked out, "Can you walk out of hearing range?"

I heard his droll amusement as he replied, "Why am I not surprised that your bladder is as shy as you are? This is me walking away." His voice got quieter until I could barely hear him.

Able to relieve myself, I did so with a sigh and then stared longingly at the shower.

Decision made, I cleaned up and crossed the room on shaky legs to switch the shower on.

Barely a few seconds had passed when Cavendish's voice cut through the noise of the water. "What's happening?"

"I'm having a shower."

"Do you think you can manage, or do you need help?"

"Absolutely not!" I practically squawked at the idea of him helping me.

He chuckled through the door. "I've seen a naked woman before, little mouse. It's not a problem."

Well, it was for me! "I'll manage, thank you very much," I answered primly.

As wonderful as the lukewarm water felt on my body, however, I burned through the small store of energy I'd gotten from breakfast. Soon I felt woefully light-headed, so I hurried through the washing of my hair and fumbled to get out of the shower. My legs almost gave way as I stepped out of the bathtub, and I had to grab onto the sink to steady myself.

I must have cried out because Cavendish sounded almost concerned as he asked, "All right in there, darling?"

How casual he was with his endearments. "Fine ... thank you."

"I procured some clean underwear and fresh pajamas from your dresser. Do you want me to pass them through?"

Blushing profusely at the thought of him pawing through

my underwear, I wrapped my body in a clean towel and opened the bathroom door. Everything was neatly folded and sitting in his palms. His gaze washed over me from head to foot.

"You look a little better."

"I don't feel it," I whispered, swaying as I reached out to take the items.

"Do you need a hand?"

To dress me? My eyes flew to his in irritation, but I saw his question was sincere and not made in perverse jest. My irritation fled. "No, I can manage."

Barely. It took me twice as long as normal to don my underwear and pajamas. As if he knew I needed some modesty, Cavendish was kind enough to select a pair of light cotton pajama trousers and a thin T-shirt.

As soon as I stepped out of the bathroom, he swept me into his arms like I was a bride. I gave a startled cry but wrapped my arms around his shoulders. "W-what are you doing?"

"You looked ready to pass out." He carried me easily and then sat me down on the bed, facing the headboard.

"Um, I don't usually sleep this way."

"Where's your hairbrush? And do you have hair ties?"

I pointed across the room to the old-fashioned dresser. I'd bought the cottage fully furnished and hadn't had a chance to put my stamp on the décor yet. "On there."

I watched Cavendish as he strode across the room to collect the items. When he returned, he sat down on the bed facing my back. I craned my neck to meet his gaze.

"Oh." He stood up to pull a phone out of his back pocket and then sat again. "You've got several missed calls."

Worry cut through me as I took my phone and typed in my passcode. Sure enough, there were texts from Jared from yesterday and four missed calls this morning. I jolted at the feel

of the hairbrush gently detangling my hair, and I shot
Cavendish another look of confusion.

His focus was on my hair, however, and the careful way he
was brushing it.

Turning toward the headboard, I called my cousin while
Theo Cavendish combed my hair. The sensation made me feel
like a drowsy cat, but I pushed through.

"Sarah?" Jared answered, sounding frantic.

"Hi," I croaked, my words nasally as I hurried to apologize. "I'm so sorry I didn't pick up. I caught a cold and I've
been in bed."

"You sound awful. You sure you're okay? I've been
worried sick. I was seconds away from jumping in the car to
come see you. Do you need me to?"

"No, no." I didn't want to drag Jared away from the farm.
"I'm really okay. I'm just sorry I made you worry."

"Don't think on it. I'm glad you're all right. You sure you
don't need me there?"

I thought of the man sitting behind me, taking care of me
... *So surreal*. "I'm all right, I promise. Just tired."

"I'll let you go, then, but try to check in with me later."

"I will. Love you."

"Love you too."

When I hung up, Cavendish murmured, "Why so many
phone calls from your cousin?"

"He worries about me."

"Aren't you a grown woman?"

I bristled. "I am. But he's more like an overprotective big
brother than a cousin."

"Sounds a little suffocating."

"No, Mr. Cavendish, it sounds like family."

The hair brushing stopped for a second, and I thought he
might say something, but the bristles gently glided through my
well-combed hair again. "I think considering the circum-

stances, it's quite all right for you to call me Theo," he suggested.

Theo.

It sounded so familiar.

To my surprise, I felt him part the hair down the middle, then he took one section and started to pull the hair together. I realized quickly that he was braiding it into two pleats.

"Where did you learn to pleat hair?"

Cavendish—*Theo* sighed. "Years ago, when I was an entirely different person, I had a girlfriend who liked when I played with her hair."

It was universally known that Theodore Cavendish was a bachelor, a playboy, and a commitment-phobe. The revelation that he'd once had an actual girlfriend whom he'd indulged in such a way was ... well, astonishing.

There was something in his tone, a slight bite, that warned me not to press him for more information. Instead, I enjoyed his gentle ministrations, my eyelids fluttering with drowsiness.

"For someone so shy, you're rather comfortable with silence."

"Doesn't that make sense?" I murmured sleepily.

"I've learned that shy people are insecure people, and insecure people tend to need to fill silence."

I huffed. "That's not my experience at all. Moreover, silence is undervalued and underestimated."

He stilled behind me. "How so?"

"Silence is a safe space. Not only does it give you time to think through what you'd like to say, it offers peace from all the things others say, all the everyday noise and clutter that mucks up everything inside our busy brains. Silence is where my imagination has space to flourish into novels."

"I'm glad that's what silence is for you. But it's not like that for everyone, little mouse. Silence is a thing some people escape because thinking *isn't* a safe space for them. People have obsessive and intrusive thoughts. Silence is the last thing they want."

I'd never thought about that, but I realized he was most likely correct. I'd had a friend at school who was diagnosed with obsessive-compulsive thoughts, and she never seemed to sit still. She was always on the go. Now I wondered if maybe she was just running away from her own mind. "Are you one of those people?"

"Thankfully not. Like you, I need silence to write."

I wondered, then, how he understood silence could be so different for other people. Had he known someone with obsessive and intrusive thoughts? The girlfriend, perhaps? "I'm sad for people who are afraid of silence."

"Yes, it must be rather tedious." His tone suggested boredom. It was that tone that I'd come to recognize as quintessentially Theo. I'd overheard him talking with North Hunter and been disappointed by him. His treatment of me that night in his room had confirmed my dislike for the man, if not the storyteller.

But now, after observing his care for me, I wondered if the perpetually bored aristocrat was a mask. And if so, why did he feel he needed to hide his true self?

"All done." He patted the top of my head like I was five years old, and I felt his weight lift from the mattress.

Turning, I fingered the long, damp braids, feeling so much better than I had this morning. Clean and fresh, if still devoid of energy and stuffed up. "Thank you."

Theo met my gaze and shrugged. "'Twas nothing." He gestured to a fresh glass of water and paracetamol. "Take those and get some rest." Then suddenly, he leaned over and took my phone off the bedstand and handed it to me. "Passcode." At my questioning look, he huffed a little impatiently. "I'm going to put my number in your phone because I intend to go out for a bit. I need some fresh air, and we need groceries."

"Oh." He was staying, then?

I opened my phone, and he took it and quickly added his number. "Call if you need me and I'll come back."

"Okay."

"Is there anything you require from the grocery store?"

I shook my head, the thought of food turning my stomach.

"You're sure? You're not due your period and need tampons or anything?"

I blushed at the blasé way he asked. Growing up with a grandfather who was loving but old-fashioned and didn't talk about those things, I wasn't used to a man being so open about the subject.

"Good God, woman," he murmured, studying me. "Is there anything body-related that doesn't make you blush like a schoolgirl?"

Scowling at the underlying mockery in his tone, I shooed him away. "I'm too tired to be subject to your charientism today, Cavendish. Off you go."

He raised an eyebrow, something lighting up his eyes. "Well, well, well, don't you have quite the vocabulary."

"Why are you surprised? You said you've read my books."

Theo full-on grinned now. "Yes, but I don't remember you using words like *charientism*. And I wasn't insulting you, little mouse."

"No, you were low-key mocking me." Even now my cheeks were hot with the confrontation. "If I'm such a joke to you, Mr. Cavendish, why are you here?"

His grin fell. "I'd think my being here was proof that I don't think you're a joke." Theo's eyes narrowed. "After that tongue-lashing you gave me back at Ardnoch, I can't believe I forgot that beneath those shy schoolgirl blushes lies a temper."

"Ugh." I pulled the duvet over my face. "I'm too tired for verbal jousting."

"Pity," I thought I heard him murmur with humor in his voice. "So that's a no on period supplies, then?"

Oh, for goodne—wait. I counted the days in my head. Damn it. I *was* due my period in two days, and I was as regular as clockwork. "Actually ..."

"What's that, darling? I can't hear you through the duvet covering your face."

Grumbling, I shoved the blanket down and forced myself to look him directly in the eyes. "I need ... tam ... Ineedtampons," I mumbled.

"Ah, so that's why you're temperamental this morning."

In answer, I used the last of my energy to throw the box of tissues at him. Theo darted out of the way, laughing. Still chuckling, he picked up the box and put it back on my bedside. Humor glittered in his eyes, making him even more attractive. "What a thanks I get for taking care of you."

Knowing he was right, but still annoyed, I murmured "Thank you" and then turned on my side to give him my back.

The bastard sounded like he was barely holding in his laughter as he wandered out of the bedroom to go on his errands.

So surreal, I thought again as my eyes drifted closed. Life was so, so surreal right now.

SEVEN

SARAH

The walls of the cottage were starting to close in on me. While I still wasn't back to full energy, my restlessness kicked up a gear this morning, and I knew if I didn't get outside for fresh air, I'd lose my mind. Growing up on a farm, I was used to constant walks in the countryside. Even working at Ardnoch, sometimes I'd take my lunch break just walking around the grounds to get out of the castle. I spent my weekends hiking or finding beaches to explore.

Four days I'd lain in this bed while Theo Cavendish took care of me. He tended to me with cavalier mothering that still shocked me. I'd learned quickly not to bring it up to him, however, because it made him prickly. It was like he didn't want anyone to think he was capable of kindness. And yet, the complicated bugger got annoyed when I suggested he was looking after me to get his hands on the film rights to my books.

I couldn't quite work him out. Or how quickly I'd grown comfortable in his presence. No, *comfortable* wasn't the right word. It wasn't like how I'd felt with Grandpa and Jared. Every time Theo appeared in my room, I got butterflies, and I never quite knew what to expect from him, so I was always a wee bit on edge. However, it wasn't like the way I was with him before. Or how I was with other strange men. Even around Lachlan Adair, my longtime boss, I turned into a nervous, blushing wreck.

But something about Theo taking care of me had created this intimacy between us. Moreover, other than when I accused him of looking after me for adaptation rights, he never seemed to take offense to anything, so I felt perfectly safe saying whatever was in my head.

Correction: If he wounded me with his arrogant mockery, I felt safe to bite back.

Usually the nervousness won out because I was over-thinking being in someone's presence. But not with Theo.

It didn't make sense considering how intimidating he could be. As an observer, I'd noted that quite a few people at the estate found the aristocrat overwhelming.

For the last four days, Theo had cooked my meals, forced me to eat what I could, kept me hydrated, and after I showered he'd insisted on brushing my hair like a nursemaid and pleating it so I didn't have to bother with blow-drying. The first few days, I'd mostly slept, but yesterday I felt better and insisted he bring me my laptop. I was still not well enough to write, but I wrote chapter summaries and answered emails.

Theo disappeared, off to who knows where, but was back in the late afternoon. We ate the pasta salad he prepared and made light conversation about Theo's writer's block, the script that just wouldn't come together for him, and the next book in the Juno McLeod series. He didn't bring up the rights.

After getting up this morning to relieve myself, I was grateful to discover that my limbs were much stronger, and I wasn't anywhere near as light-headed. I wasn't a hundred percent back to normal, but I was on the mend. And I needed fresh air.

I said as much to Theo when he arrived from the kitchen with poached eggs on toast and a cup of coffee. The man had taken to sleeping in the guest room and was an early riser because he was always up, washed, and dressed before I even woke. When I was well, I was an early bird too. But the flu was making me sleep longer.

"I'm going for a walk on the beach," I announced once I'd finished breakfast.

"I don't know if that's wise."

"It's been nearly a week," I argued. "The worst of my symptoms are gone. Even my stuffy nose is gone, and I've only got a wee cough."

"But you're still weak."

"No." I frowned. "I'm much better this morning. Look, I'm not asking. I'm going for a walk." I threw off the covers and slid out of bed, grabbing my empty breakfast plate. Hurrying past him, I heard him mutter something under his breath but couldn't quite make it out. Then I heard him following me into the kitchen. I glanced over my shoulder as I put the plate in the sink. "I don't need an escort."

"Don't you?" he murmured silkily as he leaned against the doorframe. He eyed me like a sleepy tiger.

"I'm a grown woman, Cavendish. While I appreciate you taking care of me this week, I don't need an escort and I don't need permission to go for a walk. I'm going to the beach. If I don't get out of this cottage for some fresh sea air, I will scream."

Theo smirked. "Someone woke up on the fiery side of the bed this morning."

I grimaced. "Don't be patronizing. This is my cottage. And in my cottage exists a gynarchy."

He grinned and it was much too attractive. "It's pronounced *gai-nah-ki* and your use of it is a little clumsy, darling."

Of course, his vocabulary was better than the average person's. "Are you mansplaining a word that literally means a government ruled by a woman?"

"I wouldn't say mansplaining. I am curious as to where you came about such a colorful vocabulary?"

I shrugged as I brushed past him. "I like words."

"Where are you going?"

"To get washed and dressed and then to the beach."

"Well then, I guess *we're* going to the beach."

I turned at the entrance to the bathroom to look at him. "You don't need to come along."

Theo stared me down in that intense, assessing way of his that would have made me squirm just a week ago. "If you're well enough to take a walk on the beach, you're well enough to discuss business. And we do have business to discuss, little mouse."

———

THE CAR RIDE to the beach was short and silent. Theo seemed to follow my lead as we made our way down onto Gairloch Beach. It wasn't a huge stretch of sand, but I was happy to walk the length of it a few times over to enjoy the sea breeze.

It was much colder than it had been just a week ago, but I welcomed the chilly prickle on my skin as we strode on the compacted sand near the water. The skies were a moody gray above, and the sea, if not rough, was marginally choppy. It rushed a little aggressively at the shore, and the rhythmic sound relaxed me.

However, it did not distract me from noticing Theo's attention. I could feel him staring down at me as we walked. I wasn't a tiny woman at five foot six, but a good eight inches shorter than Cavendish. He strolled at my side, and when I finally turned to look at him, our eyes locked. I knew he was staring at me.

My cheeks flushed at the intensity of his gaze. Did I have something on my face? "What is it?"

"You look much better," he stated factually. "Even with no makeup, you're rather beautiful, little mouse."

I flushed, though he'd commented with as much emotion as a robot. Embarrassed and annoyed by how contradictory he was, I huffed, "Are you trying to flatter the adaptation rights out of me now?"

Theo's eyes narrowed dangerously. "No. I'm just shocked at how attractive you are. Usually, one notices someone as attractive as you. It must go unnoticed because you skitter about like a frightened mouse, trying to stay invisible."

The comment stung. Badly. I looked away, staring at the water, refusing to respond to his mockery.

After a minute or so, Theo spoke again. "I didn't intend to insult you."

I turned back to him, drawing to a stop. "No, I think you very much intended to insult me." And I didn't understand him at all. Before he could respond, I resumed walking. The breeze blew through my hair and whispered over my skin. Needing a moment, I halted, turning toward the water. Then I closed my eyes, hands in my coat pockets, and just enjoyed the feel of nature all around me. Nothing but the sound of the water and the seagulls crying in the skies.

My legs still felt a wee bit wobbly, but I definitely had more energy than before.

I knew that I'd recovered so well because Theo had been a pushy nurse, making sure I ate (even when I didn't want to) and drank plenty of fluids. How could he go from being so casually kind and caring to being a complete and utter wanker? I couldn't even enjoy that he thought me beautiful because it was a backhanded compliment.

The man was so frustrating.

Shoving thoughts of him away, I tried to focus on being on this stunning beach. Opening my eyes, I watched the water ripple a little more wildly than usual.

I felt Theo at my side, staring out at the water too.

After a while, he spoke again. "I'll give you one thing, little mouse. You never deblaterate, and it's rather refreshing."

Deblaterate. To prattle, blab, babble. "I've never been much for prattling or small talk."

He laughed, eyeing me as if I were a new species of human. "You're very interesting, aren't you, Sarah? Or should I say S. M. Brodie?"

Another wave of flutters shook my belly, and I didn't know if it was because he'd used my name instead of that horrible pet name or because it was now hitting me that Theo, my number one choice, was here to write the screenplay of *Hollow Grave*. My life had been a strange mix of dream and nightmare this past year.

I straightened my shoulders and looked him in the eyes. "Jack Irving's production company will pay me a minimum of a hundred grand if the TV show gets made. And an option fee of £8000." I'd learned that an option fee was what a production company paid for the rights to make the TV show or movie. If they didn't produce it within eighteen months, they had to pay another fee or the rights would revert to me.

Theo considered this. "Is that for the first book only?"

I nodded.

"And how many copies has the series sold worldwide?"

"At last count, over eight million. The first book alone has sold nearly two million."

"Christ." He whistled. "Well done, little mouse."

I gave him a look and he grinned.

"Fine. When we get back to the cottage, I'll have my agent, Fern, reach out to your agent with my offer."

"Which is?"

"Ten-thousand-pound option fee for eighteen months. But I have an idea for incorporating book two into the first season, so I'd want the rights to *Hollow Grave* and *City of Deceit* and we'll work out a percentage that equates to a minimum payout above Jack Irving's offer if the thing gets made. And with me at the helm, it will."

He knew that I wanted him to adapt the books and that he had the upper hand, so why hadn't he lowballed me? "You could have offered just the same."

He shrugged at the question in my tone. "Yes, I suppose I could have."

Realizing Theo Cavendish would never explain himself, I decided not to argue about his gentlemanly offer. "Done. I'll contact my agent when we get back."

"Who is your agent?"

"Liz Mackle at Mackle & Brown Literary Agency in London."

"I know Liz. Fern and I have done film rights deals with her before. Excellent." He started to walk, his brow furrowed in thought, and I hurried after him.

"So, what is this idea of incorporating book two into the first season?" Now that we were really talking about it, my excitement was growing at the idea of seeing Juno's world on-screen.

"There's a scene between Juno and the main antagonist, Peter, in *City of Deceit*. I think it would make an excellent scene in the last episode of the first season."

I loved that he'd already mapped out the last episode in his head and was hopeful of a second season. "Is it the scene where she breaks into his house and he comes home?" It was one of my favorite scenes, where Juno begins bending the law and you start to see that Peter is fascinated by her but doesn't want to harm her. Yet. There's an attraction between them that adds a dark and complex layer to their dynamic. The reader should be part enthralled, part appalled.

Theo's eyes glittered as he stared at me like I'd surprised him again. "That's exactly the scene I had in mind."

It just confirmed he was the right person to do this. To my surprise, we were on the same wavelength. "So ... I'd like to be involved in writing the screenplay. How would we do that?"

He considered this. "Usually, darling, I'd tell you to fuck off and let me handle it."

I flushed in immediate indignation and opened my mouth to protest, but Theo held up a hand with a smirk.

"But I already know that would get me nowhere. Plus ... to my complete and utter shock, I think we need your voice in this."

I harrumphed.

Theo gestured toward the hills behind us where my bungalow stood. "How about I write the screenplay while you work on the next book? At the end of each day, you can look over what I've written and provide thoughts. We'll discuss any changes you want to make together."

"So, you'll stay with me?" At my cottage. Writing together.

"Why not?" He exhaled heavily. "This is a good place to write. And there's another desk in the guest room that I can put beside yours in the living room. You're not hogging that view to yourself."

Shaking my head at the continued weirdness of my current situation, I looked away from his handsome face. Stuck in my cottage for a prolonged time with Theo Cavendish. I didn't know whether to run from or rejoice at his proposition.

"Is that a no?" he drawled.

"I'm just ... life is strange. Don't you think?" I looked back up at him.

He studied me thoughtfully. "Life isn't strange, little mouse. People are."

"Nothing stranger than folks," I murmured. It was something my grandpa used to say.

"So ... do we have a deal?"

My stomach flipped wildly, but I tried not to let it show as I replied, "It seems we do."

EIGHT
THEO

Two days later, Sarah was well enough to start work. Although the contract hadn't been drawn up yet and it would take more time than I'd like, we decided to start work on the screenplay. It gave me an excuse to stay away from Ardnoch, and to stay hidden from my brother who had apparently run out of numbers to call me from because I hadn't heard from him in days. North had contacted me while Sarah was still ill and, for some reason, I'd lied and told him I was traveling, trying to find something to unplug the cork stuck up the arsehole of my creativity. I wasn't quite ready for anyone to know where I was.

Now that the little mouse was well again, she was up at the crack of dawn, and I made breakfast because when I was at home, I liked to cook. We took turns showering because there was only one. Being a gentleman, I let her go first.

Clean, fed, and ready to work, I strode out of the guest room and into the living room to find her perched on the couch watching something on her phone on low volume.

"Switch it off," I demanded. "Time to get to work."

Sarah shot me an impatient glance. "I think Britain might have its newest serial killer."

"Is that the tagline for the series? Hmm, I don't know. A little cliché."

"No." She shoved her phone in my face. "A third girl has been murdered down south. That's three in a year. The police said there is a pattern to the murders and are warning young women not to walk alone at night. All three victims are blond, between the ages of twenty-three and twenty-eight. *I* picked up on that. The police haven't highlighted that in their statement yet."

Morbid curiosity filled me as I read the article under the news video. Something familiar scraped across my brain at the pattern Sarah noted. I wondered if similar murders had happened in the past and if this was a copycat killer. Unsurprisingly, I read a lot of true crime, so it was quite possible it was stuck in my memory bank somewhere.

"Always the detective, little mouse. Now come. We have our own serial killer to get to grips with."

She nodded and slipped off the couch's arm, her silken hair, the color of wheat, falling over her face. I'd never seen or felt softer hair. I studied her as she walked past me and slipped gracefully into her desk chair. Her cardigan fell off her shoulder, revealing an expanse of creamy pale skin. Golden freckles sprinkled her petite shoulder, which told me she'd walked in the sun a lot during the summer. Everything about Sarah was soft, silky, and graceful. I hadn't lied to her when I'd told her she was rather beautiful. It just continually surprised me because ... well, how had I missed how attractive she was?

Strolling past her, I took a seat at the narrow desk I'd moved from the guest room. To take advantage of the view from the front window, I'd abutted the second desk against Sarah's, which meant we were sitting quite intimately.

She wrinkled her nose adorably as she glanced between my desk and hers.

My lips twitched at her obvious perturbance. "What?"

"Nothing." She pulled out her laptop and opened it.

"Am I too close to you, darling? Invading your personal space?"

Sarah shook her head a little too vehemently. "No, it's fine."

"I can move," I pushed, enjoying her discomfort more than I should.

"I said it's fine." She smiled, but it had a bite. That only amused me more.

Letting it go because I knew she was too damn polite to demand I move, I opened my laptop. While Sarah was sick, I'd begun making notes, highlighting the copy of the book she'd given me with scenes I wanted to incorporate into the script.

Scripts were an entirely different beast from novels, and I had to hope that Sarah wouldn't get too hung up on the fact that it was more difficult to understand the nuance of a scene when it was only written in dialogue and basic actions.

A few hours later, Sarah pulled me from my deep thoughts to announce she'd finished her chapter for the day. Taken aback to realize how much time had passed, and how easily we'd worked in each other's presence, I looked up from my laptop to stare out at the Highland loch beyond.

"Well?"

At her question, I dragged my gaze from the view. "Well, what?"

She shrugged and gestured to my laptop. "I was so into my work I don't know how you're getting on."

"Good." And it had been. No writer's block. "I've finished the first scene. Why don't we have lunch and then you can read it?"

Her expression was filled with curiosity as she stared at my screen. "Okay," she agreed reluctantly.

I tried not to laugh at how much she clearly wanted to read it now. "Food first," I insisted. While she might be better, she was still only a few days into her recovery and needed fuel. "Let's eat out. I fancy that little burger place down by the water."

"Burger place?" She frowned.

"Yes. You haven't seen it." I explained where I'd seen the sign.

"Oh, I hadn't noticed. Someone else must have bought that restaurant. It used to be a wee café."

"Let's try it, then."

Sarah eyed me. For someone so shy with everyone else, she had a way of looking unwaveringly at me that unnerved me a little. Like she was peeling back my layers. And I didn't want anyone peeling back my layers, thank you very much. I didn't have many. I was almost entirely layerless. Deliberately so.

"Okay," she finally agreed with a shrug.

I tried not to take offense to the fact that she was so under-whelmed at the thought of dining with me. Women usually loved eating out with me. Well ... they loved me eating them out. An image of Sarah lying flushed and naked with my head between her thighs rose out of nowhere, and I jumped out of my desk chair like the action might shove the image right back out of my head.

There would be none of that between me and the little mouse. I had rules against mixing business with pleasure.

I SALIVATED over my bacon burger while Sarah ate a small portion of mac and cheese. I thought about the scene I'd written and how complex Sarah's characters were. It was important to me that I translated the characters perfectly because there was no improving on them.

A tourist walked in as I mused and Sarah looked up. Her cheeks immediately flushed bright red, and I shot the tourist a look. It was a younger fella, handsome, rugged, outdoorsy type, and he was smiling invitingly at my lunch companion.

My hand tightened around my fork as he wandered off, still looking at her over his shoulder. His eyes met my hard gaze and he quickly looked away. Sarah glanced back down at her plate, her pretty cheeks still pink.

"Lord, you don't half blush, do you," I muttered, annoyed.

She shot me a vulnerable look that made me feel like a bastard before she took a long gulp of her cold water as if to cool her cheeks. Unfortunately, my shitty commentary only made her blush harder.

I bent my head toward her, catching her gaze, and asked her more gently, "How can someone as intelligent as you, someone who understands human emotions and psychology as well as you, someone whose writing is fierce with confidence, be so shy?"

Her stunning eyes widened ever so slightly. "I—I don't think those things necessarily go hand in hand, anyway."

"Yes, perhaps. But there must be a reason a grown woman is as shy as you are?"

"Are you mocking me?" she asked, quietly dignified in her wariness.

"No," I answered sincerely for once. "I'm genuinely curious. Do you even know why you're so shy? Especially of men." I gestured toward where the tourist now sat at the counter.

Sarah studied me for what seemed like too long. Then, "I'll tell you why I am the way I am if you tell me something real about yourself. And not something I could find out if I googled you."

The challenge made me tense, all the muscles in my body locking. I glowered at my meal. Something real she couldn't learn from Google? The only real things about me existed in the past.

"Or not," she said so quietly, it was almost a whisper.

But damn it, I was just curious enough about her to give her something. "I held my mother's hand while she died," I offered bluntly.

Shocked at what I'd revealed, I imagine I gaped at her like *she'd* said the words. Hating the pity in her eyes, I shrugged, tone bland, "Is that the kind of thing you were looking for?"

Her gaze washed over my face in understanding, and I wanted to lash out at her for it. To my relief, she didn't offer me a useless *sorry* or sympathy.

"My mum was an addict," she confessed softly instead. "It started with alcohol and then eventually whatever she could get her hands on. The substance abuse turned her into someone else. I ... She ... she abused me as well." She lowered her gaze, fiddling with her fork. "Emotionally and verbally. She ... she didn't have the nicest boyfriends either," she said in a hoarse whisper.

Sharp pain sliced up my palm.

I glanced down to realize I'd gripped the small table too hard and there was a splinter sticking out of my skin. I pulled it out and returned my attention to Sarah.

Her gaze was filled with so much hurt, I wanted to run from it. Yet I forced myself to stay. "When the one person who's supposed to love you, to think the sun shines from your arse, continually tells you that you're stupid, worthless, that you ruined their life ... you start to buy into it."

"And where was your father in all this?" I bit out, guilt eating at me.

"He died in a farming accident when I was a baby. He was Grandpa's son. Mum took me away from the farm after he was killed. But I stayed with my grandparents during the summers. Eventually, when I was twelve, things got so bad that I called Grandpa. He contacted social services and after a bit of time, my grandparents were given custody. They tried hard to undo what she'd done, but her words were tattooed on my brain. Every time I thought of asking a boy out or going to uni or going for a job I really wanted, I'd hear her voice in my head telling me that I couldn't. That the boy wouldn't want me, that I wasn't smart enough for uni, or good enough for the job."

"Jesus fuck," I muttered, horrified.

"It took everything I had to publish the first Juno McLeod book. I'd been writing the series for years and Grandpa knew about it. When Jared found out, he hounded me until I decided to self-publish it. It was the success of the series that made me start to realize my mum was wrong about me. That was solidified when a publisher, a big publisher, wanted the print rights. Then Grandpa ... not long before he died, he sat me down and told me he was worried about me. That he wanted me to go out and *live*. Really live." Tears glimmered in her eyes. "When he died, I decided I owed him to try. To go after what I want."

Understanding dawned. "Which is why you came to my room to ask me to adapt the book?" And I'd treated her like an insignificant simpleton.

All the droll remarks I'd made about being so shocked by how smart and intelligent she was, how beautiful she was, I was just being typical me. Not thinking of the harm in it.

But I realized I'd probably been inflicting much harm indeed.

"I know I'm a cold-hearted sod sometimes, and I can't promise not to be myself, but I can promise that from now on, I will never poke fun at your intelligence or worthiness again."

Sarah's lips parted in shock and then her expression softened in a way that scared the shit out of me.

So I pushed away my plate and pulled out my wallet and added blandly, "Thank goodness you realized you're far from stupid or you wouldn't be enjoying someone as *menseful* as I am."

She snorted. "You're not at all well-behaved or particularly polite. I'd say you were more *jaculiferous* than menseful."

Grinning, I stood, holding out a hand to help her from the table. "You think I'm prickly, little mouse?"

"As a porcupine."

"I have never been accused of prickliness before." I narrowed my eyes at her teasing. "But I shall try to refrain from being jaculiferous in the future."

Sarah sighed dreamily. "It's such a good word."

My smile was so wide, it almost hurt as I stared down at her, resisting the urge to pull her into my side. "It is an excellent word." We strode together to the counter to pay, and I waved away her hand as she held out her card. "*Mendaciloquent* is also a good word."

"To tell lies," she defined.

Good lord, she really did have the most exceptional vocabulary.

"It sounds better when you say it in your posh accent," she teased.

"Everything sounds better in my posh accent."

"True." Her gaze flittered to the handsome tourist from earlier before coming back to me. "Though other accents are nice as well."

Had the tourist spoken with an accent? I hadn't heard him speak. Frowning, I paid for the meal, left a tip, and then took Sarah by the elbow, blocking her view of the tourist as I led her out. "How about *crepuscular*?"

She wrinkled her nose. "I think it sounds more like something that grows on a wound than anything relating to twilight."

I threw my head back, laughing as I held open the door for her. "This is why you're a writer."

Sarah threw me a wide grin over her shoulder as she walked out of the restaurant, and I ignored a sharp twinge in my chest at the sight of it and followed her. In a desperate attempt to feel anything but that, I lobbed unusual words to test her and chuckled at her smug success with every one of them.

Nine
SARAH

"I put the fire on!" Theo shouted from the living room.

The coastal winter chill cut through my knitted cardigan. I grabbed the mugs of hot tea, delighting in the rush of heat up my arms, and hurried from the kitchen into the living room. My thick socks had slipped and were getting dangerously close to tripping me up.

Thankfully, Theo crossed the room to take the mugs, and I smiled at the sight of the flickering flames in the wall inset as I bent down to pull up my socks. "It's my first time using the fire."

The bungalow had a gas fireplace mounted inside the wall that was far more modern than the rest of the surroundings.

"It's bloody hyperborean," Theo muttered, sniffing the tea.

I smiled. He couldn't just say it was cold.

He held out one of the mugs to me, and I assumed it was my chamomile. Theo liked peppermint.

I tried not to stare at him as he sipped, his gaze drawn toward the large picture window. It was now November and another two weeks had passed. Theo had been here for three weeks in total. It strangely didn't feel that long, while at the same time, it felt like he'd been here forever.

We'd fallen into a comfortable routine that I never would've imagined in my wildest dreams. We both woke up roughly around the same early hour. We'd have a cup of coffee and something to eat and then take turns showering and readying for the day. If the weather permitted, we'd go for a companionable walk on the beach only to return to write. We'd break for lunch either at home or we'd venture out, and then we'd review the script.

In the evening, Theo would tease me about my lack of television while we watched a movie or TV show together on either one of our laptops.

It felt easy and natural, like we'd been doing this our whole lives.

Conversation didn't stall, and we talked about nearly everything and nothing. The only thing we didn't venture into was the past. Theo Cavendish had walls built around his heart that were at least a mile high and constructed of solid ice.

If that bothered me, I ignored it, just as I ignored my growing attraction to him. Before, I'd thought him handsome and I'd had a creative crush on him. Now, I didn't know what I felt. I just knew it was more. Physically and emotionally.

But I wouldn't spoil what felt like friendship for the sake of a one-sided infatuation.

Autumn had been mild for this far north. However, this morning we'd woken up to an early November winter. Our cars sat in my driveway, the windshields crusted in ice, and the floorboards were freezing beneath our bare feet. The bungalow had central heating, but I hadn't switched it up high enough, so the house was taking a while to heat up. Thankfully, we had the fire in the living room.

I searched Theo's profile, the strong, straight nose, the hard angle of his jaw, the slightly sharp cheekbones and the contrast of all that masculinity against the pout of his mouth. My belly fluttered and I dragged my eyes off him to follow his gaze.

The mountains across Gairloch Loch were snow-dusted, and the icy pale gray of the sky made the loch look like it had a layer of frost over the top. Puffy clouds reflected in the water. The naked trees were touched with frost, the roads and grass and plants too. Not quite as still as ice but glittery and magical. It was beautiful here. I'd never spent much time in Gairloch in winter, but I was never more grateful for the bungalow.

"I was up during the night working on another scene." Theo wrenched his eyes from the stunning view. "Perhaps you could look at it before you start your chapter?"

Surprised he'd been working through the night, I wanted to ask him why but knew he'd probably just fob me off with a vague, dry answer.

"Sure." I walked past him to the desk and settled in.

Theo followed, resting his mug of tea next to mine before he dragged his chair over to my desk. Our legs and shoulders brushed as he sat, and a prickle of awareness shivered down my neck.

I must have made some kind of movement because Theo frowned. He was so close I could see the silver striations in his pale gray-blue eyes. His aftershave tickled my senses with its spicy, woodsy masculine scent. "Are you still cold?"

Clasping my mug in my hands, I nodded without looking at him, fighting back the pink that wanted to bloom on my cheeks. *Think of cold soup, period cramps, of Harry Renfrew whose tongue felt like an out-of-control slug in your mouth.* I sipped at my tea, the thoughts doing the trick.

"The fire should warm up the room soon," Theo murmured, seeming to shift unconsciously closer to me as he opened his laptop.

So far, our work on the script had gone more seamlessly

than I could have hoped. Theo was a bit of a control freak when it came to his writing, but he'd proven a willing listener if I had a difference of opinion. That didn't mean he didn't wield sarcasm like a blade, but I was used to him now and didn't take his personality personally. In fact, I got the impression he quite liked it when I jabbed back.

Half an hour later, Theo's proximity was no longer forefront of my mind as I got lost in our discussion about the script.

"You need to add the sex scene here. It's the perfect transition between the scene where she's emotional and exhausted by the dead end she's met on the case, and then the scene after the intimate interlude, where she's compartmentalizing and being strong. The sex scene fits perfectly between those two moments."

Theo rubbed his eyebrow in thought. "I think it's gratuitous. You don't see that sex scene on the page in the book, Ms. Fade to Black. So why should we put it in the show?"

It was true I mostly didn't write sex on the page, but I also didn't always fade to black either. "But Juno thinks about the sex with Cameron as they're changing afterward." Cameron is Juno's friend-with-benefits in book one. She's a total commitment-phobe because of her past and her job. "She's impatient to get away from him. It surprises me that you don't understand what's going on in this scene."

Hearing my frustration, Theo quirked an eyebrow. "Well, explain it slowly, little mouse, so my feeble brain can comprehend."

Ignoring his tone, I continued, "She thinks to herself how Cameron's constantly asking her if this or that is getting her off, if she wants this, if she wants that, does she like this ... it kills her desire."

Theo frowned. "Later in book three or four, she has sex

with that ex-criminal who is dominant and aggressive, and she gets off on it."

"Exactly!" I was so into our discussion, it didn't even occur to me to be embarrassed we were talking about sex. "She spends all day every day in this traditionally masculine role, being the boss, making decisions, carrying this tremendous weight of responsibility on her shoulders. Sex is the one place she doesn't want to make decisions or think."

"She just wants to be fucked," he murmured.

Pink heat hit my cheeks and I looked hurriedly back at the laptop. Damn it. "Aye, pretty much."

I could feel him staring at me. "Okay. I understand where you're coming from. That this facet of her personality is important—"

"For women, in particular."

"Right. Well, we can talk about working it into the script in a way we're both comfortable with."

"Okay." I chanced a glance at him. His eyebrows furrowed in thought as his gaze searched my face. "What?"

"Is that what you like in bed?" Theo asked matter-of-factly. "To be dominated?"

The old me would have stuttered in mortification and, unable to find an excuse to leave, would have fled the scene. The new me clenched her fists and forced herself to stay seated.

"You don't have to answer, little mouse. I was merely curious as to where Juno comes from."

Perhaps it was his use of my nickname or the idea that he didn't see me as a woman beyond the pen behind Juno, but I straightened in my chair, causing our shoulders to brush. "I'll tell you if you tell me something real about you." I repeated my words from the diner. So far I only knew he'd once had a girlfriend he'd been extremely close to, and that he'd held his mother's hand while she died. Small pieces of a puzzle that helped me understand why Theo might be so closed off.

Theo leaned back slightly, his eyes low-lidded as he stared emotionlessly at me. I instantly felt insecure. Why on earth would Theo Cavendish share personal information he didn't share with anyone just to find out if I liked to be dominated in bed? I wasn't that interesting. My cheeks flushed, and I let out a small laugh. "Never mind. I think we should break for lunch. And then I really need to write my chapter."

"I didn't just come here to write the script. I came here to get away from my brother."

I glanced sharply up at Theo, surprised by this information, and the fact he'd offered it. "Your brother?"

He exhaled heavily, his tone bored, but I heard the edge beneath the apathy. "He wants me to visit with my father because my father has testicular cancer. Very treatable testicular cancer. He's going to be fine. But my brother, Sebastian, heir to the viscountcy and all-around perfect boy wonder, decided to camp out in Ardnoch until I agreed to return to London."

My mind whirred with speculation. "You dislike your father?"

"He cheated on my mother their entire marriage, and he punished her when she"—he made air quotes—"didn't behave like the exemplary wife of a viscount and lady of society. When she coddled me—"

"Punished her?" I glowered.

"Hid her credit cards. Banned her from leaving our house for days. Anything to get her to bend to his will. To go where he wanted her to go. To do the things he wanted her to do, including being a little less mothering toward me. As she got older, she fought him more. I wished she'd left him. She had her own money and plenty of it. But she was afraid he'd use his connections to take her parental rights away. Sebastian was afraid to be close to our mother because of Father, but he attempted to be a good big brother to me. When we were kids, anyway."

My chest ached for him. "I don't understand why your dad wanted to control your mum, to even control her relationship with her sons."

Theo sneered. "Because he considered us all possessions under his control."

"That's awful." I wanted to reach out and cover his hand with mine, but I doubted he'd like me for it.

"Yes, it was rather. But my mum refused to let go of me the way she'd let go of Sebastian. She'd rather take the punishments. And for the longest time, I was too young to understand. It's only as you get older and look back that you comprehend what was happening. If I'd known, perhaps I would have kept my distance."

"It sounds like your mother wouldn't have wanted that."

"No. But my father did try. He sent me to Eton, attended by all Cavendish men before me. Yet even that couldn't break our bond."

There. I heard it then. The utter sadness in his tone. I couldn't help myself. I smoothed a hand down his biceps, soothing, empathetic. "What happened to her, Theo?"

He unconsciously leaned into me as he replied, "I met my girlfriend, Saffron, at Oxford uni. Even though the school was about ninety minutes from home, we spent a lot of time at the London townhouse so I could spend time with Mum. Saffron got on well with Mum and even my father. Saffy kept trying to heal the breach between us, telling me my father wasn't so bad. But all I could see was the man who'd betrayed my mother over and over and treated her like a fucking commodity. He'd also pretty much given up on me at this point, and Sebastian was hyperfocused on his career. He'd allowed Father to drive a wedge between us, but I still tried to keep us tethered."

Theo looked me in the eye, and I saw the anger he couldn't bury. Bitter anger and hatred. The intensity of it scared me a little. "Mum was diagnosed with breast cancer, but they caught it too late. It had spread to her lungs and lymph nodes."

I squeezed his arm, trying to force back empathetic tears that stung my eyes.

"That bastard," Theo spat. "That festering boil of a father and husband was fucking Saffy while my mother lay dying in a hospital bed."

Gasping in horrified shock, I reared back. "Please tell me you're joking."

"Oh," he said, huffing a bitter laugh, "little darling, I wish I could. But after watching my mother cry for the thousandth time, asking why her husband wasn't there, I went in search of him. That human pustule had a bachelor flat. I knew where the key was, and I let myself in and discovered my father rutting between my girlfriend's legs."

Nausea pitched in my stomach on his behalf. "Theo ..." I didn't know what to say. What could you say to that?

"I had to lie to my mother and tell her Father was on his way the night she died. And then I had to bury her while my father played the grieving widower. He waited a stunning three months before he moved Saffy into his house and another month before he put a ring on her finger. They divorced three years later after he got bored and moved on to the next barely legal girl."

"I hate your dad, Theo," I stated bluntly. "He's a piece of turd dripping in pond scum a hundred animals have peed in."

To my surprise, Theo's expression lightened, his lips twitching. "Yes, he is rather, isn't he?"

A smile tickled my mouth, glad I could amuse him after such a woeful confession. "I won't tell anyone what you told me."

He shrugged. "It's not exactly a secret in my circle. But when you're a wealthy viscount, people tend to forgive your sins."

"Why would your brother ask you to come visit a man who did all that to you and your mum?"

"Because he's ... he's always sought my father's approval." He shrugged. "He took his side when Mum died, when Dad betrayed me with Saffy. Told me that our father was doing me a favor and I'd see that in the end. I suppose he was right. To me, Saffy was a sweet girl who liked to joke and cuddle and loved when I brushed her hair, could be kind and nurturing, and was exciting in bed. I wonder how much of that was just what she wanted me to see ... because I wasn't enough. I think, frankly, she got off on playing me and my father."

"She's a horrible person."

"Yes, well, I'm grateful to her and the lesson she taught me. She gave me an STD, which I realized she probably caught from my father. My father." He shuddered. "That was traumatic enough to make me almost obsessive with my sexual health. I like sex and I'd hate to do to someone what they did to me, so I make appointments every few months at clinics. Every time I go for my checkup ..." His gaze drifted. "I'm reminded all over again why."

I suddenly knew with absolute certainty that this Saffron person and his father were the two reasons Theo had not been in a serious relationship since. And why he kept everyone, even those he cared about, at a safe distance.

It was such a shame.

He liked to come across as this laid-back, cavalier, playboy writer ... but he cared. And he was secretly nurturing and patient. He'd looked after me when I was sick without hesitation or grumbling.

However, I'd be a fool to think he was capable of falling

for someone after the story he just told me. It wasn't only Saffron's betrayal; it was his father's and brother's too.

No wonder his walls were built so high.

"So." Theo turned into me, his legs pushing against mine with the movement. "Now that I've told you something real ... will you answer my question?"

Ten
THEO

Sarah stared up at me, confusion marring her expression. I nudged her with my legs. "Does Juno like to be dominated because you like to be dominated?"

Color flushed Sarah's cheeks and she swallowed hard as she looked away, staring out the large window. I greedily drank in the sight of all that blushing skin, eyes trailing down to her pretty lips as she nibbled nervously at them. It was strange how, just a few weeks ago, I found her blushing ridiculous, and now it filled me with an odd mixture of tenderness and amusement.

My question was definitely not appropriate, but we were both grown-ups and I couldn't deny my curiosity about this woman. She was such a contradiction. Shy, mousy reputation back in Ardnoch. Best-selling author of a stellar crime series in the real world. Disarmingly beautiful when you took the bloody time to look, and honestly, the best damn company I'd had in a long time.

Her presence was at once invigorating and soothing. I felt ... at peace here.

And in my gratitude, I was pushing her out of her comfort zone like the truly dastardly bastard I was.

"Sarah," I murmured, my tone a little taunting, "you can tell me. I'm a vault. I trusted you with something I haven't told anyone." My brows drew together. Good God, that was true. I had told her something I hadn't spoken about with anyone else. One would think I'd feel vulnerable, like several layers of skin had been scraped off, but ... I didn't.

Sarah turned to look at me. It was disconcerting how stunning her eyes were and how, even after living with her for a few weeks, they still stopped me in my thought process. "You haven't told anyone else that story? Not even North?"

Amused, I smirked. "You imagine quite the bromance between me and North, don't you?"

"You can be blasé all you want, but I know he's your friend."

It was true that I trusted North more than most. "He's a good man."

Sarah nodded. "I sensed that about him."

"Do you sense things about people, then?" I teased.

She gave me a mock scowl, and I resisted the urge to trail my thumb over the little crease it made at the bridge of her delicate nose. "As a matter of fact, I do."

Intrigued, I leaned in. "Oh, do tell. Who else have you sensed things about?"

"I knew Lucy Wainwright was a sociopathic bitch before anyone else did," she admitted. Her tone turned regretful. "I was just too shy and cowardly to speak up."

I frowned, knowing she was talking about the famous case of Hollywood actor Lucy Wainwright who, along with the estate mechanic, terrorized Ardnoch Castle and stalked Lachlan Adair. It happened a good few years ago now, before I was a member. Usually, I would bluntly say what I felt about a situation, but in this case, I was wary of hurting Sarah's feelings in the same way other people had. "You ... you weren't cowardly, little mouse."

She studied my face. "They wouldn't have listened, anyway, would they?"

"They didn't know who you really are, so perhaps not," I agreed as she took the words right out of my mouth. "*I* would have listened."

Shoving me playfully, she chuckled. "Aye, right."

Smiling, I nudged her again. "Stop avoiding my original question."

There was that blush again. She lowered her gaze, and this time I couldn't help myself. I reached out and gently touched her chin, lifting it so she'd look at me. "You don't have to tell me anything you don't want to." I wanted her to, though. I wanted to know about her. And I wanted my trust reciprocated.

"I don't know," she answered, eyes wide, sadness gleaming in them.

Shock moved through me as something occurred to me. I released her, my eyes searching her face for the answer. "Are you ... are you a virgin, Sarah?"

The woman flushed the color of strawberries, and I felt like a bit of a shit. "N-no," she stuttered, pulling back from my touch.

I hooked my foot around her chair so she couldn't escape entirely. Relieved she hadn't gone thirty-one years of her life without enjoying sex, I pressed, "Then how do you not know what you like in bed?"

"Why are you so interested?" She huffed, pressing her palms to her hot cheeks as she gazed out the window.

Disappointment flooded me, but I didn't want to upset her. "Shall we break for lunch? I was thinking grilled cheese, or do you want to venture out into the cold?"

Her head whipped back to me, lips parted, somewhat bewildered.

"Well?" I released my foot on her chair.

She studied me for a few long seconds. Then, "My first and last kiss was when I was twelve years old. It was my mum's boyfriend's son and he was seventeen."

I stiffened. "I'm horrified by several things in that sentence. First and last?"

"It wasn't a kiss I wanted," she answered sadly.

My hands curled into fists as anger tightened my throat.

"His name was Harry. His dad wasn't a good man either, and he'd learned how to treat girls from him. I remember his tongue felt like this slug that I couldn't get out of my mouth." She winced. "When I started to need to barricade my bedroom door at night and my mum wouldn't listen when I told her I was afraid of him, I knew I had to be brave and put myself first. So I called Grandpa and told him what was happening."

"I hope he ripped that little shit's head off," I whispered harshly. The thought of Sarah as a girl, cowering in her bedroom from a sexual predator living in her own home, enraged me beyond measure.

As if she sensed it, she settled a calming hand over mine. "I think Grandpa wanted to, but he is so—" She flinched, grief-stricken. "He *was* so smart. He called the police and social services instead. When they showed up, the police took me aside and questioned me. I told them what had been happening and when they relayed it to my mum, she flew at me and smacked me across the face in front of everyone. That was it. The police arrested her and social services took me from her right there and then."

Her words were so matter-of-fact, but the pain that must have caused her. Christ, this woman had lost so much before she was even a teenager. "Then your grandparents got custody?"

Sarah nodded, her expression softening. "They gave me the life I'd always wanted. They saved me in more ways than I can explain. But ... my mum left her mark on me. I ... My shyness was crippling. Maybe if we'd known better then, I could have talked to a therapist or something, but we just muddled through." She bit her lip, withdrawing her hand from mine. "I was pretty awful with men ... I mean, I *am*." She huffed out a self-deprecating laugh. "I just get so tongue-tied and embarrassed around men I find attractive. It's mortifying."

I didn't point out that she no longer got tongue-tied when she was with me because I didn't know how I felt about Sarah finding me a comfortable person to be around. "But you've had sex?"

She laughed at my bluntness, her whole face lighting up. I ignored a strange tugging in my chest. "Aye, twice."

I blinked rapidly. "Excuse me, did you just say you've only had sex twice?"

"Are you mocking me?" She narrowed her eyes into fiery slits.

"No, little darling, I'm not mocking you," I assured her. "I'm trying to digest the news that a supremely intelligent, beautiful woman of my acquaintance has only had sex twice in her thirty-one years."

"Oh." She pressed her lips against a pleased smile and then shrugged. "Well, the first time was when I was eighteen. I had two close friends in high school and they were always trying to force me out of my comfort zone, to be more outgoing. They asked me to a postgraduation party in the woods behind Ardnoch, and there was this guy. Callan. He wasn't from Ardnoch—he was a classmate's older cousin. Anyway, I'd had a few beers to try to loosen up and for some reason, he took an interest in me."

Oh, for some reason, indeed. She had no clue how gorgeous she was.

"Thinking on it now, I acted so stupidly, but he asked if I'd go for a walk with him and we did. It was pitch-black, but he had a little torch key ring. We were about five minutes from where everyone else was camped and he just stopped and tried to kiss me. I told him I didn't kiss on the mouth. So he kissed my neck." Those two pink flags of embarrassment glowed on her cheeks again. "One minute he was feeling me up, the next ... well ... And I wanted to," she reassured me. "I wanted to be like everyone else. I wanted to know what sex was like."

Dear God. "Are you telling me, your first time was against a tree in the woods with a stranger?"

She wrinkled her nose and nodded. "It was bloody uncomfortable and painful."

"And the second time?" I was almost afraid to know.

"A few years later. Before I worked as a housekeeper at Ardnoch, I was a housekeeper at the Gloaming when Gordon owned it." The Gloaming was the local village pub and hotel. "I'd put my hat in the ring for management, and he'd sent me to this managerial course down in Glasgow. The people on the course all got along, but I was shy as usual. One night, I was bored in my hotel room and went down to have a quiet drink, but one of the blokes from the course saw me and came over. Andy was his name. He'd been trying to flirt with me for the prior two days and didn't seem at all put off by my lack of social skills." She grinned at herself, and an answering smile twitched my lips. "I was brave that night and asked him back to my hotel room."

Lucky Andy.

"It was ... it was nice." She nodded. "Much better than the first time. But ... he rolled off me almost immediately, cleaned up, thanked me like I'd been his waitress for the evening, and left. I felt … vulnerable. A bit sad. Like a piece of tissue he'd just used."

"Bastard," I murmured.

"No." She shook her head. "We both knew what the situation meant. Especially when I told him he couldn't kiss me on the mouth. I just … I just hadn't expected to feel so empty afterward. Like he'd taken something rather than me giving him something. Does that make sense?"

I nodded, my pulse starting to race for some inexplicable reason. "And that's it? That's the extent of your sexual experience?"

"I'm afraid so."

It was even more impressive, then, that she wrote the sexual psychology of her characters so well. And it was a damn fucking shame that it hadn't come from more experience. "You really haven't kissed anyone since you were twelve years old?"

"I don't like it," she replied, her tone sharper than usual. "So why bother?"

Deciding not to push (for now), I shoved back from the desk. "Well, now that we've exchanged mutual trust, I think it's time for a break from all this intense talk about our past traumas."

Sarah smiled at my droll tone and gave me a grateful look. "Let's go out for lunch."

"Sounds good." I stood, pulling out her chair for her to stand. "You can tell me what's happening with Juno in the new book."

"You want to spoil it for yourself?" she asked, switching off the gas fire.

"I rather like the idea of being the first to know. And I should really, shouldn't I? Since I'm adapting it for television."

"The first two books. If you want any more, you're going to have to pay for it," she teased with a devilish smile.

I laughed, following her toward the coat stand at the front of the bungalow. "You, little mouse, are turning into a shark. It suits you."

When she shot me a grin over her shoulder, I once again ignored that terrifying tug in my chest.

ELEVEN
SARAH

It was a perfect November morning. My favorite kind. The air was crisp with winter's chill, but the low sun was a gentle heat on my cheeks and cast light over everything, making the thin layer of frost sparkle on the grass and trees and pavements.

Only one other person walked along the beach with their dog, and the water lapped gently at the shore as I talked to Jared on the phone. Theo stood off in the distance, his mobile pressed to his ear. Jared updated me on the wonders of having a second tractor that Georgie could use, and how much quicker the work was getting done. I'd insisted on paying for the new tractor to help with the workload and I was pleased it was a big help to Jared, but I was also distracted as I took pleasure in watching Theo. Butterflies fluttered in my belly. I was getting used to the sensation. The complicated Englishman wore a dark green peacoat, dark jeans, and boots. A striped navy and green scarf protected his neck from the cold, the peacoat accentuating his broad shoulders and tapered waist.

Yesterday, I'd heard grumbling and groaning coming from the guest room and I'd ventured in to find him rearranging furniture. Under his T-shirt, the lean, hard muscles of his biceps popped along with his veins as he hauled the heavy wooden bed frame across the room.

Tingles awoke between my legs as I studied him down the beach, watching him scrub his long fingers through his hair as if frustrated by whomever he was talking to.

"Sarah, are you still there?"

"Oh." I sucked in a breath, feeling guilty that I'd let my mind wander while talking to Jared. "Of course. Got a bit distracted by a cute dog that's bounding in and out of the water."

My cousin sighed. "I still worry about you being out there by yourself. Please tell me you've at least made some friends."

I rolled my eyes at the question someone might ask a ten-year-old. Sometimes, between my shyness and how young I looked, people, even Jared, seemed to forget my age. "I'm here to write a book, not make friends."

"I just ... I worry about you being lonely."

It was true that I didn't have any close friends. I'd gone on nights out with some of the girls from work and I kept in contact with my closest friend from school, Allie, even though she lived in Aberdeen now. None of them knew about S. M. Brodie. I'd often longed for that kind of female friendship. Where I felt safe. To entrust my secrets, worries, and fears to another woman.

But I didn't have enough time with my grandmother to undo the damage my mum inflicted. Her example made it very difficult for me to trust women. But I knew I needed to try harder.

"I'm fine," I assured Jared. I was not at all lonely right now. But he didn't know about Theo. He would ... my cousin wouldn't like the idea that I'd spent an entire month alone with an Ardnoch member. He wouldn't understand. "I'm too busy with writing and this deadline to be lonely. Are you lonely?"

He chuckled. "I'm too busy with the farm to be lonely. So I get your point. I'll lay off."

"I know it's just because you care."

"You'll call if you need me," he said, as he did every time we spoke.

I was distracted for a second as Theo turned to look at me. It took a minute to remember what Jared had said.

"Oh ... aye, you know I will. And I want you to call if you need me. I know it's still early ..." Our grief over losing Grandpa was still fresh.

"Aye, sweetheart. But ... I'm okay. I feel him with me," Jared said gruffly. "Every day I'm out there on the land, I feel him right there with me."

Tears thickened my throat and stung my eyes, and I turned away from Theo to swipe at the ones that escaped as I struggled to swallow back my grief. Finally, I could speak, but my voice rasped with emotion. "That makes me happy."

"I'm sorry, Sarah. I didn't mean to upset you."

"No, you didn't," I hurried to assure him. "I'm just glad you feel that way. I know he's there with you too."

"It'll get better," Jared promised. "It'll get easier to bear."

"I know." A swell of grief built upward in a way I hadn't felt in weeks, and I wasn't ready to have a public breakdown. "I better get back."

When I hung up, I turned around and let out a squeak of surprise to find Theo standing inches from me, frowning. He bent his head to study my face, eyes searching. "What happened?" he demanded.

I gave him a shaky smile as I wiped at the last of my tears. "Oh ... just something lovely that"—my breath hitched— "that Jared said about Grandpa."

Understanding softened Theo's expression. "Little

darling," he murmured in sympathy.

And for some reason, that's all it took.

The sob rose out of me before I could stop it, and I covered my face in embarrassment.

Theo made a *tsking* sound before I found my cheek pressed to his chest, his arms wrapped tight around me. At the comforting embrace I hadn't asked for, I found the courage to cry. "I miss him so much."

"I know." He pressed a kiss to the top of my head. "Let it out. It's okay. Let it out."

So I did. On Gairloch Beach, on a perfect winter's day, with the last man I ever thought would hold me through my grief, I cried all the weeks' worth of tears I'd kept locked inside.

———

I COULD FEEL Theo watching me after my episode on the beach.

Crying in his arms had released some of my tension, and I felt a bit exhausted, so we'd ventured back to the cottage to have lunch.

"I'm okay," I reassured him as we sat at the dining table. Theo was quite handy in the kitchen, and his grilled cheese was the best I'd ever tasted. It was three different cheeses and herbs from what I could tell. I took a bite and moaned. He'd made this half a dozen times already, and it was still bloody amazing.

His gaze flickered to my mouth before returning to my eyes. "You know I met your grandfather once."

I swallowed a bite, surprised. "Really?"

"At the Gloaming. It would have been about eighteen months ago. I'd not long joined Ardnoch and I'd gone to the village local to see what it was all about." He grinned. "Collum was there, and he gave me shit about my posh English accent."

I half laughed, half groaned. "I'm sorry."

"No, don't apologize. We had an excellent evening of ripping the piss out of each other. It's very hard to find someone who has skin thick enough to not only take my verbal jabs but enjoy them."

Chuckling now, I sat back in my chair, imagining it. Grandpa had always appeared gruff and a bit belligerent to everyone else. He liked people who weren't intimidated by him. "He must have enjoyed you."

Theo shrugged. "We got along well enough. I liked him."

A jagged mix of gratitude and pain flashed across my chest. "Thank you."

He nodded, watching me carefully. "Are you all right?"

"Aye," I promised. "It just ... catches me off guard sometimes."

"Grief?"

I nodded.

"I know. It happens sometimes when I think about Mum."

We shared a look of understanding until Theo's expression tightened, and I noted the discomfort in his eyes. He bit off a piece of his sandwich with more aggression than was necessary.

"Were you on the phone to anyone fun?" I changed the subject.

Theo's shoulders relaxed. "My agent. We haven't had the revised contract back from your agent."

"Should I be concerned? Should I hurry Liz up?" The thought of asking Liz to hurry with anything made my stomach flip.

"We'll do that." He waved away my offer. "But she's not being slow. These things take time. I haven't bought rights before, but I know from my peers that it can take up to a year to finalize these types of contracts."

"A year?" I gaped in dismay.

"Don't worry, little darling. There is no way I'm waiting a year. I'll be on your agent to get this done extra fast. I want Juno in production as quickly as possible. I can't legally start talking to actors I'm interested in or take the script to studios and streaming services until the contract is signed, but as soon as it's done, I'll be reaching out to actors and a few different contacts. I'm thinking Skylark World Productions, the studio behind *King's Valley*. We have a relationship, and they know how to reach that audience."

Excitement churned in my gut as it always did when I realized a TV adaptation of Juno was really happening. "Do you have actors in mind?"

"Olivia Jones for Juno."

My eyes grew round. Olivia Jones had just won an Academy Award for Best Actress in a Leading Role for a huge Hollywood film. "You know Olivia Jones?"

Theo nodded and shrugged like it was no big deal. "Before her fame exploded last year, we'd worked on a few smaller projects together. And I know she's interested in doing a British drama. I think Juno would be just the kind of role she'd love to sink her teeth into. I might not be able to approach her officially yet, but I already sent her a copy of *Hollow Grave*."

"When?"

"When you were sick. I bought a copy online and had it sent directly to her."

"And she's reading it right now?"

At my disbelieving tone, Theo chuckled and shifted in his seat to pull his phone out of his pocket. I watched him flick his thumb over the screen as I chewed a mouthful. Then he held out his phone to me.

It was a text conversation between him and someone called Olivia.

Holy crap.

Are you reading it? Theo had sent in his usual cryptic fashion.

Olivia must know him well because she'd sent an equally cryptic reply. *Yes. Just tell me when.*

And Theo responded, *I'll be in touch.*

He laughed as my jaw dropped. I shimmied in my seat with excitement. Olivia Jones would make the perfect Juno McLeod. "Oh my God!"

Chuckling, he took back his phone. "Don't get too excited. Her schedule might conflict with ours in the end. But she's interested."

"I can't believe Olivia Jones read *Hollow Grave*." I shook my head. My life was so surreal!

"You're fucking adorable, little mouse." Theo's grin was wolfish before he took a huge bite of his sandwich.

The human observer in me wondered why he flitted between the pet names *little mouse* and *little darling*. Did the usage mean something different? Was I foolish to look for some deeper meaning in them? I'd heard Theo use endearments so casually with people at the club, with strangers. He'd called me darling before he even knew me.

"What?" he asked suddenly.

"Nothing. I'm just excited about the TV show."

We finished our lunch, talking about other actors Theo was interested in and what I thought about them. Most of them I liked, though there were one or two I hadn't heard of, so I wasn't sure. He reminded me that the studio or television company he sold his scripts to used a casting director, but he had such clear ideas for Juno he wasn't sure it would be necessary.

After we cleaned up, we settled down in the living room at our desks to write.

I'd barely written a paragraph when I became aware of tingling on my left cheek.

Turning my head, I found Theo staring intensely at me.

It reminded me of our conversation four days ago when he told me the story about his family, and I told him about my sexual history. I still marveled that I'd been brave enough to reciprocate his trust. And even more so that I hadn't felt vulnerable or regretful afterward.

"What is it?" I asked, confused by his attention.

"Are you feeling better?"

"Much," I promised with a small smile.

He nodded, searching my face. "So I won't be a bastard, then, to mention that I can't stop thinking about the fact that you've not been kissed since you were a preteen."

Taken aback, I spluttered, "W-why c-can't you stop thinking about it?"

Theo shrugged casually. "Because kissing can be damn nice and even better, it can be damn hot. It's troubling that you won't let yourself experience it because of that little prick."

"I don't like kissing." I turned away from him, feeling embarrassment creep up—and frankly annoyed he'd use what I'd told him against me. *Tell him that!* Huffing, I spun in my chair to face him. "You're being a shit bringing it up like this."

He raised an eyebrow, a stupid smirk curling his lips. "I don't mean to be a shit. I'm trying to talk to you about it."

"Why?"

"Because an older boy forced a kiss on you. Of course you hated it! It doesn't mean you shut yourself off from enjoying it with someone you *want* to kiss."

"I don't want to kiss anyone," I lied. Because maybe I'd imagined what it might be like to kiss other men I'd crushed on. Maybe I'd even imagined what it might be like to kiss Theo.

"Lies." He called me out. "I've seen you looking at my

mouth."

Heat flushed my cheeks, and I cursed my pale skin and the capillaries beneath that were obviously closer to the surface than other people's. "I-I ..."

"Don't worry." Theo waved off my embarrassment. "I'm nice to look at. It's not a crime to recognize my attractiveness."

"You are such a cocky prick sometimes," I muttered hotly, looking back at my computer screen. "Now, if you don't mind, I'm trying to write."

He leaned in so quickly, I gasped, his face inches from mine when I turned to meet his gaze. His heady aftershave drifted over me and I shivered. "What ..."

Theo searched my eyes before his attention dipped to my lips. "Let me kiss you."

Blood rushed in my ears. "Are you mocking me?"

His eyes rose from my mouth to meet my suspicious gaze. "I would never," he said with rare sincerity. "I want to kiss you. I enjoy kissing. But more than anything, I want to help you move on from what happened to you." He was so close, his breath whispered across my lips. Tingles awoke between my thighs as my belly fluttered wildly. "We'll take it slow. Ease you into it. If you want to try, that is?"

My pulse throbbed in my neck, and I thought my heartbeat must be so loud Theo could hear it.

The truth was, I did want to know what kissing was like when you wanted it with someone. I'd just been so afraid because my first experience had been all about fear.

"Like an experiment?" I whispered.

Theo nodded. "If that makes it feel safe for you, then yes, like an experiment."

I knew my cheeks were bright red as I nodded. "All right, then. But ... I want to kiss you first. Not you kiss me."

Something softer than triumph glittered in Theo's eyes. "I think we can manage that."

TWELVE
SARAH

Theo had insisted we sit on the couch that faced the fire. It was a comfortable old sofa in a floral fabric not even my grandmother would have picked out. I needed to update the furniture in here.

And I dithered so I didn't have to think about the way my knees trembled as I lowered myself onto the cushion next to Theo. He shimmied closer, resting his arm along the back of the couch.

"What are you thinking about?" he murmured silkily.

"The word *gallimaufry*," I blurted out, twisting my fingers nervously in my lap.

Theo's mouth trembled with amusement as he reached out to smooth his hand over mine. I jumped at his touch. His skin was rougher and more calloused than a person might expect, but I remembered him telling me he was part of a rowing team back at Oxford and he'd continued to row alone after graduation. Were the calluses from rowing for years?

"Why are you thinking about the word *gallimaufry*?" he asked softly, his lips almost touching my ear.

A shiver skated down my spine and I turned a wee bit so

our faces almost touched. "I need to get rid of the furniture in here," I offered, my voice hoarse with tension and nerves. "Put my own stamp on the place. Something more cohesive."

"Ah." Understanding dawned. "It is quite the gallimaufry of furnishing, isn't it?"

I swallowed hard as my eyes landed on his mouth. I think I nodded. It was hard to know because I was suddenly hot and the wild butterflies in my stomach made it hard for me to concentrate on anything else.

Theo studied me before he reached out to caress my cheek with his thumb. The soft touch made me move closer. "We don't have to do this if you don't want to." His voice sounded hoarse, and there was a smolder in his eyes I'd never seen before. Like ... he was turned on.

My belly flipped, this time deeper and lower.

Be brave, I told myself as I felt his chest brush my shoulder. *Be brave and take what you want.*

I turned toward him to bridge the short distance between us. My lips brushed softly over his, tentative touches that made my mouth tingle. His lips were soft, full, and my heart rate sped up along with my gentle exploration. Theo stayed perfectly still, letting me take my time.

It wasn't scary. It was exciting.

I pressed my lips a little harder against his and, finally, he kissed me back. A gasp escaped from me into him as tingles awoke across my breasts, making them feel fuller, tightening my nipples. That same tingling sparked to life between my thighs. Wanting more of that sensation, I moved my mouth against Theo's, enjoying the way he took his time.

Who knew kissing could feel like this?

Suddenly, he pulled back, and I noted the pink across the crest of his cheeks. His gaze was low-lidded with desire and instead of terrifying me, it thrilled me. "Open your mouth, little darling."

Oh.

This was the part I was sure I was going to hate. But the only way to know for sure was to try. I licked my lips and nodded. And I was sure Theo groaned before he brushed his mouth over mine, coaxing me back into the deliciousness of his soft kisses. Then I felt his thumb on my bottom lip, pulling it down. Asking me to open.

I parted my lips and at the first touch of his tongue against mine, a rush of arousal squeezed my belly. I gasped again at the sensation, my hands coming up with a mind of their own to rest on his shoulders as I tried to mimic what he was doing with his tongue.

Theo groaned as I licked at him, and his arms were suddenly around me, crushing my breasts to his chest as he deepened the kiss.

Whoa.

Holy ... this ... this is what I'd been missing out on the whole time?

Losing myself to sensation, I matched him, moaning into his mouth as our kisses turned hungry and desperate.

THEO

I WAS HARDER than I'd ever been in my life.

At the first innocent brush of her lips against mine, I swear all the blood in my Neanderthal brain rushed south. I went from half-mast to full at the simple touch of Sarah's tongue against mine.

I couldn't explain my visceral reaction to kissing this woman.

And at that moment, I couldn't give a damn why. I just wanted to experience her.

As she moaned into my mouth, her hands drifting up the nape of my neck to slide her fingers into my hair, any last remnants of rational thinking flew out of my head.

Instead, I pulled her light weight over me until she straddled me, my cock straining against my zipper at her heat.

"Oh." She broke the kiss, those stunning eyes wide with arousal and questions.

"Don't," I practically begged her not to overthink this. "Unless you want to stop." *Please, Christ, do not say you want to stop.* I think I might have offered the universe my fucking soul to have Sarah not say she wanted to stop.

"I don't want to stop," she murmured, her cheeks flushed.

I reached up to cup her hot cheek, stroking my thumb over her soft skin. "I'm dying to know if that blush covers the entirety of your delectable body."

Her chest rose and fell with excited breaths, and despite her shyness, she forced out, "I-I suppose you're about to find out."

Dear God, she was magnificent.

I wrapped my hand around her nape, my fingers tangling in the silky strands of her hair, as I yanked her mouth to mine. I knew I should take it slow, or if I wasn't being a total moron, stop altogether, but I couldn't remember the last time I was this goddamn aroused.

To my surprise, Sarah's timidity disappeared when she was turned on. She sank into my kiss with eager hunger and rolled her hips, the seam of her jeans rubbing against my cock. Her gasp lit me on fucking fire and I took over the kiss. Needing to touch her, feel her, I slid my hands beneath her sweater and skated my palms up her slender waist to cup her perfect breasts. They filled my palms exquisitely. I wanted them in my mouth. I squeezed them, hard, and Sarah whimpered, her fingers tightening in my hair.

God, this woman. I wanted to fucking devour her.

I broke the kiss, my breathing shallow and rapid. "Take this off." I tugged at her sweater.

Sarah didn't hesitate. She seemed as impatient as I to feel *everything*.

At the sight of her straddling me, in nothing but a demure lacy bra, her hair falling wildly around her shoulders, her cheeks flushed, eyes bright ... I honestly didn't think I'd ever seen anything so beautiful or sexy in my life.

Holding her gaze, I felt her breathing grow labored as I reached around her back to unclasp her bra. Slowly, I peeled the straps down her arms until she was bare to me.

My mouth went dry.

Her breasts were ... "I'm not just saying this, love," I whispered gruffly. "But you have the most perfect breasts I've ever seen."

And I meant it. Round and perky with tight, hard, dark rosy nipples that begged for my mouth. A flush spread across her chest at my words and I grinned. "Well, you don't flush *all* over, but you certainly do flush in places other than your pretty cheeks."

That only made her blush harder until I took her tits in my hand and squeezed them.

She made a guttural sound as her back bowed into my touch, and I was lost again. "I want to do filthy things to you, little darling," I warned against her skin as I trailed kisses between her breasts. "Do you want me to do filthy things to you?"

"Yes, yes," she panted, arching into me as I wrapped my mouth around her right nipple.

As I tormented the little hard bud, my fingers opened the

buttons and zipper on her jeans. Sliding my hand inside, I found the lace edge of her knickers and slipped past those too. I felt the light dusting of hair that told me she wasn't entirely bare, and her hips jerked with feeling as I expertly found her hot little clit.

"Oh!" She gasped as I sucked her nipple and rubbed the bundle of nerves between her thighs. "Theo, Theo."

I swear I lost my mind at the sound of my name falling from her lips.

SARAH

I DIDN'T KNOW how it happened. How we went from experimenting with a kiss to me riding Theo's fingers as his mouth played with my naked breasts.

As my arousal tightened toward climax, I gasped out his name.

And then suddenly the man growled (aye, growled) and I was being lifted into the air. I grabbed onto him like a monkey, arms around his shoulders, legs around his waist.

"I need to fuck you," he explained, voice thick, "and we need a bed because I intend to do it thoroughly."

No discussion about whether we should do this and if we did, what it would mean.

And I honestly didn't want to talk about it. It would ruin it.

I wanted him to take me to bed. If our kisses and caresses were a sign of what could be, I wanted to experience the kind of sex I'd only dreamed of.

So I nodded, clinging tighter to him, and triumph glittered in his blue-gray gaze as he carried me easily into my bedroom.

He dropped me on the bed and yanked roughly on my jeans. I loved that he didn't treat me like delicate glass or a shy virgin, even as a flush of vulnerability heated through me as he tugged my knickers down my legs.

Theo's eyes blazed as he stared down at me. "Bloody hell, woman, every inch of you is perfect."

I squirmed in delight at his compliment as he whipped off his sweater to reveal the hard planes of his torso. For someone who hadn't exercised much while he was here, he certainly hadn't lost any definition. I wondered if he was naturally wiry and hard. Then I didn't wonder anything beyond wanting to explore him, to feel the smooth, hard dips and ripples of his lean muscle. I licked my lips and his nostrils flared.

"Like what you see, little mouse?"

Words wouldn't come, so I nodded.

He grinned as he unbuttoned his jeans, and the look was so cocky I found my voice.

"Smug bastard," I grumbled.

Theo chuckled and shoved his jeans and boxers down with casual confidence. My pulse increased as his cock sprang free, standing to full attention between his hard thighs. It was swollen and thick, a vein pulsing along the side of it.

The first time I had sex, I hadn't even seen his cock. The second time, I'd been indifferent to it until it was inside me.

For some reason, this time, I imagined wrapping my mouth around Theo's and felt a rush of wet between my legs.

"Have you never seen a man's cock before?"

My eyes flew to his. "Once. Not for long, though."

Theo's gaze grew low-lidded as he stepped closer to the bed and wrapped his hand around his arousal. I inhaled a breath at the sexual sight, my legs shifting restlessly. "What are you thinking?"

Oh.

"Um ...I ... that I want you inside me."

His breathing increased as he stroked himself lazily.

"And I'd like to ..."

"Like to what, little darling?" he purred.

"Taste you," I whispered hoarsely.

He squeezed his eyes closed, and I swear his cock strained higher. "Jesus, you're going to be the death of me, aren't you?" He put a knee on the bed and then something shifted in his gaze. "Fuck, condom."

Disappointment filled me. I'd been on the pill since I was eighteen to help with irregular periods, and it was on the tip of my tongue to say so. I wanted him that much. But the smart, sensible part of me that knew he had a past, decided not to offer that information up. "I don't have any."

His lips twitched. "That's all right. I do. Where did I leave my wallet?"

Relieved, I gestured to the doorway. "On the coffee table."

He studied me carefully. "Stay there and don't move. Just anticipate that when I come back, I'm going to lick every inch of that pretty pussy."

My belly squeezed low and I felt another rush of wet.

Theo grinned like he knew before he turned and marched out of the room, naked and uncaring. Why should he be? He had a long, lean body that made my mouth turn dry. His arse muscles shifted with his stride, and I imagined those muscles clenching as he thrust into me. I experienced another flood of arousal. I wanted him more than I'd ever wanted anyone. The only time I'd ever been this turned on was by myself, using my imagination.

But is this stupidity? I wondered.

Was I opening myself to a path that would lead me to heartbreak?

Should I stop it before it went any further? Or did I take the risk and finally experience what life was all about?

As if he knew my thoughts would intrude upon the moment, Theo hurried to grab the condom. His expression was fierce with need as he marched back into the bedroom, hard cock bobbing with each stride.

He reached the bed, wrapped his hands around my ankles, and dragged me toward him. I let out a cry of surprise that made him grin devilishly, and he hooked my legs over his shoulders, cupping my arse in his hands.

A flash of embarrassment flared through me at being so exposed to him.

"Is this your first time?" Theo asked, drawing a finger down the wet heat between my thighs. "The man from the hotel ... he didn't go down on you?"

I shook my head, biting my lips against my panting.

Theo stared at my sex until I swear my cheeks were hotter than they'd ever been. "So pretty ... a damn shame to leave such a pretty pussy so neglected."

I squirmed. "Theo."

He smoothed a calloused palm over my trembling belly, the touch almost soothing but possessive too. "Don't worry. I'm going to give you what you need." Then he buried his head between my legs and my hips arched off the bed, my heels digging into his back with the sensation.

I felt him groan against me, his fingers biting into my arse as he licked and sucked, his eyes holding mine the entire time. Daring me to hold his gaze, to watch him devour me.

So I did.

And it didn't take long for that coil of tension tightening deep inside me to reach its snapping point. My climax exploded, my cry filling the bedroom as my inner muscles spasmed, seeking his cock to squeeze.

For a moment, I wasn't aware of anything but my own

bliss. Then Theo braced over me, my wobbly legs spread on the bed. His expression was harsh, almost angry, as he stared down at me and rolled on the condom. Then he nudged between my thighs with his hot hardness. I stared up at him, a little dazed, a little uncertain of what his expression meant.

Until he kissed me, leaving my taste on my tongue as he stole my breath. The nudging between my legs grew more pressured and then Theo gripped the back of my left thigh and lifted it, spreading me.

He pushed in, the slight burn making me break his kiss with a gasp.

"Are you all right?" he bit out between clenched teeth. "Shall I stop?"

"No." I shook my head frantically, grabbing his waist. "Please don't stop."

The muscles in Theo's arms strained as he held himself above me. "Thank fuck. My cock has never been more desperate in its life, and I don't think it would thank me if we backed away now."

I stifled a giggle, biting my lip, and Theo grinned down at me. Then he flexed his hips and pushed deeper inside.

"Oh, fuck me," he groaned, pleasure tightening his features. "Sarah, Sarah," he panted now, looking down at his cock pushing inside me. "I've never ... fuck ... you feel ..."

My hips arched at the overwhelming fullness, and even as my thighs trembled with the pressure, I wanted more. I wanted friction. "Please." My fingernails bit into his waist. "Theo, please."

He released my thigh and I drew it up against his hips as he braced himself over me again, holding my gaze as he thrust all the way into me.

I cried out at the pleasure pain, my breath hitching as he withdrew and thrust back in. "Theo." My breath hitched at the tightening sensation deep inside my womb. "Yes, yes."

"Sarah," he groaned, tension trembling his arms. "God, it's taking everything in me not to just fuck you. You feel phenomenal."

Pleasure suffused me. "You can if you want," I panted, undulating against his thrusts.

"Later," he promised gruffly, keeping his pace slow and steady, building the tension inside me.

My heartbeat thudded in my ears as the sensation tightened, tightened, tightened. "Theo, Theo," I huffed, my hold on him biting with desperation.

Hard satisfaction filled his gaze as he held mine. "That's it, little darling, find it. Take it. Come for me. My good girl. Come for me."

And just like that, I did. The tension shattered, my body stiffening momentarily before flooding with exquisite relief. My inner muscles tightened and swelled around Theo.

Something like shock filled his eyes as I throbbed in hard waves around him. "F-fuck!" His hips jerked, and I felt an overwhelming pressure as I tightened around him at the same time he pulsed with release. His hips shuddered between my legs as he came. And came.

He ground his hips into me, his head buried in my neck, his groan hot against my skin as the last of his release shivered through him.

I rested my palms on his back, his muscles hard, his skin damp with sweat. Staring at the ceiling, I couldn't think beyond the melting relaxation flooding my limbs, making them feel like they were sinking into the mattress.

Theo's cock still pulsed inside me, and my inner muscles fluttered around him in response.

I liked the weight of him against me.

Finally, he lifted his head.

He looked a little ... stunned. Maybe even a bit fearful.

I swallowed hard, not sure what his expression meant. Be brave. "Can ... can we do that again?"

Theo suddenly grinned, whatever had been playing behind his eyes seconds ago disappearing. "Addicted to me already, little mouse?"

I shrugged, shoving off the worrying thought that I might be. "It was satisfactory."

He ground into me, making me gasp. "Satisfactory, indeed," he huffed gruffly, arousal thickening his words. "I just blew your fucking mind and you know it."

"I blew yours back," I insisted, pretty certain after what we'd just experienced that I wasn't wrong.

"Hmm, perhaps you did. Care to see if it was an anomaly?" He gently pulled out of me and sat up.

"I think we definitely need to experiment again, aye," I said nonchalantly.

He smiled at my teasing, but heat darkened his eyes. "Round two. Let's see if I can make you come twice this time with just my cock. On your hands and knees with a good hard fucking."

If he was trying to shock me, he would be surprised to discover all his words did was turn me on. Feeling confidence rise in me from how hard he'd climaxed, I pushed up to sitting, giving him a sly smirk as I turned and got on my hands and knees. I wiggled my bottom at him, glancing over my shoulder. "Go on, then."

Theo smoothed his hands over my arse, caressing me until I shivered. "I think I've created a monster."

"Is that a problem for you?"

He smacked me lightly. "I have a penchant for monsters, don't you know. Let me clean up and suit up again. And then I'm going to fuck you until you see stars."

Thirteen
SARAH

Theo sprawled on his side across the bed before me in nothing but boxer briefs. I watched him, feeling a strange mix of giddy and apprehension as I nibbled at cheese on crackers. I sat up against the headboard in nothing but a robe, in desperate need of a shower. However, Theo had insisted we eat first.

We'd just had what could only be described as a sex marathon. And I think the only reason we stopped was because I was getting a wee bit sore. From everything I'd read and heard, I was extremely impressed by Theo's stamina. Moreover, I was gleeful I turned him on that much.

Who knew?

I'd never have imagined when I knocked on his hotel room door all those weeks ago that we'd end up here.

Truthfully, I'd lost count of my orgasms today. I was exhausted and enervated all at the same time. Since we hadn't eaten in hours, Theo disappeared into the kitchen to pull together a picnic on a breakfast tray.

We watched each other as we snacked. The air of sexual tension still crackled between us. In fact, it felt heightened, which surprised me since I'd have assumed it would've dissipated now that we'd slept together.

Not that the intention had been to sleep together.

But maybe the kiss experiment had just been an excuse on both sides to give in to an attraction that had been growing for weeks.

"Well, your shyness certainly took a holiday today," Theo drawled, eyes glittering with teasing amusement and sex.

I smiled around a bite and waited until I'd chewed and swallowed before I replied, "I feel like I became another person entirely." It was true. I'd been more confident naked with Theo than I'd ever been just talking to a man I found attractive.

"You even stopped blushing." His gaze dipped down my body and back up. "I think I rather miss it."

"I'm sure it'll make a return," I replied dryly.

We fell into companionable silence again, just watching each other. Then Theo cleared his throat. "What are you thinking?" He blinked, as if the question surprised *him*.

I considered my answer carefully. I didn't want to overanalyze what was happening between us. I didn't want rules or expectations. Whatever would be, would be. That's what I wanted. But I'd been waiting for the last twenty minutes for Theo to lay down ground rules. To tell me that sex between us meant nothing. I was dreading it.

"I'm thinking I shouldn't tell you what I'm thinking because your ego doesn't need to swell any bigger."

Theo grinned. "Oh, now I demand to know. C'mon. Give me your thoughts and I'll reward you with multiple orgasms."

I laughed, shaking my head, which only made him grin harder, like a mischievous boy.

"C'mon," he insisted.

"Fine. I was just thinking that today was pretty good."

He mock glowered. "Pretty. Good?"

My lips twitched as I shrugged.

"Oh, yes, with accolades like that, my ego is tumescent with arrogance," he growled dryly.

Laughing, I grabbed grapes from the tray.

Theo huffed. "Is that it? That's all you're going to say."

"What would you say?" I couldn't stop smiling.

His eyes narrowed. "It was fucking glorious, and you know it was. My cock hasn't stayed hard that long since I was thirteen. I deserve awards for what happened here today."

I nearly choked on a grape I laughed so hard.

"You disagree?" Theo looked affronted.

I shook my head, trying to speak around my amusement. "Not at all. In fact, I'm impressed by your stamina."

"Impressed by my stamina?"

"I enjoyed myself very much."

"Sarah ..."

At his warning tone, my grin softened. "I didn't know sex could be like this. I ... for the first time in my life, I feel ... I feel truly awake." As soon as the words were out of my mouth, I wanted to take them back. They were too much. And I didn't want Theo to think that I thought what happened between us meant anything beyond two people giving into their insane attraction.

Theo's expression grew alarmingly blank.

Damn it.

I opened my mouth to explain, but he beat me to it.

"Let's take a bath. It'll help soothe that pretty pussy of yours."

"Oh."

"Do you think tomorrow you'll be able to take me again?" He took a swig from one of the two bottles of water he'd brought in. "If not, we can do other things."

Pleased my words hadn't chased him off, I shrugged as nonchalantly as possible. "You mean, like writing?"

"I mean like you suck me off while I eat you out," he answered bluntly.

And just like that, I was ready for him again. Goodness, this couldn't be normal. I blushed at my rampant horniness for the man.

Theo grinned. "Ah, there it is."

"Thigmophilic," I said suddenly.

His expression sharpened at my randomness. "A love for touch?"

I'd never met anyone who knew the same unusual words I did. It was fun being able to blurt them out randomly and have Theo understand. "Hmm. Apparently, almost all mammals are thigmophilic. I never really thought I was ... I liked a cuddle from my grandpa and Jared, but ... there was always a disconnect when anyone else tried to touch me. Now ..." I felt my breathing grow a wee bit shallow at the thought of what he'd just proposed.

"Now?" he asked quietly.

I hesitated. Again, I didn't want Theo to get the wrong idea.

In answer, he pushed off the bed and then slid one arm around my back and the other beneath my knees. I squeaked in surprise as he lifted me into his arms. "What are you doing?" I clung to his shoulders.

He didn't answer. Instead, he carried me into the bathroom and gently put me down. I watched, bemused as he turned on the bath tap, tested the water, adjusted it, and lifted my bottle of bubble bath to smell it. The room filled with the scent of citrus as he poured it into the running water.

He turned, eyes locked with mine, and tugged on the belt of my robe without saying a word. My breath hitched as the fabric fell open and he pulled it off until I was naked. Theo's gaze roamed slowly down my body and movement caught my eye. He was growing hard again.

"Ignore it," he said as he shucked off his boxer briefs. "Evidently, you naked equals me hard."

Lips twitching with delight at that, I waited to see what he'd do next.

He held out his hand.

I took it.

And then he guided me into the tub with him. We stood as the water flowed around our ankles, Theo's hands coasting down my waist, caressing, soothing. "Turn around."

I did.

His erection bobbed against my arse cheeks and I heard him suck in a breath before his heat disappeared. I glanced over my shoulder to find him settling himself against the bathtub, his legs spread. To accommodate me. "Sit," he gestured.

I lowered myself between his legs, and Theo wrapped his arms around me, a proprietary hand over my breast, the other on my stomach as he gently tugged me toward him until my back rested against his chest.

"Relax," he murmured in my ear.

He grabbed my purple bath sponge, dipped it into the rising water, and gently rubbed it over my body. My limbs melted against him until it felt completely natural to be like this together. Finally, once the bubbly water had reached our waists, he switched off the tap.

"How are you feeling?" he asked quietly.

"Good," I murmured drowsily. "How are you feeling?"

He guided the bath sponge down my torso, between my legs as his other hand began gently kneading my breast. My breath hitched. I felt Theo's chest rise and fall a little faster behind me. But he didn't answer my question.

Instead, he asked another. "Are you terribly sore?"

My cheeks grew a wee bit hot. "A little."

"Inside?"

I nodded.

He released the sponge but only so he could press two fingers over my clit. My hips jerked in reaction. "But not here?"

I couldn't speak. My fingers curled around his strong forearm as he circled the bundle of nerves at my apex, while caressing my breast at the same time. I turned my cheek against his upper chest, moaning as sensation thrummed through me.

"Theo," I whispered.

"Yes, little darling ..." His voice was hoarse in my ear. "Is this all right?"

I nodded frantically. "Aye, pl-please."

The pressure on my clit intensified and before I knew it, the tension inside me shattered. I shuddered and shivered against him as he petted and caressed me through it. Exhaustion melted through my limbs and my eyes fluttered shut.

I was aware of Theo's hand resting between my legs, not with intent ... just resting there as we drowsed. It felt possessive and claiming ... but I decided it was most likely neither. Theo wanted to claim no one and possess nothing but his career. *And that's okay*, I thought sleepily to myself. All I wanted was to experience life to the fullest. If this was all we had of each other, I could more than live with that.

I WAS ONLY half awake as Theo roused me from the now cold bath and lifted me out of it. He towel-dried me with efficient gentleness, reminding me of how he'd cared for me when I was sick with flu. That felt like a lifetime ago now.

Once I was dry, he pleated my damp hair and guided me back into the bedroom. Heavy with exhaustion, I lay down on the bed and closed my eyes, vaguely aware of him clearing away our picnic.

A few minutes later, he nudged me awake again and I held

my arms up for him while he slipped a nightdress over me. Then he tucked me into bed.

I expected him to leave. But feeling his continued presence, I opened my eyes. Theo's expression bordered on irritation as he looked down at me. Suddenly, he shrugged as if we'd just had a conversation and he rounded the bed. He slid in under the duvet and pulled me back against his chest like he'd done all those weeks ago when I'd had fever chills.

"I'll probably want you in the morning," he murmured in my ear as if by way of explanation.

Too tired to analyze whether that was the whole truth, I nodded. And then nodded off.

Fourteen
THEO

"There's a rumor going around that you're a missing person," North told me wryly.

I huffed, ear pressed to my phone against the winter breeze, as I watched Sarah walk along the beach. We were entirely alone this morning, and she was enjoying her sedate stroll near the shore. Even bundled up in a winter coat, scarf, hat, and gloves, my hunger for her stirred in the warm tightening of my balls. I'd expected my attraction to fade or to at least calm down over the last two weeks. I mean, I'd had Sarah every which way on almost every surface of the cottage. Yet, my need for her had only increased. It was bloody inexplicable.

It was utter madness, is what it was.

I didn't ... I didn't quite feel in control of it, which was disconcerting. Irritating. But I also didn't want to analyze it. I knew eventually I'd have to put a stop to it. However, I was the most selfish bastard I'd ever met, so that wouldn't be happening anytime soon. Sarah hadn't asked for a commitment. She seemed as reluctant as I to talk about what this thing between us was. So I'd decided to just give and take what I could from the situation.

"Theo?"

I shook my head, looking away from the woman who had turned me into the equivalent of an amorous, sex-obsessed teen. Bloody hell. "I ... I, uh, well, I'm not missing, as you can clearly hear."

"Where are you, then?"

"If I tell you, you can't tell anyone. There are some people I don't want knowing where I am right now, including my brother. So you can't even tell your fiancée."

"My fiancée is in the Highlands while I'm in Glasgow," he muttered almost petulantly. "I can't wait for filming on the show to end."

"I thought you were enjoying it?" The filming was set to wrap near Christmas.

"I am. But I miss Aria."

I rolled my eyes. "You see her nearly every weekend."

"It's not the same."

My gaze darted back to Sarah as I grunted.

"Is that it? No commentary on how pathetic and lovelorn I am?"

"You just did it for me."

"Bawbag," he said without rancor. "Anyway, back to the topic at hand. I won't tell anyone. Where the hell are you?"

Sarah slowed to a stop and tilted her face up to the sky. I couldn't see her expression, but I imagined her eyes were closed as she enjoyed the tranquility of the beach. My heart beat a little faster as I told North about Sarah being the author of the S. M. Brodie books. How I'd followed her to Gairloch and somehow ended up in her bed while we wrote together.

There was silence on his end of the phone.

Then, "Sarah McCulloch? As in Ardnoch's shy wee housekeeper?"

I scowled. "No, Sarah McCulloch as in Ardnoch's resident master storyteller and—" I'd been on the verge of making some droll, overshare comment about how exquisite she was in bed, but I stopped. Not because I hadn't before. I'd made all sorts of outlandish comments about my one-night stands to North and other friends. Somehow, however, it didn't sit right to speak about Sarah like that.

She wasn't some casual stranger I'd enjoyed a good night in the sack with.

I didn't know what she was, but she wasn't that.

"And?"

I cleared my throat, willing my heart rate to slow. "And ... a grown woman. She's thirty-one, not some innocent child. And you can't tell anyone about her pen name. That's up to her when she wants that information made public."

"She might as well be an innocent child, Theo, for fuck's sake. Of all the shitty things you've done, this is the shittiest."

Anger flushed through me. "You don't know a damn thing about her."

"I know she's not some gymnast from Thurso you can fuck around with." He referred to my last casual affair.

A busy line sounded in my ear and I pulled my phone away to see a London number was trying to call me. I ignored it and said into the phone, "You know, it's unlike you to be such a judgmental bore, North." But that wasn't true. The man was extremely protective of women. I just didn't think he thought they needed to be protected from me. It chafed more than I liked.

"It's unlike you to go after women who don't know how to play the game." He was pissed. "I have to go."

He hung up on me.

The little prick hung up on me.

So much for friendship.

A burn scored across my chest, and I refused to explore that feeling. Instead, I noted the voicemail message the

London number had left. Pressing the phone back to my ear, I listened to it.

"Mr. Cavendish, this is DCI Rick English of Scotland Yard. If you could contact me on 08904313002 immediately, I'd be grateful."

That was it. That was the message.

I suddenly remembered North joking that there was a rumor going around that I was a missing person. *Oh, for Pete's sake, please tell me my brother has not made a missing person's report.*

Ridiculous ass of a human being.

Grunting, I shoved my phone in my pocket with no intention of calling the bloody detective chief inspector my moronic brother had sicced on me.

Sarah turned my way, a soft, pretty smile on her face.

No, I had far better things to do today.

"I WANT to read your latest chapters." I turned my head on the pillow to look at Sarah.

She was flushed, still trying to catch her breath. Her hand rested near her cheek, her elegant fingers relaxed as her gorgeous tits trembled. "What? Now?"

I ignored the surge of desire and the ludicrous thought that if I were a painter, I'd grab a paintbrush right now to capture the stunning, sexual creature at my side. "Yes, now. You can read the revisions I made to the script while I read yours." I slid out of bed to haul on my boxer briefs.

Sarah pushed onto her elbows, a frown marring her brow. "But I haven't had a chance to read it through myself or edit it."

"I think I can manage through a couple of spelling errors."

"Fine," she grumbled, pushing out of the bed to pull on

her pajamas as she muttered, "So much for round two. Get a woman used to multiple rounds of sex and then suddenly, a book is more interesting than her vagina."

Laughing, I rounded the bed to haul her against me just as she pulled her pajama bottoms up. She made a little grunt of surprise and heat flashed through me. Smoothing her hair back as I cuddled her, I bent my head, my lips almost touching hers. "Later, I will fuck you until you can't walk straight, little darling. But first, I want to know what happens next to our Juno."

She pulled back, one eyebrow raised. "*Our* Juno?"

Trying not to smile, I released her. "Did I say our?" With a shrug, I turned and walked out of the bedroom. Despite the heating system, the cottage couldn't seem to get to a nice temperature without the fire on in the sitting room, so I hurried to grab our laptops and return to the bed.

Sarah sat crossed-legged on it, waiting for me. "Just to be clear, she's *my* Juno."

I snorted. "Dear God, woman, don't panic. I know Juno is yours. It was just a slip of the tongue. And I thought you liked that sort of thing." I wiggled my eyebrows suggestively as I slid under the duvet next to her.

She smirked as I gave her my laptop. I opened her laptop to pull up the latest draft of the next book in the series.

I was barely a page in when I felt Sarah lean against my arm. Glancing out of the corner of my eye, I found her watching me as she bit nervously at her fingernails.

Taking her hand from her mouth, I threaded my fingers through hers and held her hand in reassurance as I read the rest of her new chapter.

"Well?" she asked once I'd finished.

"It's good." It was. Her writing always was.

"But?"

Christ, she was starting to know me well. "I think you're

giving too much away about Colton." I referred to one of her red herrings. We'd already discussed at length Sarah's plans for the book, so I knew the red herrings and I knew who the real villain was. "There's almost too much information about him here. I fear readers will decide for that reason alone that he isn't the main guy."

She leaned against me, nibbling her lip. "Aye, I did wonder that myself."

"You would have caught it on your read-through."

We talked a little about which lines to cut and which to keep.

Then I prodded at something I probably shouldn't, but as soon as I'd read it, I'd felt a gnawing curiosity and suspicion. Honestly, I wanted Sarah to allay my suspicions.

"The scene where the attacker hits Juno ... you describe that well. What it feels like to be punched in the face and gut. It isn't the first time in the series that Juno is physically attacked and ... there's a realness to it ..."

Sarah met my questioning gaze. "Have you ever been punched in the face and gut?"

"My father backhanded me a few times as a child," I told her with an indifference I tried to feel. "There were a few tussles at school because I was quite an angry little shit. And I mistakenly slept with a married woman a few years ago and her husband found out and gave me a well-deserved beating."

"You didn't know she was married?"

I shook my head. "We met at a pub. He found some texts on her phone and tracked me down to said pub and clocked me in the face. Caught me unawares so I hit the floor and he kicked me in the gut before someone pulled him off."

"I'm sorry. That wasn't deserved, Theo. You didn't know. You wouldn't sleep with a married woman."

I glanced sharply at her. "How would you know that?"

"Because you wouldn't do to someone else what was done to you."

My throat tightened and I found it a little harder to breathe. Pushing through it, I shook my head. "You changed the subject. I asked you the question."

"Did you?"

Angry now, but not at her, I bit out, "Do you know from experience what it's like to be punched in the face and gut?"

I already knew the answer.

She'd told me her mother was abusive. But seeing how well she described it on the page and knowing her like I knew her now, I knew this had happened to Sarah. It seemed unimaginable that someone could take their hands to her.

"I told you she slapped me in front of the police."

"But there was more, wasn't there?"

"Mum slapped me around a bit, yes, but ..." Sarah swallowed hard. "I ... A few months before Ardnoch opened, just before Adair started hiring his staff, I was still working at the Gloaming. We went for a staff Christmas night out in Inverness. There was a guy who'd started working with us who kept coming on to me, and I wanted nothing to do with him. He got drunk and wouldn't leave me alone, so I decided to leave the bar without telling anyone." Sarah let out a shuddering breath, and dread sickened my stomach. "A man, a stranger, followed me and tried to pull me down a dark side street. Thankfully, a few girls who were out for the night saw it and came after us to chase him off, but not before he'd punched me in the face and gut to try to incapacitate me."

Unexpected rage welled within and I looked away, scrubbing a hand over my mouth to stop the reaction from spilling out.

"Those girls saved me from God only knows what."

"Oh, I think we both know what they saved you from," I snapped, turning to look at her.

She flinched at the fury in my expression and remorse filled me. I reached out to stroke a thumb over her cheek, unable to bear the idea of what might have happened to her if those girls hadn't been there. I softened my tone. "Did the police get him?"

Her cheeks flushed and she lowered her gaze. "I didn't tell the police. I ... if I told the police, then Grandpa would find out and it would just upset him, so ... so I let the arsehole get away with it, and now I have to live with the fact that he's probably done it to other women."

"Sarah." I tilted her chin, forcing her to look at me. "The likelihood is that he'd done it to women before you and even if you had told the police and they did catch him, he hadn't done enough to you to warrant much of a sentence. He'd be out again, doing it to other women, because men like that are predators with a sickness inside them. You know that. You write books about them."

She nodded slowly. "I ... it's just one more time in my life that I wished I'd been braver."

"You were brave, little darling," I murmured as I touched her cheek. "Was it here?"

Knowing I was asking her where he'd hit her, she nodded, eyes wide, perhaps a bit dazed.

Leaning in, I brushed my lips gently over her cheek, then I pulled back to brush another kiss across her lips. Pushing both our laptops aside, I moved over her and gently shoved up the hem of her pajama shirt. Her smooth, pale stomach trembled as I trailed my fingertips over the middle. "Was it here?"

She swallowed, cheeks flushed for an entirely different reason, and nodded.

Eyeing her to make sure this was all good, I bowed my head and dusted soft kisses across her flat belly. Sarah's scent filled me, and my balls tingled and tightened as blood thickened my cock. I followed a path downward and curled my fingers around her pajama bottoms.

"Where else does it hurt?" I asked thickly.

Shifting her hips to allow me better access, she whispered, "Between my legs."

"Be more specific." I tugged down her pajamas and underwear.

"Theo ..."

Throwing her clothes over my shoulder, I pushed her thighs apart, bowing my head toward her pussy. "Use your words, Sarah. Where does it hurt?"

She shook her head. As free with her body as she was when we had sex, her verbal shyness was something we still needed to overcome. Giving her mercy, I licked her and she gasped, undulating toward me.

"Is it here?" My voice was gruff with need now that I had her taste on my tongue. "Does your *wee* pussy hurt, my little darling?"

"Please!" She gasped, fingers curling into the duvet at her side.

Fuck.

I sat up, yanking her farther down the bed, before I pulled my cock free from my boxers. Needed her. Needed her so desperately. Wanted to banish all the bad memories and fill them with nothing but this overwhelming desire between us.

Prodding her opening, I groaned as I began to sink inside her. She felt even better than usual, and she usually felt phenomenal.

"Theo!" Sarah shook her head on the pillow, expression twisted with regret. "C-condom, condom, condom."

I froze.

Disbelief coursed through me as I glanced down at where my cock pushed inside Sarah. I had never forgotten to don protection. Ever.

Fierce desire made me want to sink all the way inside. In fact, I don't think I'd ever been in this much pleasurable pain in my life. The caveman part of my brain tried to rationalize that one time would be fine. But I'd never do anything a woman didn't want to do. Chest heaving with the exertion of pulling out when I was so goddamn happy where I was, I practically threw myself off her.

Glowering at my lack of control, I grunted as I leaned over the bed to where condoms lay on the bedside table. I pulled one on with jerky, angry movements.

"Are you ... annoyed?" Sarah asked uncertainly.

A tender ache filled me. "No," I told her gruffly as I spread her thighs again. "But your pussy is the physical embodiment of Elysium, and my cock likes being there naked. As it turns out, Little Theo is a bit of an exhibitionist."

Laughter spilled from her lips and despite myself, I grinned. Then I thrust inside her and her amusement turned into a cry of pleasure. "Take your top off," I demanded hoarsely.

I didn't stop thrusting into her as she did, so it took longer than usual for her to be rid of it. Then my Sarah was naked and perfect beneath me.

"Hold on to the headboard."

She reached her arms out, her fingers curling around the bars of the metal bed frame.

I tightened my grip on her thighs, hoisting her hips off the bed.

And I fucked her.

"Harder!" she begged, arms straining, breasts jiggling as I took her hard and fast. "Theo, harder, please!"

I did as she begged. It was dirty and rough and claiming and exactly as she wanted. And it was never enough, I realized with something akin to despair. I didn't think there would ever come a time when I'd had enough of this woman.

FIFTEEN

SARAH

Usually when I woke up, Theo was either just waking too or was already up and about. The next morning, however, he was awake, staring at the ceiling in contemplation.

"Morning," I croaked, my throat raspy from sleep. And perhaps from crying out in pleasure more than once last night.

He turned his head on the pillow. His eyes searched my face as his mouth turned up at one corner. "Morning."

"Everything okay?"

Theo gestured to me in answer, and I moved across the bed to snuggle into him, resting my head on his chest. His arm came around me. Tenderness throbbed in my breasts as they pressed against his side, and I remembered that dull cramps in my lower belly had woken me.

"What date is it?" I mumbled.

Theo mumbled it back and I sighed. My period was due. Had it really been eight weeks since Theo arrived at the cottage? It felt like longer.

"What's wrong?"

I still wasn't a hundred percent comfortable talking about

my monthly visitor, but I wasn't as shy about it as I had been all those weeks ago. "I've got cramps."

His arm tightened. "Do you need anything?"

"It's not too bad." I patted his chest. "What has you looking so broody this morning?"

"Broody? I don't brood."

I snorted because he definitely knew how to brood.

"Fine, maybe I can brood." He trailed his fingertips down my arm and back up again in a gentle caress. Pleasure flushed through me.

"Why are you brooding?"

It was Theo's turn to sigh heavily. "I think my brother might have put a missing person's report out on me."

I lifted my head to look at him. "Are you serious?"

He rolled his eyes. "Unfortunately. I have a voicemail from a police officer in London."

"Why ... why would he do that?"

"Because he's like my father and can't see past his own nose."

"What will you do about it?"

"Nothing. I won't play into his little games."

"But it ... has upset you?"

Theo was quiet so long I didn't think he was going to answer. Then, "Today would have been my mother's birthday. She would have been turning fifty-eight."

I felt a wee crack across my heart. "Theo ... I'm sorry. I ... she must have been fairly young when she had you."

"Young but not too young. Twenty-eight. She married my father at twenty-two, straight out of uni, fell pregnant, and had Sebastian at twenty-three. I came along five years later."

"How did she like to celebrate her birthday?"

"Cake," he answered immediately, amusement in his voice. "She loved cake. But she didn't indulge much because she was trying to keep a perfect figure. As if that would've stopped the bastard from cheating on her."

I smoothed a soothing hand over his chest.

"But on her birthday we'd have lots of cake. When I was around twelve or thirteen, I started taking her out for her birthday and we'd go for afternoon tea, except I'd arrange it so there were more cakes than sandwiches and tarts."

I grinned, imagining little Theo doing that for his mum. "I bet she loved it."

"She did. We'd have a lot of fun together. We did that every year until ..."

A deep empathy came over me and I turned, blinking back tears, to press a kiss to his chest.

"She deserved so much better," Theo whispered, such sadness in his voice. "My mother was the kindest woman I've ever known ... until you."

My tears threatened to spill.

"It seems so unfair that someone with such goodness in her was treated so abominably by the people she loved."

"Theo," I forced words past the emotion thickening my throat. "Your dad might have treated her poorly and your brother might not have been the best son, but you clearly adored her and she knew that. I know she knew that. Being that loved by one person ... it can make everything else bearable. Trust me."

His grip on my arm tightened and he squeezed me closer to him, I think to let my words percolate. We lay together in silence for a while.

Eventually, he rubbed my arm. "How are the cramps?"

My cheeks heated at how casually he asked. "A bit sore. I might see if there's a hot water bottle lying around."

"I'll get up and get the fire going in the living room and have a look. You stay here." He pressed a quick kiss to the top of my head before he slipped out from under me. Uncaring of his nakedness, he strode out of the room in search of a hot water bottle. I nestled into the sheets, soaking up the body heat he'd left behind.

Five minutes later he appeared in the doorway, totally naked still. He reached up, easily touching the doorframe above as he stretched, eyes pinning me to where I lay on his side of the bed.

We held each other's gaze for what seemed like forever, the moment charged. Sexy, yes, but more intimate than that. My heart raced.

Finally, he released the doorframe and crossed the room to me. He didn't address the moment. "Can't find a hot water bottle. Does anything else work?"

I shrugged. "Not really. I better check to see if ... well, if *it's* arrived."

Theo grinned as he braced himself over me. "You mean, your period?"

Scowling, I huffed, "You know that's what I mean."

"Say it." He tickled me under the arms and I shoved him off, laughing. "Say it, little mouse."

Laughing but growling at the same time, I tried to escape his tickling fingers. "Don't call me that!"

"Tell me you have your period or I'll keep tickling you."

"You're so immature!" I squealed, giggling as his fingers caught on my ribs.

His deep laughter filled the room. "I'm not the one who can't say I have my period."

That only made me laugh harder.

It was probably why it took a minute for us to become aware of the pounding noise and a familiar voice shouting angrily, "Sarah, open up!"

I stiffened as Theo stopped tickling me and turned his head toward the doorway.

"Jared," I whispered.

Theo looked back at me just as my cousin roared my name again and pounded harder on the front door.

"Off, off." I shoved Theo out of my way and crawled out of the bed. The sensation between my legs told me my period *was* here. Bugger. Hurrying into a robe.

"Uh, Sarah ..."

I turned around.

Theo pointed to the bedsheets, and I flushed at the spots of blood. "I'll get the door," he said, pushing off the bed to pull on some underwear. "You take care of yourself."

I flushed even harder. "If *you* open the door, Jared will lose his mind."

Still, Theo gently nudged me toward the bathroom.

"At least put on some trousers! And I need underwear!"

Theo quickly grabbed a pair of knickers out of the drawer and handed them to me before guiding me into the bathroom.

My heart raced as I hurried through cleaning myself and rummaging through my toiletries for tampons.

"Where the hell is Sarah?" I heard Jared bellow. I'd never heard him so angry.

"If you'd just calm down—"

"Calm down? Calm down? I'm this close to ending you, mate. Where's my cousin?"

As together as I was going to be in such a short time, I tightened the ties on my robe and burst out of the bathroom, hurrying into the sitting room.

Jared stood facing off with a half-naked Theo. Theo wore a mask of boredom, but I saw tension riding his shoulders. My cousin, while relieved to see me, also looked murderous.

"Jared, what's going on?" I rushed over, pressing my side to Theo's.

He stepped away from my touch and I shot him a concerned look.

"What's going on? What's going on is that I got a call last

night telling me that this prick"—he gestured angrily to Theo —"is here taking advantage of you."

Indignation and embarrassment flooded me, but Theo asked blandly, "Who called?"

Jared eyed him as if he were a disgusting bug, and my anger built. "Someone with more decency than you. Do you get off on taking advantage of innocent women?"

Theo shrugged like he didn't care about any of this.

Me? I was pissed. "How dare you?"

Jared stared at me, stunned. "How dare I?"

"Aye, how dare you? I'm not some innocent virgin child, for God's sake, Jared. I'm definitely *not* a virgin and definitely wasn't one before Theo got here."

My cousin's eyebrows raised as if this was some big surprise to him.

I scoffed. "I'm older than you, remember."

"But—"

"No buts. I appreciate the concern and I'm grateful you love me enough to drive down to check on me. But you don't get to come in here and treat me like a child or treat Theo like crap."

"He's a well-known player, Sarah. As a fellow member of his species, trust me, he's using you!"

"If he is, it's none of your business." My pulse raced.

Jared scowled. "You don't mean that. You're not ..." He eyed Theo again. "You're not the kind of woman someone plays with. You don't know the game. And you're grieving, and this arsehole probably knows that and is taking advantage. He's not good enough for you. I think it would be best for you to come home with me so this prick can go back to his own life. Away from you."

I didn't say anything because I was stunned by how high-handed Jared was acting. He'd never been this intrusive in my life before. But then he was still grieving Grandpa. He wasn't himself right now.

Unfortunately, Theo misinterpreted my silence.

"Go on, then," he uttered.

I looked up at him. He gestured with his chin, trying to keep a blank mask on his face. "Go run home, little mouse. Go with your cousin. What's it to me? I certainly don't care."

Hurt threatened, but then I noted the shimmer of sweat across his upper lip and the tension in his shoulders. My eyes drifted down. His hands were clenched into tight fists. My eyes flew back to his and he swallowed hard, his Adam's apple bobbing visibly with the movement. He tried to relax his hands, but he'd already given himself away. Theo shrugged. "Off you go," he insisted, yet there was a shakiness in his voice now he couldn't hide.

Damn this man.

I glowered at him. "I'm not going anywhere." Facing my cousin. "Outside. Now."

Jared yanked his astonished gaze from Theo and turned on his heel with a huff. I followed him, stopping to shove my bare feet into boots.

"Coat," Theo bit out.

I hid my smile as I shrugged on my winter coat over my robe and hurried outside after my cousin. As soon as the front door shut, Jared whirled on me.

"You're out of your mind."

Done with his attitude, I raised a palm. "Just stop. Stop it right now."

His head jerked.

"I'm not out of my mind with grief. I am a thirty-one-year-old woman with her own mind and her own needs. While I appreciate the intention, you do not have the right to come into my home and treat me like I'm a child."

"Sarah ..." He sighed heavily. "I'm just worried about you. This guy? This fucking guy, really?"

"You don't know him. You don't know anything about him."

"Do you?"

I shrugged, amazed by the truth in my next words. "I think maybe I know him better than anyone does."

Jared scrubbed a hand over his face. "I don't want him to hurt you. Especially not now."

"You have to trust me, Jared."

"I do trust you. It's him I don't trust. And I'm not blind." He gestured toward the house. "Surprisingly, I can see he cares about you. But I can also see that he is terrified that he cares for you, Sarah. Terrified." His shoulders slumped. "So please be careful."

My cousin's words hit home. Because that's what I saw too. I didn't see a man telling me to go because he was apathetic. I saw a man telling me to go because I scared the shit out of him. I knew Theo could hurt me. Yet, what I felt when I was with him ... it emboldened me. It felt so good, I'd risk anything for it.

I hugged my cousin tight and hard, and he buried his head in my neck. After a few long seconds, he squeezed and then nudged me toward the door. "Get inside out of this cold."

As soon as I stepped into the bungalow, I experienced a sharp throb near my heart.

Theo hadn't moved.

He stood still as a statue, hands still clenched at his sides. Like a little boy who was afraid something he wanted was about to be taken from him.

"Jared is heading home now," I said, moving to his side, using both hands to unclench one of his fists and thread my fingers through his.

Theo looked down at our joined hands, a frown marring

his brow. Suddenly, his fingers tightened in mine, and his breathing grew shallow. This man. I ached for him and all his emotional wounds.

"If you hurt her," Jared's menacing tone brought our heads up, "I will fucking eviscerate you."

I blinked rapidly because there was no denying Jared sounded sincere.

"I have farming equipment that can dice you into small pieces, and a lot of land in which to scatter those pieces. No one would find you."

Well, that was grim. I bugged my eyes out at my cousin. "Okay, we get the point."

"Do *you*?" Jared asked Theo.

Theo clenched his jaw but nodded.

A few minutes later, I hugged my cousin goodbye again and watched him get in his truck and drive away. Normally, I'd ask him to stay, but there was too much tension between me and Theo. We hadn't discussed what we were to each other, but it was becoming increasingly clear this was more than just a casual thing.

I'd barely toed off my boots and shrugged out of my coat when I found myself spun around and hauled into Theo's arms. His face was hard with determination as he carried me through the house and into the bedroom. He threw me on the bed, and I bounced with a startled yelp.

Suddenly he was over me, kissing me with a desperate fierceness that made me breathless and hot. Rationale broke through my arousal, though, and I pushed on his chest.

Theo broke the kiss, his eyes searching mine.

"I ... I think I understand you," I told him quietly.

A vulnerable light filled his gaze.

"That's why I stayed despite you telling me to go. But next time you tell me to go like I don't matter ... I will go," I warned him. "I'm not like your mother, Theo. There's no way I'll return to a life of feeling not worthy of someone, of feeling like I don't matter to someone who matters to me."

Remorse tightened Theo's expression, and he nodded in understanding. His lips were soft, gentle, apologetic on mine.

"My period." I broke the kiss again to remind him.

"I don't care," he whispered harshly. "And the sheets are already marked."

"I need to ... I need to take care of ... you know." My tampon.

"I'll do it." He kissed me again and I flushed head to toe at the idea of sex while I had my period. But Theo didn't care at all. Moreover, he took his time kissing apologies all over my body. And later as he moved inside me with slow, easy, savoring glides, he held my gaze captive in his.

We watched each other come, clinging onto one another through our lovemaking, and I felt the bond between us grow stronger, tightening its grip until it was almost painful.

I had to hope that with time, what we felt for each other would become more comfortable and easier to bear.

Sixteen
THEO

Three days after Sarah's cousin's arrival, I still felt out of sorts. I didn't want to overthink anything because I was ... well, it would probably mean the end for Sarah and me, and I wasn't quite ready for that.

Staring out of the living room window at the wintry day, I tried to ignore the fast beating of my pulse but couldn't. It felt like my heart had been racing for the last two days, and I was uncomfortable in my own damn skin.

Maybe it was the Highlands.

December this far north wasn't this southerner's optimum environment.

Soft hands slid around my waist, and I inhaled her citrusy scent as she pressed a kiss to my shoulder blade. "Good morning."

I covered her hands with mine, my pulse slowing a bit as Sarah rested her cheek against my back. "Morning, love."

"Is everything okay?" She pulled away to rest her pert little bottom on her desk to face me. Those stunning green eyes met mine. "You seem a bit out of sorts."

Yes, I was, wasn't I. Maybe it wasn't just the Highlands. Maybe it was ...

No.

It was probably because I suspected the one friend who I trusted had broken my confidence and tattled on me like a schoolboy to Sarah's cousin. It had to be North who'd told Jared I was here. He was the only one who knew. I had to admit it stung more than I liked that he thought me such a philandering bastard that I'd hurt Sarah. Not to mention the way others seemed to treat Sarah as if she were fragile and incapable of making her own adult decisions. They didn't know her. Not even the people who purported to know her best really actually bloody knew her.

She had a quiet fire and inner strength that put most people to shame.

"You're thinking pretty hard over there."

I nodded. "I think North told Jared."

Sympathy softened her expression. "I'm sorry."

I shrugged. "It's good to know where one stands."

"Theo—"

"Let's go to London," I cut her off, unable to discuss North or anything remotely related to wounded feelings.

Sarah's brows rose. "London?"

"Yes. Have you ever been to London at Christmastime? It's something to see."

"I've never been to London, full stop. I've ... I've never left Scotland."

Taken aback, I reached out to caress her pretty cheek. "Well, little darling, we need to do something about that."

"My agent is in London and she did suggest meeting when she visits Edinburgh next year, but maybe I could meet her if we go to London now," she mused.

Glad she was giving it serious contemplation, I pressed,

"And the weather is milder in London too. We could take a break from writing while I show you the sights."

"But my deadline ..."

"It'll still be there. Everyone needs a break, Sarah. You've been working every day for the past two months."

She considered this and then nodded. "All right. Let's go to London."

Relieved, knowing a change of scenery to somewhere more familiar would ground me again, I picked her up and twirled her around. Her excited giggles filled my ears and an invisible hand stroked a tender caress across my heart. Lowering her, I patted her bottom. "Go get ready."

She shoved me playfully, her face wreathed in smiles, before she hurried from the room like a child at Christmas.

I stared after her, feeling ...

Feeling too much.

Seventeen
SARAH

After Theo suggested I do some clothes shopping in London and spend a little of my money on myself, it didn't take me long to pack. We were ready to leave in record time.

I had a moment of panic when, just as we stepped out the front door, I asked, "I don't need a passport, do I?"

Theo raised an eyebrow. "You don't have one?"

"No."

"Well, you should get one. But to travel to London you just need ID. Your driver's license will do."

"Speaking of, what about my car?" I gestured to it as he led me to his rental.

"Leave it. We'll figure something out." Then he peered at my vehicle for a few seconds before turning back to me with a smirk. "We need to do something about this car, Sarah. You're making all the other millionaires look bad."

My laughter echoed off the driveway as I shoved him playfully aside to load my bag into the boot of his car.

We chatted about all the sights Theo wanted to show me when we got to London, and I let the butterflies of excitement fill my belly as I anticipated our trip. It was out of character for me to do something so impulsive, but it made me feel alive. I sincerely believed Grandpa would be proud of me for going out into the world.

Even though I was afraid it would take the shine off my excitement, I texted Jared to let him know I was flying to London. That I was spending an indefinite period of time there, but I'd be home for Christmas.

We'd just reached Inverness Airport when my phone buzzed in my purse with a response from Jared.

Ok. Have fun. Be careful. Call me if u need me.

Grateful at his measured response, I told him I would and that I loved him.

I knew Jared had thundered across the Highlands to "rescue" me out of his love and protectiveness, but I was hopeful that he was finally starting to see me as a grown woman with her own mind.

The problem with impulsivity, however, was that there were no more direct flights to London out of Inverness that day. We had to fly to Edinburgh first. Fear had cut through my nerves as I followed Theo through the airport and fumbled with my shoes and belongings at security. He guided me, though, helping me place my shoes on the conveyor belt and making sure I had all my electronics out of my bag and in the tray. The only time he broke contact was when we each had to step through the doorway sensor thingy. Then Theo's hand was on my lower back again as we waited for our trays to go through the machine sensor too.

By the time we got to our gate, I was a sweaty mess.

Theo seemed to find my first visit to the airport amusing and adorable.

"It's like watching Bambi try to walk for the first time," he teased, rubbing my shoulders as we stood at the gate.

I rolled my eyes. "Funny. Is that what the first woman you slept with said to you afterward?"

Theo threw his head back in laughter, even as he wrapped his arms around me, pulling me tight to him so my back rested against his chest. His laughter had drawn attention and I tried not to flush as he nuzzled my neck. I felt his smile against my skin.

Our teasing banter helped abate the nerves, but by the time we got on the plane, I could feel my knees shaking a wee bit. It finally hit me that I was about to find myself thousands of feet in the sky for the first time in my life.

Theo sensed the change as we took our seats. He didn't ask if I was all right nor did he smother me with protectiveness. Instead, he just quietly wrapped one of my hands in both of his and held it. He held it while everyone boarded the plane, while the flight attendants ran through the safety instructions (which I listened to harder than I'd listened to anything in my life), and he held it while the plane gained speed on the runway and thrust into the air. I squeezed my eyes closed as the pressure forced me back in my seat, and I relaxed marginally at the touch of Theo's lips on my hand and then on my cheek.

And then on my lips.

Despite the awkward position, he kissed me thoroughly, hungrily. It was an NSFW kiss if ever there was one. But I didn't care because when he finally let me up for air, the plane had leveled out.

"We're flying?" I gasped, peering past him out the window.

Theo leaned back to let me see out.

Amazement replaced my fear, and when the flight attendant came around to offer a drink and snacks, I started to enjoy myself.

Landing, however, was a nerve-racking business and I let

out a little yelp as the wheels hit the runway. Theo tried not to laugh.

Once we arrived at Edinburgh airport, we didn't have to go through security again. Theo led me through the much bigger, busier airport, and I tried to take in all the shops and restaurants as he marched with long-legged strides. He'd already told me we would eat for free in the business lounge since we were flying business class.

As we neared large glass doors with the airline logo etched across them, Theo slowed, digging into his coat pocket. "Go ahead, little darling. I'm just looking for the tickets."

I stepped toward the doors, and they slid open automatically. I'd barely taken a step inside when a woman dressed in the airline uniform stepped forward, her palm up toward me. "I'm sorry, miss, this is business class only."

Heat exploded across my cheeks and I turned toward Theo as he stepped inside.

His gaze moved over my face before he looked at the airline attendant. To anyone else, his expression was a mask of disinterest, but I'd seen the flicker of irritation in his eyes and the popping of the muscle in his jaw as he pulled the tickets out of his pocket. He handed them to the attendant and drawled mockingly, "Perhaps you should look at a person's ticket before making assumptions about what they can afford."

The attendant flushed almost as red as me as she looked over the tickets. "I do apologize, Mr. Cavendish."

"*I* don't need your apology."

The attendant could barely look me in the eye, and I squirmed in embarrassment and secondhand mortification for her. "Ms. McCulloch." She swallowed hard. "I'm very sorry for my mistake."

"It's all right," I assured her.

She took the tickets over to a desk where her colleague waited. The man drew her a dark look as he held the tickets under a machine that beeped. As Theo took the tickets from him, the male attendant said in a snooty voice, "Apologies for my colleague, Mr. Cavendish, Ms. McCulloch. She's new. It won't happen again." He gave her another dirty look, and I felt awful for her as misery cut across her expression. "Please enjoy the lounge and the rest of your day."

"Thank you for your shitty customer service," Theo replied blandly. "Please do not enjoy the rest of *your* day."

I caught sight of the flight attendant squeezing her eyes closed in dismay as Theo guided me past them and into the large lounge.

It was half-empty. There were different kinds of seating. Some bistro tables. Bench seats. Chairs with electrical sockets and side tables. Stools at high counters where people worked on their laptops.

In the center was a catering area with sandwiches and pasta, soda, water, juice, and coffee and tea machines. There were snacks and fruit plates.

I'd have marveled at what a business class ticket could buy you if I wasn't currently annoyed with my companion.

"You embarrassed her," I bit out.

Theo drew us to a halt at a table away from other people. "She embarrassed you first. All's fair, love." He stroked a tender thumb over my cheek. "Only I get to make you blush."

I flushed even harder as I gritted my teeth in irritation. "That may be, but I didn't want you to embarrass her for me. She was embarrassed enough by her error. And the way her colleague looked at her ... I feel bad for her. What if she's on a trial run and they let her go over this?"

Theo tugged my bag off my shoulder and placed it on the bench seating, a heavy sigh spilling from his lips. "You are far too nice, Ms. McCulloch."

I frowned. "You can be nice. You're nice to me."

Cupping my face in his hands, Theo murmured against my mouth, "I'm not nice. Let me prove it."

He kissed me hard and deep. Another inappropriate public display of affection.

By the time he released me, I was breathing hard, and I knew I was flushed bright red again.

"See?" The bastard grinned smugly. "Now, what do you want to drink?"

I pressed a cool palm to my hot cheek as I slumped onto the bench beside my bag. "Um ... Diet Coke."

"Anything to eat?"

"Whatever you think," I mumbled.

Despite his good-natured teasing, I was still uncomfortable with the way he'd treated the attendant on my behalf. I knew he hadn't been overly horrible to her (his last parting remark, however, was totally unnecessary), but as someone who'd spent her life being mortified by my shyness, by feeling constantly embarrassed by it, it didn't sit right with me to put someone else in that position.

Yes, the flight attendant shouldn't have assumed I wasn't flying business class (and I was not going down the rabbit hole of wondering why she'd assumed that about me), but it was a mistake. She was new. She was learning. And yes, maybe I was hyperfocusing on the incident and blowing it out of proportion because of my own issues, but I couldn't help it.

Theo returned with snacks and attempted conversation, but I was stuck in my head. Aye, Theo was nice to me. But was what I just witnessed a taste of what he was like with others? I knew he was kind to North, that he cared for North, but I didn't know how he treated other people beyond me. We'd eaten out a few times and he'd treated the waitstaff with politeness. But we hadn't had interactions with other people.

We'd been living it up in our little bubble together.

What if ... what if I didn't like who Theo was outside of our bubble?

Dread knotted in my gut.

I could feel Theo's intense study as I nibbled, no longer hungry, on the snacks he'd brought over. Surprisingly, he didn't push me to chat. Instead, he seemed to fall into his own grim contemplation.

Was he thinking what I was thinking?

I didn't know why that made me feel worse.

Not long later, it was time to gather our belongings and head to our gate. Theo took my hand, his grip firm, unyielding, as we strode together out of the lounge. The two airline attendants were still there, and my hand flexed in Theo's with uncertainty as he gestured the woman over to the desk so he could speak to them both.

She looked like she wanted the floor to open up, and honestly, I was right there with her.

Theo cleared his throat as he glanced between the man and woman. "I just want to apologize for my attitude earlier. It was a silly mistake. No need for embarrassment or admonishment." He stared sternly at the man. "Let's just forget this, yes?"

The male attendant frowned but nodded. "If that's your wish, Mr. Cavendish."

"Please. I have a feeling it won't happen again." He offered the woman a teasing smile, and she blushed for an entirely different reason now.

"Thank you." Her gaze flicked to me. "Apologies again."

I gave her a soft smile, something easing in me as we nodded goodbye. Theo's hand squeezed around mine as I hurried to match his stride.

He looked down at me as we stepped out of the glass doors, and I gazed back up at him with an expression I worried bordered on adoration.

Relief loosened the tension in him. I felt it.

By the time we boarded the plane, the tension between us had eased. Theo fussed over me, advising me what to choose on the lunch menu, making sure I had enough room, that I was comfortable.

When the male flight attendant returned to ask us if we had everything we needed for the fourth time, his bright eyes fixed on Theo, I realized he'd asked us more than anyone else and tried to contain my snort.

As soon as he was out of earshot, I leaned into Theo. "I think our flight attendant fancies you."

Theo grinned, a bit smug. "I think you might be right." Head bending toward mine, he whispered huskily, "Unfortunately for him, I rather fancy you."

I tried to smother a smile but couldn't. "It would be quite the conundrum if I fancied him."

"Don't be daft," he murmured, reaching for my mouth. "You fancy the pants off me. You have literally fancied the pants off me multiple times this past month."

My laughter was swallowed in his kiss.

I kissed him back, a feeling of utter happiness cascading over me.

It amazed me because I didn't think I could feel like this so soon after losing Grandpa. And I realized that was the magic of Theo.

On the other side of the coin, however, were the cold shadows awaiting me if he ever took his affection away.

Fear niggled in the back of my mind. I kissed him harder to chase away the unwanted emotion.

EIGHTEEN
THEO

The only part of my past life I hadn't given up was Mayfair.

My flat on Half Moon Street was an uncomfortably close twenty-minute walk from my father's townhouse on leafy Wilton Crescent. But the flat had belonged to my mother. She'd left it to me, and I couldn't bear to part with it.

Sarah stared around wide-eyed as we stepped almost directly into the living area of the Georgian townhome that had been split into apartments. The living room was to the left of the main entrance and was the largest space in the house with massive symmetrical windows that let lots of light into the flat. I'd taken a wall down so the kitchen and sitting area were one space. It wasn't a huge kitchen, but I enjoyed cooking in it. To the right of the entrance was the only bedroom. It was a suite with an attached bathroom and walk-in closet.

My taste ran toward midcentury modern, and my décor was decidedly masculine. I watched Sarah as she toured the flat, eyeing the books on the shelves in the living room with curiosity and then the rowing machine that took up too much space. I itched to use it after weeks without the familiar exercise.

"It's a great flat," Sarah offered softly.

"It was my mother's," I blurted out.

Sarah turned to look at me. "The flat?"

I nodded, scrubbing a hand down my cheek. I could probably do with a shave, but I'd noticed Sarah liked the bristles against her skin. Therefore, I was reluctant to get rid of it. "She had an entire real estate portfolio my father didn't even know about. He was just as astonished as Sebastian and me to discover it after her death." I smirked sadly. "Her parents died when she was nineteen, leaving her their fortune. Sometimes I wonder if that's why she clung on to my father so quickly."

"Looking for an anchor," she whispered, her sympathy genuine and moving and frightening. Because I worried about how easily Sarah could be hurt when she cared this much for people she didn't even know.

"Exactly." My voice sounded hoarse, so I cleared it. "Anyway, I think she must have hidden from my father what she was worth. Maybe a tiny part of her knew that she needed to protect that. And she built a real estate business behind his back."

"Good for her."

I grinned. "Yes, it was rather a lovely surprise." Gesturing to the flat, I continued, "She left me this and four other properties. All in Mayfair. All worth quite a bit. I kept this one for myself and rent out the others."

"You don't want to sell them?"

My throat tightened at the thought. "I can't," I choked out.

She nodded in understanding and then did me the favor of changing the subject. "I love the high ceilings and windows. It's gorgeous."

"Yes," I murmured, watching her as she kicked off her

shoes and curled up on the sofa beneath a window. She rested her chin on her arm as she stared out at the world passing below. Her silky hair slid across her shoulders, and I suddenly imagined her naked with soft morning light spilling across her smooth skin. I'd never had a woman stay in my flat before. I preferred to fuck them at their place so I could leave.

Guilt flickered through me, and I was reminded of the moment at the airport with the flight attendant. I hated the idea of Sarah finding something abhorrent in me. I wanted to be better for her, but an insidious voice reminded me of the truth.

I wasn't good enough for this woman.

Then she turned and smiled at me, and my selfishness won out. "Let's freshen up. I want to take you somewhere."

AN HOUR later we were in a restaurant having dinner when Sarah's phone buzzed and mine rang. It was an unfamiliar London number again, so I silenced it as Sarah peered at her phone screen.

Swallowing a bite of pasta, I asked, "Anything interesting?"

She nodded, smiling. "An email. You got the same one. It's from Liz. She says the contract is almost ready and will be back with you by the end of the week."

"Wow. They certainly pushed that through."

"You did ask her to."

"Yes, but I wasn't quite expecting it this soon. Good for her."

"I'm going to ask her about meeting up while I'm in London." Her fingers flew over the keys as she responded to the email. "Who was calling you?"

"I don't know ...," I trailed off as my gaze returned to my

phone, and I noted the voicemail notification. Sighing, I put the thing to my ear to check who it was. Unsurprisingly, it was DCI Rick English sounding more urgent now as he again asked me to return his call. "No one." I hung up annoyed. "Just my brother acting insane."

Hopefully, news of my return to London would put a stop to this nonsense.

"Anyway, my team should be able to get the contract back to Liz within a week or so. It'll probably take a few more back-and-forths from there, but we should see it finalized by the end of January, I would think."

"Aye?" Sarah's excitement was palpable.

It reminded me of what I was like when I stepped on my first film set, and it just hit me how fun it was going to be to make this thing with her. I had to have her on set, at least for the first episode. "Once that's done, we'll cast Juno and Peter and shop it out to Skylark. If they don't want it—which seems unlikely—we'll try some streaming services."

She bit her lip, eyes alight. "It's getting so real now."

I grinned. "We'll need permits to film in Dundee and Edinburgh." The first book split its time between the two cities. "And then you'll get to be there while we film."

"I can't wait."

We chatted a little more about the script and after dinner, I led her out to find a cab.

"Where are we going?" Sarah asked for the fifth time as the cab tried valiantly to get through London evening traffic.

"It's a surprise," I insisted.

She didn't seem too bothered as she gaped out the window, taking in everything. It reminded me that this was her first time out of Scotland, never mind her first time in London. I wanted to show her everything, and it was a bit like seeing it all through new eyes.

Finally, about fifteen minutes longer than it should normally take, we arrived at Kew Road.

I paid the driver and helped Sarah out. People were already filing into the gardens. Tightening my hand around hers, I guided her through the black decorative wrought iron gates situated between four stone pillars.

"Where ...?"

"Welcome to Kew Gardens, Ms. McCulloch." I gestured as we entered a Christmas wonderland.

Sarah's mouth parted as she took in all the lights.

"This is nothing," I promised in her ear.

It had been years since I'd visited Kew Gardens, but Christmastime was quite the spectacle. Trees and hedges wrapped in fairy lights, others aglow in rainbow hues cast by light shows, and archways made entirely of light. The illuminations were a little magical, and Sarah needed a little magic this year.

She took in the sights with wonderment in her eyes, clinging to my arm, gasping, smiling up at me like a girl seeing Santa for the first time. It amazed me she could have reached this age and still be filled with awe by things I'd grown used to overlooking. I was somewhat jealous. But my overarching emotion was protectiveness. For the first time in years, I wanted to protect someone else. I didn't want anyone to break her or take that wonder from her.

And I especially didn't want that person to be me.

Under a cathedral of lights, uncaring of the people walking through it with us, I halted and pulled Sarah up onto her tiptoes to reach my lips. I kissed her like it would save me.

Like it might save her from me.

A voice in the back of my head told me I needed to let her go.

But I couldn't.

Why couldn't I?

My grip on her tightened, my kisses hard and hungry, and I might have stayed there with her forever if someone hadn't wolf-whistled.

I reluctantly released her and she stared up at me, lips swollen, dazed, the twinkle lights reflected in those spectacular eyes of hers.

"There are children here," a woman practically spat at us as she passed.

"Are there?" I drawled, tucking Sarah into my side. "I thought they were poorly dressed elves."

Sarah muffled a snort, and I grinned harder.

The woman huffed and strode off.

"That there is a woman in desperate need of good sex."

"Theo!" Sarah slapped my chest, hushing me even as her lips trembled around a smile.

"I only speak the truth." I shrugged. "Fancy some hot mini doughnuts?"

She shook her head at me like I was a naughty schoolboy.

"No to hot doughnuts?" I gasped in teasing outrage.

"No to your nonsense." She tugged on my hand with a roll of her eyes. "But aye to doughnuts."

For the next hour, I led Sarah around the gardens, taking pictures, watching her as she contemplated one light display after another.

"Believe it or not," she said after swallowing a bite of hot, sugary pastry, "this is giving me a great idea for a scene in the next book. I could take Juno to London at Christmastime. Can you imagine her being stalked through Kew Gardens by her latest suspect?"

I chuckled. "Only you, sweet Sarah, could think of a thriller scene amid a Christmas wonderland."

She laughed, and I couldn't help myself. I bent down to kiss her, licking at the sugar on her lips. The way her breath hitched caused an immediate tightening in my balls. "Fuck," I murmured. "Are you ready to get out of here?"

Understanding flushed her cheeks and she nodded.

It was a tense cab ride back to my flat. I held her hand between mine, stroking my fingertips over her palm. She shivered and the blood thundered in my ears.

I barely remembered the ride or paying the driver. My sole focus was on getting privacy with Sarah. My desperation for her was such that I couldn't even take a few more steps into the bedroom. Instead, as soon as we stepped inside the flat, I used our bodies to close the door and I pressed her into it. She gasped into my kisses as I undulated against her, fumbling frantically for the zipper on her coat. Past that barricade, next were her jeans and mine.

There was just enough presence of mind left to pull a condom out of my wallet and don it before I thrust inside her snug heat. I groaned in utter relief as she cried out, her features tight with pleasure. Then I fucked her against my front door, watching her unravel, getting off on the fact that I could make her lose her mind too. My release followed on the heels of her climax.

"We're not done," I warned her gruffly as I ground into her, wanting more. "I plan on keeping you up all night, little darling."

She panted for breath, eyelashes fluttering, cheeks flushed delightfully. "No arguments here, Mr. Cavendish."

I grinned against her throat. "There's my good girl."

Her inner muscles throbbed around me and I could feel myself growing hard again. My Sarah was a dichotomy. Fucking hated it when I said anything so patronizing like *good girl* outside of the bedroom, but when I was inside her, those words definitely hit the spot.

"Come." I reluctantly withdrew from her. "Let's christen my bed before I take you against the door again."

NINETEEN
THEO

Despite rowing every day since we'd arrived in London, I still felt my muscles tiring quicker than usual. I was out of shape.

I breathed through the burn, my eyes flicking from the screen where my avatar cut through the Thames, to the television screen mounted on the wall. The machine wasn't the same as rowing on water. Since my rowing team from Oxford had found it increasingly difficult to meet up over the years, I'd taken to single-scull rowing. I'd even invested in a scull that I stored at a facility near the Thames. But it had been more than two months since I'd visited it.

Watching the weather on TV, I noted it was mild enough for the next week to go out there. The problem was I'd become a little consumed with Sarah. Today was the first day since our arrival that we'd parted. She'd wanted to meet her agent by herself, so I'd put her in a cab and sent her on her way.

Perhaps I needed to return to some semblance of my own schedule too.

That wasn't to say the last few days hadn't been fun. I wondered if I'd truly had fun in years after experiencing

London with Sarah. I'd taken her shopping on Oxford Street and convinced her to spend money on a few items of clothing she'd never have bought otherwise. I'd been admonished by a sales assistant who caught me feeling Sarah up in the changing rooms. Sarah had flushed a delightful pink, and it had been exceedingly difficult to walk away. We strolled to Piccadilly to shop some more and then returned to Oxford Street in the evening so she could see the Christmas lights. Afterward, we jumped in a cab to go eat at 34 Mayfair so I could show her their outlandish Christmas bauble display that filled the entire ceiling and dripped down into the room.

The day after that, I took her ice skating at the Natural History Museum. It had been years since I'd skated, but muscle memory was quite remarkable. Sarah had skated once in her life, so it took her a while to get her ice legs. I had to admit to enjoying having to hold her through most of the experience. Last night, we finished off the day in the West End. Sarah's grandfather had taken her to the theater when she was a teenager, but nothing quite like a West End show. I spent most of the musical watching her and the way she lit up from the inside.

In the past week and a half, I'd gotten tremendous pleasure out of introducing her to new things and was already listing my favorite international cities to take her to next.

A cheer sounded from the screen on my rower, and I realized I'd completed my row. Slowing to a stop, I reached for the water bottle attached to the equipment just as a news report on the television drew my attention.

"Scotland Yard is issuing a new warning to the public today after a fourth woman was murdered two nights ago in High Wycombe," the news reporter announced. "The victim's identity has not yet been released by police, but they revealed in their statement that she does fit the profile of victims in what they're calling the Hangman murders."

Unease flickered through me at the nickname. I'd used that same name in the *King's Valley* TV show because North's character, Charlie King, hung his victims after he'd killed them.

"Police are urging people not to walk alone at night, in particular, women between the ages of twenty and thirty years. Last year the Hangman killed his first victim in December. The second victim was murdered in June this year. The third woman, a primary school teacher, was killed in October ..."

I reached over for the remote and switched off the news. Sarah had been right. It looked like Britain had a new serial killer. Discomfort rode my shoulders, and I decided if she didn't return home from her meeting with the agent by sundown, I'd go out and meet her. She was older than the other victims, but she didn't look it. And yes, I knew the probability of Sarah becoming a victim of a serial killer was unlikely, but one could never be too careful.

Twenty minutes later, I'd just gotten out of the shower when I heard banging on my front door. A rush of pleasure filled me as I wondered if Sarah had forgotten the spare key I'd given her.

I opened the door with a grin that promptly slipped off my face.

"Sebastian."

My brother glowered at me as he bulldozed into the apartment.

"Well, come the fuck in," I snarled, outraged.

"Shut the door," he demanded like a typical, entitled peer of the realm.

Since I didn't want my neighbors to hear my business, I did indeed shut the door.

"What the fuck do you want?" I followed him into my living room, eyeing the way he studied my home with a pinched expression.

"For you to stop saying *fuck*, for starters," the pompous bastard admonished like I was a schoolboy.

Drawing on my patience, I plastered on a neutral expression. "What are you doing here, Sebastian?"

"I honestly don't know." My brother suddenly looked exhausted. "I should be at work. But my PI told me you'd come home."

I wasn't even surprised he had a private detective following me. "You're a piece of work."

"You dropped off the face of the planet, Theo. Of course I had people looking for you."

I bloody knew it.

"Well, as you can see, I'm dandy."

"Yes." He glanced around. "Where is Ms. McCulloch?"

Anger filled me and I fought hard not to show it. "You investigated Sarah?"

He shrugged like it was normal to look into who your brother was sleeping with. "She's not your usual type. A housekeeper at Ardnoch. Really?"

At the sneer in his voice, I warned blandly, "Be careful, brother."

"Don't tell me you have actual feelings for this woman? You know her mother is a junkie? She was raised by her grandfather on a farm in the Highlands. There's no record of previous relationships or any kind of a life, for that matter. She's just a quiet nobody, and bringing her into your world like this when you have no intention of keeping her is a level of cruelty I did not expect even from you."

Indignation wrapped its hand tightly around my throat and my voice was but a whisper, "You have no idea what you're talking about."

Sebastian's eyes narrowed in contemplation. "Yes, I do. I can see my words hit their intended target. Good. Perhaps you're not a complete sod after all."

"If you just came to insult me, you can leave."

"I came to tell you that Father is recovering well."

"And you thought I cared? How pathetically naive."

My brother's expression tightened. "You know what ... I wish that I didn't care about you."

I flinched. I hated him for getting a reaction out of me.

"For years, I've carried guilt for the way I handled things with you over Father and Saffron. I've attributed your entire personality change to Mother's death and Father and Saffy's betrayal ... but it's been years, Theo. At some point, I just have to admit that you're never going to be the boy I remember."

Pain slashed across my chest.

"You've turned into a selfish, self-indulgent, bitter, and uncaring prick," he spat. "And this woman you're carting all over London, spending your money on, dressing her up to play the part ... what happens to her when you grow bored? Do you even care?"

I could barely hear over the blood rushing in my ears.

"God, I hope that look on your face means you care enough not to be a selfish cur. Maybe that means there's a little of my brother still in there."

When I continued to stare blindly at the floor, I heard him huff, seconds before he strode out of the flat, slamming the door behind him.

TWENTY

SARAH

Before I left for the meeting with my agent, Theo announced we would be going to a club that evening. We were both more the pub type, but when I told Theo I'd only ever been to a nightclub once, in Inverness, he'd decided I needed to experience a proper club.

"I'm not taking you to some celeb spot like Cirque Le Soir either," Theo said with obvious distaste. "We'll go somewhere I think you might actually like."

My meeting with Liz went well—in person, she was hyper-intelligent and forthright, but warm too. She'd informed me we had three more foreign language deals on the table, which took the series to thirty-three countries. I still couldn't wrap my head around that.

My excitement about the evening ahead escalated into nervousness when I walked into Theo's flat. He was already dressed, looking incredibly sexy in an expensive, fitted three-piece suit. While he always dressed well, I'd never seen him in a suit. I crossed the room to smooth my hands over his chest.

"You look handsome." I smiled up at him.

However, he stared blankly down at me and replied,

"Thanks. Why don't you get ready? I'm sure one of the dresses you bought yesterday will suffice."

He didn't ask me about the meeting, which was unusual in itself, but he also hadn't reacted to me touching him, and Theo was surprisingly tactile and affectionate.

"Is everything all right?"

"Fine. I thought we'd eat first and then start at a bar before I take you to a club."

Feeling a decided chill and distance from him, my stomach knotted. "Are you sure everything's all right?"

"Fine. I just don't want to miss our reservations."

Letting his strange behavior go, I disappeared into the bedroom to change, hoping his mood would lift once I was ready.

I'd bought two cocktail dresses on our shopping spree. One was black and the other a green that closely matched my eyes. Deciding I wanted to blend a wee bit for my first London club experience, I chose the black. It was a simple silk chiffon dress with thin straps and a deep V neckline. It clung to my curves without being too tight and ended just above the knee. Theo had sworn it straddled that fine line between sexy and classy.

I paired the dress with the Jimmy Choo sandals I'd treated myself to. They were just as simple as the dress with a thin black suede strap over the toe and around the ankle. At first, I'd thought it ridiculous to spend that kind of money on such a basic design, but then I'd walked in them and couldn't believe how comfortable they were.

Quickly creating a beachy wave with my hair straighteners, I left my hair down and applied eye makeup and lip gloss. Looking at myself in the mirror, I smiled, feeling sexy and grown-up outside of the bedroom for the first time in a long time.

That pleasure was dimmed, however, by Theo's response

when he saw me. "You look beautiful," he opined in a robotic tone that killed the compliment.

Confused, I dazedly let him help me into my coat and guide me out of the flat. He didn't take my hand or touch my lower back like usual.

He didn't touch me at all.

Tension thickened between us once we grabbed a cab. By the time we reached the restaurant, I wanted to yell or shake him or get him to do anything but sit with that bored expression.

I wouldn't ask him if I'd done anything wrong because I couldn't imagine that I had. Truthfully, I'd spent every day until the age of thirteen walking on eggshells with my mum and her boyfriends, asking her constantly if I'd done something wrong.

I would never go back there.

Instead, I fell into a sullen mood.

He brought me to a fancy restaurant in an area called Bishopsgate. The restaurant was in a tower with floor-to-ceiling windows overlooking the city. We could see the Gherkin from it.

The food was delicious, but I wasn't that hungry. However, my mood seemed to draw Theo from the metaphorical arse he'd shoved his head up and he attempted conversation over dinner, asking about my meeting. Slowly, the tension relaxed between us, but I could still tell something was bothering him.

A few hours later, we walked about a minute from the restaurant to a hotel next door. Confused, I asked Theo where he was taking me, and he said there was a bar in the hotel that did great cocktails. That he'd been a few times with cast and crew, and it wasn't an overly trendy or A-list celeb spot. He thought we should stop there first before we hit the club.

The bar looked like it *should* be for VIPs. It was spacious with polished concrete flooring and a large bar in the center with plenty of bar stool seating. Along the room's edges were curved, plush booths around oval wooden tables. In symmetrical lines across the middle of the room was a mixture of seating. Some low benches and modern comfy chairs between gold oval tables, while others were trendy bistro tables with funky, weirdly shaped chairs. The lighting was low and atmospheric and the music playing was popular chart hits.

Theo explained there was a smaller whisky bar at the back as we strolled through the space toward the bar. I didn't know if it was because it was still fairly early, but it wasn't crowded, though most of the seats were taken.

I ordered a mojito while Theo ordered a whisky sour. Leaning against the bar top while we sipped at our cocktails, I people-watched while I tried not to fixate on Theo. Though he was trying a little harder, it was the fact that he needed to try that bothered me. Interactions between us were usually effortless. I wanted to ask him again if he was all right, but my stubborn pride forced me not to chase him for an answer.

Theo seemed happy to let me observe the room rather than engage in conversation with him.

On my second mojito, a couple started dancing to a Lana Del Rey song. I felt a pang of something in my chest. Maybe something a bit like longing as I watched them sway together, smiling into each other's eyes, uncaring that no one else was dancing.

I wondered if the song had some meaning for them.

But when the song changed to Fleurie's "Love U Already," they didn't sit down, and another couple filled the empty space beside them to slow dance.

"Well, I've never seen that happen in here before," Theo drawled, throwing back the last of his drink.

At his dry tone, I asked, "Do you like to dance?"

"Not particularly."

Disappointment flashed through me, but I turned away to watch the couples again so he wouldn't see.

"Do you?"

I shrugged, still not looking at him. "I suppose. Though ..." My cheeks flushed with embarrassment. "I've never danced with a man before."

When he didn't say anything, I wished I hadn't admitted it.

But then Theo reached over to take my glass and placed it on the bar. I frowned at him until he held out his palm.

My stomach fluttered in realization.

Warmth filled the wee ache in my chest, and I took his hand. Without speaking, he curled my fingers tightly in his and led me to where the couples were dancing. With grace and ease, like he'd done it a million times, he pulled me into his arms and slowly began to sway to the music.

Nervous and unsure at first, it took me a few seconds to find rhythm with him. Relaxing, temporarily happy, and appreciative he'd do this for me, I rested my cheek on his chest and melted as he wrapped his arms around me.

"Maybe I could get used to it," he whispered in my ear, and I smiled, those butterflies in my belly flapping their wings.

It was such a perfect moment, and I knew I'd remember it for the rest of my life.

When the song ended, replaced by a more upbeat Tom Grennan track, I lifted my head and smiled up at him. "Thank you."

Something finally softened in his expression. "Thank *you*."

"Cavendish?"

Theo jerked at the voice, and I turned with him to find a familiar good-looking guy approaching us. "Scott." Theo nodded.

"It's been a while." The dark-haired man slapped Theo's biceps before glancing at me and then taking a second glance.

"Uh ..." He shot me a smile, then turned back to Theo. "Haven't seen you at the Roebuck."

"It was becoming infiltrated."

Scott chuckled. "By A-listers, you mean? You do know you're in that category?"

Theo raised an eyebrow. "I think not. How are you, old boy?"

"Good, good. I got a recurring part on *The Beat*. Film it here, get to stay home, all's good. How are you?"

"Fine. Writing."

"I hope you'll look me up for whatever it is you've got cooking." He grinned cheekily and then turned to me, gaze ... interested. "Hi, I'm Scott Holland." He held out his hand and I suddenly recognized him. Scott was an English actor who'd starred in *King's Valley* and a British soap before that.

Surprised he'd noticed me after years of invisibility in Ardnoch, it took me a second to shake his hand. My cheeks pinkened. "Sarah. N-nice to meet you."

"You too." Scott held my hand a little longer than appropriate before turning to Theo. "Alice and Brent are here with some friends. Come have a drink with us."

I thought Theo would say no since we were technically on a date, but he surprised me by nodding and following Scott across the bar to a larger booth at the back.

Theo seemed to know a few of the people already and Scott introduced me to the group, but my heart pounded and I could barely hear over my nerves. I disliked how nervous I got meeting large groups of new people, but I decided if I was going to work on a film set with Theo, I needed to get over my old insecurities.

Theo slid into the booth next to a pretty redhead who seemed to know him. I took the seat next to his and Scott quickly sat on my other side. A waiter came over to take more drink orders and as Theo engaged in conversation with the redhead, smirking at something she whispered in his ear, I decided I needed another mojito.

"So, Sarah," Scott leaned in a smidge too close to ask in my ear, "what do you do and how do you know Theo?"

"I'm a writer." I wasn't quite ready to out myself to the world yet, so that's all I said. "You were in *King's Valley*."

He smiled, pleased. Scott was very good-looking but honestly, he did nothing for me. I was afraid no one else but Theo could now. "I was. So, a writer? Like a screenwriter?"

"Perhaps," I hedged.

His grin widened. "A woman of mystery. I love it. Is that how you know Theo?"

"Aye." It wasn't a lie.

"And I detect a bit of an accent. Are you Scottish?"

I nodded.

"My mother is Scottish. We used to spend all our summers in Oban visiting my grandparents. I love Scotland. I hope to own a second home there one day."

"Do you still visit often?"

For the next very long twenty minutes or so, I managed to keep Scott talking about himself, all the while aware that Theo was next to me chatting and laughing with the redhead. When I glanced over, she was shoving him playfully and he was rolling his eyes with that teasing smile of his.

My stomach dropped.

He was flirting with her.

By my fourth mojito, I was struggling to stay focused on Scott who, for some reason, did not leave my side. I felt sick. I didn't know what had happened today or why Theo was acting so strangely, but I'd thought our dance had broken that tension. Now he was flirting with some other woman in front of me.

I wanted to leave.

What I wanted to do was cry, but I wouldn't give the

bugger the satisfaction.

"I need to use the restroom." I cut Scott off midstream about the new role he was playing in a long-standing UK crime drama. "Will you excuse me?"

"Oh. Of course." He shimmied out of the booth to let me pass and I hurried on shaking legs toward the restroom.

A few minutes later I stood at the sink, staring at my flushed cheeks in the mirror. Maybe I should just leave.

I ... I didn't deserve to be treated like this. I knew we hadn't discussed what we were to each other, but it had been pretty clear after Jared showed up that this was more than just a fling.

So what the hell was Theo up to?

Deciding I wouldn't continue to put myself through this, I pulled open the restroom door, determined to tell Theo I wanted to leave. But as I walked out, I almost slammed into his broad chest.

He stared down at me blandly, and I wanted to scream at him to wipe that protective mask off his face and just be real with me.

"Are you all right?"

"I—"

"Scott rather fancies you," Theo cut me off. He said it like it meant nothing to him that his friend was attracted to me.

"Oh." I didn't know how else I was supposed to respond.

"He asked me if we were exclusive or if you'd be interested in him. I told him the latter."

Pain lanced across my chest.

Theo shrugged, but I noticed the telltale flexing of his clenched jaw before he forced himself to relax. "You should experience other men, Sarah. Grab life by the balls, so to speak."

"There you are!"

I flinched at the female voice seconds before the redhead

sidled up to Theo, pressing her breasts into his arm. "I wondered where you'd gone to. Come." She flicked me a dismissive look. "You owe me a drink."

"Quite right, love, so I do." Theo ignored me, turning to her and wrapping his arm around her, hand on her hip as they walked away.

Tears threatened, but I forced them back. It was painful.

Everything ... everything hurt.

I was an idiot.

Jared ... Jared had warned me. When someone is *terrified* of caring for you ... you put your guard up. Not down.

And with all his issues and trauma, Theo Cavendish was utterly terrified of me.

That didn't make this okay.

He didn't get to treat me like this.

I'd warned him.

Fury cut through my pain. I'd warned him that if he told me to go again, I'd leave.

Notching my chin higher, like I didn't have a damn care in the world, I strode toward the bar, past it, heading toward the exit. I'd almost made it when a hand wrapped around my biceps.

Stupid relief flared through me. Until I turned to find Scott.

He searched my face. "Are you all right? Are you leaving?"

My eyes flicked over his shoulder where Theo was in the booth, laughing with the redhead and the rest of the group.

I think I hated him then.

I looked back at Scott. "I'm just ... not feeling this place."

"Yeah, this place is kind of over. Would you like some company?"

And maybe because I was just petty enough to do it, I nodded and let him take my hand. Without looking back, I exited the bar with Scott, leaving Theo behind.

TWENTY-ONE
THEO

It was quite possible I was about to upchuck my four whisky sours all over the table in front of these people.

Sarah had left with Scott.

I'd pushed her to him.

Now my heart wouldn't stop fucking racing and my chest felt tight. The faces of my companions, including Alice, a costume designer I'd worked with but never slept with despite her flirtations, were blurry. Their voices, their words, became muddled noise.

It had been an hour since Sarah had left the bar with another man, and every time I thought about how I'd treated her, or how Scott might have his hands on her ... how he might be inside her ... fuck, I was going to be sick.

I couldn't breathe.

Pushing out of the booth, uncaring if I looked like a madman, I hurried toward the restroom, feeling the room tilt not from drunkenness ... with panic.

I burst into the loos and hurried over to the sink.

I couldn't catch my breath.

Fuck.

I was having a panic attack.

Trying to loosen shirt buttons that were already loose, my fingers felt numb and useless. When was the last time I'd had a panic attack?

Mum. When Mum died.

For Christ's sake.

Fumbling with the cold water tap, I tried to bury my head under it.

"You all right, mate?" a bloke to my left asked.

I didn't answer, and he departed the restroom while I rubbed the cold water into my face and stared into the mirror.

Breathe, just breathe, I heard Sarah's soft imaginary voice coax.

"Theo, you all right?" A hand slapped my back and I straightened, trying to focus.

Scott stared at me in concern.

Scott.

He was here?

"Where's Sarah?" I practically barked.

Scott grimaced. "Your little cocktease changed her mind as soon as we got back to my flat. I put her in a cab. Next time you tell me a woman is up for it, make sure she's actually up for it, mate. It's not like you to pick the prudes."

Rage filled me and I grabbed him by the shirt front and slammed him into the wall. "Did you touch her?"

Scott shoved me away angrily. "I don't touch women who don't want to be touched. Why do you give a shit? You passed her to me like she was a toy you got bored with. Doesn't exactly scream that you care, mate." He cut me a dirty look before marching out of the restroom.

Guilt tightened in my chest, but the panic receded. I needed to get to her. To apologize. To explain. Yanking my phone out, I tried calling Sarah, but she didn't pick up. I called and called the entire way out of the bar and out in the city as I tried to flag down a cab. The cab ride was a torturous forty minutes back to my place. I must have called Sarah forty times and she didn't pick up.

Worry cut through my shame. What if something had happened to her? Women weren't supposed to be out alone. What if the serial killer was a fucking cab driver?

My melodrama and fears became monstrous things over the next forty minutes, and I rushed up the stairs to my flat like I'd lost my damn mind. I burst into it, shouting Sarah's name as my eyes drifted over the living room. Rushing into the bedroom, I skidded to a halt at the sight of her missing luggage.

"No, no, no." I threw open the wardrobe where I'd made space for her, and my heart sank. The hangers were empty.

That's when I finally noticed the paper on my pillow.

Fingers shaking, I lifted it reluctantly and felt my panic build again at the words she'd scrawled in her pretty cursive.

If you need to discuss the adaptation, please do it through my agent.

Don't call me again.

Goodbye.

Sarah

My legs gave out on me as I slid down the side of the bed, landing on the floor with a thump. She'd warned me. *"But next time you tell me to go like I don't matter ... I will go."*

I'd acted like a swine.

The way I'd treated her tonight ...

All because I'd let my fucking brother get in my head.

And now Sarah was gone.

Black spots covered my vision as I struggled to breathe, hyper-fucking-ventilating.

I curled up, head pressed to my bedside table, trying to survive every second of feeling like I might die.

As a boy, I'd suffered from panic attacks that my father

dismissed as weakness and my mother tried to coax me through. They'd dissipated with adulthood, the last one being the day I buried my mother. There was nothing for it but to endure the absolute certainty that I was about to die.

Of course, I did not die.

I came out of it only to face the clusterfuck that had caused the panic attack in the first place.

Eventually, I got through the Sarah-induced attack, but by the time it was over, I was drenched in sweat and utterly exhausted.

I crawled onto the bed, turning my face into Sarah's pillow and inhaling her perfume.

Squeezing my eyes closed, I felt an overwhelming sense of self-loathing I wasn't sure I could come back from.

Why did I let Sebastian's words get to me? He had Sarah all wrong. He thought she was some kind of charity case I'd picked up and was using.

She wasn't, and I wasn't using her.

Why did I let my damn fears win?

"It's not too late," I whispered gruffly, practically burrowing myself into her scent. I could explain. I could ... I could get her back.

I had to.

Because as mortifyingly scary as giving myself to her was ... it was nothing like this terror that swept over me at the thought that I might have lost her forever.

TWENTY-TWO
SARAH

To keep busy, I put up the Christmas tree and decorations because Jared hadn't gotten around to it. He probably wouldn't bother with them at all if it was just him.

I'd always been the one to decorate the farmhouse every Christmas, and I had a particular way of decorating the tree that meant I did not welcome help. Grandpa and Jared used to tease me mercilessly, adding baubles when my back was turned and waiting for me to spot them. Which I always did.

Grief thickened my throat and tears burned my eyes. Our first Christmas without Grandpa. I wondered what he'd think of me and how I'd let myself get swept up in Theo's charm and seduction.

I was supposed to be smarter than that.

Jared had known without me saying a word when I turned up at the farmhouse first thing this morning. I'd gotten a night train from London to Inverness and then a cab from there. Dead on my feet, Jared had just led me to my old room, and I'd passed out. I'd woken up around six hours later with a note from him that he was out repairing one of the farm's dry stone walls and that I just had to call him if I needed him.

Not feeling very hungry, I'd forced down toast and then stared sullenly around the kitchen. I should be writing. I still had a deadline, but I couldn't stop picturing Theo's bland expression as he passed me off to his friend.

Even if he cared a little ... it couldn't be enough. To just give me away like that.

How fucking dare he.

It made me sick to my stomach.

He'd probably gone home with that redhead.

I was a moron for thinking he felt more for me.

Every time I let my mind replay the previous evening, I experienced this gnawing pain in my chest and a pit in my stomach. I couldn't stand it. So I decided to decorate the farm-house for Christmas. It would be a nice surprise for Jared and a good distraction for me.

It wasn't much of a distraction. Every other minute, with apparently no control over it, I'd experience a flashback of last night. Or one from the weeks before it, when Theo made me feel seen and cherished and sexy.

How he must be laughing at me now.

And his so-called friend, Scott, who took me to his flat, a five-minute walk from the hotel, all charm and flirtation, until I froze, terrified at his front door. The thought of letting another man touch me was nauseating, and I just wanted to be alone. Scott had gone from sweet and funny to cold and irri-tated within an instant, though he'd walked me back out onto the street and called me a cab. He had, however, slammed the cab door behind me, to make it very clear he was angry I'd gotten his dick's hopes up.

Most men were bastards. Hadn't I learned that lesson yet?

They only wanted one thing. Though some were worse and made you think it was more. Like Theo.

My gaze was drawn to the fireplace mantel. The fire crackled in the grate, filling the house with heat and that lovely smoky smell that felt like home. I'd hung our stockings and even hung Grandpa's because I couldn't bear not to. Framed photos of my grandparents sat on the mantel. My favorite was their wedding photo. Grandpa was so unromantic most days ... but I loved that photo and the adoring expression on his face as he looked down at my grandmother rather than at the camera. He'd been devoted to her. When she died, a piece of him went with her, and he didn't even think about looking for another woman. It wasn't an option for him.

"Where are men like you, Grandpa?" I whispered, tears spilling down my cheeks. Even Jared, who was a wonderful cousin to me, was a philandering arse with women. "You were one in a million, weren't you? Grandma was one of the lucky ones."

You've got that the wrong way around, sweetheart, I suddenly heard his voice in my head. *I was the lucky one.*

I smiled, brokenhearted. And not just because I missed him.

But because I'd moronically fallen in love with Theo Cavendish.

"Looks like I know how to pick them," I croaked to the empty room.

DECORATING WAS PAUSED while I showered and bawled my eyes out where I knew no one would disturb me. By the time I got out of the shower, my face was a splodgy mess. I took time drying my hair and putting on makeup so Jared wouldn't know how upset I'd gotten while he was gone.

The days were short this far up north in December, so he'd

finish up soon. At least the Christmas tree was decorated. Maybe he'd help me with the rest of the décor.

It was two weeks until Christmas. I'd need to go shopping in Inverness because I'd left the presents I'd bought back at Theo's flat in my hurry to leave. Not that I had many presents to buy. Just Jared and a wee something for his farmhands. Something for Mrs. Hutchinson, my old boss at Ardnoch Estate. I'd given Liz hers at our meeting. Theo's ... I'd left that behind too.

So that was it. That was the extent of it. How pathetic was that?

I was just wrapping tinsel around the stair banisters when I heard the back door open.

"It's me!" Jared called.

We had a mudroom at the back of the farmhouse where Jared and Grandpa would remove their soiled boots and work coats.

Glancing out the glass panes of the front door, I noted the sky had darkened considerably. A look at the clock on the wall to my left told me it was four p.m.

"Whoa, look at it in here." Jared's voice traveled through the house.

I finished up decorating the stairs and wandered into the sitting room. The tree illuminated the space and it looked cozy and Christmassy. I waited for it to fill me with that same sense of warmth and comfort it always used to. But there was a dreadful emptiness in place of that feeling.

Jared stood eyeing the tree. He turned to me, his cheeks flushed from the cold, his hair a wee bit disheveled from where he'd obviously been wearing a hat. Jared wasn't what people thought of when you said the word *farmer*. While our grandfather didn't give a rat's arse about appearances, Jared did. He kept his hair fashionably long on top and short at the sides. And while I was gone, he'd grown a beard that he kept meticulously trimmed. Women had always flocked to Jared, and he took what they offered without promising them much in return.

I felt a smidge of my anger at Theo transfer unfairly to my cousin who was just as messed up when it came to relationships. Didn't they know there was a drought of good men out there? Why did they all have to be so emotionally unavailable?

Jared raised an eyebrow. "What? What did I do?"

Realizing I was scowling at him, I wiped my expression. "Nothing."

He turned more fully toward me. "Do you want to talk about it?"

Understanding he meant Theo, I opened my mouth to say no but was cut off by the sound of our gravel driveway kicking up under tires. I frowned. "Expecting someone?"

Jared shook his head and strode past me. Curious, I followed him to the front door.

My cousin wasn't as tall as Grandpa or Theo. He was five eleven. But he was broad-shouldered and right now, he was using his shoulders to block my view as he opened the door. Noting his tension, I stood on tiptoes to see past, and I swear my heart leapt into my throat at the sight of Theo getting out of a rental car.

"Do you want me to tell him to leave?" Jared asked quietly, stepping aside.

Surprised he wasn't going all scary protective like he had before, I sighed heavily. "No. I suppose not."

I didn't know what Theo was doing here, but I wasn't going to be a coward. Like him.

"Can you give us a minute?" I asked my cousin as Theo slowed to a stop, determined gaze fixed on me. He looked a bit disheveled and there were dark circles under his eyes.

"Will you be okay?"

I nodded.

Jared glanced between us but said, "I'm going to shower, but I'll leave my door open. You scream if you need me."

Theo had the audacity to roll his eyes.

I glared at him, and he primly wiped his expression.

My cousin gave me one more assessing look before he shot Theo a warning glower. It lasted an awkward ten seconds at least, before he turned and took the stairs two at a time. Once I heard the creak of the floorboards above me, I focused on Theo.

It hurt to look at him, but I didn't want him to know just how much. "What are you doing here?"

"May I come in?" he asked, expression pleading now that Jared was gone.

"No."

He seemed surprised but accepting. "All right. Freezing my balls off while I say this to you seems like an excellent punishment."

"I'm not punishing you." I crossed my arms over my chest protectively. "I just don't want you in this house."

Pain slashed across Theo's face, and he squeezed his eyes closed for a second. "Sarah." My name was a hoarse plea. "I am so bloody sorry for how I treated you last night." At my silence, he took a step toward me and stopped when I retreated. Raw agony swirled in Theo's eyes, and my body trembled at his open vulnerability. "I got back to the flat about an hour after you, and I couldn't get a flight out until this morning and then I was delayed in Edinburgh. I took the chance that you'd come here rather than the cottage. If I could have gotten here faster, I would have."

"Why? Why would you do all that ... for someone you care so little for?" I swallowed hard, fighting the burning in my eyes. I would not cry in front of him.

Theo flinched. "You know that's not true."

"Not really. I tend to judge people by their actions, not by their pretty words."

Fear flashed in his gaze, clear for all to see. "Sarah ... I'd had a visit from my brother while you were at your meeting. He doesn't know that you're independently wealthy, and he made it seem like I'm treating you to the good life, using you, only to discard you later ... he accused me of being cruel and he brought up things about our past ... I'm an idiot and I let him get to me. I let him convince me that I am a selfish bastard to keep you. You deserve to experience life, to get out there, and ... and I felt like maybe I was hogging you."

"Hogging me?"

"Keeping you for myself. Not letting you experience ... other men."

Indignation made me suck in a breath. "And did it ever occur to you that the choice to experience other men is up to me?"

"Yes," he whispered. "A bit too late, unfortunately." He stepped closer, and my fingers clenched tightly around the frame of the door. "Sarah, as soon as you left with Scott, I felt sick to my stomach. I ..." He glanced away and I realized in astonishment that he was embarrassed. "I had a panic attack."

Stunned, I could only gape at him.

"Not my finest moment. Any of it." Theo huffed. That raw gaze returned to mine. "I didn't sleep with Alice. I didn't kiss her or touch her. I left as soon as Scott returned to the bar and told me he'd put you in a cab. Then, if I'm to be completely honest with you, I had another panic attack back at the flat when I saw you'd left."

Confused, hurt, exhausted, I ... "I don't know how I'm supposed to respond to that."

"I'm not telling you to manipulate you. Whether I have a panic attack is entirely my issue to deal with. I just ... I need you to know that *I* know I'm fucked up. But I want to be better."

I stepped back into the house, shaking my head against my warring emotions. A huge part of me just wanted to forgive him. To believe him. But I was scared now. "I told you. I warned you that if you told me to go like I don't matter, I would go. Well, this is me, going." I moved to close the door, but Theo shot forward, expression desperate as he pressed a palm to the wood to stop me.

"Sarah, you matter," he insisted urgently. "Don't you see that? You matter more than anybody. And it terrifies me. But ... losing you terrifies me more." Theo swallowed hard. "I am not one to beg, Sarah. Pride is one of my greatest faults. But I'm begging you now. Please forgive me. Forgive me."

Heart pounding at his declaration, staring up at this man who was so familiar to me, but saying things I never expected to hear him say ... I slumped, releasing my hold on the door.

Theo charged me, yanking me into him, but I couldn't make myself hold him.

Until it registered that he was trembling against me. "Please," he whispered harshly in my ear, "please, little darling, please forgive me. I'm going to be better. Braver. For you."

And because I loved him so much and wanted so desperately to believe him, I pulled back but only to clasp his face in my hands. His stubble rasped against my palms. "One last chance," I warned. "And I mean it. I won't let anyone treat me like that, Theo. Not even you."

He nodded, his grip tight, almost frantic. "I know. I know. You matter, Sarah. You matter more than anyone."

A tear slipped down my cheek as I held on to tenuous hope that he spoke the truth, and I melted into him as he kissed my tears away, murmuring apologies and endearments over and over as he did.

TWENTY-THREE
THEO

It was strange how effortlessly I'd gone from desiring autonomy and solitude to craving the company of a beautiful, quiet Scot and her sharp wit. Unfortunately, as much as she'd forgiven me, Sarah had put some boundaries in place for now. That meant she turned down (several times) my request that she stay at Ardnoch Castle with me. Instead, she'd decided to remain at the farmhouse. I attempted not to take it too personally, knowing she deserved space from me after what I did. Yet, I was afraid to give her too much of it.

I'd wanted to make love to her after she'd forgiven me, but she asked if we could wait until she felt safe with me again. Knowing she didn't feel safe with me was like a knife to the gut.

What had this little mouse done to me?

No one who knew me would believe anyone could have such power over Theo Cavendish, let alone a shy country housekeeper. Little did they know she was so much bloody more than that.

Since Sarah wouldn't stay at Ardnoch and I hadn't been invited to stay at the farmhouse, I convinced her to meet in the village every day. We both wrote separately in the morning (and I missed writing with her, asking her advice on a scene, or returning the favor for her) and then spent the afternoon together. Sometimes our sessions were interrupted by work calls I had to take, but at least it was something.

Though I swear it felt like I hadn't touched her in a million years.

It had been three days since I'd followed her here. I'd brought the Christmas presents she'd left behind, which won me some brownie points. But I still felt a distance between us. A disconnect. And it was painful.

I wanted to take things slow for her, but I also had to remind her about why we were so good together. If it had been only physical attraction, both of us would've grown bored by now, so it wasn't just about that. But physical connection *was* important. Today I had it in mind that I'd steal a kiss and see how it went from there.

The club was busy at this time of year, and I was a last-minute booking, which meant I was lucky to secure a room at the castle and not be ousted to one of the estate's lodges. However, my room was smaller than I was used to, and it didn't have a sea view, which was unfortunate. Closing the door behind me as I left for the day, I nodded to a few members in the corridor on my way downstairs but made no attempt to stop and chat. I was on a mission.

Walking along the balcony above the great hall, I peered down to see guests seated near the impressive fireplace. The carpeted hallway led to the landing where three stained glass windows spilled light into the gigantic space.

The great hall was exactly what you'd expect of a Scottish castle with expensive Aubusson carpets, classic lavish furnishings, and tremendous double doors that led outside. Two chesterfield sofas faced one another at the big stone fireplace, which was currently lit. Guests who were not familiar to me sipped coffee and read on their phones.

A footman dressed in a traditional black tailcoat and white gloves waited off to the side. I gestured to him as I took the last few steps down into the great hall. The young man strode smartly across the room to meet me.

"Good afternoon, sir." He bowed his head.

"Good afternoon. I'd like my rental car brought around. Cavendish is the name."

"Of course, Mr. Cavendish. I will see to that immediately."

"Thank you."

Clicking of heels in the distance drew my gaze toward the entrances that led to other reception rooms in the castle. Sure enough, a familiar, tall, and very beautiful woman appeared through the arched entrance that led to her office.

Aria Howard. Ardnoch's hospitality manager and my old friend's fiancée.

North had tried calling me three times since Jared showed up at the cottage, but I wasn't ready to talk to him.

Aria was a voluptuous, long-legged beauty who managed the estate with such efficiency and calm, she made the job look easy when it must be anything but. Her father was legendary film director Wesley Howard, and she'd grown up in Malibu. A far cry from the council estate her fiancé North had grown up in as a foster child in Scotland. I'd admired North when I'd learned his story. He'd pulled himself up from shit and turned himself into an award-winning actor.

He was a good man.

I hadn't expected the arsehole to think so little of me as to betray Sarah and me to her cousin like I was ... like I was a monster who'd kidnapped and defiled an innocent princess. Now that I knew that was what he thought of me, I didn't have time for him.

Or his fiancée.

Aria wore a neutral expression as she came to a stop. In her heels, she was the same height as me. "Mr. Cavendish, two officers from Scotland Yard are here to see you," she told me in hushed tones. "They're in my office waiting."

Oh, for Pete's sake. Had my brother not ordered his watchdogs off my back? "Wonderful," I muttered and gestured for her to lead the way.

Instead, she fell into step beside me. "North has been trying to reach you."

"Has he? What an utter waste of his precious time."

She stiffened. "He's worried about you. Though goodness knows why."

I cut her a bland look. "Yes, I, too, am rather at a loss as to why."

Her eyes narrowed ever so slightly. "You don't deserve him as a friend."

I raised an eyebrow, a mocking smirk curling my lips. "You and I must have very different understandings of the definition of the word *friend*, Ms. Howard."

Confusion flickered over her face for a second before she wiped it clean and pushed open her office door. I followed her inside.

"I'll leave you in private," she said, stepping back and closing the door behind her, leaving me in a room with a tall, broad-shouldered man who looked to be in his early fifties. His belly strained slightly against his white shirt, but beyond that, he looked like he could squash me between his large, bear-paw hands. The woman at his side was dressed similarly in a suit and winter coat, but while she was tall, she was younger and fit-looking. Her brown hair was pulled back in an efficient ponytail, and she wore little makeup.

"Look, let's save us all some time. I'm alive and well and

there is no reason, other than insanity, for my brother to file a missing person's report."

The police officers shared a look before the man stepped forward, holding out a hand. "DCI Rick English, Mr. Cavendish. This is DI Jane Hatlock. We're with the Major Investigations Unit at Scotland Yard. We're not here because of your brother or a missing person's report. We've been trying to contact you regarding the Hangman murders."

Dread instantly settled like a pit in my stomach.

"Are you aware of the murders, Mr. Cavendish?"

I nodded, feeling a little out of my body. "Yes. Yes, I've seen it on the news. I ... I ... I did note that the murders share the same name from my television show." There was a question in my statement.

DCI English nodded solemnly. "Mr. Cavendish, I'm sorry to relay this, but it's become very clear in our investigations that our perpetrator is copying the murders from *King's Valley*."

I shook my head, not wanting to believe it. "How ... I mean ... how?"

DI Hatlock said, "There have been four murders so far. Our first victim, Jennifer Parsons. Blond, twenty-four, murdered in December in Bracknell Forest. Second victim, Angela Wright, blond, aged twenty-seven, murdered in June in Slough."

Horror began to fill me with dawning realization.

"Polish primary teacher Ewa Kowalski, age twenty-six, killed in October—"

"In Maidenhead," I answered numbly.

"Yes."

Dread sank heavily in my gut. "And the fourth murder was a victim called Rachel, age twenty-three, in High Wycombe."

The police officers nodded. DI Hatlock continued, "Each

victim went missing forty-eight hours before their bodies were discovered. They suffered stab wounds to the heart and had the words *I'm sorry* carved in their torsos. Each victim was then hung in a location where their bodies were likely to be found quickly."

The killer *was* copying *King's Valley* to a tee. The show had *Valley* in the title because the murders took place in towns within the Thames Valley area. Each victim shared the same name, age, month of death, and wounds as the victims on the show. My character Charlie King found his mother hanging when he was seven years old, and she'd left a note with just the two words "I'm sorry." Charlie's victims all looked like his mother, and the idea was that he stabbed them in the heart because his mum had broken his heart as a boy. He was acting out her punishment on other women.

"Someone on our team was a fan of the show and started to put the pieces together when our third victim, Ewa, was murdered," DCI English relayed. "You should know members of the public have started piecing it together online. We've tried to shut it down, but we have our hands full, and it might not be long before the media picks it up."

"Right. Of course they would," I murmured stupidly. The room was spinning a bit. Stumbling backward, I leaned against the wall.

"Are you all right, Mr. Cavendish?" DCI Hatlock asked.

What did she think? "I've just found out the greatest writing achievement of my career has been used as inspiration to murder innocent women."

"We don't believe you are in danger, Mr. Cavendish, though we must ask if you or any of your cast or crew have received disturbing or threatening messages?" She probed.

"I haven't. I don't know about anyone else."

"We'll need a list of everyone who worked on the show."

"Of course." Renewed horror cut through me. "You don't think the perpetrator worked on the show?"

"We can't rule anything out."

"Are you here for my help beyond that? There are three more murders on the show. My character, Charlie King, murders a woman named Helen. It was his mother's name. And then he murders his father and stepmother."

DCI English nodded. "We know. We have a team analyzing the show and the murders. We just need the cast and crew list from you, Mr. Cavendish. And we wanted to make you aware of the situation personally so you can be on alert. We must caution again, however, that the reason we did not want this information released to the public was for public safety, but it's likely the tabloids will speculate."

It was a warning.

For *my* safety.

People might blame me.

Or more likely, the actors on the show.

Like North.

Fuck.

I might not be on speaking terms with North, but he'd been through enough this year.

"You have my utmost discretion in this matter," I promised. "Do you have an email? I'll get that list to you by the end of day."

TWENTY-FOUR
SARAH

I was lost in my thoughts, worrying about Theo, and hadn't even noticed the two women enter Flora's Café. My palms hugged my coffee mug, seeking the heat as nerves churned in my gut. I was worried about Theo. Other than how he was when he chased after me from London, I'd never seen him so off-kilter as he was yesterday. He'd told me about the police and the fact that they believed the Hangman serial killer was copycatting the serial killer from *King's Valley*.

We'd walked around the village while Theo made a few phone calls, the most important one being to his executive producer at Skylark World Productions, giving her a heads-up and asking for a full cast and crew list from the show that he could forward to the police. Next, he sent a blunt text message to North. I know he still hadn't forgiven him, but I also knew Theo didn't want his friend going through another year of media scandal.

North had tried to call him after the text, yet Theo couldn't bring himself to answer. Instead, he'd just stood there, staring at his phone, looking so lost and forlorn. Unable to bear it, I'd broken my promise to myself to keep my physical distance from Theo until I felt like I could trust him again, and I'd wrapped my arms around him.

He'd held on so tightly.

I tried to tell him that none of this was his fault, but he was deeply disturbed his work had been used in such a horrific way. And I couldn't blame him. I'd feel the same if someone took my books and turned them into real-life crimes.

"Sarah? Sarah?"

I blinked, my name on repeat breaking through my thoughts, and I turned to find Sloane Harrow leaning across the distance between our tables, her brows pinched with concern. She was accompanied by Monroe Adair, a primary school teacher and wife to retired Hollywood actor Brodan Adair. Brodan and Monroe were a good seven years older than me, so I hadn't been in their friend group, but I'd known that the famous couple were best friends growing up. They'd taken separate paths after high school but found their way back to each other almost twenty years later. Their story was utterly romantic. Monroe had fallen pregnant quickly upon their reunion, and they'd married in a private ceremony. Their baby boy Lennox followed a few months later.

Sloane, an American transplant and single mum to Callie, was friends with Aria, so Aria had gotten Sloane a job as a housekeeper at the estate. We hadn't worked shifts together, but the pretty American had been sweet and polite to me and brought all of us the most amazing baked goods. She'd had some trouble with her daughter's father, and Walker, a new security guard at the estate who also happened to be Brodan's ex-bodyguard, stepped in to help her. They'd fallen in love, gotten engaged, and according to Jared, they'd married while I was in Gairloch.

Sloane quit housekeeping at the beginning of summer to open a bakery that was now extremely popular in the village. It was only open three days a week, much to everyone's chagrin, but I admired Sloane's determination to run her business the way she wanted to. I shouldn't think of her as Sloane Harrow anymore. She was now Sloane Ironside.

"Hi." I shook my head, blushing at the fact she'd obviously called my name several times before I heard her.

"Are you okay?" she asked, studying me carefully.

"I'm fine," I assured her. "I hear congratulations are in order."

She grinned and held up her hand where a beautiful engagement ring was nestled beside her wedding band. "Yeah, still can't believe it sometimes."

"Well, congratulations. To you and Callie."

Surprise softened her features, no doubt because I'd never been a great conversationalist when we worked together. But these last few weeks with Theo had helped me gain a lot of confidence. If I could converse easily with someone as intimidating as him, I could pretty much talk to anyone.

I smiled at Monroe. "I don't think I got the chance to congratulate you on your marriage or your son, so congrats."

Monroe stared at me like she'd never seen me before, but then quickly recovered. "Thank you, Sarah. How are you doing?"

"Yeah, Aria said you quit the estate," Sloane remarked. "Everything okay there?"

It's time, I thought. Soon enough people would know. And ... I was proud of my achievements. Feeling my cheeks grow hot as my heart raced, I pushed through my nervousness and confessed, "I ... I started self-publishing a crime series, and ... well ... it kind of took off, so I'm writing full-time now."

Both of their eyes widened and then comically, as one, they got up from their table and sat down at mine. It made me chuckle through my nervousness as they leaned closer.

"That is amazing." Monroe beamed in genuine happiness for me.

"So amazing. Tell us more. Do you write under your own name?" Sloane asked excitedly.

Unused to such focused attention, my hands curled around my mug a wee bit too tightly, but I shook my head. "I write under the pen name S. M. Brodie."

"No way!" Monroe slapped a hand on the table, eyes round as saucers. "You write the Juno McLeod series?"

Pride and joy filled me that she'd heard of it. "I do."

Monroe turned to Sloane. "It's one of my favorite crime series. It's set in Dundee. Mostly."

"Is that the series you wanted us to read for book club?"

"Aye, that one." Monroe turned back to me. "Sarah ... congratulations. I mean, I've seen the accolades on the blurb. A multimillion-copy bestseller. I've seen the book in stores ... It's just amazing. I'm so thrilled for you."

"Oh my goodness, I have to google you." Sloane pulled out her phone and did just that while I laughed, blushing wildly. "Oh, wow. Sarah, this is awesome." She looked up from her phone. "Would you come to our book club? It's us and all the Adair women. We meet at Arro's once a month. Would you come to our January meeting?"

"No pressure," Monroe added, shooting Sloane an amused but quelling look.

"Oh, yeah, no pressure," Sloane added.

For the last few years, I'd watched the Adair family women from afar. How other women in the village envied them for their handsome husbands, some of whom were famous. I didn't envy them for that. Well, not really. I envied what looked to be a tight-knit friendship circle. If I didn't see Arro Adair out and about with Eredine Adair or Regan and Robyn Adair together, I saw Monroe and Sloane, or a mix of the pairings. Sometimes they were all together. And they looked so close. I wondered what it would be like to have close female relationships. But I'd been too scared to try. Too scared to trust.

Because of my mum.

I was done being afraid.

I wanted to be brave.

Smiling, I nodded. "I would love that."

Monroe and Sloane thanked me excitedly and then Monroe got up to grab their drinks and bring them to my table. I asked after their kids. Callie was in school, and Brodan had Lennox for the morning. Monroe had been a teacher at Ardnoch Primary but had decided to become a stay-at-home mum until it was time for Nox to attend school. "We'll see if I last that long, though," she grumbled. "I do miss class."

"Can you imagine teaching all those young kids and coming home to be a mom?" Sloane mused. "It must be so exhausting."

"Which is what Brodan reminds me every time I get broody for my class."

"And how is Callie coping with the Scottish school system?" I asked. I couldn't imagine moving to an entirely different country, even if they did technically speak the same language.

"She loves it. She's best friends with Lewis."

"Adair?"

"Yeah."

Lewis was Thane Adair's son with his first wife, who died not long after giving birth to their daughter Eilidh. Thane was now married to Regan, Lachlan's wife Robyn's younger sister. She'd been his nanny, and it had been quite a scandal at the time.

"You know Regan had her baby," Monroe offered as if she'd read my mind.

I gaped. "No, Jared didn't say."

Monroe grinned. "A wee girl. Morwenna Adair. Our clan is growing rapidly."

"It's lovely," I said quietly. "Please give them my congratulations. Family ... family is everything."

Sloane suddenly reached across the table to cover my hand with hers. "How are you doing?"

Knowing what she asked, I swallowed the grief that welled up at the slightest thing these days. "Christmas ... our first Christmas without Grandpa is hard. Sometimes it doesn't feel real that eight months have passed since we lost him, and then other times it feels forever ago. But we're okay."

"You know, you're welcome, both you and Jared, to spend Christmas with us," Monroe offered. "We're having a big Christmas at Lachlan's, and we'd love to have you."

Sloane nodded her agreement and I melted at their kindness. These women didn't know me that well and so I was blown away by their invitation.

"She'll be spending her Christmas with me and her cousin, but thank you, ladies." Theo's voice cut between us, and I glanced up in shock to find him standing there.

How had I not even noticed him come in?

My companions gaped up at him in surprise too, and I could only imagine their expressions as Theo bent to brush a kiss against the corner of my mouth. He settled into the empty seat next to me, his legs so long, his knees knocked into mine. Arm casually sliding across the back of my chair, he grinned at Sloane and Monroe. "But we'll probably see you at the Ardnoch Christmas party."

What? I frowned at him. He turned to look at me, his expression softening. "Party?"

"Yes. I want you to be my plus-one."

At the Ardnoch Christmas party?

"So you two ..." We turned toward Sloane as she gestured between us, expression unreadable. "Are you together?"

"I don't believe we've met," Monroe interrupted before we could answer. "I'm Monroe Adair."

"I know who you are. The tabloids wouldn't leave you and your husband alone for a while there." He held out his hand to shake hers. "I'm Theo Cavendish."

Monroe shook his hand. "Are you a club member?"

"Yes. I'm a screenwriter and director."

"Oh. Anything I'd recognize?"

Theo leaned into me, his expression tightening for a second. "This and that."

Sympathy sliced through me. Only a day ago he would have proudly announced *King's Valley.* You'd had to have been living under a rock not to have heard of the show. Now, it was tainted by some sick psycho.

"Will you be at the party?" I changed the subject, mind still reeling at the idea of me attending an estate party as a guest after years of housekeeping there.

"Not this year." Monroe went with the subject change, though she kept glancing curiously at Theo. "But, of course, Lachlan will be there."

"So, Theo." Sloane eyed him suspiciously. "You met Sarah at the estate?"

"Yes."

My lips twitched at his bland response. "We're working on a project together."

"Oh. That's exciting."

"And we're together," Theo added with more nonchalance than I knew he felt. "Just so there's no mistake about the nature of our relationship. I hear the gossip mill runs quick and fast around the village."

Monroe and Sloane both raised an eyebrow.

Theo looked amused. "To clarify, Sarah and I are in a romantic relationship as well as a professional one ... to save you all days or weeks of speculation."

"Sarah, you're awfully quiet about that," Monroe said with a smirk.

I might be taking my time diving back into what he and I had before, but we *were* together. I wanted to be with him. To work on returning to that place of trust. "Theo and I are dating. People will find out soon enough."

Sloane grinned. "Well, I'm glad for you both."

"We can die happy now."

I elbowed Theo. "Ignore him. Sarcasm is his first language."

"Just for that"—Sloane pointed at Theo, lips curled at the corners—"I'm going to get Walker to do a background check on you."

I chuckled as Theo shrugged. "Why bother? I am an open book. Ask away."

At my snort, he turned to me, eyes narrowed. But there was heat in his gaze that made my skin flush. It felt like years since we'd touched.

"You disagree?"

"You're an open book with me ... but no one else."

"Well, that's all that matters," he murmured with a wicked twinkle in his eyes. "Isn't it?"

I wished that it was all that mattered. But before Theo had been hit with the awful news about the murders and his show, I'd been thinking more and more that Theo needed to face some of his demons. And by face his demons, I meant his father. I was worried that if I fully embraced our relationship, something else would come up to remind him of his father and Saffron's betrayal, and I'd be the one he'd push away again.

Yet, I didn't know how to bring up the subject now that he had so much he was dealing with.

But I knew for my peace of mind, and for his, it was something I'd need him to at least consider facing.

TWENTY-FIVE

THEO

"It would just be two episodes. Two weeks in Vancouver," Miles Cooley coaxed down the line. He was the head writer and creator of a successful US crime series and I'd guest directed a few episodes of the show in the past. He wanted me out there in February to do a few more.

"I can't commit to it, Miles. I'm sorry. I have a project in development that will probably take up most of my time in the new year. But thank you."

"Okay. Well, I don't need an answer for another week, so think on it," Miles insisted.

I promised him I would, though I knew I couldn't take the job. I hoped I'd be close to getting Juno into production by February.

We hung up and I turned to look at the tuxedo on my bed. I'd had it delivered to the castle a few days ago. With the horror of the Hangman cases lingering in my thoughts, I knew I was courting distraction by asking Sarah to attend the Ardnoch Christmas party with me. The truth was, I wanted her back. Fully. And it was better to pour all my attention into winning her back than think about the show or the murders. There was nothing more I could do, anyway.

Skylark World Productions sent the police the list of cast and crew, and some of them had been contacted. The production company had their PR team fired up and ready to go as soon as this became real news. So far, it hadn't turned into that, but I had a sinking feeling it wasn't far from breaking headlines.

As such, I was concentrating elsewhere.

On the one thing that was most important to me in the world. In a few hours, I'd pick up Sarah and bring her back to the estate and we'd get ready here together. I'd spend the entire night showering her with affection and attention and proving to her that she was all I wanted.

And maybe, just maybe, she'd let me touch her again.

There was nothing quite like being denied the one thing you wanted more than anything. I longed for her, even though I'd had her. I wanted her more than I'd ever wanted anyone. Because it wasn't actually about sex. It was about connection.

She had her guard up.

I wanted to smash that guard to smithereens and prove to her she never needed it again.

Fuck, if any one of my acquaintances knew what I'd do for this woman, they wouldn't believe it. That, I, Theo Cavendish, was at the mercy of an introverted Scot.

Screw them. I'd shed my pride for Sarah McCulloch any day of the bloody week.

A rhythmic thudding sounded on my suite door, followed by, "Theo? Are you in there?"

Recognizing the deep, Scottish-accented voice, I pinched the bridge of my nose.

North.

Well, I suppose this meeting was inevitable. Crossing the

room, I grabbed my rental car keys off the side table and pulled open the door.

Sure enough, North stood on the other side, hands in his pockets, a scowl marring his brow. "You're alive." He brushed past me, pushing into the room.

"And on my way out." I turned with a beleaguered sigh, closing the door behind me. "But do come in."

North faced me, arms now folded over his chest. "I don't enjoy having my calls screened. Especially after having the news dropped on me that a bloody serial killer found his inspiration from a part I played."

"A part I wrote, old boy. Imagine how I feel. I dreamed up a twisted, complicated bastard of a character, one I was proud of ... until someone brought his wicked misdeeds to life."

Sympathy gleamed in North's eyes. "I'm sorry. I'm sorry for both of us. We created him together, so you're not alone in feeling unsettled by this."

"Don't you mean guilty?"

"No." North shook his head. "We made a TV show, Theo. Like hundreds of creators before us have done. It is not our fault some sick fuck decided to carry out those murders."

Growing agitated because he was distracting me from my distraction, I scrubbed a hand down my face. "I don't want to think about it today, so if you're quite done ..."

He cocked an eyebrow. "What? Leave? Very nice. Is that it, then? You're ghosting me like I'm a flexible gymnast you've grown bored with."

Ignoring the jab at my previous sexual exploits, I shrugged with more nonchalance than I felt. "Believe it or not, you were one of the few people in this industry I didn't mind having around. Thought I could trust you. Until you blabbed like a tween to Sarah's cousin and sent him after me."

"I won't apologize for that." North shrugged. "I was protecting Sarah. To get involved with her was wrong, Theo."

"Why?"

Anger flickered over his face. "Because she's a grieving member of staff at this estate who can barely say boo to a goose, and you shacked up with her when she was at her most vulnerable."

"Sarah is an intelligent, talented thirty-one-year-old ex-member of staff, and she knows her own mind."

"She doesn't know you."

"Do you?" I asked, losing my patience. "Do you actually know anything real about me, North, other than my work? No," I answered for him, and his chin jerked back in surprise. "You don't know a damn thing about me. But Sarah does. She knows me better than anyone. And I swear to God, if you try to come between me and Sarah again, I'll ruin you."

My old friend gaped at me, stunned. Silent.

"You can leave now." I gestured to the door.

"Theo." North took a step toward me, gaze searching mine. "I'm sorry, mate. I ... I clearly got the wrong end of the stick."

"Yes, you did. A stick that is rammed thoroughly up your arse."

The corner of his mouth lifted. "I suppose I jumped to conclusions. I've just never known you to be serious about anyone."

I looked away, still not entirely comfortable with the strength of feeling I had for Sarah but willing to deal with it to keep her. "*I* never thought I'd be serious about a woman again."

"Again?"

"There was a woman when I was younger. We met at uni and dated for a while. Thought I loved her. She ... she had an affair with my father while my mother was dying. Then she married him and stayed with him until he grew bored and traded her in for a younger model."

North's eyes widened in shock. "Fuck, Theo ... that's brutal. I'm sorry."

"Yes, well, never really had much interest in relationships after that."

"Until Sarah?"

Rubbing the back of my neck, I gave my friend a rueful smile. "She's rather special. Don't know what she sees in me."

North grinned and clapped me on the arm. "No one does, mate."

"Oh, fuck off," I said without heat, turning to the door. "Literally. I have to pick up Sarah for the party tonight."

"She's coming here?" he asked as we left the room.

"Yes. Problem?"

"Of course not. I just wondered if I could tell Aria about her writing under S. M. Brodie. She was worried when Sarah suddenly quit the estate."

It was clear from our conversation with Sloane Ironside and Monroe Adair the other day that Sarah had told them about her writing. "I don't see why not. She's telling other people now."

He grinned. "Good. I'm looking forward to seeing you two together."

"I'm never living this down, am I?"

"You once called me a brain-addled romantic and said that falling in love would end badly for me. Of course, I'm holding this over you."

"I also, if you remember, was the one who advised you to give Aria your trust. And how did that work out?"

"So, what you're saying is you've been a secret romantic this whole time?" North teased as he took the castle stairs.

"I wouldn't go that far."

"I guess we'll see tonight."

I rolled my eyes. "Please do not watch over us like we're the evening's entertainment. Sarah hasn't miraculously changed overnight. Though she's growing in confidence, she doesn't like being the center of attention. And I want her to enjoy this evening."

North chuckled. "While it's adorable you're looking out for her feelings, Cavendish, you need to get real. You're bringing Sarah to a celebrity Christmas party at the place of her former employment. People will be curious about this odd match of yours."

I scowled at the phrase *odd match*. "Pish posh. Ninety-five percent of this elitist community are too busy drowning in their own bovarism to even know or care who I am."

"What exactly is bovarism?"

"Sarah would know," I told him haughtily.

North laughed. "Oh, man, you've got it bad."

I didn't disagree. Instead, as we reached the great hall, I told him, "I'll see you tonight."

"Wait. Theo."

Turning to him, I raised an impatient eyebrow.

North looked remorseful. "I am sorry. I ... I realize now that I was a shitty friend when you've been a good friend to me."

Giving him a reassuring clap on the shoulder, I promised, "All's forgiven. Let's forget it."

My friend nodded and I experienced a rush of relief. I'd been so busy with Sarah that I hadn't realized just how much it bothered me to be in a bad place with North. I didn't have a lot of genuine friends, and while I liked to pretend I didn't need them, it wasn't true. Having North in my life had been like having a brother I could count on again.

Goodness, I'd grown maudlin since finding Sarah. Shaking my head ruefully, I gave North a gentle shove and stalked away. "See you tonight."

"Oh, aye, we will! Looking forward to it!" I heard the amusement in his voice.

With a beleaguered sigh at his nonsense, I hurried out of the castle, heading toward the mews where my rental was parked.

———

"SO WE DISCUSSED ALL THAT," I called to Sarah as she got ready in my suite's bathroom. I'd just relayed my meeting with North to her. "But I have to admit, I didn't feel like discussing the murders. Perhaps I should have. I'm sure North is concerned he's going to make the headlines again for all the wrong reasons."

"There's still time to do that," she called back. "I'm sure North understands your reluctance to talk about it. But if it's bothering you, just make it clear when you see him next that you're there for him if he wants to talk about it."

"Yes, yes. You're right." I tweaked my black velvet bow tie as I stared in the mirror. The last time I'd worn a tux was at an awards ceremony. I owned two tuxedos. This one was a burgundy velvet tuxedo jacket with black lapels. I wore it with black trousers and a white shirt. A little outlandish but perfect for a Christmas event.

"Well?"

I turned from fussing with the tie and froze at the sight that greeted me.

Sarah wore a green velvet dress. It had thin straps, a fitted bodice, and a pleated skirt that flowed from her waist to her knees. The green was dark against her smooth, pale skin. She'd paired the dress with strappy delicate heels that made her already gorgeous legs look fucking fantastic. Her hair was styled in waves down her back, and her makeup was light except for her eyes. She wore black mascara that lengthened her lashes considerably, and the green of her irises was impossibly vivid.

I was struck mute.

She was graceful and elegant and sexy as hell. It was difficult for me to believe that I'd never paid much attention to her before she came to my room all those months ago. I mean, I'd noticed her, eventually. North and I had bumped into her once, and it was the first time I'd realized she was beautiful. But ... that was just noting something physical about her. I didn't know her then.

Now I knew her. Now I knew how extraordinary she was. "You are the most stunning creature I've ever seen," I blurted out, the compliment raspy with emotion.

Sarah flushed a pretty pink, the color spreading across her chest. Tenderness and something like possessiveness filled me. "Thank you. You look very handsome."

I grinned as I crossed the room to her. "Is it perverse of me that I like that I can still make you blush?"

She rolled her eyes as I pulled her against me. "I would expect nothing less."

I smoothed my hands down her waist, desire heating my blood. "I miss you."

Understanding softened her expression. "I know." She caressed my chest. "I miss you too. We're getting there, though. I promise."

Determined to respect her wishes, even if the cost was physical pain, I stepped back. "We look like a Christmas advertisement."

Sarah laughed, taking in the burgundy velvet of my tuxedo against the forest green of her dress. "So we do." She reached for my hand, drawing me back to her. "Who cares? I think we're beautiful."

"You certainly are." I threaded my fingers through hers, drawing her close before leading her toward the door. "I'm warning you, I'm feeling very thigmophilic this evening. You can tell me to back off whenever it gets too much."

She blushed prettily again, heat in her eyes that gave me hope. "Maybe I'm feeling thigmophilic tonight too."

Grinning, I nodded. "Good. I'm open to groping. Are you?"

She smacked my arm, laughing.

"That wasn't a no, little darling."

Sarah leaned into me, wrapping her other arm around mine. "No, it wasn't, was it?"

Twenty-Six

SARAH

We met a few people on the stairwell, but I didn't recognize their faces and, thankfully, they didn't seem to recognize mine. Music cascaded up the stairwell toward us, bagpipes and accordions with fiddles leading the tune.

I'd grown more and more nervous about the Christmas party as the day progressed but was attempting to hide that from Theo. It was strange, though, to come to the castle as his guest. For seven years, I'd scuttled around the halls here, trying to be invisible. It wasn't my job I was embarrassed by. No. I wasn't particularly proud of my timidity back then. And now I felt like a fish out of water. Like I was a fraud.

Theo didn't even acknowledge the weirdness of it. Maybe for him, it wasn't weird. We were in a relationship, and he wanted me to be his date for the Christmas party.

I think he just wanted a distraction, and I was willing to suck up any discomfort I felt to give that to him.

The great hall was filled with guests. A small band, including a bagpiper, played traditional Scottish country dance music as guests performed the Gay Gordons, some successfully, others not so much.

I spotted Lachlan Adair with his wife Robyn among the participants. Years ago, my eyes would have lingered on my longtime crush. Now I looked up at Theo. "I'm having primary school traumatic flashbacks. Please do not make me country dance."

Theo chuckled. "We're on the same page. Let's find something to drink."

We skirted the edges of the great hall and followed other guests through the arches and down the corridor to the dining room. It had been transformed for Christmas. Glittering trees, wreaths, an abundance of fairy lights, and garlands everywhere. A long buffet table was set up along one side with serving staff. Tables in the middle of the room were decorated with elaborate vase centerpieces filled with gold-sprayed foliage and fairy lights. Miniature golden deer and red wreaths decorated the bases. The tableware was gold, the napkins red, and the table linens a crisp white.

Servers in the usual Ardnoch tailcoats and gloves moved through the guests with trays of champagne, offering them to those they passed.

"I used to get a peek at the décor the day of the party, but I've never seen the place filled with guests or music."

Theo gestured to a server who slowed to offer us the tray. My date handed me a glass of champagne before taking one for himself and muttering his thanks. When the server moved away, Theo turned to clink his glass to mine. "To grabbing life by the balls."

I smiled curiously. "That's our toast?"

"Yes. Despite your fears, you went after what you wanted when you came to me all those months ago. And despite my utter terror, I went after what I wanted when I chased you here from London."

Tenderness warmed me and I clinked my glass against his. "To grabbing life by the balls."

We'd barely taken a drink when my ex-boss Aria Howard appeared with her fiancé North. North and Theo greeted each other easily, which made me relieved for Theo. I knew men weren't good at admitting such things, but I believed his friendship with North meant a great deal to him.

"Aria, you're looking effulgent this evening." Theo gave her a cordial bow of his head.

She grimaced. "Was that an insult?"

I snorted into my champagne glass, but at her suspicious look, I hurried to explain, "It means *radiant*."

"Oh." Her expression slackened as she turned to Theo. "Well, thanks."

"It doesn't sound like a compliment, so I understand your confusion," I added.

Aria nodded, wrinkling her nose. "It sounds like a fungus."

Theo barked out a short laugh.

Aria shook her head, a small smile playing on her face. She did look radiant. Her envious curves were accentuated in a dark red dress that made her look like a movie bombshell from the 1950s. "Sarah, can I sneak you away for a second?"

"Of course." I gave Theo a reassuring smile, then noted his disgruntled frown. A playful side of me felt like sticking my tongue out at him, but I gestured toward North in a silent insistence that he talk with his friend while I was gone.

"You look beautiful," Aria stated as we walked toward the dining room exit.

My cheeks grew hot. "Oh. Thank you. So do you."

"I look effulgent, remember."

I chuckled. "He's trying."

Her gaze turned assessing, but a group of people cut us off and we were separated before coming together again, just at the entrance to the great hall. Aria smoothed a hand over her hair. "It's even busier this year than last."

"It's so festive." And still so surreal to be here as a guest.

"Yeah." Aria suddenly turned into me, concern marring her expression. "I know it's none of my business, but I care about you and, although North assures me that Cavendish's feelings for you are real ... I just want to make sure that you're good. That you're happy? That Theo isn't taking advantage of you in a time of grief?"

Gratitude moved me. I placed a reassuring hand on her arm. "Ms. Howard, thank you for worrying about me. But I'm fine. I'm better than fine. What happened between Theo and me was unexpected for both of us. But it happened. Neither of us can deny it. And I can handle whatever comes."

She considered this. "You can, can't you?"

"I can."

"You seem different."

"I am. And I'm not."

Aria nodded like she understood. "I also want to congratulate you on all your success. And the reason I pulled you away is that someone else would like to congratulate you." She took my arm and guided me through the crowds along the edge of the dancing.

When we came to a stop before Lachlan and Robyn Adair, those old butterflies fluttered to life.

Lachlan had a short but lucrative career as a Hollywood action star. When he returned to his family's estate to develop it into the club, I'd been in awe of him. I knew the Adairs from growing up in the same village, but Lachlan was the eldest and twelve years older. He was already working in Hollywood by the time I came to live at Ardnoch.

I'd thought him the most rugged, handsome man I'd ever met. And he hired me despite the history between his family and mine. Grandpa had not been pleased when I took the job at Ardnoch, but he knew it paid better than anywhere else in the area and that I needed to make my own decisions about these things.

Every time I was around Lachlan, I blushed like a schoolgirl. It was mortifying. And I could sense all that past nervousness and embarrassment bubbling up.

Be brave, little darling. Show them who you really are. I stiffened at the sound of Theo's voice in my head.

The reminder of him and everything we'd shared soothed me, and as Lachlan and Robyn turned to us, I let that calm take over.

Robyn Adair was a charismatic badass from Boston, Massachusetts. I'd looked up to her, even when she'd suspected me of stalking Lachlan. An ex-cop turned landscape photographer, rumor had it she'd also taught jiujitsu to every woman in the Adair family. She and my grandfather had saved Lachlan's life.

Tall with an athletic figure and large breasts, she was almost like a real-life Lara Croft. Not classically beautiful, but she had a face that was hard to look away from. And she was intimidatingly cool. Robyn was more charismatic than half the people in Hollywood.

Now, the American offered a wide, happy smile that relaxed me. "Sarah!"

"Merry Christmas, Mr. and Mrs. Adair," I offered to husband and wife.

"Merry Christmas." Lachlan bent his head to brush a kiss over my cheek and I felt my skin grow hot.

Laughing ruefully at the reaction, I almost rolled my eyes at myself.

He grinned a little smugly and Robyn nudged him not too gently. "Stop it."

The cocky Scotsman just laughed, and his wife shook her head. Then Lachlan turned to me. "Call us Lachlan and

Robyn," he insisted. "I asked Aria to find you because Robyn and I are taking off early."

"Oh." It was my understanding as hosts they stayed until the end of the night.

Robyn patted her stomach, and I noted a slight swell. "The baby isn't enjoying the dancing or the heat of all these bodies."

My jaw dropped. "You're pregnant?"

"Oh, yeah. I keep forgetting we just told the family yesterday." Robyn let Lachlan pull her more deeply into his side, and recognition cut through me at the way he stared down at her so adoringly.

I realized ... I'd seen Theo look at me that way.

Oh.

I suddenly felt a little breathless.

"Aye, Vivien is going to have a wee brother or sister." Lachlan looked so damn pleased.

"Congratulations."

"Thanks." Robyn nudged Lachlan again. "So ..."

"Oh, right." He dragged his gaze off his wife. "We heard about your writing career and all your success, and we just wanted you to know how happy we are for you and how proud. I know Collum would be so proud."

Emotion thickened my throat. "He was. And thank you."

"So he knew?"

I nodded. "The books took off a few months before he died. Losing him gave me the impetus to accept my success."

"I'm sorry that's what it took," Lachlan said gruffly. "But I'm glad he knew."

"Thank you." I smiled at them both, holding back the tears. Then to Lachlan, I said, "And thank you for holding the wake last summer for the village. I'm sorry I couldn't make it." I'd been too devastated to show my face. "Thank you for allowing me to work here despite everything between our families. I want you to know that I'm forever grateful. And I want you to know that I knew my grandpa better than anyone … and despite how he felt about the history between your families, he believed you are a good man and he respected the hell out of you."

A sheen of emotion appeared in Lachlan's eyes, and he gave me a sharp nod as his wife squeezed him in comfort. "Thank you," he forced out. "That means a lot. I respected Collum too."

"He knew that," I assured him.

A sense of peace settled over me, as if I'd done something for Grandpa that he'd lost the chance to do for himself.

Twenty-Seven
THEO

A good twenty minutes had passed since Aria swept Sarah away, and I was getting antsy for her return.

"The usual suspects are here, then?" I remarked, eyeing the guests gathered in the dining room. Most were out in the great hall, but I'd avoid that place until the traditional Scottish dancing ended.

North shrugged. "I suppose so. You have to admit, this place is pretty festive. It reminds me a bit of school."

"I wouldn't know. We didn't do traditional Scottish dancing at school."

My friend grinned. "You mean at Eton?"

I ignored his teasing. "I do want to enjoy tonight without thinking of ... well, of the murders. Selfish, yes, considering the families of the victims can't escape it for a second, let alone a night ...," I trailed off, uncomfortable with the guilt that clawed at my chest.

"Theo, you have to stop beating yourself up over this. This psycho could have picked any show to copy."

"I'm not sure of that. From my research, there must be something that triggered it. Perhaps he sees parallels between our show and his own life. I don't know." I shrugged, rubbing the back of my neck. "Anyway, that's not why I mentioned it. I just wanted you to know that if you're worried about the media, I'm here. You can talk to me. And I won't let them target you. I'll make sure they know I'm the one behind the show."

He shook his head. "We're in this together. Honestly, I don't care if they drag me through the mud again. I have Aria, I have a life I'm proud of. The most important thing is that the police find this guy."

I nodded. "I wish I had more information. Perhaps I could help them."

"Couldn't you? You wrote the show. You might know what his next move will be."

"So do they. They have a team analyzing the show. Figuring it all out."

"They should have drafted you in. You know it better than anyone."

"I was not invited, and I did offer my services." I shrugged. "Anyway, enough for tonight. I just wanted to say that."

"Well, I appreciate it." North eyed me with something akin to amusement.

I grimaced. "I know. Sarah is turning me soft."

"No, actually." He clapped me on the shoulder. "You've always been like this. You had my back when Darren's mum was sending me threatening letters, and then when I hit Preston. You had my back with Aria. I should have known better when I assumed you were taking advantage of Sarah."

"We don't need to rehash that." I glanced around, looking for my other half. "Where did Aria take her, anyway?"

"Lachlan found out from Monroe that Sarah is writing. He's known her most of her life and just wants to congratulate her."

I stiffened. "Sarah had a crush on him for years."

North chuckled. "He's a happily married man. Look at you, all jealous, mate. Never thought I'd see the day when Theo Cavendish became a one-woman man. You're not even eyeing other women here."

"Why would I?" I asked imperiously. "Have you seen my date?"

"Aye, and she's as lovely as I always knew she was."

"Yes, she is." And I hoped she was starting to realize it about herself.

North leaned into me. "Why is Angeline Potter asking after you, though?"

Fuck. "When?"

"Out in the hall. She asked Aria and me if you were attending tonight. Is it because of what happened between you two here last Christmas?"

Discomfort rode me. "I ... I made the mistake of sleeping with her a few months ago. Before Sarah, of course."

"Oh, mate." North shook his head.

"I know. It was the worst experience of my life."

He raised an eyebrow, male curiosity gleaming in his eyes. "Really?"

"I almost admire the fact that after she came, she announced she wanted to be done, thus killing my erection, but then she acted like she'd claimed me somehow and warned me off a friend who apparently had a crush on me. I realized I'd been used to stroke her ego, and you can imagine how that went down with my pride."

North snorted. "Why does that not surprise me?"

"I don't want to think about it. Or her. She's nothing to me." I craned my neck to see past guests. "Is Aria intending to bring Sarah back to me anytime soon?"

"Seriously? She's *it* for you now?"

I narrowed my eyes. "Is Aria *it* for you?"

"Aye, but we both know I was always a monogamist. Or do you not remember mocking me mercilessly about it?"

My lips twitched. "I do remember."

"But as long as I've known you, you've never had sex with the same woman more than a couple of times."

"Just because I'm an acolaust doesn't mean I can't be faithful to just one woman. Especially when that woman satisfies me in every way."

North chuckled. "Fine." Then he frowned. "What's an acolaust?"

"Sarah would know," I repeated my words from earlier.

"Sarah would know what?" Her soft voice caressed my nape seconds before she rounded me to stand at my side.

Just the sight of her eased something within. Seriously, I should be terrified by her effect on me. Instead, I replied, "What an acolaust means."

Her cheeks immediately flushed pink, and I chuckled as I reached out to caress my thumb over her cheekbone. "I'll take that to mean you do."

"Would someone like to tell me?" North shrugged, grinning at us like we were the most entertaining thing he'd ever seen.

"It means to enjoy indulging in sensual pleasures," Sarah responded first, her cheeks blooming even pinker.

My friend chuckled. "Ah. I see." He eyed Sarah as if he'd never seen her before and I felt a prickle of unnecessary jealousy. Then he glanced away and around the room. "Sarah, do you know what happened to Aria?"

"She got pulled away while I was talking with Mr. Ad—I mean, Lachlan. While I was talking to Lachlan." At my questioning stare, she shrugged, blushing harder. "He wanted to congratulate me on my success and asked me to call him Lachlan."

"Did he?" I murmured through clenched teeth.

"I'm off to find my fiancée." North clapped me hard on the chest and said under his breath, "Don't be an ass."

I shrugged him off but did my best to rein in my possessiveness.

And by best, I mean I pulled Sarah into my side as soon as North left. My hands roamed her waist as she settled against me, her expression questioning. "Contrectation."

Sarah nodded, a small smile on her lips. "An impulse to caress."

"It also refers to touching in relation to sexual foreplay."

"Do you know all the dirty unusual words?" she teased.

"It's not particularly dirty." I slid my hand perilously close to her delectable arse. "Feculent. Now *that* is a dirty word."

She giggled, and the sound scored through me. I tightened my hold on her and she rested a hand on my stomach. "You know that's not the kind of dirty I was referring to."

"Matutinal."

"How is something that occurs in the morning sexual?"

"Because I'm usually very horny for you in the mornings." I tutted. "Clever girl, you should have gotten that one."

Laughing, she tilted her head in thought. "Famelic."

"Exciting hunger. Very nice. Basial," I rejoined.

"To kiss. Hmm ... satyriasis."

Unbelievably, this little word game was turning me on. I knew I was looking at her like I wanted to eat her alive. "I may be inflicted with that when it comes to you."

Heat glittered in her gaze. "Calefacient."

I wracked my brain trying to remember the meaning of that one. "Uh ... something about heat."

"Something that produces a sensation of heat. Particularly to the body. When you touch me. Calefacient."

Blood rushed to my cock. Good God. "Concupiscence," I warned her.

Her breathing stuttered. "Me too ... Paizogony."

I blinked, searching for recognition and finding none. "Uh ..."

Sarah pulled back, glee cutting through her desire. "You don't know that word, do you?"

"Uh ..." *Come on, brain.* "I ... uh."

She shoved me playfully. "I won. I won, didn't I?"

Laughter bubbled on my lips. "I didn't know it was a competition."

"Of course it is." She tickled me and I grabbed at her hands, chuckling. "I won!"

Cuddling her close, I bowed my head, desperate to kiss her. "Tell me, then, little darling. What does it mean?"

"It means love play. Petting." She stroked my chest.

An emotion so big, so overwhelming, it was like concrete pressing on my breastbone, cracking it, propelled me forth. I needed her.

"Kiss me," she whispered, the words a little desperate.

Yes, fuck yes.

I closed the short distance between us, taking her mouth, her soft lips. It should have been just a gentle brush, a caress, but I wanted everything. I stroked my tongue against hers and she gasped, opening to me. Then she was kissing me back just as fiercely.

Until a shrewish voice cut between us. "Well, isn't this *not* a surprise!"

Oh, bloody hell, please no.

I wished her away.

But when I broke the kiss, Angeline Potter stood before me and Sarah.

Twenty-Eight

SARAH

I tensed against Theo at the sight of Angeline Potter.

Angeline was a long-standing member of Ardnoch. A bit of a British rom-com sweetheart, the world would never guess that she was so horrible.

I'd never complained about her to Mrs. Hutchinson, even though my boss had seemed to sense I was always a wee bit off-kilter after an encounter with Angeline.

I should have complained. Lachlan didn't put up with members who behaved abhorrently.

What did she want?

Theo's hand flexed on my lower back, and I felt the tension in his body as he stared at Angeline with a blank expression.

A dreadful knowing settled nervously in my stomach.

"I wondered if you'd be here tonight." Angeline flicked me a look before turning back to Theo. "Though I rather hoped you'd be alone."

I stiffened, the heat rushing out of my body.

Theo must have sensed it because he pulled me even closer. "I can't imagine why."

It was difficult for me to look at her and see beauty, but she was considered very attractive. A tall, leggy brunette with a big white smile and "adorable" brown eyes. Tonight, she wore a red dress that showcased her slender curves and ample bosom. Of course, Theo had found her attractive. Hadn't he?

She threw my date a dirty look. "I suppose it's true what they say about you, Cavendish. You never come back for seconds." She looked at me pointedly. Then her eyes narrowed in thought. "Have we met?"

I didn't reply, too busy trying not to imagine Theo in bed with this awful human.

"Didn't we work on *Much Ado* together a few years back?"

Swallowing hard, I lifted my chin. "No. I used to work here at Ardnoch." The fact that she couldn't remember me after the way she'd treated me ... I didn't hate many people. But she was one of them.

And Theo had obviously slept with her.

Instinctually, I withdrew from him.

Theo's hand tensed on my back, trying to pull me to him, but I stepped out of his touch.

Recognition lit Angeline's eyes. "You're that mousy little housemaid. Does Lachlan know you've crashed his party?"

"Unlike some people, Sarah was invited because she's liked, not because she spends so much money here, it's hard to turn her away. Even when she's not particularly wanted," Theo drawled pointedly.

Angeline blanched, gave Theo the middle finger, and stormed off, almost going over on her spiked heels in her rush to leave.

I stared blindly after her, unable to look at Theo now that I knew he'd been with Angeline Potter of all people. It brought back to harsh reality how much of a player he'd been.

Theo suddenly stepped in front of me, a dark scowl marring his handsome face. "Sarah—"

"Did you have sex with Angeline?"

"Yes," he gritted out without hesitation.

I flinched, looking down. There were people around us, laughing, talking, drinking, eating. Christmas songs played. It all blurred and fell away.

Theo gripped my upper arms, forcing me to meet his gaze. "It was before you," he explained impatiently. "So get that wounded look off your face. I won't apologize for having a sex life before you, Sarah. You know who I was. We can't keep going back there."

Fury rushed through me. "I don't need you to apologize for having a sex life before me, Theo. But I can judge you for having no discernible taste whatsoever and putting your cock in anything that offered itself up." I yanked my arms out of his hands in disgust and marched away. I needed space—and I needed a drink.

Is this what it would be like with him?

Bumping into women he'd fucked every five minutes? Women I despised.

I knew it wasn't rational or fair, but this *hurt*.

Grabbing a glass of champagne off a passing server's tray, I threw it back as I hurried out of the dining hall. Maybe I'd find Aria and North. They were kind. A shelter among these people.

The music was so loud, I didn't hear the footsteps behind me. Suddenly, a strong, familiar hand gripped my arm and I looked up to find a furious Theo. He tugged me toward the library and my champagne spilled out of the glass with the movement.

"What are you doing?" I hissed.

Two men were enjoying a whisky in the library.

"Gentlemen, apologies, but I require the room for some privacy." Theo gestured to the door with all the imperiousness of the son of a viscount. "If you please."

The two men shared a look and then smirked at me as they passed us.

I trembled with fury.

Theo shut the library door behind them and turned to me.

"You know what they think we came in here to do, don't you?" I cried in outrage. "Let me out of here!"

Theo wore a mask of hard determination that made my heart beat fast and caused an impossible tingle between my legs that I shouldn't be feeling when I was this pissed off at him!

He prowled toward me, and I stumbled back on my heels until I hit the bookshelves. With nowhere to go, I lifted a hand. He pressed his stomach into my palm, bracing his hands on the shelves above my head.

Caging me in.

Dominating.

A thrill coursed through me, and my breathing grew shallow.

"Do not walk away in the middle of a discussion. It's rude."

Indignation overtook my desire. "If I want to walk away from you, I can, Theo. At any time."

"But over this?" he hissed, and I saw the fear and hurt blazing in his eyes. "Sarah ... I can't change my past. Fuck, do I wish I could now. It's just a bloody reminder that I'm not good enough for you. I wish I could wipe away every second, so you didn't have to come face-to-face with it. And so I didn't have to witness that look when you do."

Stung with remorse, I slumped against the shelves. "I'm sorry. I ... I know you have a past. I know *why* you have a past. You don't have to apologize to me about other women from before we met. I don't want to make you feel guilty about it. It's just ... I just ... it's *her*." Tears burned my eyes and I looked away.

But Theo caught my chin, forcing me to meet his gaze. "What happened there?" he murmured, concerned.

"I hate her," I confessed. "She ... she was so cruel to me while I worked here."

The concern on his face transformed rapidly into outrage. "Cruel to you how?"

"She would always be in the room when I came to clean it. Most guests leave when they know housekeeping is coming. But she deliberately stayed and she would mock me the entire time I cleaned her suite." I mimicked her, "Ooh, how awful it must be to be an invisible little mouse, cleaning up after everyone's shit."

Theo blanched. "Little mouse?"

I smiled sadly. "It hurt when you first called me that, but it's different now. You actually made me like the pet name."

"I know, but ..." He glowered. "What else did she do?"

"She would spill things after I cleaned. Deliberately. Maliciously. She ... she once ... I was cleaning the toilet, and she sat down on it while my arm was in there with the ... with the toilet brush." I bit back the tears as shame filled me. "She ... she bloody peed on me and then laughed like she hadn't realized I was there. And I didn't tell anyone. Because I'm a coward."

A tear slipped free, and Theo caught it. When our eyes met, I froze at the rage in his.

"I'm going to fucking ruin her," he bit out slowly.

I shook my head. "Don't. She's not worth it. The housekeepers got paired up after what happened with Sloane last year. She couldn't treat me like that once there were two housekeepers in the rooms. She didn't want witnesses. She doesn't want anyone to know what she's really like."

"*I* know now, Sarah. She humiliated and bullied you. Do you think for one second that Lachlan Adair will put up with that?"

"I should have told him when I was here. I didn't. So it's done."

"And what about the next timid young housekeeper she decides to target? You were never powerless, Sarah, but you definitely are not now. If you speak up, something will be done about it."

The idea of her humiliating someone else the way she did me was sickening. "Okay. I'll ... I'll tell Agnes. My old boss. But later."

Theo clasped my face in his hands and pressed his forehead to mine. His voice was harsh with emotion. "I feel violated to have touched her even more than I did. Because I can promise you, Sarah—and trust that this is no lie—Angeline Potter is the worst fucking lay I've ever had in my life. I regretted it from the moment it started, and our encounter did not end well. I regret it ... God, I regret it even more now. I'd like to scrub every inch of my fucking body, actually."

I curled my hands into his tuxedo jacket. "It's not your fault. You weren't to know."

"The thought of her hurting you ... of anyone hurting you ... I want to kill her. First, I want to shower, though. With scalding water."

Running a soothing hand down his back, I whispered, "Or ... you could let me wipe away the memory of her."

Before he could respond, I reached for his mouth.

Theo groaned, the sound somehow as emotional as it was sexual. He kissed me back with so much feeling.

I loved the taste of him, the way he kissed, like I was oxygen to him. I sucked his tongue hard and he shuddered, his rumble of pleasure making me shiver in turn. Possessiveness filled me. I really did want to wipe every last thought of her from him. To make him mine and only mine.

His hands grabbed at my waist, the touch desperate. "I can't wait." Theo broke the kiss. "I need you. Please tell me you need me too. I feel like I haven't been inside you in decades."

We were in the library where anyone might walk in, and yet the thought of waiting one more second was like being asked to wait one more year.

His warm, rough hands skimmed over my outer thighs, pushing my dress up to my waist. With a growl of want, Theo curled his hands around my lace underwear and tugged, the sudden air between my legs making me tingle with desire.

My urgency hit a new level and so did his. We wanted to erase Angeline. To erase the murders. To erase everything bad and hold on to the good.

Our lips collided, biting, nipping, licking, as we both reached for the closure on his tuxedo trousers. He took his wallet out and removed a condom, fingers fumbling a little, and then he shoved down his trousers and boxer briefs just far enough to free his cock. My breathing increased, the fabric of my dress constricting. My nipples chafed against the velvet, wanting to be bare. Wanting his mouth. I wanted him everywhere.

Then suddenly Theo, sheathed and ready, gripped my legs, spread them, and thrust into me.

"Theo!" I cried out in pleasured shock, his throbbing heat overwhelming me.

He stretched me perfectly.

I'd missed this.

I'd missed this connection.

Theo grabbed the back of my thighs and I followed his lead, jumping into his arms to wrap my legs around him. It caused him to slide deeper into me and we gasped against each other's mouths.

"Fuck, you're so perfect, so right. This is everything. You're everything," he whispered harshly before kissing me hungrily.

He grunted into my mouth as he began to thrust. Hard. Our lips parted as he picked up speed, his features tight with need.

"Yes!" I cried out, my fingernails digging into his shoulders as he pounded us into the bookshelves, jostling books, gliding in and out of my snug channel, the slap of flesh against flesh spurring us toward climax.

All the time I was aware someone might walk in and find him fucking me against the shelves. It excited me beyond bearing.

His thumb pressed down on my clit and I blew apart, my cry of release triggering his. Theo grasped my face in his hand, his thumb beneath my chin, his fingers on my cheek, holding me there. Forcing me to look into his eyes as his hips juddered, his cock pulsing inside me with his climax. He let out a guttural groan as I held his gaze through it.

Theo panted for breath as he rested his forehead against mine. "Phenomenal," he whispered. "It's always phenomenal with you."

I smiled as he pulled back to kiss me. Soft. Tender. Then he released me, gaze searching mine. "But that wasn't how this was supposed to go." Gently, he lowered me to my feet, and I made a mewling noise as he pulled out.

His breath hitched as he cupped my face in both hands. "I wanted our first time together again to be …I wanted …"

Frowning, I smoothed my dress. I thought it had been phenomenal, like he said, so why did he look … regretful? "To be?"

Theo smirked self-deprecatingly. "I wanted to make love to you."

Wonder and hope warred with fear. I bit my lip shyly. "The night is still young."

Twenty-Nine

SARAH

Theo wore an expression that must have said "Don't even bloody think about coming near us" because we managed to escape the library and cut through the hall to the staff elevator without anyone stopping us.

The members weren't supposed to use this lift, but I knew if we tried to use any other stairwell to get to his room, we'd be stopped by some guest or other.

Inside the lift, Theo pressed me against the wall and kissed me until my lips were bruised. We were barely aware of anything as we reached his floor and stumbled, kissing and laughing, toward his room.

"Someone's going to find that condom and wonder who was naughty tonight." Theo chuckled as he let us into his room.

There was nowhere to get rid of the used prophylactic but to wrap it in tissues we found on the library desk and put it in the bin. As an ex-housekeeper, I felt bad about that and promised myself I'd sneak down in the morning and take care of it. "Oh, they'll know."

"How so?"

"There are cameras everywhere." I blushed at the thought of security having seen what we'd done.

Theo gaped. "Are you joking?"

I shook my head. "I'm sure they must have told you that when you became a member. All public spaces on the estate have cameras to protect the guests and staff."

"So ... you knew security could see us fucking?"

I bit my lip. "I forgot. In the heat of the moment."

"Are you ... bothered? Because I can talk to Walker."

Blushing, I shook my head. "It was exciting."

Theo looked ready to combust. "Fuck, you turn me on, woman."

"Back at you."

He reached for my hand, threading his fingers through mine. "Are we okay, Sarah?"

"We're okay. I'm sorry if I overreacted."

"No." He tugged me to him. "After what you told me ... you didn't overreact."

"Forget it." I brushed my fingers over his soft lips. "Forget her." Fear still rode the longing, but longing won out as I whispered, "Make love to me like you promised."

He swallowed hard, and I swear my heart grew at the sight of his expression. He looked at me like he loved me. Half of me wanted him to say it and the other half was terrified he just might. At that moment, I didn't want to analyze the latter.

Theo let go of my hand as he reached the bed and turned to face me. Holding my gaze, making my body hot without saying a word or touching me, he quickly removed his tuxedo jacket and bow tie and unbuttoned his shirt.

He whipped them all off, throwing them on the chair in the corner.

I would never get tired of looking at his beautiful body.

All lean, solid muscle. I followed the lines of his six-pack to the sexy cut of his hips, my cheeks blazing even though we'd done this many times.

But then ... we'd never expressly admitted we were "making love" whenever it happened.

I had been waiting for him to drop his trousers and let me ogle the rest of him, but instead, he sat down on the edge of the bed and looked up at me. "I'm yours, little darling. I can take the lead here or you can do what you want with me."

I licked my lips, eyeing him as he waited patiently for me to decide.

As I drank in his half-nakedness, I shivered with need.

"Take off your trousers," I ordered.

With an affectionate gleam, Theo stood and unbuttoned them. He pushed them and his boxer briefs down, his arousal throbbing to attention as he kicked himself free of his clothes.

Wanting to be close to him again, to be touching, to be connected, I kicked off my shoes and shimmied out of the dress. I stood in only my underwear.

Theo's gaze turned hot, smoldering, his cock growing impossibly harder. "My God, you have no idea how stunning you are, do you?"

It still surprised me that he thought so, but I accepted it. I believed him. It just made me happy that he felt for me what I felt for him. "So are you."

He gave me a smile beneath lowered lashes. "Thank you, darling."

I shivered, looking my fill. Wanting to be filled, while keeping in mind Theo wanted this to be lovemaking, not fucking. And so did I. We needed that emotional connection too.

I gestured to the bed. "Lie down on your back."

Shooting me a boyish grin, Theo did as I commanded, his arousal straining between his thighs for attention.

I approached him slowly, and I kept the feminine satisfaction from my expression at the way his body tensed with antic-ipation.

Getting onto the bed on my hands and knees, I held his gaze for a few seconds, noting his breathing was as shallow as mine. Then my gaze dropped to his cock.

"Sarah," he implored hoarsely.

I crawled up his legs and took him in my mouth. Back at the cottage, I'd done this with him for my first time ever. And I realized with utmost certainty that I never wanted to do this act with anyone else. I couldn't imagine wanting to.

I loved making Theo lose his mind with passion.

His scorching hardness passed between my lips, and I felt his thighs tense under my fingertips. My tongue trailed along a vein on the underside of his cock and his breathing stuttered before seeming to stop entirely as I began to suck, bobbing my head so my mouth slid excruciatingly slow up and down his length.

"Sarah," he groaned, his fingers tangling in my hair. "My love, fuck, my love, your mouth. Your mouth is a fucking gift."

I smiled around him and took him deeper.

Then his fingers clenched in my hair. "Stop, darling. Stop. I want to come inside you again, not your mouth."

With a moan, I released him and gazed at him from under my lashes. My nipples were stiff and wet slicked between my thighs.

But I forced myself to be patient. I kissed the sexy cut of definition in his right hip, my lips tracing a path along his torso as I moved up his body. Knees on either side of his hips, I shivered as I felt his cock brush against my inner thigh. Taking his right nipple in my mouth, my tongue flicking, my moan muffled against his body as I felt his rough hands cup my breasts. I rubbed into him, eager for his touch. When his thumbs brushed them, I shuddered, panting against his chest.

Theo made a pleased sound as he pinched my nipples between his fingers and thumbs. I barely had time to recover from the streaks of white-hot lightning that shot between my thighs before his right hand coasted down my stomach.

As two fingers slid into my slick heat, my back arched, giving his left hand better access to my breast, and my hips surged against his right. I panted, nearly breathless. "Theo." My eyes flew open, and he watched me intensely as he brought me to climax. I shuddered against his hand, pulsing and throbbing around his fingers, my inner muscles trying to pull him in deeper.

"You're so beautiful when you come. If I could, I'd spend every day of every year just watching you come, Sarah McCulloch."

I moved over him, my nipples brushing his chest as I braced my hands on either side of his head and kissed him hungrily as I rubbed myself over his cock. Breaking the kiss, I whispered, "I'm on the pill."

"Fuck, yes." Theo nodded, looking dazed with desire. "I got a checkup before I came to Gairloch. I'm clean. My results are on my phone if you want." The worry in his eyes filled me with tenderness. I knew it was a vulnerable subject, and I wanted to reassure him.

"I believe you." I smiled affectionately as I took him in hand and guided him between my legs. Then I slammed down on him, and we both cried out, Theo's hips jerking up in reaction.

We found our rhythm easily and with my hands braced on the bed beside his thighs, I leaned back slightly so his cock thrust into me at the most delicious angle. I moved slowly, building toward orgasm.

My gaze never left Theo's face as I moved. He made me feel sexy and adored. I loved the way he stared into my eyes, showing me everything he felt, the way his gaze darkened on my breasts as they trembled while I rode him. His hands gripped my hips, his fingernails digging in, keeping me moving at a languid pace. His features tightened as the heat between us increased and a light sheen of sweat covered our skin.

"You feel spectacular," Theo huffed. "I feel like we're one." He sat up with ease, shifting our angle so he hit me deep in that exquisite spot. I gasped and shivered around him. He slid his hand between us, feeling where he moved inside me. "Connected. I belong inside you."

He did. But I was afraid to admit it out loud. So I kissed him, pouring everything I felt into the kiss as I moved over him, faster, harder, our mouths meeting and parting, meeting and parting.

"Come for me, my love. That's it, darling," he praised gruffly. "Come around my cock like a good girl."

Lights exploded behind my lids as my orgasm shook through my entire body. My muscles clenched around Theo, wave after wave of pleasure pulsing around him.

Suddenly, I found myself moving as Theo flipped me to my back. My eyes flew open as he pressed me into the mattress, holding my hands imprisoned above my head. His features were strained with uncontrolled need, and as he crushed his mouth against mine, he began to stroke deep inside me, his movements rough and hard. He groaned into my mouth, the noise vibrating through my whole body, and I felt the stirring of another orgasm.

When his lips left mine, I stared up in wonderment, our gasps seeming to echo all around us as I pushed up against his thrusts. He let go of one of my arms, his hand disappearing between our joined bodies, and as soon as his thumb pressed down on my clit, I flew apart, my scream filling the room.

Satisfaction hardened Theo's expression seconds before his lips parted on a shout of release. His hips juddered as he came, his shout turning into a long groan as he ground himself into me, prolonging his climax.

His arms trembled as he continued to hold himself over me. Then he bowed his head against my forehead. "I ... I love you, Sarah. I'm so in love with you, I can hardly bear it."

THIRTY
THEO

"*I'm scared.*"

The image of Sarah looking up at me after I confessed I was in love with her was branded on my brain. As were the two words she'd whispered with a tearful apology.

She was afraid to say it back.

Who wouldn't be after the way I'd treated her?

But even though I recognized that, even though I'd kissed her softly and promised her I understood and told her to take her time, that I would wait patiently ... it hurt. It hurt that she didn't say it back.

It reminded me of this one girl I'd slept with just a few years after what Saffy did. I'd told the girl it wasn't serious, but we'd been screwing around for a few months. Until she told me she loved me, and I'd rejected her callously on the basis that I hadn't let her know me. So how could she love me?

What a bastard I was.

How many people had I inadvertently hurt because I was pissed off at Daddy Dearest and my ex-girlfriend?

"Where are you?" Sarah cuddled into my side on the couch.

Her cousin had been gracious enough to let me stay at the farmhouse over Christmas. Sarah wanted me there the day before Christmas Eve through to Boxing Day, and since I was turning into a giant sap, I, of course, agreed.

Jared was working. The days were so short, he worked every day to make up for it. Sarah said he'd take Christmas Day off, but she hadn't been able to convince him to take Boxing Day. The plan was that Sarah and I would cook, and we'd just returned home from the most chaotic, terrifying supermarket experience of my life. There hadn't been a Christmas since my mother died in which I hadn't finagled an invitation to someone else's festivities, so I'd avoided the Christmas food shopping hell my entire life. Until today.

Someone had attempted to rip the last bag of potatoes out of Sarah's hands and when I stepped in to protect her, they had the audacity to claim *I* was the threatening one. The wannabe thief took off when he spotted someone trying to claim the last of the carrots.

By some miracle, we managed to get everything we wanted, but it was a harried experience and reinforced my belief that there were basic elements of human nature that could not be dragged out of the cave.

"Just thinking about how we nearly died for a bag of potatoes and a turkey," I murmured back, watching the flames in the large fireplace crackle and dance.

Sarah shook against me, and I glanced down to find her grinning. "How quickly people devolve."

"I was just thinking something similar." I studied her face, feeling such overwhelming love that sometimes it was difficult to not let the fear win. To not just run. But then I remembered how I felt when she left me in London, and any thought of leaving her was obliterated.

"I can put another movie on if you like?" She gestured to

the television. We were watching an old classic, *Meet Me in St. Louis*.

I slid my hand down her leg. "I was thinking of doing something a little more entertaining."

Her eyes widened, another smile tugging at her mouth. "What? Now? Jared will be home soon."

"We can be quick," I murmured in her ear, trailing kisses down her neck. Sarah's head fell back, giving me access to her throat. At the sound of her gasp, I stood abruptly.

Then I picked her up and threw her over my shoulder with ease. Her laughter filled the house as I hurried upstairs to her old bedroom. I laid her on the bed and made quick work of undressing her. "I bet you never thought you'd have sex in here," I teased.

She pulled an adorable face. "I did have sex."

I raised an eyebrow as I unclipped her bra.

Sarah shrugged. "I had lots of very quiet sex with myself."

Chuckling, I kissed and moved over her, my hands exploring her perfect body. "Poor darling. I'm here now."

She laughed, shoving me playfully. Grinning smugly, I sat up to remove my shirt and she retorted, "I'll have you know that up until you, sex with myself was the best sex I'd ever had."

"That's because some men are selfish fuckers in bed." I pressed my lips to her slender belly, following a trail to her jeans. I unbuckled them, looking up at her from beneath my lashes. "Lucky for you, I'm a possessive bastard who wants to ruin you for all other men."

Sarah gasped as I yanked down her jeans, taking her knickers with them. "Lucky for me, you only mean that in the sense of the bedroom. We wouldn't get along—oh!" She arched into me as I licked at her clit.

"We wouldn't what, my love?"

"Wouldn't ..." She clawed at the duvet covers. "I don't ... oh ... just keep doing that."

So I did.

Tasting her, sucking, nibbling, licking, fucking her with my tongue ... pushing her to almost breaking but then pulling back before she could come. She was flushed and lost, her face etched with passion and need.

"Theo, please," she begged.

The sound of gravel kicking up under a vehicle outside cut through her panting. Her eyes widened. "Jared."

I lifted my head. "Do you want me to stop?"

Sarah looked adorably outraged. "You better make me come right now or you'll have blue balls for the next month."

Laughing, I gripped her thighs and pulled them over my shoulders, grabbing her arse in my hands to pull her deeper into my mouth.

Sarah keened and I growled against her, my cock rock hard.

I ate at her hungrily and then, just as the back door slammed downstairs, Sarah came. She clamped her teeth down on her fist as she shattered.

"Sarah!" Jared called. "You in?"

Suddenly, Sarah scrambled away from me and I collapsed onto the bed, confused. Until she jumped up and grabbed my arm. "Come with me," she whispered frantically. So I did, following her into her en suite bathroom.

As soon as we were inside, she locked it and reached into the shower to turn it on. Her cheeks were flushed bright pink as she looked up at me with laughter in her eyes. "Thankfully, Grandpa added this bathroom for me a year after I came to live with them so I'd have a wee bit of privacy."

I raised an eyebrow.

She gestured to my engorged cock. "Do you think I'd leave you in that state?"

Grinning, I let her pull me into the shower. I pressed her up against the cool tiles, kissing her, throbbing against her stomach. I pulled back to reassure her, "You know I would have waited. While I cannot handle a month, I can handle a few hours of blue balls."

Sarah grasped my cock in her hand, and I grunted as she guided it between her thighs. She was so wet. Fuck. "I don't want you to wait."

As I surged into her, one hand gripping her thigh to open her to me, the other braced on the tiles above her head, I thought, *At least I have this of her*. I knew at that moment that Sarah would never give this part of her to someone else. Trust. I trusted her as much as I loved her.

And that's why I'd wait forever to hear her say those words back.

Because I never thought I'd trust this way again, never mind love.

"Fuck, I love you," I groaned as she came around me, milking my cock and urging me closer to my own climax. I buried my head in her neck, thrusting harder, deeper, because nothing ever felt enough with this woman.

"Theo ..." Her breath hitched on my name as her finger-nails dug into my waist. "Theo."

"Yes." I lifted my head, locking eyes with her. "I'm yours, Sarah," I panted. "Are you mine?"

She nodded, grasping tighter to me. "I'm yours."

The words triggered my orgasm and sensation coursed down my spine and legs as I emptied inside her. Giving her everything.

"Good God." I rested my temple against hers as my cock pulsed. "I never knew ..." I'd never known it could be like this. I'd had plenty of sex in my life, but until Sarah, I'd never real-ized how bloody hollow all those other times had been.

I pressed a kiss to her temple, then her cheek, another to

her nose and then her mouth. Our kiss was slow, reassuring, and a sense of calm came over me for the first time since I'd told her I loved her.

She might not be able to say it back yet, but she'd admitted we belonged to each other. It was enough for now.

"How was your day?" Sarah asked Jared as we ventured into the kitchen to start dinner.

Like us, his hair was wet, suggesting he'd showered as soon as he returned home.

He shot us a look over his shoulder as he stirred milk into a coffee. He glowered at me, and I tried not to laugh. Clearly, he knew what we'd been up to. No one showers in the middle of the day unless they were a farmer returning from work.

"It was fine." He leaned against the kitchen counter, near the sink, watching us as we moved around, pulling ingredients out of the fridge. "What's happening?"

"We're making dinner." Sarah beamed at him. Her cheeks were still a little flushed from our earlier exertions. "Theo's making fajitas and I'm helping."

Jared eyed me. "You cook?"

"I do. I hope you like Mexican."

"I'll eat anything. Thanks," he reluctantly added.

"I noticed a lot of prepacked meals in the fridge." Sarah gave her cousin an admonishing look.

Jared scrubbed a hand over the back of his neck. The man appeared exhausted. "Sarah, I don't have time to cook for myself at the moment. The meals do in a pinch."

Guilt clouded Sarah's expression. "I'm sorry."

"For what?"

"Not being here."

He shook his head even as he reached out to pull her into

his side for a hug. Jared kissed the top of Sarah's head. "Never feel guilty for living your life." He squeezed her. "I'm proud of you."

I decided at that moment to forgive him his high-handedness when he'd barged in on us in Gairloch. It was clear the cousins shared a deep affection, and I was glad, after learning what Sarah had put up with in her early years, that she had Jared. I was maybe even a little envious of it.

As I chopped peppers, my phone buzzed in my back pocket. I set the knife on the counter and looked to see who was calling. My agent. What on earth ... "Fern?" I answered, sensing Sarah's and Jared's regard.

I walked out of the kitchen and into the living room that looked like something out of a cozy Christmas catalogue.

"Theo, sorry to call you during the holidays, but I thought you should know that an admin assistant here at the agency has come forward with some information that might relate to the Hangman murders."

A chill skated down my spine. "What kind of information?"

"We just handed it over to the police in charge of the investigation. I'm sure they'll be in touch, but I felt awful at the thought of leaving you out of the loop. Because ..." She sighed heavily. "Theo, it's fan mail. Addressed to you. You know when we usually receive fan emails, we either forward them to the intended or delete. These were actual letters, and the assistant thought they were odd, so she just filed the letters away to be forwarded to you later. Except she's been doing that for two years." She sounded angry. "The letters are disturbing. The person seemed to believe that he was Charlie King and wanted to thank you for bringing his story to life."

Dread coiled in my gut. "It could be him. The murderer."

"Yes. The last few letters asked for your response to the murders. He was looking for praise," she spat in disgust.

"Oh, hell." I sank into the nearest chair, feeling a little light-headed. "Can I see them?"

"The police took them. I'm sorry, Theo. I'm sorry we didn't catch this sooner. Rest assured the admin assistant will be dealt with."

"Don't fire her for a clerical oversight."

"It was a big bloody oversight, Theo."

"She wasn't to know what was in those letters. And who sends letters anymore?"

Fern sighed. "I know. I'm just ... I can't believe this is happening. My clients have been making shows like this for over two decades, and ... you never expect someone to take something they've created and use it for this kind of evil. I'm so sorry, Theo."

I bowed my head. "I'm sorry too."

"No. You have nothing to be sorry for. Nothing. I just wanted you to know what was happening."

I nodded, trying to speak around the sorrow thickening my throat. "I appreciate it ... Merry Christmas, Fern."

She laughed unhappily. "Yes. Merry Christmas, Theo."

We hung up and I stared into the fire, all the peace I'd found with Sarah upstairs turning to ash.

A hand rested on my shoulder and I jerked in surprise.

Sarah stood over me, concern marring her brow.

I reached for her hand and pressed a hard kiss to the back of it.

"Tell me?" she whispered, brushing her fingers through my hair.

THIRTY-ONE
THEO

The next day, while Jared worked on the farm, Sarah convinced me to spend Christmas Eve in the village.

That is until it began to snow and someone in Flora's told us it was to turn into a storm. Sure enough, a quick check on our phones confirmed the snow was supposed to keep falling all through Christmas Eve and Day. There were weather warnings all over Sutherland.

By the time we returned to the farmhouse, the snow was beginning to lie on the ground, and Jared's truck was parked outside the house. He was already home.

Sarah attempted valiantly to lift my mood, going on about how perfect it was that our first Christmas together was a white one. She was trying so hard while I was locked in my head about the murders that I didn't see what else she was trying hard to forget.

Instead, I got through the day on autopilot. Distracted myself by cooking. Jared wasn't one for idle chitchat, which suited me fine. The roast chicken dinner Sarah and I made was damn good, but much like the fajitas last night, I barely tasted it. I kept waiting for the phone to ring. For the police to tell me they needed me, or worse.

Sarah had arranged all the presents under the Christmas tree and stuck a few little ones in Jared's stocking that hung over the mantel. Jared returned the favor, and I watched their traditions unfold, feeling half there and half somewhere else.

We all sat down after dinner to watch a Christmas movie and then another. The ten o'clock news interrupted the second one, and I was suddenly alert at the breaking news chyron that scrolled across the screen as the newscaster announced, "The Thames Valley Police are urging the public to stay safe this Christmas after the body of twenty-six-year-old Helen Miller, a dental technician originally from Hull, was found in Slough early this morning. The police released a statement confirming Ms. Miller is the latest victim of the Hangman serial killer."

"Theo." Sarah's fingers curled around mine as I stared dazedly at the screen.

Urgency filled me. Urgency and restlessness and the utter horror that there was nothing I could do. "There are only two victims left," I whispered hoarsely. "Charlie King murders his father and stepmother before he kills himself."

"Then we have to hope the police figure out who he is before it comes to that," Jared said from across the room.

I looked at him. For the first time in our acquaintance, he wore an expression akin to kindness.

That made me feel worse.

I turned to Sarah. "I'm sorry, my love. I just need ... I'm heading to bed." I pressed a quick kiss to her forehead before she could object.

Later, when she came to bed, I pretended to be asleep.

At some point during the night, my mind finally shut down out of sheer exhaustion.

Guilt would find me in the morning again. But not for the same reason as the night before.

I woke up, the bedroom still dark, and turned to find the space beside me empty. Confused, I reached for my phone to check the time. It was barely five o'clock in the morning.

Worry coursed through me, and I got out of bed. The floorboards were freezing beneath my feet, and I hurried to pull on socks and then a sweater over my T-shirt. The farmhouse was old and bloody cold.

The stairs creaked as I made my way down them, a glow from the living room guiding me.

The sight that greeted me made my heart throb in my throat.

Sarah stood by the unlit fireplace, her head buried in the stocking that hung on the mantel. The one that was her grandfather's. Her shoulders shook as quiet sobs wracked her body and pain flared in a sharp, stinging ache across my chest.

She was grieving, and I'd been so wrapped up in my own demons I hadn't noticed.

Cursing under my breath, I crossed the distance between us.

Sarah lifted her tear-streaked face seconds before I reached her and came into my arms without hesitation.

Her sobs grew louder, though muffled against my chest as I held her tighter. "I've got you, my love," I promised her gruffly. "Let it out. I've got you."

She pulled at my sweater as if trying to burrow deeper into me. "I—I m-miss h-him so m-much," she stuttered through her cries.

I squeezed her tighter, wishing I could take it all away. There might not be anything I could do for the victims of the sick fuck who was out there copying my show. But I could be here for Sarah. I could get her through this because I knew what it was like to lose a parent I adored. "I know, my darling.

I know." I kissed her head again. "You just have to miss him. There's nothing else for it. Some days it will feel like this. Fucking unbearable. But most days, you will bear it. I promise."

She nodded against me, crying a little harder.

"And"—I lifted her head, holding her tear-filled gaze with mine—"on the days you cannot bear it, I will be here to bear it for you. Okay?"

Sarah's face crumpled with a different emotion and she nodded again. "Th-thank you."

"You never have to thank me for that." I gently led her to the couch and sat her down. Then I made quick work of lighting the fire.

I could feel her watching me and was glad to hear her voice had calmed as she whispered, "Where did you learn to build a real fire?"

I glanced over my shoulder at her with a small grin. "Haleshall Manor. My father's ancestral seat. It's this three-hundred-year-old manor house on the Suffolk Coast, and it's bloody freezing in the winter. We'd spend Christmas there, and I learned from the staff how to light the fires. They had many to light in the mornings."

Sarah wiped the tears from her cheeks. "I sometimes forget that you grew up so differently from most people."

"I suppose I did." I stood once the fire was burning.

"Theo."

"Yes?" I turned to her.

"There's only one Christmas present I want from you this year ... but I'm afraid to ask for it."

Frowning, I crossed the room to sit beside her. "Should I be worried?"

"I ... I know you and your father have an ugly past."

I stiffened at the mention of the bastard. "That's putting it lightly."

She hesitated at my acidulous tone but then forced out, "I want you to go speak to him. To forgive him. Not for him. For you."

Despite how I'd found her this morning, I felt a surge of anger. "Sarah ... how could you even suggest such a thing? I know you're grieving your grandfather, but my relationship with—"

"It's not because I think family should forgive each other because life is short," she cut me off. "It's because ... it's because the bitterness you feel toward him and Saffron is eating at you, whether you're aware of it or not. We almost lost this," she said, gesturing between us, "because of it."

"But we didn't," I clipped out, my heart racing.

"I'm afraid we still might."

Her expression from the night I told her I loved her for the first time filled my mind. *"I'm scared."*

"I'm worried that if you don't make peace with the past, it'll find us, Theo. That you'll walk away from me again when it begins to hurt too much."

Angry, I huffed. "And have you had a heart-to-heart with your mother? Have you forgiven her?"

Sarah sighed wearily. "I forgave her a long time ago. People can't help who they are. And we can waste our lives feeling bitter that they won't change for the better for us, or we can just accept who they are and try to be better for the people we love. So that we don't repeat their mistakes."

I looked away, glowering, because what she said made sense. But it didn't mean I liked it.

"I wrote an email to my mum when I was fifteen telling her how I felt. She wrote one back, bemoaning that I blamed her for everything. But it didn't matter. Because it was good to know she was aware of my feelings. Have you ever told your father how you feel about what he did?"

I shrugged like I didn't care. "Not in so many words."

Sarah was quiet for a long while. Then she whispered sadly, "I only have to mention it and you pull away."

I looked sharply at her, opening my mouth to argue ... then stopping. Because she was right. "Fuck," I bit out furiously.

Her barely there smile was sympathetic. "Just think about talking to him. Please. Do it for you. And for us."

Studying her precious face, I suddenly experienced some of the complicated emotions I'd been writing about for years. How it was possible to adore someone with every fiber of your being ... and yet resent them a little, too, for having such power over you.

Sarah had such power over me.

And it would make me promise something I never thought I could. "I'll think about it. Now come here." I drew her into my arms and cuddled her against me. "Let's talk of nicer things this Christmas morning. Why don't you tell me about your first Christmas with your grandparents?"

I felt her smile against my chest before she began to talk. Eventually, her words soothed me, my heartbeat found a calmer pace, and I let myself forget about the promise I'd made.

At least for a little while.

THIRTY-TWO

SARAH

I t was difficult to leave Jared after Christmas. We'd intended to stay through New Year's, but DCI English had asked Theo to come to New Scotland Yard in London. His call came only four days after Christmas.

Jared assured me he was fine and would spend New Year's Eve at the Gloaming with the rest of the village. Still, I felt like I was abandoning him, torn between my cousin, who'd been there for me for the last few years, and Theo, who was hurting over these murders.

It was my cousin who'd decided for me because he'd seen Theo's pain too.

"He needs you," Jared told me while I was wavering over what to do.

And Theo had been there for me while I grieved Grandpa. Despite my fears—despite so far being unable to choke out the words *I love you*, even though it was obvious to everyone I felt them—I needed Theo to know he could count on me.

Sitting curled up on the large couch in Theo's London flat, I stared out at the buildings that stretched along Half Moon Street. The sky peeked above the proud rooflines, cloudy and dark and ominous. It matched the roiling in my gut. I'd wanted to accompany Theo to Scotland Yard, but the police wouldn't let me join the discussion and Theo saw no reason in dragging me along.

I'd protested that I just wanted to be with him, but I got the feeling in the end that Theo needed space to process. I understood that.

My phone rang in my lap, startling me, and I scrambled to pick it up, fumbling and dropping it before I finally got a look at the screen. Even though I'd known it was too early to hear from Theo, I was disappointed it wasn't his name. It was Liz, my agent.

I answered it, forcing a smile into my voice. "Hi, Liz. How are you?"

"Sarah, I'm good. I'm good. Just calling with a few updates." My agent was originally from Newcastle and had never lost her Geordie accent. Usually, I could listen to her speak all day, but I struggled to concentrate at the moment.

"Okay."

"Is now a bad time?"

I shook myself, sitting up. "No, of course not."

"Great. First up, the film rights contract is almost complete in absolutely record time. I've never had a film rights contract go through this fast, which is exciting. We've just sent it back to Cavendish's people, so they'll be sending it to you for your signature soon."

"Wonderful."

"Cavendish must be very eager to get this into production."

"He is." I cleared my throat, my heart racing a wee bit. "Liz, you should know that Theo and I are ... we're more than writing partners for this script. We're seeing each other."

"Right, right. Good to know," she answered briskly, as if it mattered but it didn't. I relaxed for a mere two-point-five seconds before she continued, "Now that you've decided to no longer remain anonymous, your publisher would like you to do an interview with *Rise and Shine Britain*."

I blinked rapidly. "The ... the biggest morning television show in the country?"

"The very one. It's an exciting opportunity, Sarah. And this isn't just slotting you into the book section of the show. It's a proper interview. Your publisher would love to use the opportunity to announce the film rights deal with Cavendish."

My body flushed hot from head to toe. "I ... I ..." I didn't want to disappoint anyone but, "Liz, I'm not ready for something like that. I haven't had any media training—"

"We can set that up."

"I'm not ..." Bloody Nora, the thought of going on national television made me want to upchuck. "No. I'm not ready. I'm sorry."

"That's okay. How about a national magazine instead?" Liz swiftly moved on. "*HEY!* Magazine wants to interview you. It would involve some photos and questions about your rise to success."

Even though that still filled me with nerves, I nodded. "I can do that."

"Amazing. I'll let your publisher know and they'll communicate all the info."

We chatted a wee bit longer about a few more foreign deals, and I promised Liz I was almost finished with the latest Juno book and would send her the final manuscript as soon as edits were completed. Self-publishing the e-book meant I still paid for editorial services and then would send the final file to Liz for her to forward on to the publishers for the print edition. I had to be very disciplined about the deadlines because we had to coordinate the release. Being swept up in an affair with Theo Cavendish should have been a recipe for distraction from the book, but being who he was, I was more inspired than ever.

At that thought, after I got off the phone with Liz, I made a coffee and grabbed my laptop. Instead of worrying about Theo, I was going to be productive and try to write at least one new chapter.

My phone sounded with several new text messages over the next few hours. One from North checking in to see if all was okay. He knew Theo was talking with the police today. Another from Aria asking pretty much the same. One from Jared. And, surprisingly, one from Sloane Ironside asking how I was, when I would be returning to Ardnoch, and if I'd still like to do coffee when I got back.

At her text, I stared at my phone in wonder.

I couldn't remember the last time this many people had been interested in my well-being.

It felt nice.

I replied to them all and told Sloane I wasn't sure when I'd be back home, but I'd text her as soon as I did. I asked after her and we texted back and forth for a bit before she was distracted by a cake order.

Another thousand words later, Sloane texted me a picture of the cake. It was a three-tiered wedding cake decorated with a sweeping band of icing flowers that draped down over the tiers in a spiral. The flowers were so beautifully crafted, they looked real. I told Sloane so and then snapped a picture of the page I'd just written.

She texted back:

Did you just send me a sneak peek of your new Juno book? Monroe is going to be so jealous! DYING *skull emoji*

My shoulders shook with laughter.

Saving my manuscript, I closed the laptop and got up to wash out my cup. I hadn't eaten anything since Theo left because I'd had low-level nausea all day.

Releasing a slow breath, I stared up at the clock on his kitchen wall. Shouldn't he be back by now? At least five hours had passed.

As if I'd conjured him, I heard the lock on the front door turn and I rushed out into the living room to see Theo enter the flat. His expression was drawn, his shoulders hunched with exhaustion as he closed the door behind him.

He looked haunted.

I rushed across the room and pulled him close. His arms bound tightly around me as he buried his head in the crook of my neck and inhaled deeply.

We didn't say anything for what felt like a long time. Eventually, Theo released me, stroking a thumb tenderly over my cheekbone.

"What happened?" I finally asked.

Stepping back, Theo shrugged out of his coat and hung it on the hooks by the door. "They have a primary suspect."

My heart jumped. "Isn't that a good thing?"

Theo scrubbed a hand down his face, his fingers scratching over his stubbly cheeks. "Hopefully. His name is Quinn Gray. They found his DNA on the skirt belonging to Helen, the last victim. He's in the system for stalking a girl at university a few years back. His parents died in a car accident when he was eighteen. It was not seen as suspicious at the time. He stalked that girl a few years after the accident, but she moved abroad after graduation, so she, thankfully, escaped him."

"What happens now?"

"The police are gearing up to release a statement. There will be a manhunt for Gray. And we need to find him fast because ..." Theo squeezed his eyes closed, his expression drawn. When he opened them, there was that haunted look again. "Sarah, I spoke with their team of analysts. They told me what their expert psychologist thinks, and it lines up with the thoughts I shared with DCI English. The last two victims in my show were the father and the stepmother. Gray has neither, but he will find an alternative to fit the sick narrative he's playing out. And they—we—need to figure out who he might hurt next."

My stomach twisted with dread. "We? Theo ... you know this isn't up to you?"

Anger flashed in his eyes. "I wish that were true. But I feel responsible for flipping some fucking switch in this bastard. Sarah ... you didn't see what I saw today. The horror and the pain ... and it was so eerily similar to *King's Valley*. Seeing that inflicted on real women, human beings with lives and families ..."

"Sweetheart," I whispered, reaching for him.

He hugged me hard again. "We have to find him."

I was afraid we did. I was afraid if Theo didn't have some part in bringing Quinn Gray down, he'd never let go of the guilt.

THIRTY-THREE
THEO

The shock of my visit to police headquarters had worn off a little. Now that Quinn Gray's name was out there and the public knew who he was, I had relaxed marginally. It was hard to hide these days, and I hoped someone would see him and call the police. The public rage toward him was terrifying but ultimately useful in this case.

People wanted him caught. They were tired of being scared.

I wanted it over. For the victims' families, for the public, for myself, and Sarah.

I'd just signed the contract on the deal for Juno McLeod and sent it to Sarah for completion. Colleen was gearing up to sell the idea to Skylark with the actor Olivia Jones attached to play the role of Juno. Just a few short months ago, I was impatient to get to this point, and now I was nauseated. It didn't feel right to put a crime series into production that followed a subplot about another serial killer.

But I couldn't disappoint Sarah, and this was my job.

Sarah stirred beside me in bed and I sat up, swinging my legs out, elbows braced on my knees, head buried in my hands.

Gentle fingertips skimmed my naked back. "Are you all right?"

I couldn't voice my doubts aloud. I ... I'd already let her down enough. So much so, she still couldn't bloody well tell me she loved me.

Instead, I surprised even myself by announcing, "I think it's time to face my father."

At her silence, I glanced over my shoulder. She stared up at me, sleep-rumpled and wide-eyed. "Are you sure?"

It was as good a distraction as any.

Moreover, I was afraid. I was afraid if I didn't try to let go of my bitterness toward the old man that Sarah was right. I'd eventually fuck up what was between us because of it. And what she and I had was the only bloody thing holding me together right now.

"Yes." I turned, sliding back into bed and bracing myself over her warm body. "But after I make love to you."

Sarah opened herself to me, caressing my chest, arching her hips in invitation. For a while, I didn't have to think about anything but the bliss I found inside her.

"Wow."

The word echoed off the marble floors as Sarah gawked at my family's London townhouse on Wilton Crescent. There were five floors to the home. Four above us, plus a roof terrace, and one below us.

The spacious entrance hall led to an impressively wide staircase with an elaborately carved balustrade that swept upward, curving along a balcony that overlooked the hall from above. To our side an open archway led to a library/sitting area. Beyond that were double doors into my father's study. He'd barely updated the furnishings since my mother's passing. It wasn't exactly contemporary, and the hallway walls were cluttered with paintings of our family and our ancestors.

I noted the painting of my mother at the bottom of the stairwell and blocked out the swell of emotion that threatened. This place held a strange mix of treasured memories and pain.

"You grew up here?" Sarah whispered as my father's butler went to announce our arrival.

"If you think this is something, you should see Haleshall Manor," I murmured back sardonically. At her uneasy expression, I threaded my fingers through hers.

I knew Sarah and I came from opposite sides of the track, but I didn't want her using that to put any more distance between us.

I was no longer the Honorable Theodore Merrick Cavendish, second son of Viscount Stephen Jerome Cavendish. I'd buried that boy long ago.

The butler, whom I didn't recognize, reappeared but disappeared down the staircase at the back of the hall. However, my father had followed in his wake.

Obviously fully recovered from testicular cancer.

He looked like he'd never been sick.

With a heart like his, Stephen Cavendish should have been a balding, fat, ugly little man. Instead, I got my height and lean but strong physique from him. That was where the similarities ended. Sebastian looked more like him. Dark hair, black eyes. Eyes like the fucking devil. I had my mother's fairer complexion and coloring.

Stephen Cavendish was almost sixty-one years old, had just battled cancer, and yet he didn't look a day over fifty. He was, regrettably, a very handsome man. Until you looked a bit closer at his insides.

His dark gaze moved from me to Sarah, and I had to fight the urge to stand in front of her, block her from his regard. "You must be the writer I've heard so much about."

I stiffened. Sebastian had been talking.

My father scowled at me. "My son doesn't keep me updated on his life, so I have to find other ways. I must say I'm extremely surprised to see you here, considering you couldn't be bothered to visit me while I was recovering from cancer."

Rage suffused me, but Sarah's hand tightened in mine, bringing me back. Centering me.

Somehow, for my sake and hers, I had to let this go.

But first, he needed to know why.

"We need to talk," I replied, gesturing to his study. "Shall we?"

He couldn't quite mask his curiosity. "All right."

Sarah squeezed my hand again. "I'll wait out here."

I nodded, pressing a kiss to the back of her knuckles before reluctantly releasing her. She didn't look at my father as she eased onto the chaise near the front door.

My father stared at her a little too long for my liking, and I moved in front of him, blocking her from view. "Lead the way."

As soon as we were inside, he closed the doors and rounded me to sit behind his desk. It reminded me of the times I'd gotten in trouble at school, and he'd brought me into his study during the school holidays to lecture me on my behavior. Sometimes those lectures had been accompanied by a smack across the face.

I shoved out the old memories.

"I must say, she's rather lovely for someone of such commonness."

I stiffened. "Excuse me?"

My father glowered. "I can see the appeal, Theodore. Truly. But you do know that her mother has a criminal record and is a drug addict. Her father was a farmer." He spat out the last word like it was filth.

Sebastian had done a lot of talking.

"You didn't know." He sat back smugly. "I thought not."

Only a year ago, I would have been enraged by his smugness. By his judgment of Sarah.

Now ... now I saw a pathetic man who cared about things that didn't matter in the real world. Who derived pleasure in control and humiliation.

He was a sad piece of shit.

And I wouldn't let him pull me into his games anymore.

"I know about Sarah's background," I told him calmly. "I know everything about her. Also, I'd quite like to take this moment to remind you that your ancestral estate survived off the backs of farmers for centuries."

He rolled his eyes and waved off my comment. "Yes, but my ancestors would have had someone shot if one of their children was discovered courting a farmer's daughter."

Courting.

I grunted. "I wish you would join the rest of us in the twenty-first century. And I'm sure once you do, this little piece of information will delight you. I could not care less about Sarah's mother or where she comes from. It won't stop me from marrying her one day. If she'll have me."

"Then you're an idiot, but that's nothing new," my father scoffed. "And you'll grow bored, like always."

"Like you, you mean? What's it now, Father? Marriage number ten?"

He glowered. "Don't you dare speak to me in such a disrespectful manner."

Sighing, I shook my head. His study was filled with leather-bound books in reds, greens, and browns. A large window overlooked the gardens, the walls covered in rich paneling, and old worn carpets worth a fortune decorated the wooden floors. Leather chairs with metal studs. It was like something from the past. And that was the world my father lived in. Some forgotten heyday of the aristocracy, of gentlemen and privilege. Where the viscount was master of his home, his staff, and his family.

He was utterly detached from reality.

"I didn't come here to argue with you about the appropriateness of my girlfriend. I came here to tell you why we haven't spoken in a decade."

My father waved his hand. "Oh, do tell. I'm sure I'll enjoy this fictional examination of our past. It's what you're good at. Writing little imaginary scripts."

I gave a huff of laughter because he really was quite the unbelievable bastard. "I don't want anything to do with you because you cheated on and abused my mother for the entirety of your marriage and then you had an affair with my twenty-one-year-old girlfriend while Mother was dying."

He stiffened, rage filling his expression.

"Now you can warp the facts to suit your conscience, but those *are* the facts, Father. You did betray my mum and you did betray me."

"It was complicated," he insisted.

"No." I shook my head. "It wasn't. It was disgusting and selfish. And for a while, I thought it was unforgivable."

My father leaned forward expectantly. "And now?"

"I forgive you," I released the words on a whoosh of air, like they'd been locked inside me for years, desperate for freedom. "But not for you," I hurried to explain. "I forgive you for me. For Mum. I have to. I don't want *your* actions to ruin the rest of *my* fucking life. So I forgive you. But I don't want to have anything to do with you ever again. Don't call. Don't set private investigators on me, and for Pete's sake, leave Sebastian out of it."

"And if I don't?" he seethed.

"Then I will file a restraining order," I told him calmly.

His face slackened with shock. "You cannot be serious."

"I'm very serious. I don't want you anywhere near my life

or the people I love. If you cannot abide by that, I will make sure you abide it by law." I turned before he could say another word and pulled open the doors.

I half expected him to shout something vile after me, but there was only shocked silence.

Striding into the hall, I halted upon finding Sarah standing beneath my mother's portrait.

She turned as I approached. "Are you okay?"

I nodded, taking her hand. "It felt good to be the one in control for a change."

Her smile was soft, tinged with a little sadness, as she turned back to stare at my mother. "Is this her?"

"Yes. This is Mum."

"She was beautiful, Theo. You look like her."

"He didn't deserve her." The painter, a famous artist called Raphaella Forbes, captured the warmth and kindness in my mum's eyes. "She was so good to everyone. Even him. He didn't deserve her," I repeated, wishing like hell she'd had a better life.

"No, he didn't." Sarah squeezed my hand.

"I worry I don't deserve you," I confessed hoarsely. "That everyone will agree because of my past."

She turned to me, expression solemn. "You have done nothing but take care of me while empowering me at the same time. Do you know how rare that is? To hell with everyone else."

Warm gratitude filled the hollowness in my chest. Relief too. I brought our clasped hands to my mouth and pressed a hard kiss to her knuckles. "My mum would approve of you." I looked up at the painting, into Mum's soft eyes. "Wouldn't you, Mum?"

A beat later, I looked down at Sarah. "She says yes."

She laughed softly, eyes still filled with an understanding of my grief that made me love her even more. Pressing a kiss to my fingertips, I rested them against the painting. "Miss you, Mum."

Swallowing hard, I stepped back, tugging on Sarah's hand. "Let's go, my love."

As we turned to leave, my feet stuttered at the sight of my father standing beneath the archway of the library. For just a second, he wore a stricken expression that shocked me.

However, he quickly covered it, smoothing his countenance to that blank expression I was more familiar with. I knew that blank expression. I'd worn it many times myself to cover up my true feelings.

I realized then that perhaps my father was human after all. That maybe he did experience remorse and guilt. But he was too scared to admit those feelings, too afraid to reveal he was fallible. Terrified, perhaps, to let those emotions in, in case they swallowed him whole.

And in the end, my father's fear would leave him with nothing and nobody but one son who stuck around out of duty.

It hit me then, as we left the house on Wilton Crescent, with more clarity than ever, why Sarah asked me to do this. I couldn't lock my feelings away like my father did. I'd only lose everyone who mattered to me. And there was no way in hell I'd ever risk turning out to be just like Stephen Cavendish.

I wanted to be better.

Not just for Sarah.

For me too.

Thirty-Four
THEO

I n an effort not to come off as a suffocating, overprotective Neanderthal, I hadn't expressed my concern about Sarah heading out into the city. It was the day before New Year's Eve and London would be teeming with visitors. I had to trust Sarah would be safe, however, meeting her agent for drinks at a bar near Charing Cross.

Thankfully, morbid distraction came in the shape of an encrypted file sent to my email by DCI English's team. They'd agreed at our visit to let me read the fan mail that had been sent to me in case there was a clue that perhaps only I might pick up on.

I poured myself a whisky and sat down on the couch with my laptop and exhaled slowly before opening the file. My stomach churned as I read the scanned letters in chronological order. The first few praised and marveled at how I'd brought his story to life on-screen. Though he never signed the letters, I thought of him as Quinn Gray. He shared how he'd been raised by his father and stepmother after his mother committed suicide in front of him when he was seven years old. The similarity to Gray's story and Charlie King's was uncanny and alarming. Charlie hung his victims after he murdered them because his mother hung herself. All his victims looked like his mum.

I shuddered, rubbing at my tired eyes, before continuing. The letters began to read like a son seeking approval.

I know only you can understand these dark desires that drive me. Somehow you know me. You sent Charlie to me as a message. Charlie and I are one and the same. I am Charlie. And you give me permission. You give me permission to do the things I need to do, things other people will never understand.

Nausea swarmed in my gut, guilt rising as I reached a letter that coincided with the first murder.

Father, I did it. I unleashed this driving need inside me. And it was glorious. She got what she deserved, and my soul fed on her. But it's opened up a yawning hunger I can't ignore. I need more. Tell me you understand.

"Fuck," I bit out, and then my heart raced faster at his next letter.

I thought you approved, but you're nowhere in sight. Don't you see what I'm doing? Why aren't you speaking up? Why aren't you telling the world that I'm just doing what you said I should do?

And the last letter:

You bastard, you've left me. You've left me just like him. And for a woman? I should have known. Well, I won't stop. I can't stop. And you will know how very disappointed I am in you.

Understanding dawned in a sudden and terrifying realization.

No.

I scrolled back up.

Father, I did it.

"No, no, no." My chest tightened as I scrolled to the last letter. *And for a woman?*

Lunging off the couch, my laptop crashed to the floor but I ignored it, racing for the kitchen counter where I'd left my phone. My fingers trembled as I hit Sarah's number.

Fear made my breaths shallow as her phone went straight to voicemail.

"Fuck!" I yelled, hanging up but only to hit DCI English's number. The phone rang as I grabbed my keys and jacket, throwing myself out the door.

The detective chief inspector picked up on the seventh ring. "Cavendish?"

"He's coming for me and Sarah," I panted, hurrying down the stairs. "In one of his letters, he referred to me as 'Father.' The letters read like a son seeking approval. And when I didn't publicly talk about the similarities of his murders to *King's Valley*, he got angry. He says 'You've left me just like him. And for a woman.' I think he's referring to his father and step-mother. And he's most definitely referring to me and Sarah. We're his alternative. He's coming after me and Sarah. She's at the Lute, a bar near Charing Cross. I'm on my way now."

"I ... Oh, okay. I have to get my team to look at this, Cavendish."

"We don't have bloody time!" I bawled, racing down the street, searching for a cab.

"She's in a public place. Sarah will be fine. Let my team look at this, and I'll be in contact."

"Fuck!" I hung up on him in a rage and threw my hand in the air at the sight of a black cab with its light on. It pulled over and I dove inside. "The Lute. And I'll pay you double to get me there in half the time."

Thirty-Five

SARAH

"You should really think about doing *Rise and Shine Britain*, Sarah." Liz waved a perfectly manicured hand. Everything about Liz was immaculate and classy. She wore a chartreuse green silk shirt that looked stunning against her dark umber skin. Her high-waisted pencil skirt was black, but her stilettos were a matching chartreuse. Her dark braids were swept up in an intricate bun and she wore delicate gold rings on every finger. She had a similar style to Aria. And like Aria, Liz was brisk and businesslike but warm and friendly too. "You've got something about you, Sarah. People will love you on interview. I can tell."

We'd spent the last two hours sipping cocktails and talking about work, our lives, and my plans for Juno. What was next after Juno. Now we'd circled back to the interviews my publishers wanted me to do.

"As much as I appreciate that, I am not ready to do national television." I blushed just thinking about it. "I admit I've come a long way in confidence these past few months, but I didn't miraculously change overnight."

"Aye, I get that," she replied in her Geordie accent I loved so much. "I promise I get that. But just think on it a bit more. When this deal with Cavendish is announced, people are going to be very excited about the author behind Juno. Moreover … you should be prepared to find yourself in the public eye if you're in a serious relationship with Theo. He's traversed that impossible crossover into celebrity director. Not all directors do that."

My stomach flipped at the thought of the public being interested in our relationship. We'd made so much progress in such a small space of time. I was so proud of him for facing his dad. So much so, I felt ready now to give him those three little words back. I'd just been waiting for him to say them again.

But to have to share him with the country? That I was not looking forward to.

I'd do it, though, to be with him.

"I hear you." I nodded, pushing my chair back. "And I promise to think about it. But for now, I need to pee. One too many mojitos."

Liz chuckled and pointed toward the bar. "The restrooms are back there."

I weaved through the crowded pub, walking along the edges of the actual bar area, searching for a sign pointing to the restrooms. Liz and I had ordered chicken wings to soak up the alcohol, so while I was buzzed, I wasn't drunk. My skin, however, was hot from the cocktails, and hot skin made me think of Theo.

I grinned wickedly at my plans of jumping him as soon as I returned to the flat.

Seeing the sign for the restrooms, I strolled past the counter and down a corridor. It branched off to the right toward the kitchen and to the left down another dimly lit hallway. I noted three doors, two on the left and one at the end of the hall.

The second door on the left was the ladies' restroom and

there was a big fat OUT OF ORDER sign on it. "Bloody hell." Guess it would just have to wait.

I spun away and almost ran smack-bang into a male chest.

"Sorry," the man muttered, his face half shadow in the low light. He wore a black shirt, black tie, and black trousers like the other waitstaff and bartenders. "Ladies' restroom is out of order," he explained unnecessarily but gestured behind me. "You can use the staff one if you like."

"Oh, thank goodness, thanks." I walked toward the door at the end of the hall. "It's this one?"

There was no answer, so I assumed he'd gone back to work. I pushed open the door, realizing a second too late that I'd just opened an exit and not a restroom door.

I might not have been drunk, but the alcohol had definitely slowed my cognition because I stumbled out into the dark, narrow alley behind the bar before I could stop myself. Rolling my eyes, I moved to turn to go back and find the door he'd meant, when what felt like steel bands wrapped around me and something covered my mouth.

I jerked in fright as a chemical smell filtered up my nose and I heard the male grunt behind me as a hard body shuffled me farther into the alley.

Knowing I only had seconds before I passed out from what I suspected was chloroform, I reacted instinctively. And dropped like a sack of potatoes.

My assailant didn't expect it, and I had time to turn and punch him hard between the legs with a shriek of rage. Just like Jared had taught me after he'd heard about the attack on Sloane at Ardnoch.

Muttered expletives fell from the guy's mouth as he clutched his crotch and I scrambled back. Flashbacks from that night in Inverness all those years ago looming, but I knew I couldn't panic. Panic would get me nowhere.

Then renewed horror filled me when light from a security lamp above caught his face.

I knew that face.

All of Britain knew that face. Handsome, but with empty eyes.

It was Quinn Gray.

A sense of surreal terror threatened to overcome me, but the survivor in me took control. I shoved up onto my feet, scrambling and slipping on food waste that had spilled out from the bar's rubbish bins. Beyond the tight alleyway was the street. I could see cars passing, people walking past.

I just had to get to them.

It felt like I was running in slow motion.

A tight pain scored across my scalp and down my spine as something caught in my hair and pulled me back with such force, I lost my footing.

I screamed as Quinn dragged me back down the alley, but music throbbed from inside the buildings on either side of us and the traffic beyond drowned me out. I clawed at his hands, dragging my nails down his arms, and he growled like an animal. Suddenly, he threw me against the damp, brick wall, and my cheek scraped against it, leaving a stinging pain in its wake.

I spun, jabbing out an elbow blindly but catching him in the chest. Rage suffused his expression, and I could barely hear over the blood rushing in my ears as he came at me.

Before he could grab my arms, I raked my nails down his face and he stumbled back, cursing. "You fucking bitch," he hissed, his gaze searing as he whipped a penknife out of his back pocket and brandished it. "You're nothing. Nothing to him. A nobody. I'll teach you that you're nothing."

Nothing.

Nothing.

A word my mum had used to describe me.

How fucking dare he? This sick, twisted fuck of a stranger.

Fury unlike anything I'd ever felt surged through me, like a live flame burning through my blood, propelling my body forward. I charged him like a wild thing, grasping the wrist of his knife hand as I shoved with every ounce of adrenaline coursing within. It took him so by surprise, Quinn moved with the force until I slammed him into the opposite brick wall.

His head connected with a sickening thud and the knife clattered to the ground.

I lunged for it, but a weight crashed down on me, Quinn's breath puffing against my nape as my chest hit the ground. Struggling to breathe as my panic surged, I grappled for the knife on the wet, cold ground and then smashed my elbow back into his face. He jerked back just long enough for me to turn and slash out at him, but he dodged the blade and then grabbed my wrist.

We wrestled for the knife as his weight forced me onto my back. I knew if he got the weapon, it was over.

I screeched in pain and rage as he squeezed the bones in my wrist until I thought they might break. My fingers involuntarily let go of the knife and he grabbed it.

No!

I couldn't see his expression in this light, but I could sense his dark triumph. Tears of fury and fear sprung to my eyes. It couldn't end like this. Not just for me but for Theo.

If it ended like this, it would end him.

I screamed with renewed determination as I snagged at his wrist, trying to fight for the blade.

Thirty-Six
THEO

My phone rang just as the cab pulled up to the Lute. I answered it as I shoved twice as much cash at the cabbie than was required.

"Someone spotted Quinn Gray in Covent Garden two hours ago. We're on our way to that bar," Rick announced without preamble.

Fuck.

"I'm already here."

"If you see him, do not engage."

"If he's anywhere near Sarah, you'll be lucky if you don't take him out of here in a body bag." I hung up, charging into the crowded bar, searching for a familiar dark blond head.

I spotted Liz by herself at a bistro table near the back.

"Fucking move," I muttered belligerently under my breath as I tried to get through the crowds.

"Hey, watch it!"

"Rude, bro, rude!"

I ignored them until I'd woven my way out of the crush and around the tables.

Liz spotted me, her dark eyes widening as I approached. I

didn't like to think how I looked, but whatever my expression was, she stood up. "Theo, is everything all right?"

"Where is Sarah?" I practically yelled.

She blinked in surprise. "She went to the restroom about five minutes ago. I was just about to go in search of her, actually."

"Oh, fuck." Nausea rose with my fear as I pushed past Liz and shoved like a bulldozer through the crowds around the bar. As soon as I was free, I ran down the hallway. The ladies' restroom was out of order. I pushed inside, kicking at the door stalls.

Nothing.

I checked in the men's, but there were just two guys pissing.

Heart racing, I zeroed in on the door at the end of the hallway.

I ran, realizing on approach it was the exit door to the alley. Then I swore I heard a scream.

"Sarah!" I shoved outside.

Light spilled across the alley only so far and on the edges of the shadows, I saw two figures. A man astride a woman, his arms raised above her as she wriggled and fought beneath him.

Just a hint of light glinted in the darkness.

Off a knife.

Her hair spilled across the ground in dark blond strands and the light caught on a blue shirt. The blue shirt Sarah was wearing.

I processed all of this in two seconds, leaving me just enough time to run like my world depended on it.

Toward him.

Toward Gray.

And the knife he was about to bring down on my fucking reason to exist.

I roared with rage at the thought of what he'd done to Sarah before I'd gotten here and I tackled him off her.

Pain sliced into my side as I wrestled Gray to the ground. The knife in his hand was now covered in blood, and the agony scoring up my side told me it was mine. Fighting through the burn, I grabbed his wrist and slammed it down on the ground over and over until he released the knife. We grappled and wrestled as sirens filled the air. And then I pounded my fist into his face over and over.

Blue and red lights flashed around us, and I glanced up in time to see the police cars blocking the end of the alley. No. I wanted to kill him first.

But suddenly, we were surrounded and I was being pulled off the murdering psycho.

Police pulled Gray to his feet, cuffing him as he wobbled unsteadily in their hold. Blood dripped down his nose and over his mouth, staining his teeth as he grinned maniacally at me. "You know this isn't how it ends. We'll see each other again."

"I see you again, you sick fuck, and I'll kill you."

He choked on a laugh as the police dragged him off.

Suddenly, the pain in my side registered and I felt something warm and wet drip down my torso. Black spots crowded in on the edge of my vision as my knees began to give out.

"Sarah!" I yelled hoarsely as an unfamiliar voice asked if I was hurt.

Then she was in front of me, her beautiful face tear streaked, bruised, and bleeding as she grasped at mine. "Theo, Theo," Sarah whispered. And then her eyes filled with horror as she looked down. "Theo, you're hurt."

"I ... Sarah."

She looked up at me, panic in her eyes.

"I ... I love you," I choked out just before everything switched off.

THIRTY-SEVEN
SARAH

There were monitors and tubes attached to Theo, all of it scary, except for the one that beeped in time with his heartbeat.

I focused on that and that his hand felt warm in mine as I hunched over his bedside in a private room in the intensive care ward. When I'd used the restroom earlier, I'd seen inside the room opposite his and the woman was hooked up to so many machines, including a ventilator.

Theo didn't need a ventilator.

He was incredibly lucky after throwing himself at a knife-wielding murderer. And by lucky, I mean he hadn't died of the stab wound, even though Quinn Gray had hit a major artery.

"No vital organs," the surgeon assured me. *"And we've repaired the damaged artery. We'll need to monitor your husband. Only time will tell whether the hemorrhaging caused damage to the muscles and nerves."*

After the police left us at the hospital, I'd lied and told the nurse I was Theo's wife so they would keep me updated. They wanted ID. But then a man I didn't recognize was there and said he was Theo's brother.

Sebastian.

For some reason, he corroborated my lie.

Those long hours waiting while Theo was in surgery were interrupted by a phone call to Jared I barely remembered making. I'd tried to calm him, but I was pretty certain he was on his way to London. Then DCI English and DI Hatlock returned. They needed a statement about what happened at the Lute. Sebastian, this stranger related to Theo, stayed with me while I relayed the story like a robot. I felt like I was outside of my body, watching down as I told the harrowing story of fighting off a serial killer and having the man I love stabbed by the bastard.

"You fought bravely," Hatlock said, squeezing my arm. *"You gave us time to get there. Be proud, Sarah."*

Proud? I didn't feel pride. I felt like I was sitting on the lid of a box inside me, wrestling to keep it sealed. To keep a panicked rage monster inside from bursting out and taking me over.

"I never told him I loved him," I'd confessed dazedly to his brother as we sat on the hard chairs in the waiting room. *"He said it so many times and I was afraid to say it back and then I wasn't. And now it's too late."*

"It's not too late," this stranger who looked a little like Theo but more like Stephen had insisted.

"Why are you here?"

"I have a friend in the police department who alerted me to what happened. And because he's my brother."

The relief was almost excruciating when the surgeon appeared to update us. Theo was alive. Only recovery would reveal if there was any long-term damage.

I didn't care.

I knew Theo would care.

But I was with him. I wasn't going anywhere, no matter what.

Sebastian forced me to drink water and eat a snack, and then he was with me when they let us in to see Theo. He'd rubbed a soothing hand on my back as I cried with relief over Theo's sleeping body.

He would take a while to wake up from anesthesia.

Finally, Sebastian spoke again. "I need to go home and update my wife. And change. Would you like me to bring anything with me when I return?"

I looked up from staring at Theo's handsome face and blinked, trying to process his words. "I'm okay."

Sebastian nodded and moved toward the door. "I'll be back in a few hours."

"Wait." I turned to meet his questioning gaze. "Thank you for being here."

He appeared uncomfortable. "Of course."

"But you were wrong. When you came to see Theo before Christmas. You were wrong. I'm not some innocent waif he was using. I'm a grown woman with a successful career ... and he loves me. I think he loves me more than he's ever loved anyone. At least that's how he makes me feel." A tear slipped down my cheek. "It was the last thing he said after he saved my life last night."

Remorse tightened Sebastian's features. "I know I was wrong, Sarah. It isn't easy for me to apologize. I'm afraid it's rather a flaw in the Cavendish genes. However, I shall apologize to my brother as soon as he's awake."

"He wants nothing to do with your father."

"I heard."

"You won't badger him to change his mind." I lifted my chin stubbornly. "I won't allow it."

A slight smile curled the corner of his mouth. "I've made peace with the fact that the relationship between my father and Theo is beyond repair. But it gave me hope to hear that he'd forgiven Father. Perhaps he … perhaps he can forgive me for not being a better brother."

"I know he can."

His jaw tightened as if fighting off emotion. Then with an abrupt nod, he slipped from the room.

I didn't know how much time passed as I sat there, waiting for Theo to wake up. His nurse, a warm, middle-aged man named Fred, came in to check on us.

My eyelids grew heavy, and I rested my head on the bed. It was uncomfortable and I knew my neck would pay for it in the morning, but I'd just add it to the aches and pains I was beginning to feel after the fight in the alley. My cheek was scratched and bruised from being smashed against the wall. Muscles burned and felt heavy from overuse. But I was alive, and so was Theo.

And I just had to wait for him to wake up so I could tell him I loved him.

I WAS RUNNING but going nowhere. Screaming but no sound came out. I didn't know what I was running from or screaming about, but I knew it was evil. I knew I was terrified.

Running and silently screaming through a pitch-black hallway that seemed to stretch on for—

"Sarah," a voice called through the darkness.

Then I felt a hand on my shoulder, gently shaking me.

"Sarah."

My eyes flew open and I blinked against the brightness of the room.

I groaned as pain burned up my neck. Lifting my head, I startled at the sight of Aria, North, and Jared. Everything rushed back and I cried out, my head whipping toward Theo as fire flared up my neck with whiplash. I winced, disappointment settling over me at finding Theo's eyes still closed.

I looked back at my cousin and North and Aria.

Jared pushed past them to pull me gently from the chair. He hugged me gingerly. "Oh God, Sarah, I'm so glad you're all right. Fuck."

I squeezed him hard, inhaling the familiar scent of grass and earth and spice. "I'm okay," I promised. "Theo got to me in time."

Jared pulled back to cup my face in his hands. "I suppose this means I have to like the bastard now?"

I laughed, but it quickly turned into a sob. Jared cursed under his breath and embraced me as I cried quietly against his shoulder. Aria and North were anxious to take their turns hugging me.

"How's he doing?" North asked, concern creasing his brow as he studied Theo.

"The knife hit an artery. They repaired it. The surgeon said they'd have to run some tests when he wakes up to make sure there's no nerve damage."

North scrubbed a hand over his face. "Fuck."

I watched as Aria wrapped a comforting arm around him. "He'll be fine. Cavendish is made of stern stuff."

"I'm never going to let him live this down," North joked, a sheen of emotion in his eyes. "I always knew the prick was a hero underneath all his stiff upper lip shite."

I chuckled as I leaned into Jared. "Hopefully, he'll wake up soon so he can contest that himself. We know he will. All evidence to the contrary."

"Are you sure you're not hurt?" Aria asked.

Shaking my head, I winced as pain scored up my neck again. "Just a few aches and bruises."

Her gaze flicked down my body and she blanched. Looking down, I saw the dark stains across my blue shirt. On close inspection, it was obviously blood. "Theo's," I explained hoarsely. "He lost a lot ... he needed a transfusion."

"Would you like me to get you a change of clothing and bring them back?" Aria offered.

"You don't have to ..."

"Please. Give me something to do. You know I need to have something to do."

"Um ..." I glanced around, looking for the purse Liz had brought out to me as they were loading Theo into the ambulance. I snatched it up and pulled out the keys to Theo's apartment. "Theo's flat is in Mayfair." I held out the keys to Aria. "I have clothes in the wardrobe. I'll text you the address."

"I've been there," North assured me as he guided Aria toward the door. "We'll be back soon."

"Thank you."

Once they left, Jared rubbed my shoulder. "How are you really?"

I sighed heavily. "I don't know how to feel. It was like some awful nightmare and it's like I'm here, but I'm not."

He nodded in understanding. "It's the shock and the exhaustion. Why don't I grab you a coffee?"

A coffee sounded pretty good. "I think there's a machine on this ward somewhere."

Jared squeezed my shoulder before he left the room to hunt down some caffeine.

"I need all the caffeine," I told Theo quietly as I sat back down beside him and took his hand. "But mostly I just need you to wake up."

As if on cue, Theo's eyelashes fluttered, and his fingers twitched in mine.

Excitement thrummed through me. "Theo? Theo, it's me."

Like weights were holding them down, it took a few more seconds for Theo to force his eyes open. He flinched against the light, blinking a few times as his gaze moved down his body before coming to me. Recognition filled his eyes. "Sarah? Sarah ... what ...?" His voice was raspy and dry. "Fuck, I hurt."

I laughed, tears streaming down my face.

He groaned. "Are you laughing at my pain, sadistic woman?"

"No, I'm just relieved you're awake."

Suddenly, Theo's eyes widened. "Sarah ... Gray ...oh, fuck."

"It's okay." I pressed a kiss to his hand, stroking a soothing palm over his chest. "You're okay. I'm going to let the nurse know you're awake. But first, I can't let another second pass without telling you that I love you. I am so in love with you, Theo Cavendish."

He cracked a weary smile, still handsome, even with dark circles under his eyes and a pale complexion. "Well then ... I think that was worth getting stabbed for."

It was such a Theo retort, my laughter spilled from my lips even as tears slipped down my cheeks.

His expression turned strained. "Come here, my love. I'm all right. Come here."

Gently, I kissed him and then rested my head on his chest. "You're s-stuck w-with m-me now, you y-you realize," I stuttered through my tears.

"Good." Theo caressed my hair. "I wouldn't want it any other way. Probably because I love you rather a lot."

I smiled against his chest, holding him a little tighter. "I love you rather a lot too."

Thirty-Eight

THEO

SIX MONTHS LATER

E*lstree Studios, London*

"And cut!" I called, waiting a beat before crossing into the paths of the cameras. Olivia and North turned to me on the soundstage, and I ignored the grotesquely realistic dummy corpse lying on a prop morgue table. "I think we need to try it without North's last line. There was this expectant pause between you before that moment, and it was perfect just like that. Try it again?"

"Agreed." North nodded congenially. "Liv?"

"Yes, that works for me." She nodded but turned to look out toward the soundstage. "I feel some sweat on my upper lip. Do I need a touch-up? I don't want to be shiny on camera."

"Makeup!" I called, striding out of shot to a waiting Sarah. "We'll start rolling in five!"

Even though filming for the Juno McLeod TV series had started a week ago, it apparently wasn't losing its excitement for Sarah. She was practically bouncing on her toes as I approached her.

"Their chemistry is perfect," Sarah whispered. "Maybe we need to make some changes from the books."

"You mean North and Olivia's? I think so too." Our shoulders brushed as we leaned conspiratorially into each other. While North didn't want to be typecast as a serial killer, especially after we all found ourselves splashed across the news for a few months again after Gray's attack and capture, he did want a part in the show. After a screen test with Olivia, I thought him perfect for playing her younger male partner at work. In the books, Sarah had written an antagonistic relationship that started with a power struggle between them. Over time, North's character grows to admire her. Sarah's writing also hinted that perhaps he had romantic feelings for Juno that were never returned. Never even crossed her mind.

"I think it might work to hint at a *mutual* attraction as the show goes on."

I pressed a quick kiss to her lips. "You took the thought right out of my head."

Sarah grinned giddily. She was bloody adorable.

Chuckling, I left her side to approach our first cameraman, Jim. "Move in a little more on their faces toward the last half of the scene. I don't want the corpse distracting the audience as they talk."

Jim nodded. "Got it."

I stepped away as Olivia's makeup artist hurried off set. "Rolling in five, four, three ...," I trailed off, mouthing two and one as I counted down with my fingers in the air.

Sarah's right, I thought as Olivia and North delivered their lines with such ease and tension, even I forgot for a moment it wasn't real. And that's when you knew you had magic in your hands.

Juno would be a success. I could feel it in my bones.

"SOMEONE TOOK a photo of us walking to the studios this morning." Sarah thrust her phone in my face as I lounged on the couch. There were two photos of us on the screen—one of us holding hands as we walked with coffee cups, and another of me kissing her hungrily on the street. I remembered she'd tasted of hazelnut.

"That's a keeper. Makes me horny looking at it." I grinned as she pulled the phone back with an eye roll.

"What doesn't?"

"When it comes to you, I am a caveman controlled by my libido," I cracked as I scrolled through a streaming service looking for something to watch.

"Your libido aside, why are people still interested in us?" Sarah huffed, throwing her phone on the coffee table.

I turned my head on the back of the couch, running a soothing hand over her legs resting across my lap. "Because you are the enigmatic and beautiful best-selling author of the number one book series in the country, and I am the second son of a viscount turned reformed playboy director. We make a good story."

"It's our story." She pushed up, moving to straddle me.

I immediately dropped the TV remote to rest my hands on her hips. "Hello there."

She grinned wickedly as she smoothed her palms over my chest. "I don't want to share you with the world."

"You don't," I assured her. "No one knows what's between us but you and me." She slipped her hands beneath my T-shirt and I hissed. "Bloody hell, your hands are cold."

"Blame it on this unseasonably cold and damp day." She wriggled on top of me and I felt my blood rush south. "Why don't you warm them ...," she trailed off as her fingertips traced over the healed knife wound. There was barely any raised skin on it, but Sarah could find the wound blindfolded. It still upset her to see the dark red scar left behind.

Frankly, I wore it like a badge of honor. Not only had I protected Sarah from Quinn Gray, but I'd been the luckiest bastard on planet Earth to walk away mostly unscathed. My surgeon, Dr. Hyatt, had run tests once I was awake and well enough. No nerve damage. I could feel all my little toes and fingers.

Recovery was a bit of a bastard because I proved to be an impatient patient, but I tried for Sarah's sake. I didn't want to drive her away now that I finally had all of her.

During those weeks, we worked from my flat on getting the show on its feet. Skylark bought it, and I made sure Sarah's percentage was more than fair. Moreover, we'd have to buy rights to the other books if the series did well, which would prove very lucrative for her.

I also talked with my brother a little more. Our relationship might never be perfect, but I'd heard how Sebastian had shown up for Sarah at the hospital. And he apologized. I supposed I owed him something of an apology, too, for refusing to make amends. Everything wasn't miraculously perfect overnight between us, but we were working on it. As long as he didn't expect me to welcome our father back into my life, we'd keep working on it.

As for Gray, we'd delayed filming to be witnesses in his trial last month. It was all very public and had brought scrutiny back on us, *King's Valley*, on North ... but we all got through it. Thankfully, helping bring Gray to justice had not only eased some of my guilt, but it fostered a positive public opinion of me and North.

It hadn't been easy.

Sarah had just gotten over her nightmares when the trial brought them all up again. This was the first week since Gray had been sentenced to life in prison with no parole that she'd slept through the night. I think working on Juno had distracted her well enough.

It had distracted me too.

From the memories. And from the victims' families whom I had to look in the eye in court. They were gracious, perhaps too gracious to me, considering it was my work that had been warped. They even thanked me for bringing Gray to justice.

I told them it was a team effort because it had been.

The police who'd gotten Gray's DNA.

Sarah, who'd fought him off like a warrior, giving us time to get to them.

I couldn't even bear to imagine what might have happened if she hadn't.

"Hey." She brushed her lips over mine, crushing her delectable tits to my chest. "Where did you go?"

"I'm right here," I assured her, sliding my hands under her top as I reached for her mouth again. When I broke the kiss, I held her stunning gaze with mine and whispered, "I'm always right here. With you. No matter where you are."

Her expression softened as she melted into me. "What would people do if they knew just how much of a romantic you are, Theo Cavendish?"

"They wouldn't do anything." I grinned wickedly as I tightened my embrace and launched off the couch. She squealed in surprise and clung to me, legs wrapped around my waist as I carried her into the bedroom. Dropping her on the bed, I whipped off my sweater and started unbuckling my jeans. Sarah gave an excited little laugh that warmed me through, and she shimmied out of her own jeans. "They wouldn't do anything," I repeated, "because you aren't going to tell them."

"I'm not?" She breathed, whipping off her T-shirt.

"No. You'll be far too busy coming around my cock. Many, many times." I crawled over her.

Her cheeks flushed like I knew they would, and she wrapped her arms around my neck, drawing me down with her. "Then stop talking about it and come inside me."

I laughed against her lips as I guided my cock to her entrance. She gasped as I pushed inside her snug heat. Groaning, I braced myself over her. "That's it."

"Oh, yes." She gripped my waist. "Yes, more."

"Take more." I pumped harder, deeper. "That's it, good girl."

Her inner muscles pulsed around me, and I smirked knowingly. "You take my cock so well, my love."

"I love it." She gasped, arching into my thrusts. "I love you!"

"Don't," I gritted out as sensation shot to my balls. "Fuck, you know you can't say that."

Sarah's eyes gleamed. "I love you."

I tried to think of other things as I pumped into her. "Don't you want this to last? Fuck!"

We'd discovered that her telling me she loved me while I was inside her was a rather unfortunate trigger that could make me spend like a callow youth. Being loved by Sarah McCulloch was my goddamn kink.

And the little she-devil loved it.

Sarah's orgasm was sudden as she arched with a cry, throbbing around me. "I love you!"

My climax ripped through me as I yelled and shuddered between her pretty thighs, emptying everything I had into her. "I love you too." I bowed my head in the crook of her neck, panting for breath. "I think I might need to see a sex therapist if we're ever to have sex that lasts again."

Sarah shook with laughter beneath me. "We have sex that lasts. I just knew I was going to come fast and I wanted you with me."

Gently pulling out of her, I hardened at the sight of my come coating her skin. "Well, looks like round two won't be far off, anyway."

She reached for me, but I grabbed her wrists, pinning them to the bed.

"This time, keep the *I love you* until after we've come."

Sarah pouted. "I thought you liked it."

"Too fucking much, and you know it," I growled, kissing her hard. Then languidly. Tasting her, devouring her. We made out like teenagers, lips bruised and swollen by the time we came up for air. I brushed the hair off her flushed, sweat-dampened cheeks. "I'm so bloody glad you knocked on my door last winter."

Her smile was slow, but it lit up her whole face. "I'm so glad you knocked on my door too."

Epilogue
SARAH

FOUR MONTHS LATER

Ardnoch, Scottish Highlands

The Gloaming was filled with chatter and laughter, the clinking of glasses, and the crackling of flames in the fireplace at one end.

There had been many surreal moments in my life in the past eighteen months, especially the past year, and this moment was another to add to the list.

It had taken me thirty-two years, but I had a friendship circle.

Our group had taken up the largest booth in the Gloaming. I was tucked into the corner with Theo next to me, one arm slung over my shoulders while he clasped his pint glass with his free hand. Across from me sat Aria, North at her side.

On North's other side was Aria's twenty-year-old sister Allegra, visiting from the States.

Across from her, next to Theo, was Jared. And beside him was Walker and Sloane and across from them sat Brodan and Monroe. Their children were being watched by family members so we could all catch up while we were in Ardnoch visiting.

Theo and I would be traveling on to my little cottage in Gairloch to write.

It was wonderful seeing everyone and feeling part of a community, even when I wasn't physically here. And while I was enjoying catching up, my attention kept straying to Allegra as she talked with Jared. She was asking him all kinds of questions about the farm and my cousin indulged her, but I was a wee bit worried by the gleam in her pretty eyes. Allegra was a stunning young woman and maybe in a few years, Jared might take notice. But I knew my cousin. He preferred his women older, worldlier, and not the daughter of a Hollywood legend.

Aria leaned across the table toward me. "Does your cousin have to be so attractively rugged? Farmers are supposed to be jolly old men."

I chuckled at that and waved off her concern. "Jared would never." He was a player, but he had lines he wouldn't cross.

Theo ducked his head into our conversation. "Are we talking about the flirty Lolita?" He gestured comically with his hand.

I squeezed his thigh under the table. "Try not to be so obvious."

"And don't bring up Lolita in any sense of the word." Aria threw a peanut at him. "It's creepy."

Theo laughed, raising his hands in surrender. "Apologies."

"You could be helpful and rescue Jared from the conversation," I whispered.

My boyfriend smirked at me as if I were adorably naive. "My love, I do not think the good farmer wants to be rescued from this situation."

I frowned and cut a look at Jared. He was staring a wee bit too intensely at Allegra as she smiled and chatted to him about wanting to see the farm, if he might let her set up her easel on the land so she could paint. Jared shrugged noncommittally as he scrubbed a hand over his perfectly trimmed beard.

Allegra stopped talking as if waiting for a proper answer. The rest of our table chatted on, Theo joking with Aria and North about the article that had just come out in which Angeline Potter denigrated Ardnoch. Aria took his teasing easily, considering it hadn't harmed Ardnoch. Everyone in the know knew Angeline's membership had been cancelled after I'd told Agnes Hutchinson what had occurred during my time there. To my surprise, a new housekeeper had come forward with similar complaints. Theo had been right. Angeline had found someone new to bully.

My thoughts drifted, however, and drowned out the conversations at the end of the table as I watched Jared and Allegra stare at each other. Goose bumps rose on my arms as I witnessed something silent pass between them.

And then Jared shook his head slightly, as if coming out of a daze, and he suddenly turned to Walker. "Mate, can you let me out?"

Walker and Sloane slid out of the booth to grant Jared's exit, and I saw Allegra follow his movements as my cousin cut across the bar toward the restroom.

For a while, I fell into discussion with my friends, Allegra engaging with us too. But then I noted after some time that she noticed Jared hadn't returned. I watched her look for him and find him at the bar, flirting with a local named Sadie. She was a hairdresser at Ardnoch's only salon, a single mum, and about ten years older than Jared. I knew from rumors that they'd slept together a few years back.

Apparently, Sadie wasn't sore that it hadn't turned into anything because she and Jared left the pub together.

He never looked at Allegra again.

Aria's pretty sister frowned at the table, lost in her thoughts.

I opened my mouth to speak, but I didn't know what to say.

Theo covered my hand with his and smiled tenderly down at me. "Leave it, my love."

Aye, he was right. There was no point making something big out of nothing.

"Sarah, you have to tell me what happens in the next Juno book!" Monroe suddenly yelled down the table. "We were just updating Brodan and Walker on the cliff-hanger you've left us all on."

I laughed at her disgruntled expression. "I'll tell you soon once *I* know. I start writing it next week."

"Oh, you must have an idea, though."

"I do."

Theo chuckled at my smug secretiveness.

Monroe huffed. "Do we not get the friendship sneak peek? Come on."

The friendship sneak peek. That sounded nice. "Well ..." I heaved a dramatic sigh. "Since it's you, I *can* tell you that Juno will live."

"We know that! It's the Juno McLeod series."

Chuckling, I leaned into Theo. "Should I tell them?"

"Herrings," he whispered in my ear. "Tell them just the red herrings."

"Don't listen to whatever he is whispering in your ear. I can tell he's not on our side." Sloane pointed a pretend angry finger at Theo.

Theo chuckled. "She knows me well."

"Not as well as I do," I murmured.

"No one knows me as well as you do," he offered with casual surety.

I stared at him in awe, disbelieving that this once closed-off, cynical aristocrat's son could make me feel like I was the most important person in the world and do it every day. As I stared up at his handsome face, with my friends begging to know more about my books because they were genuine fans, I didn't think I could get any happier than I was at that moment.

ONE WEEK LATER

GAIRLOCH, Scottish Highlands

"IN OTHER HEADLINES THIS EVENING," the radio newscaster announced as we drove the winding, dark roads toward Gairloch, "serial killer Quinn Gray, sentenced to life in prison back in May of this year for the Hangman murders, died today from multiple stab wounds. Paramedics were unable to resuscitate him as he succumbed to his injuries before reaching hospital. Police have yet to name suspects but have released a statement confirming Gray was attacked by a fellow inmate.

"In entertainment news, crowds gather at Wembley tonight as global star Koda kicks off her UK tour ..."

Switching off the car stereo with trembling fingers, I noted

Theo's hands clenched tightly around the wheel. "Are you all right?"

"The bastard's dead," he replied hoarsely. "He can't harm anyone else. So, yes, I'm all right." He glanced at me. "Are you?"

"Is it wrong that I'm relieved?"

"No. No, it's not wrong." Theo reached over to squeeze my hand before returning his to the wheel.

We drove in silence for a while, lost in our thoughts at the sudden and strange news until the headlights lit up the sign for Gairloch.

"'When the moonlight's on the mountain / And the gloom is on the glen, / At the cross beside the fountain / There is one will meet thee then,'" Theo recited softly as we drove along the winding coastal roads into Gairloch.

The moon cast a glow over the loch below and the snow-topped hills made me shiver with anticipation. It had been a year since I'd stayed at the cottage. With Theo.

It would forever be our place, and I loved the idea of us staying there for a few weeks every year.

"What's that from?" I asked, wanting a distraction from the news that had dampened my excitement with dark memories.

"'When the Gloom is on the Glen,' by William Makepeace Thackeray. It's a love poem." He glanced at me. "Have you never heard it?"

"No. It's pretty. We should write a poem about us and a glen."

"Hmm, how so?" he asked.

"We had to climb mountains to get here. To have this." I gestured between us. "It took us a while to find the glen that would let us pass through."

He flashed me a smile, but I couldn't tell if it reached his eyes. "How very poetic, my love. And very true."

I reached over to smooth a hand down his arm. "I'm here if you need to talk about this."

"I don't," he promised. "It's finally over, Sarah. That's a gift."

Hearing the sincerity in his voice, I nodded and let it go.

A few minutes later, Theo pulled into the cottage's driveway and then we bustled inside out of the cold, only to walk into more cold because the heating had been switched off. Even so, as we flipped on the lights, illuminating the desk Theo had pushed next to mine this time last year, all dark memories were obliterated. Old beautiful ones flooded in. Those days when I didn't know what these intense feelings between us meant, but they were exciting and new and I wanted to experience every second of them, no matter what.

Theo slid his arm around me, his gaze on the desks that sat at the window overlooking a view obscured by winter darkness.

"This is my favorite place in the world," he whispered, turning to me, all the love I could ever hope for burning in his eyes.

Now that we were here again, I couldn't imagine only visiting once a year.

"Mine too," I whispered back. "It's good to be home."

He pressed a tender kiss to my temple and agreed, "Isn't it, though? And I've thought of a new name for it."

"What's wrong with Haven's View Cottage?" I thought it was pretty.

"Nothing, really. But I thought perhaps Through the Glen Cottage suited us a little better."

I sighed happily, loving that only I got to see how utterly romantic Theo could be. I snuggled into his warmth. "Aye. Through the Glen Cottage. It's perfect, Mr. Cavendish."

***

Intrigued by Jared McCulloch? Read his story next in Skies Over Caledonia (The Highlands Series #4)
Out May 9, 2024 in Kindle Unlimited, paperback and audio.

He's a down-to-earth highland farmer. She's the rebellious daughter of Hollywood royalty. They might seem like they're from different worlds, but that won't stop them from engaging in a marriage of convenience...

It's been five years since Jared McCulloch's grandfather Collum passed away and he inherited his farm in the Scottish Highlands. After his grandad saved him from his past life, Jared is determined to honor Collum's legacy. But not only has a series of bad luck put him in danger of losing the farm, his estranged father is disputing the will. In a desperate situation, Jared realizes he'll do just about anything to save the land.
Even marrying Allegra Howard, a woman he's avoided at all costs.
A woman who tempts him beyond reason.

There's only one place that makes Allegra Howard feel safe; one place that feeds her artist's soul. Allegra wants to settle down in Scotland and expand her business. But there's a hitch: immigration intends to return her to US soil.
Panicked, Allegra finds the one person just as desperate as she is. The same person she's lusted after for years. In exchange for marrying her, she'll invest financially in Jared McCulloch's farm.

However, living together only forces them to acknowledge their searing mutual attraction. And with it comes an undeniable emotional connection Jared's not sure he's ready for.

Yet, blurring the lines of their arrangement is the least of his concerns when someone begins terrorizing the farm. Allegra and Jared came together to save what matters most and now that might just be each other. And unless they can figure out which of their pasts has returned to torment them, they could lose their chance at a real future together...

Read on for the bonus novella *A Highland Christmas (The Highlands Series #3.5).* This novella was included in the multi-author holiday anthology *Lights, Snow and Mistletoe*.

A Highland
Christmas
A Highlands Series Novella

By Samantha Young

Copyright © 2023 Samantha Young

Edited by Jennifer Sommersby Young

PROLOGUE
HAYDYN

FIVE MONTHS AGO

Ardnoch, Scottish Highlands

As soon as I opened the door and saw Kenna Smith standing on the other side of it, I immediately thought, *No way in hell*. It was bad enough interviewing people to replace Jean, a woman Michael adored and who'd made our lives easier for the last ten years, but there was no bloody way I was hiring an attractive young thing who'd get the whole village yammering.

A few years back, all anyone could talk about was the gorgeous American nanny Thane Adair had hired. The one who was thirteen years his junior and living on the property. I usually wasn't privy to local gossip, but the parents wouldn't shut up about it at school events, plus Thane's son Lewis was in my son Michael's class.

As it was, rumors turned out to be true that Thane was carrying on an affair with his nanny. He married her.

I would not put Michael in the position of having his father and new nanny gossiped about.

Kenna beamed up at me from the doorstep. "Dr. Barr?"

I felt a *flutter* in my belly at the sight of that gorgeous smile. Aye, this definitely wasn't happening. The next ten minutes would be a waste, but it would be unprofessional and illegal to shut the door in her face because she was gorgeous. "Kenna Smith?"

"That's me." Sunlight captured gold striations in her chestnut-brown eyes and I was struck dumb for a second. I'd never seen such beautiful eyes. Her smile dimmed. "Is ... oh, have you already filled the position?"

Tell her yes. I cleared my throat and stepped back to allow her entrance. "No, please come in."

Years ago, just before Michael started school, I'd decided I wanted to bring my son up in a village much like the one I'd grown up in near Aberdeen. After searching for plots of land to build a house, I found one on the outskirts of Ardnoch. It meant a two-hour round-trip commute to the university where I worked, but the village was everything I wanted for Michael. It had since turned into a bit of a tourist trap when local gentry and ex-Hollywood actor Lachlan Adair turned his family's estate into a members-only club for the Hollywood elite, but it was still a quaint and friendly place to raise a child.

Despite the fortune few knew about, I'd built a modest but luxurious three-bedroom home on the village outskirts. It had everything Michael and I needed.

"Your home is stunning," Kenna opined, eyes wide as she took in our open-plan living area. Kitchen, dining, and living space all in one with floor-to-ceiling glass windows to the front, overlooking our private driveway and the trees surrounding it. Sliding doors behind the kitchen led out to the back garden. It wasn't a huge space out there, but we were surrounded by picturesque woodland.

"I had an interior designer do everything," I admitted as I gestured for her to take a seat on the couch. "Tea, coffee?"

"A coffee, please. Milk, no sugar." She gazed around. "The designer did a great job. They really captured that modern midcentury look."

My mouth tugged up in amusement as I moved into the kitchen to make the attractive brunette a coffee. "You sound like you might know a thing or two about design."

"Oh no, not really. I just love home renovation shows." She chuckled and the husky, throaty sound caused heat to flare where it shouldn't.

Damn it.

Time to hurry this up. I quickly made her a coffee and sat across from her once she'd taken it from me. I was careful not to touch her in the exchange, though I noted her elegant long fingers and even longer legs as she crossed them. As she sipped the coffee, I saw a flicker of nervousness in her eyes that her cheerful friendliness was doing an imperfect job of hiding.

I knew from her application that Kenna was twenty-seven years old, had a qualification in childcare, and had been an early years' practitioner for five years. She'd moved on to working as a nanny but only had one previous employer for that on her résumé. I'd called her in for an interview, anyway, because I'd only had four people apply for the position. It wasn't easy to hire a nanny in rural Scotland.

"So," Kenna spoke before I could, "may I ask why you're looking for a nanny?"

Who was doing the interviewing here? I straightened in my armchair, greedily taking in her stunning face. She wore very little makeup, from what I could tell. A bit of mascara, maybe. Her olive skin was naturally tan, and she had a healthy flush to her cheeks that didn't look manufactured. I didn't think I had a type, but if I did, Kenna Smith was it.

Pointless, pointless interview. Still, I answered, "I hired Jean when Michael was a baby. She was a widowed nanny looking for a fresh start, so she moved out to Ardnoch to be with us. However ..." I smiled, happy for her, even though we'd miss the hell out of her. "She met someone on a dating app. Together, they've found a new lease on life. They want to travel."

Kenna grinned. "That's a good reason to lose her."

"Oh, very much so. And as she keeps reminding us, we're not really losing her."

"I bet not." She cocked her head. "So, is it just you and Michael?"

"Oh ... well, yes, since he was an infant. But without going into the details, Michael's mum has come back into his life." Deena's return had made me a nervous wreck this past year, but I'd do anything to make my son happy, and he wanted a relationship with his mother. "Anyway, I should ask you some questions," I remarked pointedly.

She flushed a delightful pink and some very bad thoughts sprang into my mind. "Of course."

I tapped my phone screen, looking at her résumé as an excuse not to look at her. "May I ask why you left your last employer and decided to move from Inverness to Ardnoch?"

Her hesitation made me look up. "We ... um ... I needed a change, and I have a cousin who lives in Ardnoch. She was looking for a new roommate."

There was something like unease in her eyes, suggesting that wasn't the whole truth. However, her last employer had given Kenna a good reference when I'd called her to confirm it, so I wouldn't push the subject.

"It's good that you already have accommodation because this isn't a live-in position." *Not that you're getting the job.*

After years of mistrusting women because of Deena, resulting in nothing but casual hookups, I'd finally decided it was time to stop letting one woman ruin my future. It would be nice to have someone to share a home with, for Michael to have a stepmum who cared. Unfortunately, there had only been two women who captured my interest in the last few years, and two other lucky bastards had beaten me to them. Since casual hookups no longer did it for me, it had been six months since I'd last had sex.

And I was not putting a long-legged brunette with eyes I could drown in, in temptation's range.

"Aye. My cousin lives in a flat on Castle Street and I'll stay with her until I can find my own place. And I have my car, so it's no problem for me to get here and take Michael to school and back." She gestured out the window. I'd been so busy looking at her, I hadn't even noticed the very nice Audi Q5 parked in my driveway. How did a twenty-seven-year-old nanny afford a fancy SUV? I turned back to her, and she shifted in her seat before taking a quick sip of coffee.

Fuck it. "Nice motor?"

She heard my nosy question in my tone and sighed. "It's a long story."

In other words, mind your own business. Difficult for me to do when I was supposed to put the care of my most precious possession in this woman's hands. The subject was moot, anyway. I'd already decided that I very much wanted to get to know Kenna Smith in the way a man gets to know a woman. I would not be hiring her, but I did want her phone number.

I'd allow some time to pass after our interview and then I could seek her out in Ardnoch to ask her for a date. I opened my mouth to bring the interview to a short end, but an engine sounded and cut me off.

I glanced sharply out the window to see Innes Williams

parking behind Kenna's Audi. What the hell? The back passenger door of the old SUV flew open and Michael jumped out, hurrying toward our front door.

"Problem?" Kenna asked.

"My son's home early."

He was supposed to hang out with his best friend Grant Williams and his mum all day, so I could do these interviews.

"Dad!" Michael flew into the house as I stood from the armchair. "Mrs. Williams told me you're interviewing new nannies."

Bloody Innes. I cleared my throat. "I am. Michael—"

"Don't you think I should be here?" He crossed his arms over his chest and tilted his chin stubbornly. Even as he tried to stare me down, his gaze kept flicking to Kenna. He was lucky I found him adorable because he was also a pain in my arse. Deena and I had brought a smart kid into the world. Michael was precocious and too switched on for his age. Because it had just been him and me for so long, he believed everything should be decided as a team.

The only times I was reminded he was still a child were his excitement at Christmas and the way Deena had a way of turning his emotions upside down.

Before I could argue that no, I didn't think he should be here to interview his nanny, Kenna stood and held out her hand to him. "Hi, Michael, I'm Kenna."

Michael's arms dropped as he stared up at her as if she were an angel from heaven.

Fuuuuuck.

He shook her hand, suddenly beaming from ear to ear. "Do you like video games?"

"I do, and I'm really good at them. But I also like walking and football and going for bike rides."

His eyes widened in delight. "I like all those things too."

"No way." She grinned that enchanting smile. "So, what's your favorite video game right now? Let me guess ... *Fortnite*?"

"Of course."

"Cool. I like *Mizuki*."

Michael was practically bouncing on the balls of his feet. "You really play it? Do you want to play now?"

The front door opened before Kenna could reply, and Innes popped her head through. Her expression apologetic, she said, "I'm sorry. It slipped out and then he wouldn't stop pleading to come home."

"It's fine, Innes." It wasn't, but it wasn't her fault either. "I've got him."

"Okay. Have a nice ..." Her words trailed off when she caught sight of Kenna. "Day," she squeaked out and then shot me a look.

I'm pretty sure my expression begged her to help me.

Her lips pressed together like she was trying not to laugh. Then she waved at Kenna. "I'm Innes Williams. My son's best friends with Michael."

"I'm Kenna."

"My new nanny," Michael offered, making my stomach drop. "So you'll see her around. Come on." He grabbed Kenna's hand. "Let's play *Fortnite*."

Kenna looked at me.

I could feel Innes watching us.

My gaze dropped to Michael, whose eyes had grown round like a puppy dog, begging me not to disagree.

This ... this was why I didn't want him involved in the interviews. I would pick a friendly, warm-spirited older lady much like Jean. And Michael would pick the stunning twenty-something who knew who the characters in *Fortnite* were.

And because I was terrified of disappointing him the way Deena had his whole life, I knew at that moment I was sentencing myself to an indefinite period of blue balls.

ONE
KENNA

Present day

*C*hristmas Eve, Ardnoch

HAVING LIVED in Scotland my whole life, I knew it was just the luck of the draw whether we got a white Christmas or not. For the first time, I wished for no snow.

So, of course, as I sat in Flora's, the most popular café in the village, I glanced up from my phone to see white flakes dropping from the sky.

Oh, vomit on cow turd. Eff my life.

"Mom, it's snowing!"

I turned toward the slightly accented voice to see Callie Harrow, a pretty blond in Michael's class, gaping excitedly out the window.

"Yeah, it is!" Her mom high-fived her, just as excited.

Our eyes met, and despite my worries, we shared a grin.

Sloane Harrow and her daughter were California transplants. We'd shared friendly hellos at the school gates and I'd bought delicious baked goods from the bakery Sloane owned across the street. She was engaged to a dauntingly massive fellow Scot, and I had it on authority from the gossiping mums at school that my boss, Haydyn, had shown an obvious interest in the gorgeous American before her fiancé won her over. I'd tried to ignore the flare of jealousy I felt at that information, just as I'd tried to ignore any romantic feelings I had for Haydyn.

It seemed he and Michael shared taste, however, because I was pretty certain Michael had a crush on Callie, who was a mini version of her mum. He teased her constantly and was highly competitive with her. More telling, however, was that before I came along, word had it he and Lewis Adair were pretty friendly. But the two boys had gotten into fights over Michael's teasing of Callie, who was Lewis's best friend.

I smelled jealousy on Michael a mile away, but he was too young to understand that's what he was feeling.

Time would only tell, and I'd keep my eye on the situation. It shocked me that ten-year-olds were talking about crushes and boyfriends and girlfriends, but when I thought back on it, I'd had a wee boyfriend in my last two years of primary school. In P7 we used to kiss behind "the huts," the mobile classrooms where they taught religious education. The memory made me snort inwardly.

"First snow?" I asked Sloane and Callie.

Sloane ruffled Callie's hair, the stunning diamond engagement ring on her finger winking in the light. "Second snow, but it's still pretty exciting for us." A look crossed Sloane's face that I didn't understand until she asked, "Will you be all right? If the snow gets heavy?"

Understanding dawned. The downside of living in a village was that everyone knew everyone's business.

When I moved to Ardnoch, I'd planned to get out of my cousin's flat and into my own home as soon as possible. The problem was that property was scarce in Ardnoch, and the only homes that had come up for sale were way too big. I could afford them, but I didn't need that much space. However, Una, my cousin, had proven impossible to live with. She didn't know how much money I'd inherited, but she knew I had money, and I'd noticed money going missing from my purse. Then she'd started asking for more money than I owed in rent and utilities. From there, she began raiding my closet and wearing my clothes without asking. It just got so weird and strained between us that I ended up securing a caravan on a caravan site out by the water. It was owned by a retired businessman. Gordon. He was lovely. And he'd given me a good deal on renting a caravan for as long as I needed it. I'd been in the caravan since late October, and it was bloody Baltic. Something I lied about every time Haydyn asked.

A bungalow had come up for sale just yesterday, though, and although it needed renovating, it was perfect for me. I'd viewed it, put in an offer right away, and it was accepted.

I told Sloane as much.

She frowned. "But that means you'll still be in the caravan over Christmas? While it snows?"

Not wanting to explain to her that I was spending Christmas alone and would be freezing if it kept snowing, I told her the same lie I'd told Haydyn. "I'm staying with family for Christmas."

She relaxed immediately.

I'd told Haydyn the same lie because things were strained between us too. I blamed Halloween, too much truth, too much bonding, and the electric chemistry that had zipped between me and my boss since he'd opened his door to me.

I knew he was a mistake as soon as I saw him. Dr. Haydyn Barr. A professor of civil engineering at the University of Highlands and Islands in Inverness. Handsome, clean-cut, chiseled jaw, almost pretty with his large dark, thickly lashed eyes and full mouth. Laughter lines around his eyes gave him some rugged weathering I found way too attractive. He was six feet tall, stylish, classy, intelligent, warm, a doting father—and ten years my senior.

The whole time he'd been interviewing me, I knew, despite how desperate I was for a new job and a new beginning, that I couldn't work for him. Not after what happened at my last job. However, Michael had blasted into the house, adorable and smart, and so desperate for female attention. I'd later learn that his mother abandoned him when he was a baby and hadn't reached out again until last year. Haydyn had taken the reconciliation with Deena slowly for Michael, but Michael wanted to get to know his mum. It was going well so far, though I knew it was still a worry for Haydyn.

When Deena asked to have Michael for Christmas, Haydyn had wanted to say no, but Michael pleaded to go and won. I was nervous about it too. Deena was married to a solicitor and they lived in Inverness. They had no children of their own, and the guy seemed nice enough, but I wasn't convinced he was interested in Michael.

Only time would tell.

So Michael was in Inverness for Christmas, and I'd told Haydyn I would be as well. That I had a friend back in the city who'd invited me to stay. That wasn't true. All my friends were back home in Aberdeen, and not one of them had thought to invite me for Christmas.

Even though they knew it would be my first alone.

Tears thickened my throat and I fought them back. "I better get on the road before the snow gets too heavy."

Sloane and Callie bid me goodbye and I waved to Flora, the owner, before I ducked out of the café. The cold white flakes weren't falling fast, but they were starting to stick.

Oh, bugger.

I burrowed into my scarf and hurried across the street to Morag's to pick up some last-minute groceries. I planned to watch a marathon of romantic comedies on my laptop and try very hard not to think about the fact that I was all alone.

Morag, a lovely middle-aged lady with pink-rinsed hair, owned the deli and grocery store. We chatted for a bit before I bid her a happy Christmas and opened the door to leave with my bag of premade meals I could heat up in my microwave, as well as wine, chocolates, and other snacks.

I hurried outside and smacked into a hard body.

"Oof." I staggered back, dropping my bag, as gloved hands grabbed my arms to steady me.

Blinking rapidly, my stomach flipped as I looked up into familiar dark brown eyes. Eyes that narrowed on me. "Kenna?"

"Haydyn," I squeaked out, looking and sounding like I was caught in a lie. Avoiding eye contact, I lowered to my haunches to pick up my fallen wares.

Unfortunately, so did Haydyn. He shoved my meals and the thankfully unbroken wine bottle into my bag and handed it to me.

"Thanks," I murmured.

"Shouldn't you be in Inverness?" he snapped with uncharacteristic belligerence.

"I-I'm just leaving," I lied.

Haydyn scowled. "And you're taking premade meals with you?"

"I—"

He held up a hand to cut me off. "I swear if you lie one more time, I'll … I'll …"

Amusement cut through my embarrassment as he failed adorably to find an appropriate punishment for me. Suddenly, the image of him taking me across his knee filled my mind and I squirmed, my cheeks flushing.

As if he read my mind, Haydyn's gaze turned low-lidded as it fell to my mouth.

And this was absolutely why he'd been avoiding me since Halloween. Every time we were alone, this sexual chemistry sparked between us, and it didn't take a lot to ignite it.

Seeming to shake himself, Haydyn straightened and cleared his throat. He wore a scarf knotted stylishly and tucked into his fitted black peacoat. The man dressed like he'd just walked off the pages of *GQ*, and it really did it for me. I'd never shown much interest in the way a guy dressed, but since meeting Haydyn, it was something I noted about the men I met.

"You lied. You're staying in that damn caravan over Christmas. Alone." His full mouth pressed into a disapproving hard line.

I shrugged. "You're staying alone."

"In a fully insulated home. Not a tin can off the coast of the North Sea."

I rolled my eyes. "Exaggeration."

"It's snowing!" he yelled and then seemed to remember we were in public.

"I'll be fine," I promised, not wanting his or anyone else's pity. "And it's temporary. My offer was accepted on a bungalow yesterday. Happy Christmas." I darted around him before he could stop me and practically ran toward my parked Audi.

However, I couldn't resist looking up the now snow-crested street. Haydyn stood under the dim glow of a street-light, staring in my direction. An ache of pure longing filled me as I remembered how he'd been on Halloween. How our night together was the first night since my life blew apart that I'd felt happy. Like I'd found home again.

Blanching at how wrong I'd been, I dove into my car. Yet as I made my way carefully through the falling snow toward the coast, the memories cascaded over me, anyway.

Two
KENNA

Three months ago

H*alloween, Ardnoch*

"THAT'S GRANT AND HIS MUM!" Michael yelled from the living room.

Hearing the childish panic in his voice, I darted around his room looking for those damn twin ninja daggers me and his dad had been reluctant to buy for his costume. Seeing the plastic blades peeking out from under his bed, I grabbed them. "Found them!"

Rushing out into the living room, I tried not to smile at how cute Michael looked as a dragon ninja. I'd spent hours on YouTube watching tutorials on how to paint scales onto his cheeks and forehead. Makeup littered the kitchen island, his dirty dinner plate on the counter, and he'd somehow managed to dump half the contents of his bedroom into the living area.

"Thanks!" Michael beamed up at me.

A few minutes later, Grant and Innes were in the house. Grant was also dressed as a dragon ninja, but his scales were blue while Michael's were green. He also didn't have face-painted scales, much to his chagrin.

"Thanks for outparenting me," Innes teased. "I'll never hear the end of this."

I chuckled as the boys stood together for the photos I insisted on taking. "You work full time, Innes. It's amazing what you accomplish."

"Thanks for saying that." She grinned at the boys as Michael slung an arm around Grant's shoulders and they posed with their plastic twin daggers. "The school is going to murder us if anything happens with those daggers."

"Or take them off them before they even get past the doors."

"Great," she muttered. "I'm looking forward to two very annoyed dragon ninjas if that happens."

Laughing, I took a few quick photos. Unfortunately, Haydyn was working late, so he'd asked me to make sure I got some snaps of Michael before he left for the school Halloween dance. Michael wouldn't be back tonight as it was a Friday and he'd be sleeping over at Grant's after the party.

We were making sure Michael had everything he needed for his sleepover when a car pulled into the drive. Ears perking, Michael rushed away from me to the window. His whole being lit up. "Dad's home!"

Warmth filled my chest as I watched Haydyn hurry out of his SUV. He must have gotten out of his meeting early so he wouldn't miss Michael. For the last few months, I'd watched Haydyn juggle a full schedule as a senior lecturer at the university, as a researcher, and as a freelance advisor on projects, not just around the UK but internationally. He did all that as a single parent. Yes, he hired a nanny because his life would be impossible otherwise, but I saw how hard he worked to make sure Michael never felt like he was missing out.

I'd found him physically attractive from the moment we met, but getting to know him had only intensified that attraction.

My stomach fluttered like a schoolgirl's as Haydyn burst through the door just as Michael flew at him. He laughed, embracing his son tightly before holding him back to study his costume. "Well, don't you look amazing!"

"I thought you were working." Michael grinned up at him.

Haydyn gently gripped his son's chin to tilt his face in the light. "I had to see my dragon ninja, didn't I? And look at you. You look awesome."

"Kenna did my scales. They're sick."

Haydyn sighed wearily at Michael's use of the word *sick* but grinned, nonetheless. "So they are."

"We better get going," Innes said, nudging Grant toward the door.

"I'll pick Michael up tomorrow." Haydyn stepped aside.

"I promised them breakfast at Flora's, so there's no rush."

"Okay, thanks, Innes."

"Bye, Kenna!" Michael waved at me and rushed out the door.

As soon as it closed on them, Haydyn turned and surveyed the room before his eyes fell on me.

There was that stupid fluttering again. I shrugged sheepishly. "I wasn't going to leave it like this for you. Let me tidy up."

"Don't worry about it."

"No, let me clear this all away." I gestured toward the hob

as I began cleaning the island. "I left some pasta and garlic bread for you."

"You're an angel," he murmured as he strolled by. I tried not to inhale the scent of his expensive cologne. A few seconds later, he said, "There's a ton here. Have you eaten?"

I glanced up from tidying. The answer was no and I was starving, but I'd been too busy feeding Michael and getting his costume ready. "Oh, I'll eat at home."

"There's plenty, and I can only imagine how rushed off your feet you've been today. I'm putting out two plates."

TEN MINUTES LATER, I was seated across from Haydyn at the small bistro table off the kitchen. It didn't take much to convince me to stay. Mostly because I wanted to be around Haydyn, but also because I was avoiding my cousin's apartment as much as possible. Things were not good there.

Since I was driving, I stuck with a glass of water with my meal while Haydyn poured himself a glass of wine.

"Long day?" I asked to distract myself from the sight of his fingers caressing the wineglass stem.

Haydyn swallowed a bite of pasta and met my gaze. "I'm close to finishing up a project, and it always feels a little manic toward the end. Plus, midterm papers."

I nodded. I'd kept Michael busy the past week because Haydyn had so much marking to do.

"You've been a lifesaver these past few months," he told me, eyes on his plate. "I was worried when Michael hired you, but it worked out."

I chuckled at his teasing, even though it was technically true that Michael offered me the job before Haydyn could. "I'm glad you're happy with his decision."

He shot me a smirk, but before he could say anything, his phone buzzed on the table. He reached for it and frowned at the screen. With a sigh, he turned it over and dug back into his pasta.

Finding myself more and more curious about my boss, I blurted out, "Everything okay? Someone bothering you?"

Since I'd started working for the Barrs almost three months ago, there had been no sign of Haydyn dating. If he was seeing someone, it was happening in the hours he spent in Inverness. Otherwise, he was totally dedicated to his son. Michael talked about his mum, Deena, after his visits with her, but I still didn't know the story there. Haydyn was a professor. However, that income didn't account for their luxurious home, car, and the designer clothes they both wore. Or the fact that Michael had everything a kid could ever need or want, including the fancy holidays Haydyn took them on every summer.

There was so much I didn't know about them, and I could only piece together the bits of information I'd gleaned over the last few months. Tonight was unusual for Haydyn because, although he was friendly with me, he tended to keep his distance as much as possible. Perhaps it was the sudden lowering of his guard—him inviting me to share dinner—that made me ask my slightly nosy question.

Haydyn looked up from his plate, his gaze searching mine. He looked handsome but tired. "It's a text from Deena asking to see Michael tomorrow. She asked to have him this Halloween, and I've already said no because she went behind my back last weekend and asked Michael to spend Christmas with her."

I knew Michael was spending Christmas with Deena because he'd been excitedly talking about it all week, but I hadn't known the decision was made without Haydyn. "Oh. That's not cool."

He pressed his lips together in a hard line before continuing, "Now I can't tell Michael no because he's excited, but I never planned for her to have him during such an important holiday. It's been less than a year since she came back into his life."

"She's getting pushy."

"Aye."

"You can tell me if this is none of my business, but how long was she out of Michael's life?"

Haydyn smirked unhappily. "His whole life, Kenna."

My lips parted in shock. "Are you kidding?"

"Nope." He took a sip of wine, and I could see it was to distract himself from the anger still brewing within. "I came home when Michael was six months old to find him alone, screaming the house down, sitting in his own filth. Deena had packed her things and left us. I could maybe get over her leaving us if she hadn't left my baby alone. She could have called a neighbor and asked them to stay with Michael until I got home, but she just left him. Anything could have happened."

At the fear in his eyes, I couldn't help but reach over to cover his hand with mine. "I'm so sorry."

"She had postpartum depression," he said. "I didn't know that until she wrote to me last Christmas, asking for forgiveness and to see Michael. There was a lot of back-and-forth between us for a few months before I asked Michael what he wanted to do."

"And he wanted to meet his mum." I lifted my hand off his and my palm still tingled from the touch.

"Aye." Haydyn dug into his pasta again.

"Did she explain where she'd been? Why it had taken so long?"

He nodded. "She'd started drinking to deal with her depression. She's been sober for two years."

"So she got sober, married a solicitor, and now she wants

to be in Michael's life because *she's* ready to be in his life."
Annoyance cut through me.

"Don't people deserve second chances?"

"Yes, but she also has to remember that it's just been you
and Michael for ten years, and she can't waltz in and start
making decisions without your consent."

Haydyn's gaze gleamed and that familiar spark of tension
lit between us. The one we'd both been trying so hard to
ignore. "I'm trying to play nice so she doesn't go after
custody."

I didn't want to worry him, but he needed to be realistic.
"Haydyn ... she's going to go after custody, eventually."

His expression tightened. "They always favor the mother."

"No, not true. They're not going to favor a mother who
abandoned her child for ten years. At the most, she'll get visita-
tion rights. So stop letting her get away with making decisions
without your involvement. Christmas is done. But she can't
get away with manipulating you and Michael like that.
Michael is the one who'll end up hurt. The next time she pulls
that crap, put your foot down. And if she threatens you with a
custody battle, you remind her of the ten years she abandoned
her child."

Haydyn sat back, watching me with an intense expression.
"As much as I admire your fierce protection of us ... I sense a
wee bit of reluctance to forgive."

"To forgive Deena? I've nothing to forgive. I'm just stating
my opinion." My cheeks flushed at the thought of him finding
me uncaring.

"No, I mean ..." He shrugged. "I don't know what I mean.
I suppose ... What's your story, Kenna? I've told you some of
mine. You've been working here for almost three months, and
I have no idea what really brought you here."

My pulse raced a bit as I prepared to tell Haydyn the truth.

"Kenna?" His brow furrowed in concern.

I licked my lips nervously, fighting back the grief that still threatened to choke me. "My parents died on Boxing Day last year. They'd visited me for Christmas in Inverness and were driving home to Aberdeen. An oncoming car took a hairpin bend on the wrong side of the road. My parents died on impact."

Emotion brightened Haydyn's eyes and he whispered, "I'm so sorry, Kenna."

I knew Haydyn's mum was still alive and that they visited her in his home village near Aberdeen, and I also knew Haydyn's dad had died, so he had some understanding of my pain.

My smile almost collapsed into tears as I explained, "Between their life insurance, pensions, the sale of their house ... they left me a fair bit of money. That's why I have the nice car ..."

"And is that why you moved to Ardnoch? To be closer to family?"

The thought of my cousin acting like real family made me snort bitterly. "No. My cousin ... I don't think I'll be staying with Una much longer. She's not the easiest flat mate, and I'm pretty certain she's stealing money from me."

Haydyn sucked in a breath. "Why didn't you say anything?"

I shrugged. "I'm handling it, looking for somewhere to rent until something appropriate comes up for sale."

His brows drew together. "I don't understand, then ... why move here?"

My pulse raced harder, my cheeks flushing. "Because ... because the mum at my last job ... she and I got friendly. As you do when you're looking after someone's child. Her husband worked a lot, and she's a full-time teacher. And her daughter could be hard work sometimes. I tried to be as supportive as possible. Plus, she was so kind to me when my mum and dad passed. She gave me time off and was always checking in to see how I was doing."

"Okay ..."

"One night, about five months after my parents passed, she asked me to stay later for a girls' night. Her husband was away for work. After we watched movies and had pizza, she put her daughter to bed ... I made to leave ... and she kissed me and grew arms and legs when I tried to push her off. I had to shove her off me."

Haydyn's eyebrows rose.

I laughed, embarrassed. "Everyone always expects it to be the dad." I got up and began clearing our now empty plates. Haydyn stood, too, and followed me into the kitchen.

"So what happened?" he asked, taking over the rinsing of the plates.

"She apologized. And I told her I didn't feel that way about her but that we could just forget about it. I assumed it was just a slip-up because of the wine."

"It wasn't?"

I leaned against the kitchen counter as Haydyn cleaned up. "She tried at first ... to forget. But about a month later, she told me she had to let me go. She was too embarrassed and I think afraid I'd tell her husband. She offered to give me a good reference in exchange for leaving quietly."

Haydyn stopped loading the dishwasher and straightened. "Wow."

"Between that and the fact that I was fresh in my grief, I came here for a change of scenery."

"Has it helped?"

I lowered my gaze. "I'm feeling things here I didn't think I would ever have space to feel again after losing my parents." I looked away. "But it hasn't been all roses. Una's an awful roommate, and my friends back in Inverness seem to have forgotten I exist. I have some family back in Aberdeen. Una's mum, an uncle... but they were pretty awful after my parents died because they expected an inheritance. Everything got left to me, and I've had a few texts and calls asking for money."

"I'm sorry."

I looked at him. "Money really brings out the worst in some folks."

He nodded and settled against the counter beside me, our arms brushing as he crossed his over his chest. "Can I tell you something very few people know?"

"Of course. I'm a vault." Pleasure filled me at the thought that Haydyn trusted me so much.

He stared out of the main picture window that captured the trees surrounding the drive up to the house, and I recognized the grief in his eyes. "My parents divorced when I was fourteen, and my parents agreed that I'd live with my dad most of the time. I spent the summers with my mum and they alternated the holidays ... but it was mostly Dad and me. I adored him." He gave me a pained smile. "About a year after Michael was born, with Deena gone, we were living with my dad so he could help out with his grandson. And ... he won the Euromillions Lottery."

Shock froze me.

That was not what I'd expected him to say.

Haydyn glanced at me. "We didn't tell anyone except his financial advisors, bank, etc. We went on a fancy cruise together with Michael, and Dad bought the car of his dreams but kept it at a garage where no one knew him."

"Because he knew everyone would come out of the woodwork looking for money?"

"Exactly. So ..." Grief tightened his expression. "When he died suddenly the next year, and he'd left every penny to me ... I decided not to tell anyone."

I gaped at him, everything making sense. "Why are you telling me?"

"So you know you're not alone. Keep your inheritance to yourself as much as possible, Kenna. Money does strange things to people, and you've already seen a glimmer of that. I mean, my mum doesn't know Dad won the Euromillions, but she knows he left me money. She makes snide wee comments now and then about how she spent years with him and got nothing ... even though I paid off her mortgage with my inheritance. Sometimes, for some people ... it's never enough."

I couldn't help myself. I reached out to curl my hand over his forearm. "I'm sorry, Haydyn. That you lost your dad too. He sounds like he was a good man." Tears spilled down my cheeks as I thought of my parents. My parents who I'd run every life decision past, who I still went on holidays with ... my parents had been my best friends and the two people in the world who made me a priority. Losing them was like losing a huge chunk of who I was. "I miss my mum and dad so much."

"Kenna." Haydyn turned and pulled me into his arms. His embrace was tight, comforting as I cried against his throat. "I've got you," he whispered hoarsely. "You're all right."

Three

HAYDYN

PRESENT DAY

The snow was sticking.

It coated the roofs of the quaint buildings on Castle Street, dusted car hoods, and sprinkled over fences and walls. Powdery whiteness lightly covered the cobblestones and pavements. The old-fashioned Victorian-style streetlights had come on, and it felt very much like we were just an hour's snowfall away from being in a Dickens novel.

Kenna drove away two minutes ago, and I was still staring after her. Yes, I'd been avoiding her, and yes, I should keep avoiding her ...

I glanced up at the sky, at the snowfall that looked nowhere close to stopping.

"Did you see the news?"

The male voice brought my gaze down, and I locked eyes with an older male villager. I shook my head. "Not yet."

He pointed upward. "This came out of nowhere, but they say it's going to snow from now until tomorrow evening. We'll be lucky if we can get out our front doors by the time it stops."

Shit.

"Just getting some more supplies for the wife before we shelter in for Christmas. Thankfully, our daughter and grand-kids arrived yesterday, or they'd never have made it up here."

I nodded at him as I strode toward my car. "Merry Christmas."

"To you too!" he called as I picked up my pace.

It was bad enough that this was my first Christmas without Michael in ten years and the house felt horribly lonely without him, but now I was about to do something I knew could break me.

Driving toward the caravan park where Kenna stayed, I cursed myself for going to her, even as I cursed myself for allowing her to stay in that damn caravan over the winter. Fear had kept my mouth shut. Fear of what I'd do if I let her close. And I had a right to worry about my actions after what happened on Halloween ...

THREE MONTHS earlier
Halloween

I'D ASKED Kenna to stay and watch a movie or two with me. The thought of sending her home after her crying jag didn't sit right. Moreover, it didn't seem like her flat with her cousin Una was much of a home.

It truly was an innocent suggestion. We settled on the couch, snacks on the coffee table, and she'd told me a bit more about her parents and how close she'd been to them. I could fully empathize. The hardest thing I'd ever done was hold myself together for Michael after my dad died. All I'd wanted to do was fall apart. But I couldn't.

Soon Kenna's spirits seemed lifted. As if merely by talking about her parents and letting it all out, a huge weight had eased from her. That made me feel good, and my guard lowered. We chose a comedy, and I loved the sound of Kenna's laugh. Anytime something funny happened, we both looked at each other as we chuckled to see if the other found it funny, happy to discover that we laughed at all the same parts and groaned at all the jokes we felt fell flat.

Afterward, reluctant to lose her, I suggested we watch another movie. It was getting late, but I intended to offer for Kenna to sleep in Michael's bed so she didn't have to drive home in the dark. Kenna agreed easily to another movie.

We didn't know what to watch, so we ended up picking a new psychological thriller that sounded good.

Unfortunately, it was an erotic thriller.

A very graphic erotic thriller.

I tried to ignore my reaction to the sex scenes and why my reactions were heightened by the beautiful, kind brunette at my side. But when I snuck a glance at her out of the corner of my eye and saw her breasts heaving with her shallow breaths, desire struck me hard.

Her fingers were curled on her knees, her cheeks rosy pink.

"Kenna," I half groaned, half whispered as the sexy moans and whimpers of the couple in the movie played in the background.

Kenna's gorgeous gaze flew to meet mine. Whatever she saw in my expression made her reach out with a trembling hand. She placed it on my thigh and slowly moved it up, caressing me. Blood thickened my cock and it strained to break free of my trousers. Her hand had almost reached my dick when I grabbed it tightly in mine.

All rational thought had fled south.

I tugged on her wrist, yanking her against me, heat flushing across my skin at the sound of her excited gasp. A noise I swallowed in my kiss as I slid my palm beneath her hair to grip her slender nape. My kiss was voracious, and she met it with equal ferocity.

The taste of her. Fuck, the taste of Kenna Smith was unbelievable. It was right.

Her fingers sank into my hair as her whole body melted into me, and I tugged her over so she straddled my lap.

Months of pent-up sexual tension, and this was the explosion.

My skin burned and my nerve endings sparked and I was desperate to be inside her. Kenna's fingers flexed in my hair as she moaned into my mouth. My arms tightened around her waist, drawing her closer. Her breasts crushed against me, the kiss changing from passionate to pure sex. It was suddenly biting and wet, our tongues tangling and licking and learning every inch of each other's mouths.

It wasn't enough.

I squeezed her perfect arse and pushed her down on my lap so my hard-on rubbed her directly between the legs, but there was too much fabric between us. She whimpered, rubbing harder, seeking the friction, riding me until our mouths parted in brief increments to catch our breaths.

With a growl of impatience, I tugged her thin sweater off and Kenna raised her arms, our movements hurried and frantic as I divested her of the top and then her lacy white bra. Her small, gorgeous tits bounced with the movement.

"So perfect," I murmured hoarsely, cupping and squeezing them gently. "So fucking perfect." I captured her right nipple with my hot mouth and she cried out in pleasure.

Lustful madness took control of me, and I pushed Kenna down onto the sofa. She watched with a fiery, low-lidded gaze as I whipped off my shirt and then unbuttoned her jeans. Her eyes lowered to my abs, and the way she licked her lips hungrily made me thankful for the many hours spent at the university gym. Yanking down her jeans and knickers, I threw them to the floor. The whole time I devoured the sight of her. Perfect olive skin. All slender curves and long fucking legs. Plump lips parted on excited pants. Eyes flared with arousal.

So beautiful. So beautiful I'd lost my mind.

I came down over her, our lips crashing together, her hard nipples brushing my naked chest, her thighs gripping my hips. I still wore my suit trousers and her kisses turned desperate as she reached for the button and zipper on them. She pushed them and boxer briefs down and slid her hand inside to grasp and tug my cock out.

"Fuck!" I groaned at the sensation of her tight grip. I was throbbing and hot and hard and I needed either her hand or pussy. Preferably her pussy.

"Jesus." I thrust into her palm as she pressed my mushroomed head against her clit. She released me to grip my waist, tilting her hips as I teased her with just the head. I kissed her hard, feeling her wet against my tip. Needing her tight heat, I slid my cock to her entrance and began to push inside.

She grasped my buttocks, fingers biting as she moaned, "Haydyn, yes, please, fuck me."

Something about her saying my name cut through my fog. I froze, staring down at her flushed face and impassioned expression.

Hours ago I'd held her in my arms while she cried, grieving for her parents.

Kenna was vulnerable.

My son's nanny.

And I was about to fuck her. Bare.

Shit.

Her eyes widened. "Haydyn?"

I scrambled off her, horrified by my selfishness. I yanked up my boxers and trousers and dove to pick up her jeans. "Kenna, we can't."

I didn't get a chance to explain why I'd stopped. Kenna had jumped off the couch, hauled on her knickers and jeans, red-faced and angry. She'd stormed out, ignoring my pleading calls of her name.

MY SKIN BURNED from the memory of that night as I pulled my SUV into the caravan site. Driving slowly past the caravans, I stopped at the sight of Kenna's Audi. It sat beside a static home. It was at least in the back row, farther from the water and tucked in between two other caravans. But it looked like no one else was on site, and the snow was sticking here too.

The next time I saw Kenna after that Halloween, I tried to broach the subject of what happened between us, but she said she just wanted to forget about it. And I was afraid to lose her from our lives, so I didn't mention it again. It stung that she'd decided she didn't want me after all, even though I knew it was for the best, so I'd avoided her.

Shrugging off all the reasons I shouldn't be here, I concentrated on all the reasons I should. There was no way Kenna should be living in a caravan during a snowstorm and no way she should be alone on her first Christmas without her parents.

Slamming out of the car, I hurried toward the narrow steps and didn't even make it to the door before it opened. Kenna stood there, still wearing her coat and shoes. A frown marred her pretty brow.

"You followed me?" she huffed.

"Grab your things."

Her eyes grew adorably round. "Excuse me?"

Impatience rode me. "Grab your things and get in the car. There's no way in hell I'm letting you stay in this caravan during a snowstorm."

She raised an eyebrow. "*Letting* me?"

Four
KENNA

J ust because he'd been bossy and domineering, I gave
Haydyn the silent treatment as we drove to his place. It was
childish. The truth was, though, my emotions were already
heightened because of the time of year, and I was frustrated that
I actually did need to be "rescued" by my boss. Staying in the
caravan was silly, and possibly dangerous, in a snowstorm, so
when I saw his car pull up I'd already decided that if he asked
me to stay at his, I would. No matter the consequences.

But he didn't ask. He demanded.

Instead of parking out on the driveway, Haydyn reversed
his car into the garage he only used during inclement weather.
As soon as he cut the engine, he turned to me. "I'm sorry."

I reluctantly looked at him.

His dark eyes filled with remorse and concern. "I'm sorry I
made you feel like you had to lie to me about your plans. And
I'm sorry for being a belligerent bastard about it. It bothers me
that you were going to stay out there alone. It bothers me
you're out there alone, period."

My heart beat fast. What did that mean? Obviously, he

cared about me. But was that it? Was that why he threw himself off me on Halloween, as if he was disgusted? I tried to find my voice. "It's temporary."

Haydyn nodded with a heavy sigh. "Let's get in the house."

The garage was attached, so we didn't need to trudge back out into the snow. Haydyn let us in through the side door and I followed him into the warmth of the house. "You can sleep in Michael's room."

His words reminded me that he was all alone today too. He'd apologized for his attitude, so I decided to forgive him and put it aside. "How are you doing? With Michael at his mum's for Christmas?"

Haydyn shrugged out of his coat and scarf. "Honestly, it only hit me when I woke up this morning and he wasn't here. On Christmas Eve, we have our traditions. In the morning, I make chocolate chip pancakes and we watch *Rise of the Guardians*. Then we venture into the village, grab hot chocolate from Flora's, walk around for a bit, and then come home, have homemade chicken burgers and fries, and watch a marathon of Christmas movies until bedtime. Then I wait until he's asleep to bring out his gifts hidden in the locked closet in my bedroom. It's always been exciting for me too."

His expression was unbearably sad as he took my coat and scarf to hang up. "It's depressing knowing I won't be doing that tonight for the first time in ten years."

Sympathy ached in my chest. "It's just one year," I promised him.

Haydyn scrubbed a hand down his face. "Is it, though? And even then, I suppose this gives me a taste of what it'll be like in a few years when he's too old for this stuff. He already told me this year that Santa isn't real."

"Oh, he told me that too." I strode toward the kitchen.

"And I could see the hopeful, pleading glint in his eyes practically begging me to tell him different."

"Really?"

I turned at the smile in Haydyn's voice. "Aye. Really."

"What did you tell him?" He watched me curiously as I pulled a pan out of the cupboard and set it on the hob.

"I didn't want to outright lie, so I just shrugged nonchalantly and said, 'I wonder how Santa would feel about you saying that?' and left it at that."

He chuckled. "Nicely maneuvered."

"My point is," I continued as I pulled a bar of chocolate and milk out of the fridge, "Michael is still a boy, and you still have plenty of time with him."

"Hmm." Haydyn leaned against the kitchen island, arms crossed, the position straining the fine knit of his cashmere sweater around his biceps. "What are you making?" I glanced back at the hob as I dropped the chopped-up chocolate into a pan and then poured in milk, cocoa, and light brown sugar.

"Homemade hot chocolate." I glanced over my shoulder. "I thought we could keep some of your traditions alive. And it's snowing, so hot chocolate is a must."

His gaze searched my face almost tenderly. "I'm glad you're here."

Skin hot, I turned back to the hob. I was so confused. Haydyn had attempted to talk to me about Halloween, but I didn't want him to say to my face that he wasn't interested because I wasn't sure I could take it. Usually, I wasn't so fragile, but with Mum and Dad on my mind, that big gaping hole in my heart, I couldn't handle emotions as well as I usually could. And the truth was, I'd fallen in love with my boss. I'd fallen in love with both him and Michael. For months I'd been trying to convince myself that I was just lonely and latching on to the first people who came along who seemed like family.

However, even desperation couldn't fabricate the chemistry I had with Haydyn. It just *was*. I'd never wanted anyone the way I wanted him. I'd lost all sense of everything else but him that night on his couch.

I thought his springing off me like he was horrified meant he didn't feel the same way and had just gotten turned on by the movie we were watching. But now and then, I find him staring at me with his heart in his eyes, and it confused me ... because ... he stared at me like he might feel the same way back.

Sighing inwardly, I stirred the mixture until it melted and then I whisked it. Haydyn reached into the cupboard and pulled two mugs down. "Whipped cream?" I asked him.

He retrieved the can of fresh whipped cream from the fridge while I poured the hot chocolate into the mugs. Our fingers brushed as I took the can from him, and tingles shot up my arm. I expertly topped the mugs with whipped cream and then shaved chocolate over the top.

Handing one to Haydyn, I smiled but couldn't quite meet his eyes. "Happy Christmas Eve."

"Happy Christmas Eve, Kenna."

I shivered at the way his voice rumbled around my name and hastily took a drink.

Haydyn followed suit, his eyes widening. "This is delicious."

"Thanks. It was my mum's recipe." Rounding him, I made my way over to the sofa and tucked myself into the corner, getting comfy. The Christmas tree I'd helped Michael and Haydyn decorate stood in the corner. Fairy lights glowed around the edges of the large picture window. Snow fell outside, weighing down the trees and covering the empty driveway. It was a winter wonderland. So peaceful.

I sensed Haydyn taking a seat on the couch a little farther down. We sat in perfect silence, watching the snowfall, and it was ... lovely. Comfortable and lovely. For a while, I forgot to be sad about Mum and Dad.

When I was finished with my hot chocolate, I turned to Haydyn and found him watching me. I raised a questioning eyebrow.

"Are you okay? I know it's the first anniversary of your parents' passing in a few days."

Pain cut through the loveliness. "Do you want the honest answer?"

"Of course."

"I don't think I'll ever be okay. I think some years it'll hurt worse than others ... but losing them will always be with me because when I lost them, I lost a piece of myself. But I think we can be not okay about one thing and still find happiness in another." I gestured to the snow outside. "Hot chocolate on a perfect snowy day ... it's not too shabby."

When I looked back at Haydyn, he stared at me in awe. "Your parents would be so proud of you, Kenna. And I'm ... I'm so grateful that someone like you is in Michael's life."

What about your life? I felt like asking. *Are you grateful for me too?* Yet, I didn't want to ruin the moment with a possible truth that might hurt.

"Let's watch a Christmas movie," I blurted out.

Haydyn gave me a soft smile that was far too sexy for my own good. "Sure. You pick. I'll grab some snacks. What do you want to drink? I have a bottle of Laurent Perrier I got from my Secret Santa at work."

Alcohol plus Haydyn. Hmm. Dangerous territory. Still, champagne was my Achilles' heel. "Ooh, someone splashed out for Secret Santa."

"We had a fifty-pound budget," he explained.

"And someone at that uni knows how you spend fifty quid."

He chuckled as he stood and took my empty mug. "A glass of champagne it is, then."

FIVE
KENNA

The champagne was a bad idea. Not because I got drunk. But because the bubbly alcohol loosened me up. And when I loosened up, I suddenly thought it was a very good idea to seek out the truth and to speak it.

We'd been having a lovely afternoon and evening, considering we were both missing Michael, and I missed my parents. There was no need for dinner because we'd been munching on snacks throughout the day. Though I'd been nursing each glass of champagne, I was now on my fourth because Haydyn preferred wine to champagne, so the entire bottle was mine.

It's a Wonderful Life played on the television, and I partly blamed the movie for making me philosophical. Truthfully, Jimmy Stewart made me question why I wasn't forcing a confrontation with Haydyn. If I had feelings for him, why was I sitting on them? So what if he didn't return them? If I didn't speak up, we would never be together. And what if we were meant to be? What if Haydyn and Michael were my future and I let them slip through my fingers because I couldn't be honest? All these questions seemed perfectly acceptable in my tipsy brain.

I waited until the movie finished because Haydyn was enjoying it.

"They don't make actors like Jimmy Stewart now," he observed as the film ended.

"Nor Katharine Hepburn. Or Lauren Bacall."

He grinned at me. "That was when movie stars were movie *stars*."

"Hmm," I agreed. *Just do it. Just say it.* I took a breath. "Why did you stop us on Halloween?"

Haydyn blinked rapidly, clearly taken aback by my question. "Uh ..."

I turned to face him fully, encouraged by Jimmy Stewart and too much champagne. "Well?"

His gaze seared into mine. "Because you were grieving. And I didn't want to take advantage."

My lips parted in shock. That was not what I'd expected. "You weren't taking advantage. I knew what I was doing. I'm a grown woman, not some girl just out of school."

Haydyn grimaced. "Grief ... it can skew our feelings and emotions."

"So you stopped because you thought you were taking advantage of me at a vulnerable time?"

"That ... and you're my son's nanny. He cares about you, and I don't want to jeopardize that just because you're attractive and I haven't gotten ..." He trailed off, blanching.

Oh.

My stomach dropped in horror.

"Because I'd be a convenient fuck," I muttered, looking away as hurt flared hot and blinding.

"Kenna, no," he denied. "I didn't mean that at all."

"No." I couldn't look at him but my tone was soft, accepting. "It's fine. I get it. You're being a good dad. Michael ... Michael should always come first. And I wouldn't want to jeopardize my job if I'm just a convenient fuck to you. That's smart. You were thinking rationally. Thank you."

"Kenna—"

"I need a shower." I stood abruptly. "Do you mind if I use Michael's bathroom? Yes? Okay." I strode out before he could stop me and practically dove into Michael's room.

Of course, it was only physical for Haydyn. Why would he want me for anything more? None of my friends and family seemed to think I was worth remembering, so obviously I lacked that quintessential something that made people care.

My fingers trembled as I stripped off my shirt and jeans. It was true, then. When my parents died, I lost the last two people on earth who really loved me.

The thought was terrifying. I blinked past the tears, suddenly wishing I could jump in my car and keep driving. I was lost. Staying in one place I was lost, so I might as well be lost on the move, right?

The door to Michael's bedroom suddenly flew open and my heart sped up even faster with surprise as Haydyn strode inside. His nostrils flared at the sight of me standing in nothing but my red lace bra and green knickers. I'd considered the combination festive and hadn't thought anyone else would see them.

His gaze dipped between my legs, and my clit pulsed in response.

"Haydyn?" I whispered.

His hot gaze drank in every inch of me.

"If I was just looking for a convenient fuck, I'd go out and find a woman. You were never just a convenient fuck." Whatever he saw on my face made his eyes glimmer with tenderness. "This whole time, I've been worried what people would think if you and I got together. The other parents, the villagers. If it would subject Michael to gossip. But Thane Adair's children seem perfectly happy, don't they?"

Knowing he referred to Lewis Adair's father who married his nanny, I nodded, heart in my throat with hope I was scared to embrace.

"Why shouldn't we have what we want? We're grown-ups. And .... and I hate the idea that you think all I see when I look at you is an attractive woman. Every time I'm with you, nothing feels more real than our connection. It's not just physical attraction, Kenna. Though I've never wanted anyone as much as I want you. The last few months have been absolute torture." He gestured ruefully to his crotch.

Blood rushed in my ears at his declaration, my gaze falling to see his jeans straining with his erection. Oh my God. My skin flushed from head to toe, and my breasts suddenly felt heavy with need.

"In fact," Haydyn continued hoarsely, "I can't think straight. I feel like I'm coming out of my fucking skin ... and ..." He took a step toward me, hunger etched in his features. "That if I don't have you in every way a man can have a woman, I'll never be truly happy again."

Wow.

"Haydyn—"

His eyes flashed. "I want to hear you say my name as we make love."

Yes, please.

"Haydyn—"

"But first, I want to hear you say my name as we fuck."

I moaned. Because YES, PLEASE.

Then he rushed me. Our bodies collided seconds before our mouths did.

Haydyn's kiss was ravaging. It was a man's kiss. Dark, deep, and sexual.

His hand fisted in my hair as he held me, and I grasped on to him as he plundered my mouth. I whimpered against his tongue as his other hand gripped my arse to pull me into the erection straining the zipper of his jeans. The whimper turned to a moan, reverberating into his mouth. Haydyn ground his hips harder into me, squeezing my arse. I slid my hands under his sweater in answer, shivering at the delicious feel of his smooth, hot skin beneath my fingertips.

He groaned as I touched his nipples. The sound rumbled in my mouth as we kissed harder, messy, sexy, wild kisses I'd never experienced before in my life.

I needed him inside me.

Fumbling for the button on his jeans, I silently told him as much.

Then suddenly, I was in Haydyn's arms for a few seconds before finding myself on the bed, Haydyn covering my body as we tugged at each other's clothing. Well, he tugged at my underwear. Haydyn broke our kiss to unclip my bra with a deftness of touch that told me he was well experienced in unclipping bras. He took hold of it and ripped it away from me, throwing it over his shoulder. His fiery eyes devoured my naked breasts.

"One day—before Halloween—I came home early from work," he said as his hips undulated against me with a mind of their own. "You were helping Michael with a science experiment for school."

Bemused, I asked, "The potato osmosis lab?"

"Aye. For some reason it involved water and Michael was being a typical kid and splashing tap water everywhere. He drenched you. I could see your nipples, see your shape." He cupped me, squeezing my breast, and I pushed my hips into his undulations. Haydyn's hungry gaze moved to mine. "I had to hide in my room from you like a teenager because I was hard."

"Really?" I'd never have known. I remembered him being a wee bit brusque that afternoon but I hadn't known why.

He nodded. "That night was the first night of many I

showered with my hand wrapped around my dick, fantasizing about fucking you."

Wet slickened between my legs. "Haydyn."

He caressed me, plucking at my nipples as they tightened into hard points. "I lost interest in dating other women. I couldn't be with anyone else when all I could think about was you. And all the ways I wanted to make you mine."

"Do it," I begged, my mind a haze of lust. "Haydyn, please. I want you too. So badly."

His answer was a triumphant, plundering kiss.

I frantically pulled off his shirt, breaking the kiss to do it, wanting to explore his beautiful body ... but then he bent his head to my breasts, sucking a nipple deep into his mouth, and I forgot about everything but what he was doing to me.

I cried out, arching against him.

His long fingers curled around my underwear, and he tugged them down my thighs. They got caught around my ankles, and I kicked to get them off. My patience was obliterated. "I need you, Haydyn. I need you so much."

"Fuck," he murmured, his eyes wild with want. "I could only dream you felt the same way." He kissed me again, slow, languorous, torturing me with pleasure.

In answer, I fumbled for his zipper. As I slid my hand inside his boxers to feel his throbbing, hard heat, he slipped his hand between my legs, sliding his fingers into me. The wet he found there made him groan into my mouth. He tore his lips from mine, and my chest rose and fell in frenzied breaths as he stared into my eyes with a tenderness that filled me with certainty.

"You're beyond ready, sweetheart." His expression turned harsh with need, and he gently captured the hand I had wrapped around him and removed it. He pinned my hand to the bed.

Anticipation made me squirm beneath him. Haydyn

never broke eye contact as he shoved down his jeans and boxers just far enough to release himself.

Then he captured my other hand and held me down by the wrists. My panting filled the room, and I let my legs fall open wide as he nudged against me.

He pushed into me with a long, relieved groan.

My desire eased his way considerably, and that overwhelming fullness I'd been desperate for caused a pleasure pain to zing down my spine.

"More," I begged.

"Fuck, Kenna," he growled, his head bowing into my neck as he pumped into me.

I was mindless with want for him. My whole being, existence, became about Haydyn and the hot push and pull of him inside me. My hips rose to meet his hard thrusts, my cries and his groans filling the room.

He was surprisingly dominant, and it turned me the fuck on. I knew I was going to come quickly. The tension inside me tightened, tightened, tightened every time he pulled out and slammed back in.

"I'm close," I gasped because I'd never come with just penetration. "Haydyn, I'm going to come."

He released one of my hands to grab my thigh and pulled it up against his hip, changing the angle of his thrust. I reached for him blindly as the tension inside me shattered.

"Haydyn!" I cried out. Loudly. Disbelieving. Euphoric.

My orgasm rolled through me, my inner muscles rippling and squeezing around Haydyn. His hips pounded faster and then momentarily stilled before he cried out my name, his grip on my thigh bruising as his hips jerked with the swell and throb of his release.

As his climax shuddered through him, he let go of my thigh and slumped over me. Haydyn's warm, heavy weight surrounded me, and I slid my hands across his back.

Our labored breathing rasped in my ears.

My heart pounded.

Haydyn and I had finally given in to our attraction.

I'd just had the best sex of my life and it might even mean something much deeper than that.

But we'd also just had sex without a condom and Haydyn had come inside me.

Six

HAYDYN

Kenna lay soft and warm in my arms. I woke up about half an hour ago, but she was still asleep.

After we'd first fallen over each other like horny teens, so clouded by lust we'd forgotten protection, I'd made sure to don some when I took Kenna into my room to make love to her. She made me laugh as I carried her out of Michael's room, anxious about throwing his bedcovers in the laundry all the while assuring me she thought she wasn't in the right place in her cycle and we should be okay.

Despite what I'd said to her, there was still a part of me worried that I was going to be the one who got my heart broken. That Kenna was still grieving and looking for a place to latch on to in her grief. That when she finally started to heal, she'd realize that and leave us.

But seeing her look so hurt thinking I only wanted her body, I couldn't let it stand. I couldn't bear to see her in pain.

And I wanted her so badly.

So I gave in.

Even as worries spun in my head about how this would

affect Michael, I couldn't deny how perfect she felt in my arms.

Brushing her hair off her neck, I trailed light kisses over her soft skin. She squirmed in her sleep, undulating her perfect arse against my cock.

Jesus, she was turning me into a teenage boy.

Reaching back for the nightstand, I grabbed protection and suited up. Then I set about waking Kenna with my fingers. Hot blood thickened my cock from semi to full mast in an instant at the feel of her warmth. I found her clit and circled it.

Kenna moaned, her eyes fluttering open. It took her a second to get her bearings. She glanced over her shoulder and her expression softened at the same time her lips parted on an excited gasp. "Haydyn?"

"Happy Christmas, sweetheart."

"Happy," she moaned, her fingers tightening around the pillow beneath her head. "C-Christmas. Ahhh, Haydyn."

Feeling her grow wet, I couldn't wait any longer. I gripped her hips and nudged her legs open. Finding her, I surged inside, squeezing my eyes closed at the perfection of her snug heat around my cock.

Our groans and cries filled the bedroom as I gently made love to her.

We came together. "Kenna," I groaned, shuddering against her as I trailed my mouth down her shoulder. "You're so perfect."

"That was certainly the perfect way to wake up." She giggled, and the sound filled me with a strange mix of happiness and desperation.

I didn't want to lose her.

Not yet.

Thus, I wasn't going to push the subject. We'd just enjoy

each other today. We'd help each other forget about the people we were missing.

Just as I returned from the bathroom after cleaning up, my phone rang on the bedside table. "It's Michael," I told Kenna as she sat up in bed.

She smiled but bit her lip shyly, making me want to kiss her. Instead, I grabbed my phone, eager to hear my son's voice.

"Happy Christmas, Michael," I answered.

"Dad! Happy Christmas!" He sounded excited and a pang of longing hit me. "I can't wait to come home and open my presents!"

I'd told him Santa would drop off his presents from me here at the house so I could still experience a bit of Christmas with him when Deena brought him home tomorrow.

"Did Santa bring you cool stuff at your mum's?"

"You can stop with the Santa stuff. Jim told me he's not real."

Anger tightened my throat and I choked out, "Jim told you Santa isn't real?"

I heard Kenna suck in a breath and looked at her. She glowered ferociously and mouthed "Fucking asshole" and I think I fell just a wee bit more in love with her.

"I'm ten, Dad, nearly eleven. I kind of already knew."

"Well, Santa doesn't visit people who don't believe in him, so that's probably why Jim thinks he doesn't exist."

"Dad." Michael laughed. "You don't have to pretend. Okay?"

I wanted to fucking kill Jim. It was bad enough Michael was growing up so fast ... did we as adults have to force them out of childhood? When I was a kid, there was nothing more magical than believing in Santa. Yes, it was heartbreaking when I discovered he wasn't real, but I wouldn't trade it for how bloody magical those eleven years of my life were when I still believed in him.

Changing the subject, I asked him what they were up to. Michael chatted away about the new phone Deena had bought him and games for his games console. Then he got quiet and asked, "Can I stay at home for Christmas next year?"

My heart lurched. "Why? Are you okay?"

"Yeah, yeah, it's fine. I just ... I like our traditions better. And I thought maybe I could just stay with Mum one weekend a month instead of at Christmas."

I smiled as I sat down on the bed. "We'll figure something out. But if you want to spend your Christmases at home from now on, you can."

A soft palm pressed against my back and I turned to see Kenna smiling at me. She slid her hand around my shoulders as she moved to press a kiss on my nape. The move made her naked breasts press against my back and arousal rose in me again.

Terrible timing.

"Do you think it's okay if I call Kenna?" Michael suddenly asked.

I stiffened, and Kenna felt it. "Uh, of course you should call Kenna. I'm sure she'd love to hear from you."

Kenna pulled back, eyes wide. And then she was scrambling out of bed. If she wasn't so fucking gorgeous, it would've been funny to watch her hurry naked from the room, presumably to get dressed and find her phone.

"Okay, I'll call her next."

"You do that. I love you, son. I can't wait to see you tomorrow."

"Love you, Dad. Bye!"

Less than a minute after I hung up, I heard Kenna's phone blaring and then her sweet voice answering, "Happy Christmas, Michael!"

My heart beat a wee bit faster. Because I wanted her to say

that to my boy. I wanted to hear her say it to him every year. But could I trust that's what she wanted?

———

I PUT my worries aside for the day. Instead, I enjoyed Christmas with Kenna. She talked me out of calling Deena and giving her an earful for letting Jim tell our son Santa wasn't real. We made breakfast together, and I tried to shrug off my annoyance. Kenna was playful and flirty in the kitchen, so that helped take my mind off it.

After breakfast, we sat down by the tree and opened our gifts to each other. Kenna had left the presents under the tree before Michael had departed for his mum's and she'd, thankfully, forgotten to take the gifts we'd bought her home.

She'd clearly snuck a look at my toiletries because she gifted me a bottle of my favorite aftershave, as well as a bottle of my favorite (and too expensive wine). "You shouldn't have," I murmured against her lips. "Thank you."

Kenna kissed me long and deep. When she pulled back, she whispered, "Someone needs to spoil you."

It was on the tip of my tongue to beg her never to leave. I cleared my throat and handed her the gift from me. It was a designer cashmere scarf I thought would suit her coloring. She smoothed her hands over it and oohed and aahed, like I'd given her the world.

Then I handed her the gift from Michael.

Her lips parted as she unwrapped it to discover the blue box with Tiffany & Co. on the front. It was an extravagant gift and one I thought would look better coming from Michael. "Haydyn," she whispered, tears filling her eyes as she opened the box to reveal the black velvet interior. Nestled on the velvet was a delicate 18K rose-gold necklace with two interlocking circles accented with carved Roman numerals.

"The girl in the shop said the necklace is part of a collection about taking time into your own hands and treasuring what matters most. The circles reminded me of your parents too. I thought it—Michael thought it was something you could wear to remember them."

Tears spilled down Kenna's cheeks as she stared at me as if she might feel the same way about me. "This is all you, isn't it?"

I shrugged. "It's from us both."

"It's the most beautiful gift anyone has ever given me. Thank you." Her fingers trembled as she took the necklace out of the box. "Can you help me put it on?"

I nodded, taking the necklace. Kenna turned, swiping her hair out of the way, and I gently fixed it around her neck.

When she turned, her palm covered the circles. "You're the most thoughtful man I've ever known, Haydyn Barr."

My heart hammered in my chest. "You bring it out in me."

Kenna's answer was to throw her arms around me and kiss me like there was no tomorrow. So I lowered her to the floor and made love to her like I might never get the chance to again.

SEVEN

HAYDYN

The next day, knowing it was the anniversary of Kenna's parents' death, I was watchful and perhaps a wee bit too much of a hoverer.

We spent a wonderful Christmas Day together, one that could've only been better if Michael had been with us. However, at night, we played in my bed, and we could be as loud as we wanted, which was phenomenal.

My first thought on Boxing Day was of Kenna, however, and I was disconcerted to realize she wasn't in the bed beside me. She was already up and dressed and making breakfast for us. She assured me she was okay, but there was a deep sadness in her eyes that I wished like hell I could take away.

It was an awful feeling of powerlessness to know that I couldn't.

The snow stopped overnight, and in typical Scottish fashion, the temperature had risen to a point that it was already melting. I'd just suggested we go for a drive to get out of the house for a bit when my phone rang.

It was Deena.

She wanted me to collect Michael.

"I thought you were dropping him off," I said, irritated on multiple levels.

"I can't. Sorry."

I hung up and explained to Kenna. I felt shit for leaving her. "Why don't you come with me?"

"No." She shook her head. "I'm not in the mood to see Deena, sorry."

"No, of course. I understand."

"I ... I should leave. Michael won't understand why I'm here."

"No!" I said louder than I meant. Kenna raised an eyebrow. I smiled apologetically. "Please, stay. I'll tell Michael I invited you over for Boxing Day."

"Oh. Won't ... will that not confuse him?"

Studying her, I realized she was asking more than just that question. She was asking me what we were and where we went from here.

Did I trust Kenna to know what she wanted when she was still grieving her family?

When she was in my arms ... the way she looked at me ... I didn't want to doubt that. But I had more than myself to think of. "We'll, uh ... we'll talk about that after, yeah."

Her expression dimmed, and I hated that I had to leave her. I pressed a hard kiss to her mouth. "I'll be back soon."

Kenna nodded, but I saw insecurity flicker in her gaze.

Damn it.

I'd need to make a decision and make it soon. I wouldn't be one more person who hurt this woman. It was difficult when I had my son to think of.

MICHAEL RAN straight into the house, calling Kenna's name.

Hearing the crack in his shout, I closed my eyes in a tight

press, curling my hands around the steering wheel. I had to get a handle on my anger. I couldn't let my son see it.

Two hours ago, he had his mum back in his life and he was sweet and forgiving and excited about it.

Now ...

The conversation I'd had with Deena just a little over an hour ago played around and around in my mind.

"We need to talk," my ex had said as soon as I stepped into her townhome. It was in a nice area of Inverness and while the house was narrow, it had three floors and was luxuriously appointed.

"Where's Michael?" I was already agitated that I'd had to leave Kenna when Deena was supposed to be driving my son home to me, and now this.

"Upstairs. In here."

I followed Deena into an office. "What's going on? Did something happen to Michael?"

"No." She leaned against the desk, nibbling nervously on her lower lip. She wouldn't meet my eyes. "Jim got offered a new job, and we can't turn it down."

"Okay?" I frowned.

"It's in London."

Fear scored through me. If she thought for one second I'd agree to Michael living with her that far away ... I imagined a horrible custody battle ahead and what that would do to my son. "Deena—"

"Look." She held up a hand, still not meeting my gaze. "Before you worry about me trying to take Michael with me, that's not happening."

Why did that make me feel even fucking worse? "So ... you're just going to leave him?"

Her cheeks reddened, and she finally looked at me before glancing away in shame. "This is a big opportunity for Jim, and we've talked about it and we know we won't have time to give Michael the attention he needs."

I hated this woman. At that moment, I truly hated her. "So, to be clear, after begging to have Michael back in your life, you're walking right back out again?"

She pushed off the desk, tone pleading. "We'd love to have him at Christmas every other year."

"No."

Deena flinched like I'd hit her. "What do you mean no?"

Seething, I hissed, "You do not get to play with my son like he's a fucking toy. You're in or you're out. If you leave for London, you don't get to see Michael again. If, when he's eighteen, he decides he wants you back in his life, that's his choice. But right now, it's my choice to protect him from his selfish mother."

Tears glittered in her eyes. "I knew you wouldn't understand."

"Oh, I understand, Deena. I understand that you want Michael on your terms and that's not what parenting is. You are a terrible mother, and I will never let myself forget that again."

Her tears spilled over. "And if I said I'd fight for custody after all?"

I huffed, no longer afraid of that threat. "I might actually have some respect for you if you tried, but one, I have a feeling your husband doesn't want a child around full time. Two, I don't think you could handle sitting in a courtroom being reminded that you abandoned your child. And three, thanks to my father, I now have more money than God, and you can bet your selfish arse that I will use every fucking penny to keep you out of Michael's life."

Deena swiped at her tears, angry defensiveness burning in her gaze. "I would have thought some time with me was better than nothing."

She didn't get it. "Deena, you abandoned him when he was a baby and he gave you a second chance without even blinking. Because he is so desperate for his mum to love him. And now you're going to tell him that you're leaving him again and you only have time for him every other Christmas? Do you not realize how much that's going to hurt him? Or do you just not care?"

She flinched again. "I ... I don't want to hurt him, but ... I didn't realize Jim would be so against having a kid when I wrote you that email last year."

"And Jim is more important than Michael?"

Deena's answer was silence.

To make it worse, she refused to tell Michael herself, and I had to tell him while we were driving home. He called Deena because he didn't want to believe me, and she reluctantly confirmed that she was leaving for London. That they wouldn't see each other for a while.

Michael had sobbed on the phone, telling her he hated her before he hung up. Then he cried and raged about it being Jim's fault. That Jim didn't like him. I hated my son had felt that from the bastard. Grief thickened my throat, and I'd had to pull the car onto the side of the road to comfort him. He fought me, wanting to be angry at everyone, before he finally collapsed against me in tears.

My own tears had slipped free, and all the old hurt and rage I'd felt toward my ex resurfaced. Yet I was angry at myself, too, for letting her back into Michael's life to do this.

The rest of the car ride home I tried to talk to my son, but he wasn't up for conversation. I'd told him Kenna was at the house and as soon as we'd arrived, he rushed out to her for comfort.

Controlling my emotions, I got out and strode into the house. I heard murmuring from Michael's bedroom, so I followed the sound and stopped in the doorway.

Kenna laid on Michael's bed and he was snuggled into her side. She stroked his hair and whispered soothing words. Her eyes met mine, and I saw the flash of rage in them before they filled with sad concern.

"I'm okay," I mouthed.

"You'll never leave us, Kenna, will you?" Michael cried, sounding so much younger than his years. "You'll never leave us."

Was it wrong that I wanted her to say she wouldn't? That I wanted her bound to us.

She searched my face and whatever she saw there made her expression soften with awe. Then, "I'll stay as long as you want me to," she promised.

And I knew then I trusted her. If not with my heart, I trusted her with Michael's. She'd never make that promise if she had even the tiniest bit of doubt.

Relief and joy cut through my anger, and I sank against the doorframe. "That would be forever, then."

Kenna sucked in a breath. "Really?"

Michael burrowed deeper into her. "Really," he and I said in unison.

That was the magic of Kenna Smith. She could take a traumatizing, sad day and uplift it with just her presence, like the sun through clouds. Even on a day that was painful for her too.

What had we done to deserve someone like her? Whatever it was, I wasn't looking a gift horse in the mouth.

"Forever," I repeated.

Kenna smirked. "Forever is a long time."

I grinned, more than happy at the thought of coming home every day for the rest of my life to this woman. "It goes by fast when the company's exceptional."

Epilogue

KENNA

FOUR YEARS LATER

"Mummy, can we get a cat?" Willow asked from the child's play desk that sat in the corner of the living room. I noted the cat she was drawing as she watched an animation with singing felines.

"Perhaps when you're older," I hedged. Haydyn had bad pet allergies, so it was doubtful, but I was in the middle of cooking dinner and I didn't want to deal with my precocious three-year-old having a meltdown.

"Ask Santa," she pushed.

"I did. He said maybe when you're older."

Willow narrowed her eyes in suspicion and I almost cursed us for giving birth to such an intelligent child.

Thankfully, the perfect distraction was riding his bike up the driveway. This year, Haydyn had finally allowed Michael to ride his bike back and forth to school. I'd been nervous about it, but we'd agreed to give him that independence. The winter months bothered me the most, so we'd agreed he couldn't ride his bike during the short winter days and I drove him to and from school.

The schools just finished for Christmas break yesterday, though, and I'd given Michael permission to ride into the village to see his friends, as long as he came home before it started to get dark.

He'd only left an hour ago, so I was surprised to see him so soon. "Look, there's your brother."

Joy flooded Willow's little face, and she threw herself away from her desk with all the exuberance of a puppy, her brown curls dancing around her chubby cheeks as she rushed across the room. My heart ached at the cute sight of her bouncing on the balls of her feet, her hands clasped as she waited for her big brother.

There was no one Willow adored more than Michael.

Worry flickered through me, however, at the sight of Michael jumping off his bike and throwing it into the grass by the side of the house. He marched up the drive, disappearing from sight, but not before I caught a glimpse of the thundercloud that marred his expression.

He burst through the front door.

"Mikey!" Willow rushed him.

"Not now, Wills," he snapped impatiently and practically ran through the house without looking at me.

His bedroom door slammed.

And his baby sister burst into wailing tears.

Switching off the hob to see to her, I'd barely rounded the island when I heard my stepson's footsteps. He hurried back into the living room and swooped Willow into his arms, expression filled with regret. "I'm sorry, Wills." She hugged her big brother tightly, needing his reassurance. "Just in a bad mood. Ignore me, eh. Shh, Wills. I'm sorry. Let me make it up to you. Do you want to watch *Rise of the Guardians*?"

Willow sniffled and lifted her head from his shoulder. She wiped a chubby hand over her runny nose. "Yes, please."

Michael had sprouted in the past three months and was only a few inches shy of six feet now. Willow looked tiny in his arms as he hugged her close and carried her over to the sofa.

Pride filled me. I didn't know what had happened to put him in a bad mood, but I knew what it was like to be a teenager. To have my hormones all over the place and feel like I had little control over my emotions. The fact that Michael prioritized his baby sister over his mood spoke volumes about the kind of man he was growing into.

Just like his father.

I let Michael reassure his sister, let them watch the movie together, and didn't push to know the details of his bad day. I'd wait until Willow was asleep.

Haydyn returned home in time for dinner, and Michael, though quiet, still conversed with us. My husband, ever the observant father, noticed, however, and I managed to murmur the story of Michael's stormy return home to him while we cleaned up the kitchen.

"I'll talk to him," Haydyn had assured.

Later, after I'd read Willow's favorite book to her two and a half times (she drifted off during the third reading), I wandered into the living room to find Haydyn on the sofa.

"I made you a cup of tea."

I thanked him, grabbing the mug before snuggling in beside him. He'd switched off the main lights and just left the Christmas tree and fairy lights on. It was cozy.

My engagement ring winked against my wedding band in the light as I lifted my mug to my mouth. "Did you talk to him?"

Haydyn nodded, a wry smile on his lips. "Lady problems."

"Oh." Of course. Michael had had "girlfriends" before, but he was fourteen now. Girlfriends were starting to mean something a wee bit more serious. "Did he go into detail?"

He nodded. "He met up with his friends today. Callie Ironside was there."

I think I knew what was coming, and my heart broke a little for Michael. "Did he finally ask her out?"

"Aye. And she told him that she liked him but she was into someone else."

"Let me guess: Lewis Adair."

"She wouldn't say, but that's Michael's guess too."

"He really likes her, doesn't he?" I sighed, wishing I could give the boy everything he wanted. After Deena walked out of his life again four Christmases ago, she phoned now and then, but Michael was still angry. Instead of persevering through his anger, showing him she cared enough to deal with it, Deena gave up. Michael hadn't heard from her since.

But my son had a naturally open heart and he called me *Mum* now and I was honored.

Haydyn had involved Michael in his proposal six weeks after we started dating. It seemed fast to everyone else, but we knew we were meant to be a family. And I kind of loved the fact that Haydyn proposed before I could tell him I was pregnant with Willow. I'd barely begun living in my new bungalow when we decided I'd just rent it out and move in with them.

A lot of people probably assumed Haydyn married me because I was pregnant, and I decided not to give a shit what anyone else thought. We loved each other, and that was all that mattered. I was six months pregnant when we got married in a private ceremony with just Michael as our witness.

It was perfection.

"As much as a teenage boy can like a girl, I suppose," Haydyn replied.

"You don't think teenagers can fall in love?"

He grinned at me. "I think it's a different kind of love. I think ... the right girl will come along for Michael when it's time. I had to wait thirty-seven years for mine, but I'd have waited thirty-seven more. And so will Michael. It's just ... everything feels bigger when you're a teen. Everything's so life or death. I wouldn't go through all that again if you paid me."

I was still glowing from his "I had to wait thirty-seven years for mine." Snuggling deeper into his side, I shrugged. "As lovely as that is, I don't want him to have to wait for anything. I want him to have what he wants. He's had a crush on Callie forever."

"Maybe she'll come around." Haydyn shrugged. "There's a bit of a legend going around, though, about the Adair family."

I'd heard of it. "That once you fall in love with an Adair, you're a goner forever?"

"That's the one."

"Well, I don't believe it. I think the Barr men can give the Adairs a run for their money."

He grinned down at me. "I guess we'll just need to wait and see." Then he kissed me. It heated quickly and Haydyn reached for my mug, putting it on the side table so he could pull me more thoroughly into his arms.

We were so busy making out like teenagers that we didn't hear Michael walk in.

"Oh, gross." His voice cut across the room. "Aren't you both too old to be doing that?"

Haydyn and I broke apart, and I shot our son an affronted look. "How dare you? What age do you think I am?"

He grinned, seeming much more like himself after his talk with his father. "Old."

"Thirty-one is not old."

Michael poured himself a glass of water. "I hate to tell you this, but it kind of is, Mum."

"Wait until you're thirty-one. I think you'll have a different opinion then."

"Aye, aye, that's ages away." He threw back the water. "Carry on, if it makes you feel young."

"Santa is taking back all your presents!" I called quietly after him.

I heard his soft chuckle before he disappeared, and I turned to Haydyn. "You're a good dad."

He raised an eyebrow. "What makes you say that?"

"Because he's better after you talked to him. I love you so much. You know that, right?"

His voice was gruff. "I love you too. More than I knew was possible."

"Thanks for letting Michael hire me all those years ago."

My husband grinned at the reminder. He'd since told me that he planned from the moment he opened the door that morning to absolutely *not* hire me because he was too attracted to me. "My son always was smarter than me. But don't tell *him* that."

Laughter fell from my lips, and Haydyn ducked his head to swallow the sound with his kiss.

After another delicious wee make-out, I rested my head on his shoulder and we gazed at the Christmas tree lights. My fingers caressed the necklace he and Michael gave me our first Christmas together, and I thought of my parents. The sadness I felt didn't hurt as much now. I knew wherever they were, they could see I was more than okay. That Haydyn, Michael, and Willow had given me family again. That I was just as loved by them as my parents had loved me.

Knowing they knew that gave me peace I hadn't realized I'd needed.

"Happy Christmas, Haydyn," I whispered.

He kissed the top of my head and murmured, "Happy Christmas, my love."

Printed in Great Britain
by Amazon

47301989R00219